The NIGHT in Question

The NIGHT in Question

SUSAN FLETCHER

UNION
SQUARE
& CO.

NEW YORK

UNION SQUARE & CO.

NEW YORK

Original edition published in the UK in 2024 by Transworld, part of the Penguin Random House group of companies.

This 2024 hardcover edition is published by Union Square & Co., LLC.

ISBN 978-1-4549-5255-8
ISBN 978-1-4549-5256-5 (e-book)

For information about custom editions, special sales, and premium purchases, please contact specialsales@unionsquareandco.com.

Printed in the United States of America

2   4   6   8   10   9   7   5   3   1

unionsquareandco.com

Cover design and illustration by Kimberly Glyder
Cover images by Shutterstock.com: KK.KICKIN (dots);
Galyna Lysenko (bushes); Lukasz Szwaj (background)
Interior design by Gavin Motnyk

This book is for my grandparents,
Gerry and Celia,
and Alastair and Claudia

and for my parents,
John and Jane

with gratitude and love

CONTENTS

The NIGHT in Question

1

Someone Is Crying

Four weeks ago, a man died. He fell—out in the wildest part of the grounds where the nettles are, where ivy and bindweed have climbed up the plinth of an old stone cherub so the cherub can't be seen now. It's an overgrown place with a foxy smell. No one goes there, as such. But one warm May evening, Arthur Potts wandered to this part of the garden—who knows why?—and he tripped and struck his head on the edge of the plinth, just once, with the bright, hard *tap!* of an egg; his pipe cracked, his spectacles shattered and his wrist, too, made a snapping sound. "Oh help," cried the person who witnessed it. "Please help."

The staff did their best. They ran out, knelt by his side as they waited for the ambulance. *Arthur? Hold on.* But Arthur Potts died, as they waited: his lifetime's warmth seeped into the dark, Oxford-shire earth, his mouth stayed open and his eyes grew still so that, in the end, they all understood they were kneeling by what remained of Arthur, not by Arthur himself. A stillness descended, like dew. They sat back on their heels, glanced at each other. And he must have seemed smaller, suddenly, as people do when they die.

Florrie wasn't there. She didn't see this happen. But she's heard about it, from those who did, and she's imagined it many times since—his mouth, that *tap!*, those spectacles. She's wondered if Arthur felt cold, as he lay there. She's wondered, too, if he'd known he was dying—and, if so, had he fought against it? Been afraid? Or maybe, being Arthur, he'd accepted it all with a mild, child-like wonder: ah—so *this* is how I go.

It is nearly midnight. Everything is quiet. Florence Butterfield sits up in bed, in her floral nightdress, and stares at her bookshelves without seeing them. It doesn't help, she knows, to dwell—but she can't stop it. It isn't merely Arthur's death that saddens her: Florrie can't bear *how* he died—for whilst one rather expects death at Babbington Hall, it mostly comes through the slowing of hearts or the filling of lungs; an indoors death, at least. Who could have expected this? The cracking of a skull on an ivied plinth? And how could it have happened to Arthur, of all people—when he'd been so lively and affable, so fond of puddings and horse racing and of his tobacco pipe, which had made a gentle *put-put* sound as he smoked it? He'd been young, too—in his mid-seventies, which is no age at all. There are some here who are over one hundred years old, yet it was Arthur Potts, not them, who was taken away in an ambulance and didn't come back.

Florrie looks down at her lap. She misses her friend so much, at this moment, that she thinks to announce it, to say, I do miss you, you know, as if Arthur were sitting in front of her in his thinning corduroy trousers—which maybe he is? In an invisible form? If so, he's smiling back at her. *Florrie. You daft old thing.*

Ah, well. For what can be done now? Arthur is no longer living in the proper way of it—but Florrie still breathes in and out. Her heart still thumps, still wants to keep going; how glad she is, every morning, to open her eyes on to this Artexed ceiling with its pink tasseled lampshade, to know that there's a whole new day ahead of her which will have wonders in it, for days always do—even now, at her age.

At this, the church bells start to chime for midnight. Florrie adjusts her bed linen; she lifts off her spectacles and sets them on her bedside table, alongside her novel and dried lavender, and counts the twelve sonorous bongs of St. Mary's. She listens for the lovely, deep hush that follows them.

But, tonight, the hush doesn't come.

Rather, as the twelfth chime fades, a new sound takes its place. *What is . . . ?* Florrie holds her breath to hear it better. It's a trembling, curious sound—like wind on a wire fence, or a cello's string. Or it's the lonesome call of the tawny owl that lives in the beechwoods so that Florrie reaches, then, for her hearing aids and turns up the volume, hoping she may hear the owl more clearly—for she adores owls and has done since girlhood.

But it's not the owl or cello music.

It is crying. There's no mistaking it: someone is crying beyond her bedroom window—a tender, private crying, as if the person cradles an injured thing. The sound drifts between the parted curtains into Florrie's room so that she stares, wide-eyed, and thinks, *Who on earth can this be? Crying at midnight? On the white-painted bench outside her window?*

But Florrie knows the answer.

It isn't just Florrie who misses Arthur Potts.

Renata. How she must glow at this hour—with her white-blonde hair and pale skin. How tiny she must look on that bench—folded, angular, all wrists and collarbones; for whilst she has always been small, she seems even smaller than she did before Arthur died. Indeed, there's such a sadness in Renata these days that Florrie would love to dismantle her, to take this sadness out of her as if it were an actual, tangible thing like a swallowed button or a kidney stone. For whilst they all mourn Arthur's death and the way of it, Renata blames herself, too. Florrie knows this because she's overheard her—murmuring *I should have* or *If only* at his funeral. Renata had pressed her fist to her chest as though it physically hurt. No one else thinks Renata is to blame. Yet it seems that, being the manager of Babbington Hall, she feels she should have foreseen the fall and prevented it, should have cleared the plinth of bindweed or nailed a sign to the crooked gatepost that said KEEP OUT OR BE CAREFUL, or roped off that weedy corner. But what difference would it have made? Arthur didn't die because of bindweed or rickety brickwork. A shoelace had been the cause, in the end: Arthur died for the lack of a lasting double knot on his left shoe—so Arthur himself had been to blame.

Poor Renata. Dear creature.

What to do? Florrie wants to help. She wants to take Renata's hand and comfort her; she'd like to dab those crying eyes with a cool flannel whilst murmuring, "There, now," as a mother might. Perhaps she should call out through the window? Or she could pull the emergency cord that's installed in the corner and summon the night staff so they could rush to Renata, arms out, and lead her inside—and, briefly, Florrie considers this idea. But then Renata cries *here*, of all places—in the darkest corner of the courtyard, near the potted hosta and crumbling wall where the wren makes her nest. Nobody lives in this part of Babbington except for Florrie herself, who is hardly any trouble, being eighty-seven, one-legged and as deaf as a saucepan without her hearing aids. She suspects, therefore, that Renata doesn't wish to be helped.

So Florrie doesn't pull the cord. Instead, she unhooks her hearing aids, sets them down and takes a sip of water. She adjusts her bed linen until she's satisfied—and turns out her bedside light.

This, she decides, is how she can help: she will give flowers. Tomorrow, Florrie will wheel herself out into the grounds of Babbington Hall Residential Home and Assisted Living and pick some flowers for Renata Green. It's only a small gesture, but whose heart cannot be lifted with a flower or two? Also, isn't late June the finest flowering time? These gardens aren't perfectly kept, it's true, but this has allowed for a tumbling of buttercups and ox-eye daisies, for lavender and larkspur, for cornflowers and poppies to self-seed from the margins of the neighbouring farmer's field, and there's an abundance of dog rose in the hedgerows, and near the church gate there's a thick, lovely bed of borage which hums and shakes with bumblebees—and all of these would look quite beautiful in the old chutney jar from the village fete that Florrie's kept for just such a purpose.

Yes. She is pleased with this idea. And, on turning onto her left side, Florrie remembers, too, that tomorrow is midsummer's day—the longest day, full of warmth and sunlight. There can be no better day for her small, flowery task.

With that, Florrie sleeps. She dreams of old, past things—of her childhood garden, of rain against a window, of Arthur *put-putting* on his pipe. But there is something else, too, in this dream. A person? It seems to be—although Florrie can't quite tell who this person is, being too far away to see clearly. There's a mist also—soft, autumnal—so that she might be staring at a gatepost and not a person at all.

She says, Hello? Can I help?

There is no answer at first. But then the mist thins to reveal Pinky Underwood—which is rather unexpected, but unexpected things can happen in one's dreams.

Pinky (*Is* it Pinky?) does not answer. She only smiles, says, This is the beginning.

Florrie frowns. The beginning of what? How? For even in this dream, she knows her age and circumstances: there can't be many beginnings left in Florrie Butterfield's life. But Pinky (for, yes, it's clearly Pinky, now—with her bristled fringe and chipped incisor, the wise, loving air she always had) is perfectly certain about it.

"A beginning? Really?"

"You'll see, Butters—you'll see."

2

The Gathering of Flowers

Until sixteen months ago, Florrie had not required care of any kind. She'd been living on her own in a cottage called Far End—with hydrangeas, a freestanding bath, a hedgehog in her garden and a view of the Malvern Hills from her upstairs loo. Every day, she'd walk into town with her stick. She'd take coffee at the Coffee Pot, flirt gently with the greengrocer; she'd wave across the street at acquaintances. But then at Christmas, Florrie fell. It had been entirely her fault. She'd been barefoot in her dressing gown and, excited by carolers at the front door, had tripped over her own feet. In the act of falling, she'd slopped a pan of mulling wine—with cloves and cinnamon sticks—onto her left shin, which scalded her so badly that, in time, it exposed the bone. The burn became infected; the infection only grew worse. No injections or pills could help it. In the end, the surgeons removed Florrie's left leg, or the lower half, at least, on Valentine's Day, which seemed a rather unfortunate date for the dissolution of a partnership that had, for the most part, worked very well for over eighty years. She cried afterward—from pain, from shock, from fear of being *dependent*, which seemed such an awful, dark-coloured word. She mourned, too, her left leg. (I never got to thank it, she thought; I never said goodbye.) But in time, Florrie steeled herself. For didn't she still have her right leg? Which had, in fact, always been the slightly better one? And anyway—it might be nice to have a little daily help.

The help was called Vera—with her bright, gossipy nature and talcum-powder smell. She made a fine cup of tea, too—leaf, not bag. But Vera, in the end, had not been enough: the cottage still had its stairs and narrow doorways; taking a bath had become impossible. (Aren't there any relatives? Vera had asked softly. But no, there hadn't been.) So, in the spring, Florrie and Vera began looking for residential homes. Mostly, it was a disheartening affair: very few places accepted wheelchairs, and those that did tended to overlook multistorey car parks or petrol station forecourts; a curious odour, like luncheon meat, seemed to hang in the air. Florrie, being Florrie, would look for positives: how friendly the staff seemed, or how jolly the fabric flowers were on the reception desk. But, in truth, such efforts did not stop her deep despondency. They didn't prevent her from wondering, in the car, how on earth it had come to this; how she was looking at care homes for the elderly when she still felt twenty years old inside, still believed she could do headstands, and when there was still so much that she wanted to *do* with her life—like swim the English Channel or ride across plains with proper cowboys, learn the trumpet or walk the Camino de Santiago with all her belongings on her back. How might she do these things now? Where had the time gone? What was left of her one, brief life? One afternoon, she came away feeling so desolate that Vera, sensing this, ground the gears of her rusty Fiesta and took Florrie to the Coffee Pot, where they ordered two huge fruit scones with cream and blackcurrant jam and ate them slowly, watching the rain.

That night, Florrie conversed with her reflection: *Don't lose heart, Florence; come on, now.* For she was still alive, at least; she still had her wits, such as they were. She would make the most of whatever lay ahead of her—even with one leg, even if her windows looked onto electricity substations. She reminded herself of her various family mantras (there is joy in the world; there is so much still to come) and these roused her, as they always did.

A few days later—quite by chance—Florrie heard of a place that accepted wheelchairs in the village of Temple Beeches, in rural Oxfordshire. It was mentioned in passing, in Mrs. Pringle's Book Bazaar, and that name—Temple Beeches—appealed to Florrie instantly so that she took out her pencil and wrote it down. She imagined deep, autumnal beechwoods, a certain reverence. Her childhood, too, had been spent in Oxfordshire, so there was a pleasing symmetry to the thought of returning to it. Excitement simmered in Florrie, like milk in a pan. She put on her best brooch for the visit. She made cheese and pickle sandwiches for Vera and herself, which they ate in a gateway, looking at sheep—and, on arrival, they pulled on the handbrake and wondered if they'd been given the wrong address or if the little talking box on Vera's dashboard had offered the wrong directions entirely. For this place was glorious. It looked more like a university college than a residential home—with deep-red brickwork, sash windows and a long herbaceous border. A nearby church clock chimed midday. And as Florrie wheeled herself toward the gates, a tortoiseshell cat emerged from a bush, tail up and mewling; it rubbed itself against her remaining leg. And Florrie felt so very grateful—for the cat, the church, the weathervane, the brickwork, the elegant font on its gold-edged sign that said BABBINGTON HALL—that she had to dab her nose with her handkerchief. What could be better? Where? It would be costly, yes— but Far End, she knew, would sell quickly. (Victor, too, had been so kind.) And what better way to spend her savings than on a place where a talkative cat slept in the undergrowth? *Here*, she'd thought. *This place.*

Florrie recalls Renata, too. How polite she'd been—meeting them with an outstretched hand, asking about their journey, offering tea and remarking on the jackdaws that squabbled near the chimneypot. She'd seemed so delicate, even then—radiant, ethereal, as neat as a pin in her matching skirt and blazer. She wore a gold badge that said R. GREEN—MANAGER. "You're in luck, Ms. Butterfield," she'd said. "One accessible room has just become available—and, truth be told, I think it's the loveliest room of all."

The next day, Florrie wakes, rises and opens the curtains onto a hot, brilliant morning. The wren fossicks in the undergrowth; the white-painted bench looks back at her. "Splendid," she says to the waking room.

Little by little, Florrie washes and dresses herself. Such things were far easier with both legs but she has learned of momentum, of the usefulness of elbows. Also, she responds very well to her own commentary: *One, two . . . three!* Nothing can be done quickly or with grace. But she performs these tasks herself, at least—opening her curtains, making her daily ablutions, making herself toast in her kitchenette with the radio on so that she could almost be back at Far End with its view of the Malverns and its flagstone floor.

In fact, Florrie's breakfasting routine is much the same as always. She is in *assisted living*; this means, therefore, that Florrie is allowed to boil her own kettle, cook an egg if she chooses to—and she can eat her meals from her own crockery, which is mismatched and chipped, but it's hers, all the same. In these rooms they're allowed their own furniture, too—so that Florrie can still have her rosewood writing desk, and her Nepalese prayer flags strung up across her bookcase; she can still sleep beneath her own linen with its broderie anglaise trim. Indeed, the only real difference in Florrie's life these days is that she has *support*—a word that has changed its meaning with age. In her youth, support had meant family money or a good brassiere. Now it means emergency cords, a folding plastic seat in the shower, the Babbington Hall minibus rides into Oxford and back on Mondays and Thursdays, a laundry service, various communal spaces and weekly entertainment nights. There's a dining room, if she feels like being cooked for. And there are carers, too—in pale-green uniforms, as

fresh as peppermints—who breeze in and out with medicines and clipboards. Florrie knows all their names. She likes all of them, of course.
But, in truth, there is one carer of whom Florrie is particularly fond.

And at this moment—as if Florrie has summoned her—this
very carer arrives. There's a casual knock on the door and Florrie is
greeted—*Miss Florrie?*—in an accent that's as thick and dark as treacle.
With that, Magda saunters in. And what an extraordinary creature
Magda is—with kohled eyes, thumb rings and hair the shade of an
overripe plum. She has, too, tattoos of stars on her inner wrist, fingernails of a midnight hue, and there are various hoops and bolts in
her ears that Florrie would rather like to fiddle with. All in all, Magda
projects the air of a nonchalant warrior queen.

She sets down a paper cup. "Your pills."

"Thank you, dear Magda. How are you this morning?"

The carer shrugs with one shoulder. "I do not like this weather.
It is too hot for me—too hot in the day and too hot at night. And my
skin—look. I turn red like meat. I will get you water." Magda drifts
into the kitchenette, led by her hipbones; she returns with a glass that
she passes over. "And it makes people cross, too. Some people are not
nice in hot weather. You notice that? There is one lady this morning . . . I tell you, she is too rude. I say this to her face but she only says
bad words back to me. I do not like her—*nie.*"

It would not, Florrie feels, be polite to press further. But, in truth,
she does not have to. Several residents are known for their disconso-
late natures but there's one, in particular, who's as sour as a lemon with
her words. Marcella Mistry arrived in December. She'd ignored greetings; she'd disliked the paintwork; she'd pushed away her food and
declared it was poison, not fit for dogs, which made quite an enemy of
Clive the cook. Marcella has quieted now—but Magda is not one to
forget readily. "I wonder, Magda," offers Florrie, "if Marcella is merely
sad." After all, any recent death will bring a sadness to the corridors.
And growing old (heaven knows) is not an easy thing.

But this means nothing to the girl. "Sad? She is sad about no one. And anyway, I tell you this: a sad mouth can still say, 'Thank you, Magda.'"

Florrie can't argue with that. She takes the paper cup of pills.

"Also, I have headache. I have bad headache in the middle of my head and this morning my nose bleeds—and you know what this means?"

Florrie does not. She swallows a pill, entranced by the silver piercings.

"Thunder. It will thunder later—I know it. My *babcia* calls me witch for this. The sky will break by nighttime—you will see."

Florrie considers this. Rain has not been forecast. She peers through the window, thinking, *Surely not?* But as she wheels herself outside—in a floppy sunhat with a pair of rusty secateurs in her lap—she acknowledges that there is a curious tension in the air. Certainly, rain is due. For five weeks now they've had the baked, dry heat of other countries, in which one perspires by elevenses and keeps one's curtains closed. At first, the residents had welcomed this sunshine; they'd sat against south-facing walls and looked up, their faces following the sun's trajectory as sunflowers do. There'd been, too, a new, genial air between the residents: bowls began to be played on the lawn; deckchairs were taken into the orchard—and one afternoon, amongst those deckchairs beneath the apple trees, Florrie had talked with Stanhope Jones until the shadows lengthened, until the first star appeared above the church and they'd both agreed it was getting chilly and time, perhaps, to go in—and those had been such a lovely few hours.

But rain is needed now. The few *spit-spats* (as Prudence would have called them) haven't been enough for Babbington's grounds. Nothing is dead, as such, but certain places have a rather thirsty look about them—the lavender patch, the weeds that sprout between paving slabs, the nettlebed that marks the end of Babbington land. And wouldn't it help the residents? This heat has meant, at best, an increase in their grumbling. At worst, there's been heatstroke, a fiery exchange between Babs Rosenthal and the Ellwoods about nothing in particular—and last Tuesday, Velma Rudge fainted dramatically, with one hand to her forehead, clattering into the cutlery table in the dining room with a proclaimed "Oh my!"

As for Florrie herself, she doesn't mind the heat. She has, after all, known far hotter places. She knows to keep the windows closed till evening, to pop a damp flannel in the icebox of her fridge and apply it, in the evenings, to various parts of herself. She has learned, too, the importance of a sunhat; for Florrie has what was known as *the Butterfield complexion*—that is, she inherited her father's freckled, rosy appearance, the reddish hair that would (in her younger days) turn, in summer, to the hue of buttermilk. A childhood of blisters and calamine lotion has meant, for Florrie, an adulthood of sensible summer clothing: long, voluminous sleeves, linen dresses, chiffon scarves to protect her décolletage; for a time, she even owned parasols— wandering through spice markets or botanical gardens feeling not unlike a Victorian lady, albeit with a little more girth. She opts, in heat, for the paler colours, too—pinks and mauves, powder-blues; but then these were always Florrie's favourite shades, regardless of the season, believing their femininity and grace might compensate for her own personal lack of either of those qualities. For Florrie has, too, *the Butterfield physique*—which is a gentle way of saying that she is short and round. She's always been so. And whilst, in her early days, Florrie had hoped for the adjectives that accompany diminutive women—*petite, elfin, dainty*—it's largely been others that have come to her: *comely, ample,* even *matronly.* (At Miss Catchpole's school she was called "oafish"—by Miss Catchpole, no less—and who forgets *oafish*? Or *Florrie Butterball*?) For a while, Florrie despaired. Oh, to be a great beauty! To not have thighs that clapped as she ran! Couldn't she have inherited the Sitwell physique instead? For, yes, her mother was clumsy and forgetful, and, yes, she sometimes thought it was

Wednesday, not Thursday—but what long limbs Prudence Butterfield née Sitwell had had. What height, what prettiness! What hair, as shiny as a conker! What a clearly discernible waist!

Never mind. What could be done? Other than try to soften this dumpy appearance with sweet pea colours and a favourable neckline? The sort of skirts that fill, bell-like, when one tries to pirouette? Thus, the teenaged Florrie came to accept both complexion and stature. She made friends with her pendulous bust, with her bottom that stretched fabrics so much that, on bending down, floral prints appeared mis-shapen, or polka dots grew wide. *I am fortunate.* She told herself this and believed it: capable was better than cute or gamine. Hers would, after all, be a body that could withstand all the adventure she was hoping for: crossing deserts on camelback, hacking her way through jungles or summiting the Eiger in winter conditions; a body that might bear children one day. It might not be pretty, as such, nor fast— but it would be enough.

And it has been. It's served her exceptionally well, all in all. And it also happens to be a physique that's adapted very well to a wheelchair. Florrie is nicely anchored, unlikely to tip; the upper arms that had once been described (again, by Miss Catchpole) as "meaty" are adept at propelling the rest of her so that she can, if necessary, travel at quite a pace. And so Florrie (indeed, the marshmallowy Florrie, as she was described by Sybilla Farr to the mah-jongg group a few weeks back so that they'd all tittered behind their fingertips), with her sunhat, her freckles and tremulous bosom, pushes herself onward, away from the bay windows, past the Grecian urn and between the crisped box hedg-ing. She turns corners adeptly, reverses when required.

Prudence. During her better spells, Florrie's mother might be found in the garden. She'd talk to everything in it: to earthworms or earwigs, to a freshly pulled carrot; she'd commend a honeysuckle for a particularly good show. It was Prudence who'd introduced her daughter to the real, tiny joy of flowers in a chutney jar, and so Florrie thinks of her mother—not Sybilla—as she snips at buttercups, at the borage and daisies, as she inhales an apricot rose.

She snips until her lap is wholly covered.

"Well, *look!*"

Pleased with herself, Florrie turns toward Babbington Hall. And it's only as she approaches it that she realizes she's no longer alone in its grounds. Breakfast is over; other residents are emerging, taking their exercise before the sun gets too high—or before the thunder comes. The Ellwoods walk arm in arm, chattering like magpies. Babs Rosenthal does her flamboyant stretches near the horse chestnut tree. In the orchard, Florrie spies Aubrey Horner setting out his easel in his precise, regimented way, laying down his brushes in descending size order and cracking his knuckles in preparation. Marcella Mistry—Magda's bête noire—has claimed the shade of the old pergola and sits so still that she might be a sculpture, with her gold-rimmed sunglasses, *Good Housekeeping* and a fixed, exaggerated pout. Reuben—one of the carers—is talking to the Lims. Florrie notes, too, the absences: Odelle Banks and Sybilla Farr are on a cruise of the Danube at the moment, which means the mah-jongg club has been temporarily disbanded. Bill Blewitt, too, is visiting somewhere. (A model-railway convention? Florrie can't recall.) And isn't Stanhope Jones near London, visiting his son? But it is someone else's absence that she feels most keenly: she slows, to see a particular empty chair—wrought-iron with its matching table, tucked against the ivied wall. For Arthur used to sit there. He should be sitting there now—with a frothy coffee and a copy of the *Racing Post*, dabbing his forehead with the creased gingham handkerchief that he'd also use for blowing his nose in such a loud, trumpeting fashion that Nancy Tapp had yelped, once, with the shock of the thing.

Arthur. *These things happen*—so said the Ellwoods, who'd never cared much for Arthur anyway. But do they happen? In all Florrie's lifetime, no one else has ever died from an untied shoelace. And, for her, the Arthur-shaped spaces feel no less than they did a month ago; she still notes the silences that his single boom of laughter (*Ha!*) would have filled. And with Arthur in mind (and a wish to avoid the Ellwoods), Florrie suddenly changes direction; she pulls sharply on her left wheel so that she pivots, turns her back on Babbington Hall and takes a narrow path beyond the old sundial, which leads her to the farthest, wildest, most forgotten part of the garden. There's no gravel or brickwork to speak of; it's a track, that's all—through waist-high grass that patters against the backs of her hands.

At the path's end, Florrie puts on her brakes. And as she catches her breath, she considers the place: a half-moon of fir trees encloses her; the cherub—mostly hidden in ivy and bindweed—stands in the middle on its fractured plinth. But it's the ground that Florrie studies most of all. She seeks the indentations that were, perhaps, made by the knees of staff members—Magda, Georgette, Reverend Joe—as they tried to help her darling friend, saying, *Hold on, Arthur. Do you hear?* She looks, too, for any sign of him.

But there is no sign. There is only moss, that foxy smell and no view to speak of except that, where the fir trees have thinned, Florrie can see a tiny portion of St. Mary's Church—its northwest corner, its vestry door, its downpipe secured by ornate, greenish brackets. If she straightens in her chair, she can see the church path. Reverend Joe is standing there, at this moment, with his hands on his hips, staring into the yew. He's admiring the bird feeders he hangs on its lower branches—filled with peanuts, mealworms, sunflower hearts.

Why here? What on earth had Arthur been doing *here*? There are far lovelier parts of Babbington in which to smoke one's pipe. Why this place, above all others? Florrie has no idea. Nor had Nancy Tapp, who'd clutched Florrie's forearm in the aftermath and said, "What was he *thinking*, Florrie? I can't begin to guess at it." Poor Nancy—for whom *dainty* would be the right word. She'd witnessed Arthur's fall; she'd screamed for help like a deer in a trap.

Florrie will probably never know why Arthur Potts came here, with a trailing shoelace—not now.

But there is another question that troubles her far more. Ever since he died, it has hovered near her, fly-like, and with such persistence that she's thought, at times, to physically swat it away. The question is: What did he mean? For in the hours before his death, Arthur had passed Florrie in the dining room—whilst carrying a tray of peach cobbler and custard so that he'd been unwilling to linger for long—and said, "Florrie, I've uncovered something. About someone here."

Uncovered something? She'd blinked at him. "What is it, Arthur?"

He'd shaken his head, glanced left and right. "Not here, Florrie. I'll find you later." But he didn't find her.

Florrie gazes up at the church tower. How handsome it looks, against the blue sky.

Some questions will never have answers; she has learned that much, in her eighty-seven years. Things happen. Loss comes. Hearts stop loving and cells divide. Sometimes there is no explanation and yet Florrie wishes—oh, how she wishes—that she could know what Arthur had longed to tell her on that airless May evening; what had made his eyes glitter like gems, behind those spectacles, in the hours before he'd died.

3

Miss Renata Green

Half an hour later, Florrie finds herself wheeling past sun-warm bricks and window boxes with a chutney jar of flowers wedged between her thighs. And, as she goes, she acknowledges—not for the first time—her lasting gratitude to the stranger in Mrs. Pringle's Book Bazaar who'd mentioned this place as he'd browsed the historical fiction section, fourteen months ago. Babbington Hall is more than Florrie could have dreamed of, in those early one-legged days.

It is, at its heart, a small stately home. The oldest part, to which she is heading, is nearly three hundred years old. Here, its corridors are wood-paneled. There are tapestries and marble fireplaces; certain rooms have that wonderfully dense, musty smell that one finds in churches or bottom drawers. Here, too, there are portraits of various Babbingtons, to whom the hall had been home for nearly three centuries, so that to roll through its reception hall is to pass beneath their black-eyed stares and stiff collars. The family money (as Florrie understands it) came from the invention of a certain type of piston that advanced the ventilation of mines. But he, the inventor, was not the only Babbington of note. There was also a Babbington actor, a Babbington fraudster who died at Tyburn, a Babbington mistress of King Edward VII and (Florrie's personal favourite) a Babbington breeder of pigs.

Yet there had, too, been a Babbington gambler—and so their family seat was sold, in the end. In the last months of the old millennium, it became a residential home. The oldest part—its entrance, ornate staircase and most of its ground floor—remains exactly the same. But elsewhere, there have been changes: old rooms have been swept and reconfigured, and the unused outbuildings (a stable, a coach house, a host of enormous pig sties ("How big," asked Vera, "*were* those pigs?")) have been transformed into a dozen or so little homes. Of these homes, one is Florrie's. It had, years ago, been the Babbingtons' apple store—smaller than other buildings, but with large enough windows to let the wind blow through, keeping the apples crisp and dry. Those apples are long gone. In their place are a kitchenette, a shower room and a main room (which is to say, a sitting room and bedroom combined), all of which are designed for Florrie's new dimensions. She can wheel herself from room to room without her knuckles skimming the paintwork. Sinks are the perfect height.

In short, whilst Babbington retains its sense of history, it has also been modernized. There are door-release buttons, lifts with glass doors, ramps that will adjust their gradient electronically and little white boxes that deliver hand gel by sensor; place one's hand beneath this box and it whirrs, clicks and drops a translucent blob into your palm—and such things are remarkable to Florrie. (How on earth does that little box *know*?) Every time she pushes a button to open a door, she shakes her head at its cleverness.

It is all extraordinary, really—this technology. And Florrie hears there is even more equipment on the upper floors. For Babbington Hall is divided into two. The ground floor and the outbuildings are for the assisted-living residents: sixteen of them, at full capacity. Several of these adapted homes are designed for couples (or, in one case, for a pair of gossipy sisters-in-law); but most are singly occupied. These ground-floor residents have their physical restrictions, such as arthritic hips or a missing left leg, yet they're otherwise perfectly able.

On the first and second floors of the main house, however, are those who are not so able. Those residents have both carers and qualified nurses on hand. For they have dementia, in varying stages. They are still themselves, inside; their hearts still beat and their chests still rise and fall, but their minds have thinned, as cotton can, so that they'll look into the middle of a room blankly or be unsure of the names of people who love them. Florrie will see them sometimes—guided into the quieter corners of the grounds by their spouses or children, held by the elbow. Some seem strangely radiant. Others seem emptied so that if the wind blew over them, as it might blow over a discarded bottle on a low-tide beach, she believes she would hear a single, quavering note.

Florrie slows. She looks up at the upper floors as one might look up at a stained-glass window: wide-eyed and with reverence, with an enormity of love. For whilst Florrie loves many, many things—such as owls and good metaphors and crystallized ginger, the still-life painting of a bowl of lemons that hangs above her bookcase, the French language (which has, she feels, all *les mots justes*), sweet pea–coloured clothing and proper leaf tea—she has a particular love for the residents on the first and second floors. She feels tender just thinking of them. How can she miss her leg? Or mind her loss of hearing? Or ever feel disheartened about her receding gums or the apple-brown skin on the backs of her hands? How can she ever feel lonely—as she does sometimes? It is by chance, no more, that she's able to live on the ground floor. It is by chance that her memory has stayed by her side, like a faithful dog. And sometimes, at night, Florrie imagines packing this love of hers into a parcel, wrapping it in brown paper and sending it up to the first and second floors, where it might unwrap itself, like magic, and enter their thoughts and dreams.

There is also a third floor. But it has only one resident: up in the eaves, the old servants' quarters have become the manager's lodgings. Renata wakes there in the morning; she retreats to it at the day's end— and she hardly ever leaves her third-floor flat, even on the weekends, so that the Ellwoods have whispered, What on earth does she *do* up there? And what must it be *like*? What on earth is *wrong* with her?

Florrie glances there now. Its dormer window is closed; Renata's curtains are drawn against the day's heat, which is how she, Florrie, used to leave her own curtains when she lived in various equatorial countries in her thirties and forties, which feels like both a whole other lifetime and five minutes ago.

Indoors, Florrie ascends and descends a carpeted ramp, presses various door-release buttons and knocks on the polished oak door. MANAGER, says the brass plaque. The door opens cautiously—a few inches, no more, through which a single blue eye appears. On seeing Florrie, the eye widens.

"Florrie?" Renata steps back, opens the door fully. "Come in."

Initially, the manager seems as she always does. That is, she appears so composed and tidy in her navy-blue dress and pinned hair that Florrie wonders, briefly, if she's imagined the midnight weeping on the white-painted bench. But once inside the office, Florrie inspects her more closely: she notes the pinkish eyelids, the slight slackness in Renata's posture, as though her muscles are too tired to hold herself fully erect. So, no, she didn't imagine it.

Florrie retrieves the flowers from her thighs, proffers them. "For you. I thought they might be cheering."

At first, Renata merely stares at Florrie with the pale, expressionless beauty of a Florentine sculpture so that Florrie wonders if Renata heard her at all. But then the blue eyes blink; they see the ox-eye daisies. "Gosh. Flowers? For me?"

"For you. From here. The south borders, mostly. The buttercups—I think they're so cheery, don't you? Like little lanterns—are from the boundary with the farmer's field."

"There are so many of them . . ."

"I know. The weather helps, of course. All this sunshine! It goes on and on. Mind you, Magda said it might thunder later."

"Really? I can believe it. The air is so . . ." But Renata abandons the sentence. Her attention is entirely taken with the chutney jar and its perky, fragrant contents. "Daisies. A rose. And this is a petunia, I think? What a colour. It's too pink to simply be *pink*, don't you think? How lovely it would be to wear something that shade . . . a dress, perhaps"—said in sad wonderment, as if owning a bright-pink dress is as unlikely for Renata as a trip to the moon. The manager glances up. "Cheering . . . You think I need cheering?"

"Perhaps we all do a little. After Arthur."

"Perhaps. Well, thank you, Florrie—they're lovely. Too lovely, really, to be kept in here."

Florrie looks around: the manager has a point. Her office—being hers—is immaculate. There isn't an atom of dust in here, nor a crease. But it is, too, a rather gloomy affair. The wood paneling makes it so— but there are also dark tapestries, heavy red curtains that are held back loosely with gold-tasseled cord, and the window itself is half covered with Virginia creeper so that the baked light of late June doesn't find its way here. Also, the furniture is dispiriting: filing cabinets and card-board boxes, a black leatherette chair on wheels. The only part of the room with any vibrancy is Renata's desk, to Florrie's right. Here there are various bits of paper: letters, reminders and pamphlets, to-do lists and thank-you cards—all laid out methodically. Looking down, in the wicker wastepaper bin, Florrie sees a magenta envelope, as luminous as the petunia itself, with FOR RENATA GREEN written on it in dramatic, Gothic script. Above this, there's a noticeboard where the building's fire-escape plan and emergency numbers have been pinned, and a cal-endar on which dates have been highlighted or blocked out with Post-it Notes or circled in felt-tipped pen. This calendar, she sees, is of Parisian scenes; June, specifically, is of Le Jardin du Luxembourg, as viewed from the south—and Florrie makes a small, private *Oh!* on seeing it, so that Renata looks up from the flowers and follows Florrie's gaze.

"Paris? I've never actually been there, would you believe? But ever since I was little, I've had dreams of walking by the Seine, of having coffee and dainty pastries in a café near Notre Dame. *"La Vie en Rose"* on an accordion. *La Rive Gauche* with a handsome man on my arm. . . . Clichés, I know. But even so . . . we all have dreams, don't we? Even I have them."

Florrie had not expected this. Renata offers so little of herself; any glimpse of the woman (as opposed to the manager) is a rare, transitory thing, like a mouse running the length of a wall. Yet here she is, speaking of childhood dreams and handsome men so that Florrie turns to examine Renata more closely, as if to make sure this really *is* Renata Green. She notes the white-blonde hair, the neat nose; she studies the lightly penciled eyebrows that have been plucked into tidy, identical crescent moons and the vertical creases between those brows that suggest her life has, so far, contained her share of private contemplation. Is she forty years old? In her early forties? Renata certainly isn't old. Yet there is the weary, wise sense to her of someone older than that.

Even I have them. It seems a strange thing to say. Why shouldn't Renata have dreams, too? Everyone has hopes and ambitions—or a right to have them, at least, and Florrie opens her mouth to say this when Renata carries on.

"Those gardens? I've had daydreams of sitting there—in that very chair, to the left. And the museums! The galleries . . . I've daydreamed of those, too. But lately, I've been wondering if I should finally stop all this daydreaming and actually *go* there—to Paris. To be in it properly, I mean, and not just in my head." She looks back to Florrie. "Have you been?"

"To Paris? Yes. I lived there for a time."

"You did? When?"

"Oh, a long time ago now. I wasn't much more than a child, I suppose. I typed letters for the British Embassy, took minutes—that sort of thing. I lived in Montmartre, on the rue Seveste. I could see Sacré-Coeur from the bathroom window. And I fell in love—"

"With a man, Florrie?"

"No, no—well, not in Paris, anyway. No, I fell in love with almond croissants. Let me tell you, there's nothing quite like one of those! Dusted with icing sugar and just . . ."—Florrie shimmies her shoulders, remembering—"*délicieux*."

She wants Renata to smile. Yet Renata does not. Instead, she stands very still—with her left hand pressed against her sternum as if she's eaten too quickly. Her eyes seem to glaze over—and Florrie wonders if she's not, in fact, in Babbington Hall at this moment but opening shutters from the top floor of a Parisian apartment or eating an almond croissant for herself, on her own terms. Does her right hand tremble a little? Do the buttercups nod their heads?

"Paris isn't so far away," Florrie offers. "And there's the train these days—that goes under the sea! *What* a thing. One could pop down to London, to St. Pancras, and . . ."

"Ah, Florrie." How sadly she smiles! "It's not quite as easy as that."

Florrie doesn't fully understand; but she leans forward in her chair, lowers her voice. "Miss Green? Renata? I hope you don't mind me asking, dearest, but are you quite well?"

The manager stares in surprise. "Am I well? It's been a long time since anyone asked me that."

"I don't mean to pry, honestly. It's just . . ." Florrie dithers: Does she mention the white-painted bench? The private weeping, like a cello's sound? The sadness Renata seems to carry, like a kidney stone?

"I know that. I know you don't pry, Florrie—not like the others. I know what people say about me. A cold fish: I heard Babs Rosenthal say that—and I know the Ellwoods have little good to add. Am I well?

I don't know. I've not been sleeping much. Last night I ended up walking around the grounds at midnight."

"The heat?"

"Yes, partly the heat. It's worse—up in the eaves. But it's more than that. I just feel so . . . *full*. Full of thoughts; thoughts, turning over and over."

"Arthur," Florrie offers, "wasn't your fault."

"Wasn't it? I should have roped off the stone cherub or asked Franklin to cut that bindweed down. If I'd done that—"

"If you'd done that, Arthur would simply have fallen somewhere else. It was his shoelace. A shoelace, of all things! I wish he hadn't died but it wasn't your fault, and everybody knows it. Even the Ellwoods. Even the mah-jongg group."

Renata's smile is small but grateful. "You were fond of him?"

"Arthur? Yes. Very much." We were, she thinks, so similar—being the last ones left, of our friends. We were both on the edge of things.

"See, Florrie? You're kind. You're so cheerful, all the time. I remember thinking that when you first arrived; most new arrivals are downhearted, which I understand because they're giving up freedoms; they see they're growing old. But you? You were excited to be here. We talked about the jackdaws—do you remember? You wore such a pretty dress."

She does remember. They'd discussed the intelligence of corvids, how Florrie had known a woman called Middle Morag who had tamed a hooded crow by leaving cake crumbs on the kitchen windowsill—and, yes, Florrie had been excited to be at Babbington Hall, so much so that she'd flexed her five remaining toes with happiness (a trait which, like her complexion, comes from her father's side).

"It's more than Arthur, though. Today? Midsummer? I find it a hard day. And it's *here*, too. It's *this*"—she looks up at the ceiling so that, momentarily, Florrie thinks Renata means the Artexed paintwork and ceiling rose and wonders what's wrong with either. But then she understands: Renata means being here, in general—here, at Babbington Hall. "I'm feeling . . . awake? Yes, that's how I feel: I'm not sleeping yet I'm also intensely *awake*—seeing and hearing things for the first time. I've been here for four years now—long before you came—and in the beginning, I thought that if I just worked hard, if I threw myself into a job that mattered, that *helped* people, that would be enough. And it has been enough, I suppose. I live a quiet life, I know that; I've tucked myself away and that's been my choice; I've never minded it. But lately . . . Oh, lately, it's not been enough at all. And I've found myself thinking of what else is out there—because there *is* so much out there, isn't there? There's so much more than the third floor of Babbington, more than Oxfordshire. And why shouldn't I see it? Why shouldn't I go to Paris? I don't want to leave my job—at least, I don't think I do. But I want more, Florrie—more adventures, more *life*. Before it's all too late."

Florrie thinks, *Oh, dear sweet thing.* Because she understands these feelings exactly. She had them in the house on Vicarage Lane; she had them in Soho, in a cocktail bar. In her childhood, when adventures were seen as a male's prerogative, the six-year-old Florrie had stamped her foot and announced, emphatically, that she, too, would fly a plane or swim with whales or become prime minister—because why shouldn't she? (Even at six, she'd sensed there was so much to *do*.) And she has a sudden, huge longing to reach out to Renata. She wants to fold her hand—her crooked, mottled hand with its prominent knuckles and pea-green veins—over this smaller, delicate one and to tell her that the Ellwoods and the Farrs and the Mistrys of this world are not to be listened to; that Renata may think herself awkward or small or *less* somehow but she isn't those things—not in the slightest; and that one's time on this earth whittles down so quickly that we close our eyes on our twenties and open them again to find we are sixty or seventy or eighty, with rheumatoid arthritis or varicose veins that can be prodded, like blancmange, with a single fingertip, and that

Renata must enjoy it all *now*, whilst she's able. She must laugh and run and cartwheel whilst she can. *Do not cry on a white-painted bench.* Above all, Renata must forgive herself, for Arthur. She must move forward and leave the guilt behind her. *Please don't be haunted by it.* But who on earth is Florrie to say these things?

Renata looks down to the flowers. She turns the jar slowly, admiring each one. But after a moment, her eyes flicker back up to meet Florrie's and she gives a shy smile. "Not in Paris, you said. When I asked if you fell in love with a man, you said not there. So you've been in love elsewhere, Florrie? Do you mind me asking?"

In love. To hear the words causes something to stir in Florrie; it lifts its head, as a dozing horse might when somebody whistles or calls its name. "Me? Oh, a few times. Here and there."

"What was it like? Or what *is* it like? I'm sorry to ask—it's all so personal, of course." Renata puts one hand to her cheek. "You see, I'm in love, Florrie—*I* am. Me! That's why I ask. It's why I feel so . . . different. I'm in love—and I haven't been before."

"Oh, Renata, dearest! How lovely!"

Renata sets down the flowers, glitter-eyed. "*He* is lovely, Florrie—*he* is. He is so . . . Oh, I don't know the words for it. I don't know what to do and I don't know how to *be*. I thought being in love would be easy."

"Oh, my dear. It never is."

Somewhere, in the distance, a door closes. Nearer, a woodpigeon calls. And Florrie thinks, *How different we must seem: one woman is in her early forties—blonde and buttoned-up, with a translucent quality to her skin; the other nearing ninety, as soft as butter with a few missing molars, in a pale-yellow dress with an elastic waistband.* They couldn't, she's sure, appear less alike. And yet Florrie feels wholly connected to Renata at this moment—as if a thread has been tied between them both, tied from rib to rib, and that, by having spoken of Paris and life and being *in love*, that thread has been tugged so sharply that something's revealed itself in both of them. A trapdoor has bounced down on its hinges. (Florrie imagines the singular sucking sound that comes with the breaking of an airtight seal.) And Renata must be feeling this, too, because she's looking at Florrie directly, without embarrassment. She is examining Florrie's face, as Florrie's examining hers. In doing so, Florrie can imagine the child that Renata must have been, with a serious, removed expression. A little lonely, perhaps.

"Would you mind, Florrie, if I talked to you?"

"Talked?"

"Yes. I mean, I'm talking to you now, I know—but properly? About . . . love? Men?" She blushes. "It all sounds so pathetic, doesn't it? But it sounds like you have stories and I think you'd understand me."

"Me? Gracious. I'm not sure I'm the right person. Don't you have someone nearer your own age? A friend who—"

"No. I don't have anyone to speak to about this. And no one must know, either—not yet. But Florrie, the fact that I've said this much to you already makes me think that you *are* the right person. You brought me flowers. You know Paris. You don't play mah-jongg." They share a smile at that. "Would you? Talk to me about your . . . experience of things? Advise, even? I'd be very grateful."

Florrie nods. For didn't she want to help Renata? Hadn't that been the purpose of the chutney jar?

At that, Renata smiles freely, with relief. "Oh, thank you! Tomorrow, maybe? I'll be feeling more myself tomorrow, I'm sure. And would you mind if I asked about Paris, too? Because I'm going to go there in the autumn, Florrie. I *am*. That will be a start, at least, won't it—of being *in* life and not just looking on? Would you be able to recommend places? Where to buy those almond croissants, perhaps?"

Florrie could do much more than that. It's been seven decades since she lived in Montmartre; most of the cafés and jazz clubs must, surely, be gone. Yet she could still offer the best hour of the day to see Sacré-Coeur; she could find, on any map, the street corner on which she'd paused once, looked up and watched the pigeons roll out across Paris—and cried, for how lovely it was. *"Oui, ma chérie. Bien sûr."*

How much lighter Renata seems now! How much colour is, suddenly, in her cheeks and eyes! "We could meet on the terrace, perhaps? Clive does excellent pink lemonades, if I ask him nicely; we could pretend that we're already on La Rive Gauche. We could *parler en français*. I've been learning for years and never used it—not once!"

It sounds so delightful—so *new*. And they smile at one another—fondly, with ease, as if they've been friends for years and one has murmured to the other, Remember when . . . ? They observe the face of the other as simply and quietly as one might observe the moon.

"Tomorrow, then—at two o'clock? And thank you again for the flowers, Florrie; that was so thoughtful of you."

4

The Keepsake Box *or* Thunder Comes

lorrie returns to the old apple store. She closes the door behind her, removes her sunhat and sets it on the bedknob.

"*What* a thing." None of that had been expected. Earlier, as she'd wheeled herself along toward the manager's office, Florrie had only supposed that Renata would take the flowers and thank her; there might be a light, passing conversation about Arthur and the weather, how fragrant the rose was—but nothing else. There'd been no possibility of Renata saying, Florrie, would you mind if I talked to *you*?

She doesn't fully know what to make of it. Yet, as Florrie makes herself a pot of tea, she is aware of a growing happiness. She tends toward happiness anyway. (She had, indeed, loved those jackdaws; she loves them still—squabbling on their nest between the chimneypots, streaking the tiles white.) But as the kettle rattles to a boil, and as she pops a spoonful of tea into the pot, Florrie finds that she's feeling that quiet, rather girlish happiness that comes with being chosen, as when a sparrow will take crumbs from her saucer—hers, not someone else's. Renata picked *me*.

What's more, as she pours water into the teapot, Florrie also considers how long it's been since anyone asked her a proper question—that is, one that doesn't concern her sleep patterns or bowel movements, her various aches and pains. When was she last asked for advice? Or visited at all? Mostly, no one sees beyond what Florrie has become; they assume she's always been a one-legged woman in her late eighties with (if not careful) a whiskery chin. Florrie learned, long ago, that society forgets an old person was ever young. It can't believe that a pensioner who shuffles across the road or fumbles for their change, apologetically, was ever sprightly or articulate, or could dance till sunrise; it can't believe that thinning hair was ever lustrous or long. Has Florrie ever thought this way? As a child, perhaps: to her, Mrs. Fortescue next door had always been rickety; Mr. Patchett, the shopkeeper, had never had front teeth. But then she grew older—and, in doing so, Florrie came to understand that everyone on earth has been physically young, at some point; also, that nobody ever *believes* their age. And this morning, Renata saw in *this* Florrie the Florrie she used to be: boisterous, healthy, capable of vaulting a gate or of drinking a pint as quickly as a man; the woman who'd fallen in love more than once—and, on occasion, been loved in return. That Florrie isn't really gone. She's still inside this one—with her silver-rimmed bifocals and hearing aids, whose skin on her upper arms has acquired the thin, pluckable texture of a deflating balloon. And isn't that quite something? That Renata *saw* that adventurous, bright-eyed Florrie? Who is, one might argue, the real and proper one? To be *seen*. It feels so invigorating— and so very kind that, in truth, it makes Florrie a little emotional. And heaven only knows when she last had pink lemonade.

Florrie pours tea into a cup and wheels herself back to the sitting room. There, she sets the teacup down, counts to three and manoeuvres herself into the armchair she loves for being the rich, dark, iridescent green of a mallard's neck. She flexes her toes with contentment as she takes her first sip.

But there's another feeling, too.

Beneath the happiness, she senses it. It's dark and slow-moving; it's watchful, like a pike. And Florrie, not wanting this feeling, pauses in her sipping. What is it? Fear? Shame? But she knows exactly what it is.

Florrie looks down.

Beneath her television stand, on a shelf, there sits a wooden crate. It's small—two shoeboxes in height and width, no more. It has a snug wooden lid with *Botley and Peeves* embossed on it; beneath this, in elaborate script, it says *Excellent Cheesemongers—Est. 1816.* It had, once, contained cheeses and pickles, but it doesn't contain cheese now.

These days, it is her keepsake box. In it, there are fragments of everything that she's loved, from her favourite rag doll, as a child, to her grandparents' Bible, to a fading photograph that was taken at Vicarage Lane on the very last day before Bobs went to war so that all four Butterfields are in it, smiling and healthy. (Even Gulliver is there, performing his toilette with a vertical back leg.) This box holds Herbert's police badge. It holds Prudence's fruitcake recipe—a Sitwell secret—written out in pencil. There are postcards and birthday cards and all of Victor's letters; there's a drawing, in crayon, from Pinky's youngest boy. There is the woven bracelet of scarlet thread which a Buddhist monk had tied to Florrie's wrist, as a blessing, and which she'd snagged on an apple tree in Dorset so that it snapped and fell off her wrist, thereby removing the blessing entirely. (She'd kept the bracelet, nevertheless.) There's a dried Scottish thistle. A pale-blue silk cravat.

All this love. A whole box of it: nearly ninety years of love condensed into something that's probably about eighteen inches by twelve, if she measured it. Parental love, filial. Agape—which is, she knows, a love for everyone. How lucky she's been. How full her heart has been.

But Renata hadn't been speaking of agape.

Romantic love. Erotic, even. Those are the sorts she'd meant. And if Florrie were to reach farther into the crate—to plunge her hand into its deeper parts, past the rag doll and cake recipe—she knows her hand would close around small, private treasures that she hasn't really talked about, not even to Pinky Underwood. *It sounds like you have stories.* Oh, Florrie has. She's felt all of love's varieties, all its fire and pain and magic—and yet what remains of such love now? Only

memories. Only what she keeps in this old cheese box: a heart, whit-
tled from driftwood; her name written in Arabic, rolled into a scroll. In
these depths is a feather—breath-soft, lovely, no longer than her little
finger—that came, she was told, from a nightjar, and Florrie, knowing
nothing of such birds, could only believe the man who told her this.
Does it? Gosh. And farther down still, at the very bottom of the crate,
there's an emerald with no apparent inclusions. "Best I've ever found,"
Jack Luckett had told her, offering it as Florrie walked toward her plane,
leaving him. She'd refused the gift, of course. She'd said she couldn't
possibly. But on unpacking her bag at Vicarage Lane, the emerald had
skittered across the bedroom floor.

So you've been in love?

A few times. Here and there.

Five times, in fact. Who'd have thought it? That her octogenarian
heart has felt as much as it has? That, even now, her heart is resolute
and huge, thumping away like a wooden spoon on an upturned biscuit
tin? And who might have thought that other human hearts, of varying ages, might have loved the oafish Florrie in return? Good men.
Complicated men.

Florrie sips.

She stares at this crate. *Botley and Peeves. Est. 1816.*

What exactly is Renata hoping to hear from her? A general sum-
mary of being in love? Or is she expecting to learn about these men,
specifically? *Your experience of things.* It sounds, Florrie thinks, rather
like the latter. And if that's the case, Florrie wonders how she feels
about telling those stories—because she hasn't talked about these six
men for so long. (Yes, *six*: she decides, suddenly, that she will include
Victor Plumley in her list. How could she not, all things considered?
Florrie has been in love with six men, not five.) How might it be to
say their names again after thirty, forty, seventy years? How might it
feel to lift, say, Hassan abu Zahra (metaphorically speaking) into the
daylight when, for so long, she's kept him in the dark? All that time

has passed. So many changes have happened in the world. Yet sitting here, in her mallard chair, Florrie can still see the precise musculature and colouring of Jack Luckett's forearms. She can still hear Dougal Henderson breathing beside her, smell his woodsmoke and whisky and brine.

"What a thing." But she says it with less conviction, now. For the pike, she knows, has not gone. In fact, it seems even closer to her, more clearly defined than it was before. *Shoo!* she thinks. But it will not be shooed.

"Right." Florrie smacks her palms together, as if ridding them of flour. So be it. Never mind. She will push this dark, unsettling feeling back down into its weedy depths. And, yes, she *will* speak of love. She will not be afraid. Tomorrow, Florrie will sit with Renata over pink lemonade and speak about those six men. And most likely she'll speak of others, too—for love is not unlike a strawberry plant in that it sends out its runners left and right so that she's loved so many other people: her parents, Bobs, Pinky, Aunt Pip, Gladness, Middle Morag with her fresh coffee that would keep Florrie jangling for days. She may even speak of Gulliver, who'd mew with pleasure as he stretched himself out with all the length and girth of a draught excluder.

To speak of those men, Florrie accepts, may make her a little sad. That can't be helped: she will miss them, she knows that, and she will miss her younger days in which so much still felt possible, so much still lay ahead. But won't it also be like dancing with these men? One by one, and for the last time? Tomorrow, Florrie Butterfield will regain her youth and missing limb and her thick, gingery, waist-length hair; she'll wear (in her head) a dress of pink satin and have one final waltz (or six final waltzes) on the terrace of Babbington Hall.

That evening, after supper, Florrie takes herself outside. Magda was right: thunder is coming. There's a purplish air to the courtyard, a sense of being watched. There's no clattering of trolleys, no closing of doors—and, as she pulls on her brakes, it is Jack Luckett that Florrie thinks of: how he'd watch the wildebeest circling each other, lifting their noses. Four minutes, he'd tell her, watching the sky. We've got four minutes.

Who, then, were these six men? He, Jack Luckett, was one. So, too, was Gaston—with the damaged hand that he set down on the table, allowed her to examine. (Frostbite, he told her; Nanga Parbat—as if this was explanation enough.) Victor, of course, was another—with his cravats and joie de vivre and poor timekeeping, with his habit of greeting everyone like they'd been missing for years: How *wonderful* to see you! Come in, come in! Hassan, who'd look for her in his rear-view mirror with such longing that Florrie has wondered, later, if it was this longing that she'd loved most of all—his need for her, his attentiveness—because she'd felt alone, sometimes, in her Cairo days. And later, from her quiet, Scottish life, there was Dougal Henderson, whom Florrie could have married, for when he'd asked her she'd almost said yes; the word had risen inside her, found its way into her mouth. "Florrie? Will you?" He'd waited. He'd waited for weeks and months. "I'll wait," he'd said, "forever." But no one, in truth, can wait that long.

And Edward Silversmith.

Enough. Florrie feels a drop of rain. It taps on the back of her hand so that she looks down, sees it. Then a second comes—on her forearm. A third. A fourth.

She turns her gaze skyward. And, in doing so, two things catch her eye.

The first is Tabitha Brimble. She is sitting, as she often is, in her window on the first floor. She is in her usual pose—which is leaning forward very slightly with her hands cupping the armrests, looking across the fields with rounded, watchful eyes, as a ship's figurehead might lean toward the squalls and imagined shorelines. Her silvery, plaited hair lies over one shoulder, tapering to a point. Despite the thinning weft of her mind, she, too, is sensing the rain.

And above her, on the third floor, there is more. Its small dormer window is open. Its curtains have been pulled back and the chutney jar is sitting on Renata's windowsill—the rose, that pink petunia, the five bright yellow buttercups. Florrie smiles to see it there.

The storm breaks late at night. The first rumble of thunder is so close that it shakes the mechanism in Florrie's carriage clock, the glassware on her shelves. She sets down her novel, grasps the bedside table.

Florrie cannot be *in* the thunderstorm—not now. But even so, she'd like to be near it; so she counts to three and heaves herself onto her remaining leg. Once balanced, she takes hold of the windowsill; she clears her trinkets so that she can lean her unfettered bosom across the sill and push the window wide open with one determined shove—and, like this, Florrie is suddenly amongst the draughts and noise of the downpour, as much as if she were running through it.

"Look!" She breathes the air.

This feels like a celebratory act. To stand, precariously, and watch this thunderstorm celebrate rain and earth, her own existence; it celebrates friendship and love in all its lovely, intricate forms. It celebrates, too, surprises—for how could Florrie have predicted this request for her company? For a little advice on *les affaires de coeur*?

But gradually, Florrie's smile begins to fade. Her balance grows weaker. And she realizes, to her horror, that the pike—that wise, dark feeling that has skulked in her depths all afternoon (that has skulked all her adult life)—is so close to the surface that it's almost floating. It fixes her with its eye. *Oh, I know you.* Of course she does. Love summoned it. Love beckoned it out from its brackish cave—and it will bite her, if it can. It has, in the past, seized Florrie and dragged her under so that she's surfaced, days later, with bruises, a fraction of herself.

Oh! She clutches the bedknob to stop herself from falling.

For Florrie understands this: if she's to speak of love in an honest fashion, surely she will have to speak of *It.*

What happened.

The Hackney thing.

You know what I mean, Butters.

Florrie has kept this secret for seventy years. But when she was seventeen years old (seventeen years, six months, three weeks and five days old, to be precise), something happened which changed Florrie entirely. It changed who she was. It changed her dreams, who she could be in her adulthood. Because of *It* (also known as *that London business*), there have been two versions of Florrie: the Florrie before— who tobogganed with her brother and picked blackberries, dreamed of adventures, the cheerful Florrie who'd clamber through the undergrowth using her elbows and knees; and the Florrie after—who, outwardly, seemed exactly the same but who'd close the bathroom door, look at her reflection and see the dark, terrible internal differences—as well as her newly scarred hands. She'd think, Who *are* you, now? What have you become? No one would believe it possible: that she—Florence Butterfield, who greets wildlife as she passes it, who is matronly and ample and marshmallowy—could have clawed at human faces or bitten them, could have slammed her fists against a wall shouting, Open the damned door! No one could dream that she's lived like an animal— snarling, wild, incapable of language—or that she's rinsed the blood of others from her forearms, in a sink.

It. Hackney. You remember Hackney?

The business with Edward Silversmith.

Only one person knows the truth of it. Or rather, they *knew*—for Pinky died thirteen years ago and she never told anyone else. Even Pinky's husband had no idea what Florrie—his wife's best friend—had done, once, in her teens.

You never speak of it. Not even to me.

No—because she couldn't. Because she has never been able to. Because even to think of *It* has always brought forth a rush of feelings, like a breaking dam—shame and rage and heartbreak, and a wish to physically pluck at herself until she is bleeding. But here it is—*It*, in this room.

Talk to me, Butters. Talk to anyone. Please?

I can't.

You need to.

Leave me alone.

But could she? Now, at eighty-seven? Florrie, clutching a windowsill in a thunderstorm, wonders if Pinky had been right, all along. What if speaking of *the London thing* might have always been the better way of it? Might have made Florrie's life a little easier somehow? And what if the person to speak to has never been a vicar or a policeman or a friend or a woman called Gladness or a doctor—but is, in fact, the manager of a residential home? *This is the beginning. You'll see.*

It is an extraordinary thought: to confess, after all this time. And a small part of Florrie thinks, *Yes*. For the first time in her life, Florrie Butterfield has the urge to open her mouth and speak, after seven decades (seven!), of Hackney and Teddy and Pinky's great-aunt Euphemia, of a linen cupboard and lacerations and the sour, pervasive smell that stayed with her for months; of that night, which altered everything; of the real, lasting meaning of the words *loss* and *joy*.

To set it down, like cards on a table. *Here, Renata. See?*

But no—she can't. It's just impossible. For Florrie is in her final years now; she is practised in keeping secrets, or *this* secret, at least—and what good would come from speaking of it? It would appall people. It would hurt. Just as one's hands would be bloodied and torn by trying to lift a real, physical pike from its watery home, so Florrie knows that speaking of *what happened* might hurt her so much that she might not survive it. They would hate me, she thinks; they would.

So no. It is decided. Florrie will only speak of those six beloved men.

With that, she turns for bed. Tomorrow will be a big day. But as Florrie pivots—unbalanced, whispering to herself to be careful, now— she hears a sound. It isn't the broken guttering or thunder. It isn't the window, shaking in its casement.

It is, unquestionably, a scream. A woman's scream—high up.

Florrie stumbles, grasps the windowsill. *What?* A single flash of lightning illuminates the lawn and path and the white-painted bench. But it illuminates something else.

An object is falling.

It is a pale, indistinct, disordered thing. It falls with the fractured quality of footage from a cine reel—staccato, bone-white.

There are two arms, two legs.

It strikes the ground. For a few seconds, there's darkness. But lightning comes again and there she is, clearly.

No no no, cries Florrie. Yet she knows exactly what she saw.

She clambers across her bed, pulls the emergency cord and keeps pulling, over and over, as one might ring a church bell to summon the village in a time of fire or flood or invasion—*Wake up! Wake up! Oh, help her!* For Renata Green lies, eyes open, bleeding in the rain.

5

The Butterfields

Florrie's life began in a house on Vicarage Lane, in the village of Upper Dorbury, not far from the town of Woodstock in the county of Oxfordshire. The road had ended at the Butterfield property, with its steep drive and thatched roof, its porch of Wellington boots. In spring, snowdrops grew by the door. On summer evenings, Gulliver would sit on the gatepost, as upright and tidy as an owl. He was vocal, plump and gingery in colour: clearly, said her father, a Butterfield cat.

Her parents had met as parents invariably do—which is by chance, in the wake of a single, small decision, which, if not made or made differently, would have changed everything: Prudence had called the police. Her bicycle had been stolen—a brand-new Pashley and Barber, she'd wailed, as red as a cherry with a basket on the front. And since PC Herbert Butterfield—aged twenty-eight, portly, a man of shiny buttons and crooked centre parting—had answered the phone, it was PC Butterfield who put on his policeman's helmet, checked his reflection and rode down to the scene of the crime.

He looked for that bicycle for weeks. He checked every lamppost and railing, phoned the stations at Charlbury or Burford; he dreamed, he said, of hearing its little brass bell. He never found it. But over time, Herbert started to hope that, in fact, he might not— for he rather liked dropping by the Sitwell residence every week to inform them of developments or the lack thereof; he liked the tea and fruit cake he was offered, the parrot in its cage which had learned to blaspheme. And one evening, as he polished his buttons, he suddenly wondered if it wasn't, in fact, Prudence he liked seeing—with her ballerina dreams and girlish observations, her eyes that mirrored the birds flying over. If Herbert found the Pashley and Barber, he might not see her again.

Three months later, they were married. For a while, they lived in his parents' house on Bagnold Street, wedging his slippers between the bedstead and the wall to soften the giggles and rhythmical blows. Three months after that, Herbert became a sergeant—and they bought the ramshackle house in Upper Dorbury. Eight months later, Robert was born. And nine years later still (nine, in which Florrie imagines there were efforts and losses, doctor's appointments, inopportune bleeds and heavy sighs), a daughter was conceived. Florrie was born in the autumn—healthy and full-voiced, arms stretched wide as if to say *It's me!* And, in the same month, they acquired Gulliver—that is to say, Gulliver, tired of his travels, had tried the armchairs of all the households on Vicarage Lane and had found, after some deliberation, the Butterfields' most pleasing to him. (Gulliver acquired *them*, perhaps.) And so, by September 1932, their family was complete.

Of the house itself, Florrie remembers the floral bedspreads, the brass coal scuttle, the sash windows that stuttered in their movements, how the evening sun moved down the wall of the staircase incrementally; she remembers the greenish staining in the bottom of the bath. Of the garden, there are words that, even now, take her back to it: *trellis, rosehip, hydrangea, trowel*. She recalls the earthy space behind the garden shed with its damp, secret smell. As for Upper Dorbury, it could have been the very definition of how a village should be—with a green, a church, a cricket pitch, the Royal Oak pub with its hanging baskets, Mr. Patchett's shop where she'd spend her pocket money on marzipan or licorice sticks that she'd share with Pinky, swinging their legs from the railway bridge. They had summer fetes, bonfires, carol concerts. They'd all build snowmen on the village green.

To Florrie, it was perfect. But the best part of her childhood—which is, in fact, the best part of most things—was the people within it. Prudence? She was all limbs and daydreams, half believed in fairies. She was, too, prone to strange headaches that blinded her, caused sickness, took her to bed where she'd stay for days with a cloth across her eyes—and on those days, Florrie and Bobs were told to *keep it down*. But when Prudence was well again, she'd sing tunelessly to herself, perform unexpected, elongated ballet moves in the kitchen without warning or explanation; she'd wander through the garden, conversing with weeds. She had a vagueness to her, a tendency to worry—but her worries were never about anything substantial; she'd be unconcerned about the abdication crisis or the advancement of Nazism but she'd fear, terribly, for her seedlings in a drought, at the sudden disappearance of a button from her sleeve. ("What if a mouse took it, Herb? *Ate* it, even?") There was, however, no vagueness in her cooking: Prudence would turn out food with such a robust, blackened, crispy appearance that Herbert would open a window or start fanning with a tea towel whilst saying, always, how delicious it looked. "Just how I like it, Prue!"

For he, in contrast, was a grounded, sensible man. Whereas Florrie's mother would lose all track of time, her father checked his watch against the speaking clock. Whilst Prudence might set all her attention on the various autumnal changes to the quince tree, Herbert was concerned with the world beyond Upper Dorbury—Chamberlain or dust bowls or the Spanish Civil War. He had a solidity about him, like a concrete post. Yet Herbert was playful, too. He could fashion a trumpet out of cardboard; he'd advocate hat competitions, funny voices, sliding down the stairs on Bakelite tea trays. And despite his pragmatism, he never stopped marveling at the world, or at being in it: bird migration, photosynthesis; the perfect sweetness of a peppermint cream; the deep, sonorous sound of rain on a dustbin lid; the ten perfect toes of his riotous daughter; the human capacity for good. Herbert marveled, too, at his job. ("Helping people! What could be better?") And at the end of his working day, Sergeant Butterfield would sit down at the kitchen table, crack his knuckles and explain his latest discoveries to his two children: "His alibi didn't stand up, you see." Or "We let him off with a caution." Or "I smelled Shalimar in the stairwell, Florrie, and *that's* how I knew."

And there was Bobs. Dearest Bobs. He was nearly ten years older than Florrie yet he'd dip for minnows with her, without embarrassment; he'd climb trees slowly to allow his cumbersome, puffing sister to keep up. Having dreams of batting for England, he taught Florrie all there was to know about cover drives or defensive shots, or how to clonk balls into the privet hedge. ("Butterfield wins it! A six!") And it was Bobs—mop-haired, gangly, with a penchant for raspberries and Gulliver's favourite—who introduced the notion of traveling to Florrie: he drew a map of the world with his fingertip on a floury tabletop, spoke of mountains and languages and monsoon season. "I'm going to go here," Bobs told her—"and here." (He favoured, she saw, the cricket-playing nations.)

"Can I come with you?" Anywhere, all over.

"Flo, of course you can."

This isn't to say Bobs was perfect. His belches could make candles gutter. His boots emitted a vinegary smell that filled the porch like a fog. One summer, Bobs fell so in love with Dr. Winthrop's daughter that he'd slam doors, reject food, claim that no one in this house understood what it was *like* for him and, when Florrie trotted behind him, he'd wail, "Leave me alone!" Yet she adored him no less. She'd tap on his door with a raspberry tartlet and say, "Are you in there,

Bobsy?"—knowing that he was. And he'd emerge, accept the tartlet before taking it down to the kitchen where he'd divide it in two with the butter knife and give her, his sister, the fruitier half.

Did she think it would always be this way? Florrie supposes so. As a child (or a lucky one, at least), one believes all beds will be toasty. One thinks that these voices you hear downstairs or calling for you at dusk, through cupped hands, will always be there—loving and healthy and strong. But life knocks at the windowpane. Bones lengthen. Birthdays come and go. War against Germany was announced so that one blustery, grey-coloured day, Bobs Butterfield set off down Vicarage Lane with a new haircut and duffle bag, and, as she watched him, Florrie felt a tap in her eight-year-old heart that told her she might not see her brother again. He waved once more before turning the corner.

"We must send him our love—because it'll help."

"Send love?" Florrie wasn't convinced. One could send parcels or letters, yes; but those were physical objects. How could love be wrapped in brown paper? Sent to northern France?"

"One *imagines* it," Prudence answered, with a sigh. "Love—making its way through the air, over fields . . ."

Florrie remained unsure. "But how will he *know* when it's reached him? If it can't be seen or heard?"

"He'll feel it—like a hug. He'll look up from a letter or cup of tea, or from polishing his boots, and think, *Ah! There it is!*"

This was a very Prudence-y notion, of course. But despite the logistical questions it posed, Florrie chose to believe it wholeheartedly—and that night, having been kissed by both parents, she turned to face the southern wall of her bedroom and sent her best, sisterly love to Bobs. She gestured physically—*Go!*—as if releasing a bird.

Perhaps it did find him. Perhaps, at some point, Bobs did turn in the ruined street of a French village and feel a sudden calmness; perhaps he was shaving in a cracked basin when Florrie's love arrived, as a pigeon might. But love, she learned, could not protect the person—or not, at least, their skin and bone.

In early 1945, Robert Sitwell Butterfield caught fire in a place called Clervaux. His tank had exploded, charring Bobs to a new, blackened shape and texture. He survived it, but Bobs was so disfigured by the explosion, so melted and charred and rearranged, that Florrie hardly recognized the man who came back to Vicarage Lane. He trembled by day. He raged by night, shouting *Get out! Oh, Jesus, no no no . . .* He couldn't hold cutlery with his stumped hands so that Florrie, twelve by then, would sit at the kitchen table with this man who she understood was Bobs, holding spoonfuls of soup to where his lips had been. "They should have left me to die," he slurred. "Why didn't they leave me to die?"

After this, Aunt Philippa came. She was Prudence's older sister, but, aside from their similar height, nose and tendency to burn supper, one might never have known it. She (Philippa, Pip, Pippa to the coalman) was a smart, violet-scented woman who'd escaped a bad marriage, rolled up her sleeves and started making clothes for a living. She arrived with a dressmaker's mannequin and proper, seamed stockings. She came, too, with a pink sugar mouse, which she pressed, like a secret, into Florrie's hand. "We'll manage this. I'm here."

Noise and bustle came in with her. Pip took charge of the ration book, dusted off the chessboard; she made a skirt and matching bodice from a leftover blackout curtain and, in the evening, told stories about the Sitwell parrot that even Bobs half smiled at. ("It told the vicar to bugger off! Do you remember, Prue? Quite right, too—awful man.") The household laughed again, for a time.

But there was more loss to come. And, later, Florrie would wonder if this loss was her fault somehow—because she'd stopped sending love. Once Bobs had come home, she'd seen no point in doing it; he was here now, after all. But should she, in fact, have kept sending it?

Not to France anymore but to nearer places? Such as into the lanes of Upper Dorbury? Or through the bedroom wall?

Florrie had been fast asleep when Herbert died. On a frosty November evening, eleven months after Clervaux, a thief was chased down Paternoster Street. He ran over the canal bridge, on to Tuppence Lane and into the old blacksmith's yard where the only light came from the glittering frost, and, on being cornered, he'd snapped open a knife with an ivory handle and swayed, from side to side, steaming like a bull. *Put it down, lad.* (Her father would have been coaxing and gentle. *Come on, now. Enough's enough.*) But the thief lashed out—just once.

The news came at first light. There were four knocks on the door—one for each person in the house; all four of them rose obediently, like ghosts, and came out on to the landing. Prudence, in her dressing gown, descended the stairs. The chief inspector himself was there, looking so sad that Florrie, at that moment, wished to run down and comfort him. "It was quick, Mrs. Butterfield, if that helps."

Florrie grasped the banisters, watching. Did it help her mother, to know this? That the knife had found a place called the carotid artery? That there was nothing to be done? It didn't seem to. Pip hurried down to join her sister as Prudence sank, gracefully and without a sound—at last, a ballerina—onto the flagstone floor.

What followed was a different life. The remaining Butterfields (for Pip was deemed a Butterfield, by then) adjusted to a new rhythm of days, the empty chair at the kitchen table. Neighbours brought flowers or pies. In church, a service was held in which Herbert's helmet sat on a plinth and Chief Inspector Maltby talked of Sergeant Butterfield being one of the very best and a credit to the force. Later, Prudence remarked on the turnout—for the church had been full. "How good of all these people to come," she murmured—as if not sure why anyone was there at all.

Financially, they just got by. Herbert's pension helped; so, too, did Pip's adjustments—helping the neighbours to make do and mend. And when Florrie turned sixteen, she began to work a few hours a week at a department store called Berriman's on Oxford's Broad Street, selling soap and lavender water. It all helped—not least to care for Bobs, whose lungs rattled so much that Dr. Winthrop impressed on them all that he must never catch influenza. "It would kill him, most likely. Understand?"

They got by in other ways, too. When Prudence's headaches took her to bed, her sister walked into all the Prudence-shaped roles. She'd press kisses on Florrie, without warning; she'd make valiant efforts at steamed puddings or stews. Neighbours, too, continued to be kind. But these two losses—Herbert's life, and the life that Bobs had dreamed of having—changed Florrie's understanding of her own time on earth in that it felt now as frail and unpredictable as old floorboards might be. Nothing, she thought, stays the same. Nothing is ever truly safe. And whilst some teenaged girls might, at this knowledge, choose to marry quickly, to live their whole lives within a quarter-mile radius of Upper Dorbury's village green, Florrie chose differently. It strengthened her wish to *do*—to live, to try, to open the doors that said DO NOT OPEN. She'd answer the murmurs of *Why* with a bright, emboldened *Why not?* And wasn't that the better way of it? Aunt Pip—the sister who'd marched out of a loveless marriage, who'd enter the Royal Oak on her own to order a pint of stout and a bag of pork scratchings, and who'd wear a feathered hat for no other reason than she wanted to— seemed to be in agreement. One night, over the chessboard, she said, "Florrie? All of this . . . Don't let it stop you. There will be other sorrows, I'm afraid; you must expect them because, heaven knows, they will come. But hiding away won't stop them. Nothing stops them, in fact. So walk into your life. Do what you *want* to do, Florrie, always— because a timid, obedient woman is quite the tragedy." Pip sat back in her chair, looked at her own reflection in the nighttime window. "Life . . . What a shame we only get one shot at it."

Florrie sees all of this now. She knows she's at Babbington Hall; the staff are with her, lifting her by the elbows. ("We've got you, Florrie. It's OK.") Yet she sees a knife with an ivory handle; she sees buttercups and a dressmaker's mannequin, a ginger cat on a gatepost and the word CLERVAUX—and she burbles of these things to the carers, of trellises and batting averages, so that, in the end, Florrie is offered a pill which she takes meekly, without protestation. She opens her mouth like a chick.

Magda, she knows, stays with her. She holds Florrie's hand as blue lights wheel over the bedroom ceiling, and she speaks of Poland—of forests and rainfall, the absence of bears. She brings her face close to Florrie's, as if assessing it. But Florrie can only think: *She is dead. She is gone now.* How can that be? How can it be over when it had barely started? With so much left unsaid, so much still undone.

6

By the Compost Heap—Part One

The next morning, the medication leaves its mark. Florrie's brain feels cloudy—like water in which a paintbrush has been dipped. She needs help to enter her chair and, feeling seasick, longs to have Renata step into her room, pin-tidy and living, saying, *Let me.* But it is Reuben who comes to her aid: a sturdy, fragrant boy of nineteen with a shaving rash and a slight lisp so that certain words are indistinct—and Florrie reaches for him, thinks to tell him how lovely he is, that she's so grateful for his help. He puts his arm around her. "On the count of three?"

Later, Georgette crouches beside her. "Do you need anything, sweetheart? Tea?"

Florrie shakes her head. "I'm perfectly fine." Of course, this isn't true. Florrie's wrist is tender; she's not sure what day it is. Also, she would rather like to cry. But she imagines that these nurses would like to cry, too; they'd like to grieve for their colleague but can't yet because they have pills to hand out and temperatures to take. Florrie won't add to their burdens.

Renata is dead. Renata, who'd liked the petunia's colour. Renata, who had welcomed Florrie on her very first morning here and addressed her directly—not Vera, but her. *Welcome to Babbington Hall.*

Florrie trembles; she steadies one hand by grasping it with the other. And she looks at her still-life painting of lemons, which she bought on impulse from a shop in Frinton-on-Sea—for it's so pretty and charming and restful, with its yellow fruit in a bright-blue plate, so simple, so perfectly done. She could tap that plate with her finger. She could pick up one of those lemons right now, slice into it, squeeze it or add it to tea—and it occurs to Florrie then that she has no proof that Renata is dead. Has anyone spoken of it? Has anyone actually *said* that she died?

Florrie needs to know. What she saw last night was dreadful—but precisely how dreadful depends on the outcome of the fall. Is there police tape outside, as there was with Arthur? Does Renata's little body—as daintily proportioned as a doll—lie in a mortuary now? She is unsure who to ask. She can't pull the cord: the cord is for emergencies (although Marcella Mistry, she knows, has pulled her own for a biscuit tray). Nor does she wish to trouble the carers. So, who?

Then—perfectly timed, as if he'd been summoned—there are two firm raps on her open door. "Ms. Butterfield. May I come in?"

Dr. Mallory is a brisk, handsome gentleman of indeterminate age. He is, Florrie supposes, in his forties, but his hair (slightly gelled, holding the marks of his comb) is greying at the temples and there is a deep vertical line between his brows, both of which give him an older air. He's pleasant, certainly; all the doctors who come here are. And she's relieved that he's come with his sense of authority, with his black leather case with its embossed initials—like the bag that Dr. Winthrop used to have. But, in truth, Florrie likes Dr. Laghari a little better—largely because it was Dr. Laghari with her expressive face who'd tended to Florrie last summer when her left leg had mysteriously throbbed at night. She'd feared she was losing her mind. (How could her leg hurt when it wasn't physically there anymore? When it had been incinerated at the John Radcliffe Hospital and—she likes to think—sprinkled on a flowerbed?) But Dr. Laghari had understood this entirely. Phantom pain, she'd assured Florrie, is very real. She'd given her little pink pills.

Dr. Laghari, however, is on maternity leave. So it's Dr. Mallory who enters the old apple store, sets down his leather doctor's bag.

"Ms. Butterfield. Forgive the intrusion. Georgette asked me to come to see you. She tells me that you saw what happened last night—and that you raised the alarm? What an appalling thing to witness. I'm so very sorry to hear it." He sits on the edge of the mallard chair. "You must be shaken."

"Me? Oh, I'm quite all right."

"Yes. Well, even so. Let's just make sure, shall we?"

How does one enquire about a death? It should be easy enough. It wouldn't upset Dr. Mallory: after all, he's delivered babies and popped joints back into place, and he will have seen dead bodies many times. But even so, she hesitates.

The doctor sets to work. He takes Florrie's blood pressure with the Velcro armband; he asks about her memory, her shock, the sleeping pill. He peers at her eyeballs, saying, "Look up for me? Look down?" Also, he takes her wrist in both hands—and this is how, for the first time, Florrie sees that a bruise is appearing on it. Dr. Mallory brings the wrist closer, peering as a jeweler might study a gemstone for flaws. "Does this hurt?" he asks, pressing it. "Or this?"

She sees the old scars as he turns her wrist over. "Only a little. Not too bad."

"Am I right in thinking you fell?"

Florrie explains that she'd wanted to see the thunderstorm, that she'd been balancing and . . .

Dr. Mallory sets her wrist back down in her lap. "There's no break to the bone. My main concern, to be frank with you, Florrie—May I call you Florrie?—is that you might have hit your head, as you fell. Do you remember doing so?"

"I'm quite sure I didn't." She'd collapsed on her bed like a laundry bag. And it's as he turns his attention to his bag that Florrie asks him directly. "Dr. Mallory, is she dead?"

He doesn't look up, at first. But he slows in his movements, setting down the stethoscope. "Miss Green? No, she's not dead."

"Oh!"

"But! *But,* Ms. Butterfield"—he holds up a hand, as if stopping traffic—"I'm afraid Miss Green is gravely ill. She fell from a considerable height and landed on a hard surface. There's bleeding on the brain and all manner of internal injuries—as she intended, I suppose. Florrie, she's in a coma. Do you understand what that means? And it's true that surgeons can do wonders these days; it's extraordinary what can be done. But even if Miss Green survives this—which I must say is the least likely outcome—she may have difficulties in her cognitive function, in language or movement. Her memory might be compromised. So, I think, I'm afraid, that you must prepare yourself." He looks regretful, shakes his head. "I'm so sorry to have to say these things to you. As if Babbington Hall hasn't been through enough of late . . ."

Florrie stares. She hears and understands—and, yes, Florrie knows of comas and where they tend to lead. But there was something else the doctor said that has struck her far more forcefully. It has woken her up, as if the doctor has slapped her cheek. Which part? Florrie sifts back through these words. *Internal injuries. Cognitive function.*

As she intended.

Dr. Mallory stands. He mentions aspirin and rest, plenty of water, but Florrie bats these words away, uninterested in them. "Doctor, I don't understand. She fell. She fell from her window. I saw it."

"Yes, she fell. But, Florrie, may I ask: How much did you see? I mean, did you see her at the window itself? Or only the fall?"

Florrie blinks. Only the fall, she concedes—and the landing.

The doctor winces, looks down at his feet. "You see, the police seem to think that . . . well, there's no knowing how someone's truly feeling. But I think we all know how upsetting that business with Arthur Potts was for her. I've spoken to Miss Green once or twice since then, and—well, I can't divulge what we spoke of, of course, being her doctor, but I think it's evident that she's been troubled. Lonely. How she's lived—all alone, like that, on the third floor." He watches her intently. "Florrie, you understand my meaning?"

Florrie blinks again.

"Like I say, you must rest. Tell a staff member if you have any headaches at all, or blurred vision—that's important, Florrie. Do you hear? Any anxiety or bad dreams—let me know and I'll come straight away because these things can . . . Well, you've been through a traumatic incident. It may take time to feel yourself again."

A traumatic incident.

He adjusts his sleeves, considers her. "And, Florrie? Please—no more standing. I commend you for your efforts but you're fortunate, in this instance, that the wrist did not break. We aren't as young as we were, are we?" He fastens his black leather bag with a single, bright *snap!*

Afterward, she sits. She stares at the lemons but it's not the lemons she sees. Rather, Florrie sees those limbs, striking the air, and the moment of impact. She sees the white-blonde hair.

Renata is gravely ill. Yesterday, it had been her heart that Florrie had thought of—a metaphorical soreness. But now the damage is literal—a sort of rupturing. And it is not merely the heart but also the liver and kidneys and lungs so that Florrie recalls the butcher's shop in Oxford where steaks bled into the ice they were laid on, and organs were brownish blobs that quivered if she knocked on the counter. And what of Renata's brain? Her teeth? Her jawbone? What of the hipbone? Her two little knees?

And this: *as she intended.*

Florrie wants the garden. She wants trellises, the sound of trees—so, despite her bruised wrist and the doctor's advice, she lifts her sun-hat from the bedknob and wheels herself outside.

The overnight rain has transformed the grounds. Hollows have filled and silvered with water; droplets hang on the tips of leaves. In different circumstances, Florrie would have marveled at this—the smell, the blackish earth, how the nettlebeds splay. But she doesn't marvel. She's too confused and tender. She would rather like to hide.

She chooses the compost heap. Once in a while, Franklin the groundsman might empty his wheelbarrow here or Clive, the cook, may upturn his bucket of vegetable peelings—but otherwise, it's a quiet place. Indeed, it is one of few places in Babbington where no one ever finds her, where she can sit for hours without human interruption. Here she can unfold Dr. Mallory's words in her lap in peace.

Florrie puts on her brakes.

She sits with her cotton handkerchief—lace-edged and mono-grammed in pink. The compost heap steams silently.

Had Renata intended to die? It's a thought too terrible to coun-tenance. Yet Florrie must try to. She must handle this possibility, feel its weight in the palm of her hand. She must ask herself, *Does this feel right? Instinctively?* As when she gropes, at night, across her bed-side table, seeking her glass of water—dismissing the lampshade or her alarm clock or her tube of hand cream before finding the smooth, cool texture of the glass and thinking, *That's it. That's my water glass?* Does she have any conviction that Dr. Mallory is right?

It's evident that she's been troubled. Yes, there's truth in that. Whilst Renata has always been small, Arthur's death reduced her suddenly—as stormy seas can pick away coastlines overnight so that, in the morning, people gather to blink and murmur, not quite believing the change in what they knew. And she'd cried, of course, outside Florrie's window. But this is hardly enough. It isn't enough whatsoever. And Dr. Mallory might think he knows Renata—but he wasn't there in the manager's office yesterday. He didn't hear Renata speak of flowers and futures, of how much more there is to life. He didn't hear her ask Florrie, coquettishly, "May I speak to *you*?"

Florrie blows her nose noisily; she folds her hanky, blows again. And once this is done, she lifts her head—for there's a sound. At first, she assumes it's a bird, for it's quiet, understated. But this sound comes from the path. It's rhythmical, too—a repeated *dab, shush . . . shush*—which is not the sound of any bird or insect she knows of.

Dab, shush . . . shush.

Florrie's second male companion of the morning comes into view rather slowly, with the dab of his walking stick and slightly shuffled step. Today his shirt is blue—that deep Venetian blue that was powdered into pigment; his braces are as yellow as a yellow courgette. Mostly, Florrie applauds such choices; she wonders, however, if today's an appropriate day to be wearing such celebratory colours. But perhaps he only owns bright colours, as Florrie only owns mostly pastels and white.

He pauses for a moment, unaware of her. He appears to be watching a bumblebee.

Florrie doesn't know much about Stanhope Jones. He arrived at the residential home in the week before Christmas—entering the dining hall with such a benign, hopeful expression that, on seeing it, Florrie had lowered her spoon and imagined his schoolboy days, and how this man might have peered into a classroom one September morning with a cloth cap and satchel, his whole life ahead of him. She'd thought (as a mother might), I hope he makes friends. The Ellwoods had rushed to his side like doves—"Do sit with us!"—and wouldn't leave him. Velma Rudge had simpered, taken to wearing more rouge. But a few days later, they—Florrie and Stanhope Jones, just the two of them—had met by chance by the Christmas tree. Their first conversation had been about tinsel. Most of the discussions they've had since have been just as light and inconsequential, about the wind's direction or a spillage to be careful of—the exception being that a few weeks ago she and Stanhope sat for several hours in the old orchard, musing on the best Shakespeare play and agreeing in the end that one couldn't simply pick one, and that had been a splendid conversation, rich and unexpected. She had carried its loveliness for days.

As Stanhope considers the bee, Florrie considers him further. He wears large, square spectacles with a tortoiseshell frame. His moustache is trimmed very neatly and the colour of—what? The fleece of a fellside sheep, perhaps, or a much-loved white garment that's been washed so many times that it's acquired a greyish tinge. And Stanhope Jones is tall. This is perhaps his most striking feature: most people would speak of his height before anything else because, even with his age and slight stoop, he's far more than six foot tall. In the orchard, he'd knocked his head against branches.

Florrie sighs. She had not wanted to be disturbed. She still doesn't, really—but what choice does she have? She can't hide behind the compost heap. Nor is it in Florrie's nature to be rude. And if someone had to find Florrie at this moment, she'd prefer it to be Stanhope than Aubrey Horner or Marcella Mistry or (worst of all) an Ellwood. After all, Stanhope strikes her as kind. A few weeks ago, he'd congratulated Clive on his rhubarb crumble; he will greet people by raising an invisible hat. And he seems to be speaking directly to the bumblebee, which is something Prudence Butterfield née Sitwell would have done—or, frankly, which Florrie herself might have done on a happier morning. And anyway, doesn't Magda like him? Florrie recalls how the carer had stood, one hand on hip, trying to find an adjective for the new, tall arrival. Nice, she'd offered, shrugging one shoulder—which was, for Magda, high praise.

As she intended. Bright blue and yellow.

Stanhope turns and sees her. "Florrie. There you are."

They sit, side by side—she, in her wheelchair, and Stanhope, on a cracked plastic chair that he's found in the bushes, retrieved and set down near Florrie but not too near. Before sitting, he'd noticed bird droppings on it and had dithered momentarily, hoping there might be a cloth near at hand. But he'd sat down anyway.

So here they sit. Stanhope looks up at the sky in a deliberate fashion. Florrie looks down at her handkerchief, which is a little damper than it was. In the orchard, they'd spoken so easily—quoting Shakespeare in turn as if gently throwing a ball back and forth. But today is a different day.

Stanhope adjusts the grasp on his walking stick. "I rather think— in fact, I'm sure—that this is my favourite part of the garden."

"The compost heap?"

"I don't mean that the rest of the grounds isn't lovely, of course, because it is. Well, it mostly is. But compost heaps have a certain . . . excitement to them—don't you think? Things happen here. One might not think it, but they're busy places—full of life. When I was a boy, we had a hedgehog that lived in ours. Toads, too—as big as pudding bowls, or so they seemed to me. And I've seen a grass snake here."

"Here?"

"Right here. See that part there? Catching the light? A very fine specimen likes to bask there." He holds out his hands to say, *This long.*

Florrie isn't sure how to answer this. There is no obvious response. And it occurs to her, briefly, to reciprocate, to speak of the shrew she'd found on Vicarage Lane, under the ottoman (one of Gulliver's questionable gifts to the household) and how she'd cupped it, carried it and released it into the bramble patch. It had felt like a magical act—and she'd wondered if, on meeting again, the shrew might recognize her voice or smell, if they might even become friends, in a way. But she doesn't tell Stanhope this. "Do you often come here?"

"To the compost heap? Sometimes. I find it a good thinking place. Florrie?" He turns toward her. "I have no wish to intrude on your thoughts. I merely wished to see how you are, after last night. The whole thing is just so very . . ." He drifts away from the end of the sentence. "Tell me to go if you'd like to? I shan't be offended."

Yes, she'd wanted to be on her own. But Stanhope is here now—in his luminous braces and speaking of toads like pudding bowls in such a gentle voice that she doesn't particularly mind. She thinks to reassure him, to say that she's quite all right, thank you, and hasn't the rain done wonders for the garden? But there's something about Stanhope's expression—the long, saintly face, the shiny nut-coloured eyes behind their thick lenses—that stops her from doing this. She can't lie to him. She can't lie very well, in general, but particularly not to a face that's so uncomplicated that it reminds her of a book opened on its centrefold; that is to say, it's a face entirely without shadows. Not many faces are like that.

Florrie sniffs. Sensing a drip, she wriggles the edge of her handkerchief into a nostril to catch it. "I'm not at my best," she says.

"If I may say so, I'm not in the least bit surprised. It's all dreadful. I only got back this morning—from my son's, in Princes Risborough. I'd no idea about any of it until I went into the dining room for breakfast—well, a second breakfast, I suppose it was, because I had eggs and bacon with Peter before leaving. But anyway, in I went—and the Ellwoods came straight to me with the news. Oh, the shock of it! It's shaken everyone. One of the carers was sobbing by the condiments. The lady with the rouge—I can never remember her name—was fluttering about, quite inconsolable. And Nancy Tapp looked terribly pale, but I suppose it brings it all back for her, doesn't it? Arthur, I mean." He shakes his head forlornly. "It brings it back for all of us, if indeed it ever went. But, Florrie, you *saw* it—the fall? At least, that's what they're saying. I can't imagine . . ."

"Stanhope? Do you know how she is?"

"Renata? I'm afraid they're saying she's not well at all. *Serious but stable*—that's the term. She's in the John Radcliffe Hospital on a machine that breathes for her, or so Georgette told me, which doesn't sound very promising, does it? But I don't know much about these things."

Florrie imagines the machine. It inflates and deflates Renata's tiny lungs. Or it measures, perhaps, her heart in green, regular blips on a screen. Most likely, its cable is off-white and plugged into a wall that has slightly scuffed paintwork where trolleys have knocked it— for Florrie knows hospitals. She remembers being wheeled down to an operating theatre—under lights, under signage, under chins and clipboards, under her own reflection in the metal grilles of the ceiling lights—and thinking, *I'm going to lose my leg now. They will chop it off.* But what's that, compared to what Renata is living through? How many needles are in that poor child's arm? "And what are they saying about it? About what happened, I mean."

He shifts his weight on his chair. He adjusts his grip on the walking stick, tests this new grasp by tapping the ground three times— and Florrie knows he's choosing an answer. He's trying, she thinks, to be kind.

"They're saying that she tried to kill herself, aren't they?"

A blackbird hops into view. They both look up, watch it. It has detected a worm and listens, head cocked, before stabbing the leaf mulch with precision. Its beak is the colour of Stanhope's braces. "Yes. Yes, I'm afraid they are saying that. Most are saying they can't believe it, but some . . ." Stanhope opens and closes his grip. "Well, some aren't surprised. Babs Rosenthal says she saw it coming, that Renata is clearly of unsound mind."

"Unsound?"

"Because of how she lives—like a hermit. No guests, no interests. No apparent social life. The Professors Lim are saying it's probably for the best, that the previous manager was far better and could we get that person back? Marcella Mistry seems entirely indifferent to it all—but I suppose Marcella is indifferent to everything. And those sisters . . ."

"The Ellwoods?"

"They were gossiping away in the dining room, saying that standards have lowered since Renata came here anyway and that they hadn't liked *where she was taking* Babbington. I don't know what that means. Where could it be taken? Anyway, they didn't seem particularly upset."

"Standards have lowered?"

He opens a palm, shrugs with one shoulder. "Less clean, apparently. I think everything's very clean here. I do have a cobweb in the kitchen, but I don't mind that in the slightest. The spiders were living there before I arrived, after all."

A rare sensation is stirring in Florrie now. She is grieving, shocked and her wrist still hurts her—but these are all secondary feelings. A slow fire starts to rise. Anger is a rare emotion for Florrie but it's growing in her now, like speeded-up footage of a seedling in mulch, so that she presses her lips together, tightens her grasp on her plastic armrest and her one remaining foot gives a little indignant stamp on its footrest so that Stanhope flinches and the blackbird darts into the undergrowth. Florrie Butterfield—who would wait without complaint in a telephone queue, who'll forgive theft or lateness or political incompetence, who didn't mind the slightly patronizing air that Dr. Mallory had shown earlier (he meant well, she tells herself; what does he know of being a woman, or old?)—is animated with rage, for a moment. She balls her hanky; her eyes glitter like a sunlit puddle and words pour out of her with all the noise and volume of an upturned bucket. "How," she says, "can people be saying such things? How can they be so busy thinking about standards (standards!) when that poor creature is lying in a hospital bed with tubes and needles? And they say her life is empty, but how do they *know* it is? How can they measure her life against their own choices, against what they think makes for a happy lifetime? Why can't people just live as they choose? And anyway, she'd been so full of plans, Stanhope—Paris, for example! She was wanting *more*—she told me this: more life, not less! And we were going to have pink lemonade together—today, at two in the afternoon—and it was going to be perfectly lovely, and do the Ellwoods know that? Of course they don't. They just like to gossip like two sparrows in a hedge."

With that, Florrie stamps her foot once more, ending it.

They glance at each other in surprise. They both seem a little breathless from this outburst—she from talking, he from trying to keep up—and there is, too, a slight embarrassment; they are only acquaintances, after all.

Florrie pats her hair. He adjusts his braces.

Something rustles in the compost heap.

"I see," he says. But Stanhope does not expand on what he sees exactly.

Florrie's anger soaks away. It had filled her unexpectedly, as a burst of sea might fill a cave, but now it retreats to leave its damage and various flotsam, and she's rather stunned to know the wave rushed in at all. She wonders if he is regretting his gesture of sitting beside her on a plastic chair.

"Paris, you say?"

"Yes. She told me this yesterday. I went to see her—about eleven o'clock, I think it was. She wanted to eat pastries in sight of Notre Dame. Stanhope, she was so . . . *alive*. She said she was also in—" But Florrie stops herself. It doesn't feel right to speak of love, not yet.

"I saw her yesterday, too—in the corridor. Around lunchtime, so not too long after you'd seen her, by the sound of it. She seemed in excellent spirits, I must say. I commented on it, actually; I said how sparky she seemed—that was the word I used—and she said, *I feel sparky, Stanhope*; I remember that distinctly. We went on to have a lively conversation about Wimbledon fortnight; it starts in a week or so, I think, and she told me she loves tennis, which I didn't know—did you? I'm partial to a game myself, or used to be. I was known for my double-handed backhand." He smiles to himself. "Sparrows in a hedge . . . yes, very good. One hears them before one sees them, don't you find?"

Florrie studies him. From her lower viewpoint, she sees his pores and wrinkles, and a thumbprint on one of his lenses. There is, too, the nick of a razor near his bottom lip—and it reminds her once more that this elderly gent is still a boy, in some ways, as she is still a girl, fashioning a trumpet out of rolled-up newspaper or chasing Bobs down the garden, his bare soles flashing ahead. She's still blowing out ten birthday candles. We don't leave the children we were. We simply grow around them like a tree will, in the end, grow around a bicycle that's been left against them—and Florrie pleases herself with this comparison.

Stanhope glances down. "Your wrist. I say. Are you in pain?"

"It looks worse than it is. Things do at our age, don't they?"

He doesn't seem convinced. "Well. If I can help with anything . . . I mean, I'm not sure *how* I can. But *if* I can, in any way, you will ask—won't you? Arthur and now this. It's . . ."

"Yes. Thank you."

Briefly, his expression is very serious—and she wonders if he has more to say. But then Stanhope announces the time. "Lunch. Well, nearly. Shall we?"

They head back toward the Hall, side by side. *Do we look foolish*, she wonders? Florrie is so short, in her wheelchair, and Stanhope is so tall that the distance between the tops of their heads is enough for its own temperature change, for birds to fly through. He must bend like a tent peg to pass beneath the buddleia. Where the path narrows, he says, "After you."

They're quiet, as they go. Their only other exchange comes when the path diverges. "Will you be coming to the dining room for lunch?"

She shakes her head. "Not today." Mostly Florrie prefers to take lunch on her own. "But, Stanhope? Thank you for having come to find me." She means it; his company and the compost heap have both done her good.

"Well. In difficult times, we must . . ." And he narrows his eyes, gazes toward the squat, grey tower of St. Mary's that peeps above the beech trees. Florrie waits for the end of the sentence, but it doesn't come. Rather, Stanhope turns, looks down at her. "I was wondering. What you said, back there at the compost heap—about Paris, and how Renata was wanting more, not less. Does that mean you don't believe what they say? That Renata . . . chose to do this?"

We are skirting, she thinks, around the word *suicide*. We dare not say it, as if the word is sleeping. And Florrie realizes then, with absolute certainty, that no, she doesn't believe it; that, having weighed this notion in her hand—that is, Renata's solitary life and midnight tears versus their conversation about flowers and love and rue Seveste, and the fact that they'd intended to *speak* to each other, as if they were actually long-lost friends or mother and daughter—Florrie will not subscribe, in any way, to the view that this fall was a deliberate choice. "No, I don't believe it at all."

He meets her gaze with those round, brown eyes—the shade of steeped tea or a polished conker. "I must say I'm glad to hear it, Florrie. Because no, nor do I."

As Florrie returns, on her own, to the old apple store, she pauses to look at Renata's landing place. It isn't roped off. There is no indentation. The brickwork path seems undamaged so that no one might know she'd fallen at all. The only clue is a few fragments of glass that have been missed by Franklin's sweeping; they crunch beneath Florrie's wheels, along with buttercups.

Florrie attempts an apple and cheese for lunch. She nibbles on this in the kitchen, staring at the draining board. Two o'clock comes and goes.

Not suicide. Not a deliberate act. Then . . . what?

An accident—as Arthur's death was. A stumble, a misjudgment. *These things happen.*

Two falls in a month. It's quite a coincidence, she thinks; but then, what other explanation can there be? They are both perfectly certain that Renata did not intend to die.

But she may die yet. Florrie lowers her slice of apple and imagines it—Renata's heart sputtering to a stop, like a car engine; a nameless doctor in a white coat deciding, regretfully, to turn off a switch so that the residual warmth of a small human body lessens and dissipates until it is cold. She abandons the apple and thinks, *Absolutely not.* Renata cannot die: Florrie will not allow it. And—as if the poor girl's fate is, indeed, in Florrie's hands—she brings together all the love and warmth and longing she can muster, imagines pressing it all together like dough and sending it over the rooftops and motorways of Oxfordshire. *Hold on, Renata. Don't go.*

Prudence Butterfield, née Sitwell, had sought comfort in the world. After her widowing, a white feather on the doorstep gained a new meaning; a certain shaft of sunlight would be Herbert, passing by. She decided—in her particular dreamy way—that if one truly believed something would happen, it was more likely to. And whilst Florrie was never really swayed by this notion, what harm could come of believing it, now? "Renata," she announces, "will survive." The time will come when they'll smile at each other, across a tablecloth, and speak of six different men.

To that end, Florrie must prepare. She must gather all that she'll need to tell her stories, to give advice. In the past, when she and Victor would move to other countries, Florrie used to write down what would be required for that move—visas, head coverings, quinine tablets, bars of Pears soap, a spare brassiere, a guide to Arabic, her supply of crystallized ginger, a few more cravats from Savile Row. It made the whole thing an easier affair. And thus, Florrie decides that, from now on, she will use her evenings for preparation. She will work out exactly what to say, and how. She will pour herself a whisky, each night, and practise (as it were) with these six gentlemen; she'll find, within her Botley and Peeves crate, the secret remnants of those six *liaisons amoureuses* which are the only evidence left that Florrie knew those men at all.

Florrie does this now.

She wheels herself toward the cheese crate. She slides its lid onto the floor.

Look . . . Reaching down is hard but, with care, it can be done, and Florrie runs her palm across its surface of photographs and Christmas cards, as one does with water. Where will she start? What small, strange memento will she bring into the light? The dried thistle from Dougal? That emerald from Jack?

Paris. Of course. She will start with Paris: for it's Renata's intention to walk through it, with coffee and "*La Vie en Rose*." But also, it's where Florrie met Gaston Duplantier; or rather, Paris led to their meeting, which wasn't even in France, as it happens. But without Paris there would have been no Gaston—no frostbitten hand, no *ma petite reine*; no quickened heart in that bluish Alpine light.

7

La Vie Française de Florrie Butterfield

I t happened. That night. *The Hackney business*. And, in its aftermath, the seventeen-year-old Florrie was wholly undone. She
returned (or rather, she was carried, like a child) to the house of
Pinky's Great-Aunt Euphemia—a townhouse in Notting Hill, where
a mattress had been set down in the linen cupboard for her. Here,
she grappled and slept. She tugged at the dressings on her hands. She
pressed her face into the pillows to muffle her grief and fury; she
feared, too, the police and shouted in her sleep, sometimes, so that
Pinky would race down from the attic in her nightdress, as quick and
soundless as a breeze.

"You must speak to someone. Your aunt? Bobs?" This, in the linen
cupboard, late at night.

"No. I don't want to."

"But you must tell them something. Won't they see your hands?
Won't they ask?"

"We aren't going to tell anyone, ever—yes? Promise me."

Pinky was reluctant. She rubbed her eyes. She sighed slowly like a
punctured tire and looked along the line of ironed sheets and pillow-
cases before agreeing, heavily, to saying nothing—but only because
she loved her friend. "Yes, then. I promise."

With that, they linked little fingers, said *one, two, three—*
because this was how they'd make a lasting promise back in Miss

Catchpole's playground, before everything. It was how they sealed a secret up.

Only Aunt Pip noticed the scars. Back on Vicarage Lane, she found Florrie by the hydrangeas and she asked her about them in a quiet, private voice. "What happened to your hands? Your knuckles—look."

"Glass," Florrie told her. "I broke a mirror."

"Lord. Don't tell your mother. That's seven years' bad luck."

Otherwise, they saw no change in Florrie beyond how much longer her hair was and the new, pale-blue tea dress that she'd found on Petticoat Lane. They asked about double-decker buses, the Thames, the prime minister ("Did you actually *see* him?" asked Prudence, as if Mr. Atlee simply strolled around the pavements, tapping his brim with the top of his cane and saying hello to the general public). As for her supposed secretarial course (the one she'd claimed she was going to London for), Florrie demonstrated her newly learned typing skills on an invisible typewriter, at the kitchen table. "Like that—see?"

But she couldn't say more—nor stay. Everything at that house reminded her of what she'd done. *I am not the same. You have no idea.* Several times, Florrie would need, urgently, to find a place to cry in— behind the garden shed or beneath the railway bridge; she'd muffle her sobs with a flannel in their copper-stained bath. She'd have nightmares, sometimes, in which she'd be taken back to London and chained up and whipped like a hated animal—and it felt wrong to have such dreams there. With Clervaux and a bone-handled knife, the house on Vicarage Lane had enough nightmares of its own.

Thus, a little after her eighteenth birthday, Florrie announced that she would like to go to France.

"France? The country?" Prudence lowered her tea.

"There's a secretarial post at the embassy. They've offered me the job." (This wasn't strictly true. The woman called Euphemia had secured the job for Florrie—having known the right people and having *had a quiet word*. But no one needed to know that. No one, she thought, ever will.)

It seemed, at first, too much. France involved a new language and currency, a new cuisine of which Mrs. Fortescue, next door, had heard worrying rumours. The country's name alone still retained a sense of war. And Florrie felt so guilty for making this request when her time in London had already asked so much of the remaining Butterfields. But she wanted to live her life fully. And, after Hackney, how on earth could she stay?

"France . . . ," sighed Prudence. "Is that where the lovely cows come from?"

"Which cows?" asked Pip. For neither Florrie nor her aunt were entirely sure. And when Prudence drifted into the garden, Pip reached over the kitchen table, between the cups and saucers, and grasped Florrie's forearm: "I'll look after them, Florrie. I promise."

As for Bobs, he fumbled with his bedding, tried to open his eyes. "Go," he told his sister, as if pleading. "For God's sake, go."

She rented an attic room in a lodging house in Montmartre for forty centimes a week. It was eight storeys up yet had no view at all except in the shared bathroom, from which, if Florrie stood on her tiptoes, she could see half an inch of Sacré-Coeur. She bought bread downstairs from the elderly Madame Sorre; she befriended the cats that slunk over rooftops. To reach the British Embassy on the Rue du Faubourg Saint-Honoré, Florrie would take the metro to Madeleine and emerge into sunshine and bustle and *les jardins* and think, *Look where I am.*

The embassy staff were kind to her. The other secretaries—Marigold, Delphine, Marie-Thérèse—invited Florrie to cafés that served *escargots* and *asperges blanches*: "After all, you are in France now!" They encouraged her with her French, introduced her to gentlemen who'd take Florrie's hand and say *enchantée*—and they'd compliment Florrie on her skirts or hair when Florrie knew, very well, she was not *jolie*. But what did it matter? She had not come to Paris for that.

She smoked Gauloises; she discovered *pastis*. She'd wander the city on foot, on the weekends, hungering for anything that was new to her, that had no shadows to it. She tried to read Proust in French and failed. But then a student called Emmanuel—observing Florrie's efforts at reading this, in Les Deux Magots—decided to dedicate his summer to improving her French. "We will talk," he declared, "of literature, *oui*?" And Florrie barely recognized herself—strolling over bridges or through Les Tuileries as this earnest, dark-eyed, attentive young man spoke, in French, of Baudelaire. In her letters home, she'd write of her adventures. *The sunrise can be pink-coloured. There's a pastry called mille-feuille.*

Mostly, it was lovely. Mostly, it worked. Yet one night, in a bar, an acquaintance of Emmanuel's had set down a curious greenish drink—*pour toi, ma chérie*—and she'd tried it out of politeness but hadn't liked it much. It dismantled her somehow. Florrie vomited in the shared bathroom; she stayed in bed for three days and watched the light change on her ceiling, held out her knuckles for self-examination—and felt so old, suddenly, so stupid and lonely and sad.

She heard, through Marie-Thérèse, of another job.

Florrie wrote to Vicarage Lane: *It's in Nice. Would you mind?*

Our dear Flo, came the reply. *If you are happy and safe and enjoying life* (Aunt Pip had underlined the word twice), *how could any of us mind? We're having good weather. It helps Bobs—and there's a robin nesting in your mother's wellington boot, which makes her ask,* What if it rains now? *I tell her she can borrow yours. Also, we've got a whole pat of butter today—and sultanas! Can you believe it? So I'll attempt some scones this afternoon and we'll miss you as we eat them. Bobs is reading more and sleeping better. Gulliver is perfectly contented—growing old and fat, which*

perhaps we all are. Florence, our darling, we all send our love with this
letter—and more besides.

How desperate Florrie felt, on reading this; what a huge, crashing wave of love broke in her, at that moment, so that she pressed the
page to her chest and let tears spill down her cheeks. She looked out
across the Parisian rooftops and cried for how much she loved them
all—even the scones, the Wellington boots. But Florrie still couldn't
go back.

In Nice, she taught English to four precocious, black-haired children
in a house with a garden that brimmed with mimosa. She passed her
nineteenth birthday *sur la plage* with them. *La fille anglaise*, they called
her—although Florrie was fluent in French by then.

In the autumn, she moved on again. She heard there'd be jobs in the
Alps, at this time of year. So, after three trains, a bus and a thumbed
lift over the Swiss border from a man with a cigar, Florrie arrived in
the resort of Zermatt with no address, no real plan, no thermal under-
wear and no proper winter coat. Ah, she thought, feeling foolish. It
was getting dark when she arrived. She headed for the nearest hotel,
with its welcoming porch light.

L'Hôtel Petit Palais was, they said, looking for maids. Her shorthand skills wouldn't be needed. "We require," said the proprietor, in
wearied English, "the beds to be made and the floors to be mopped.
Et les toilettes aussi. Oui?" Florrie nodded, wide-eyed. Why not? There
were worse things, she knew that much. Also, the job came with its
own little room, in the eaves; she could, he said, start straight away.
And as she unpacked that night, looking out of the sash window at the
Matterhorn, Florrie wondered if there was magic here, in Zermatt—in
its strange, glittering light.

What does Florrie remember of her time at L'Hôtel Petit Palais?
Making beds; eating her meals in a windowless room; chasing away the

dog that liked to *déféquer* on the hotel steps. At night, the mountains seemed to adjust, creakily, to their new weight of snow. The lobby was decorated with framed sepia photographs of long-dead Alpine climbers, with hard stares and notable moustaches—and Florrie came to know their faces as she polished their glass. Most of the guests paid no attention at all to the plump, freckled maid who dusted the crampons set above the door. But some did notice her. Some greeted her or thanked her. Some asked if she was English. (No one assumed she was French.) Once a climber—muscular, clanking with metal—asked Florrie casually if she might like to join him for hot wine at Le Bar de Glace that evening, and she'd blushed until she was wine-coloured herself. *"Non, monsieur. Merci."*

She was away for nearly two years. She missed her family with a literal ache—choosing, as distraction, to scrub bathrooms on birthdays and anniversaries, to clear plugholes of hair. She missed events, too. In the spring, Pinky got engaged to an ophthalmologist; a month later, with only two witnesses, they married near Kew Gardens. In the autumn, Bobs managed to walk down to Patchett's shop on his own, without assistance, which Florrie knew was a real, exhausting achievement for this man who had, once, hoped to stand on the equator or throw his own children high into the air. Also, on a morning of blizzards, Florrie lifted a copy of *Le Monde* to read of the death of the British king. The proprietor had passed it to her and shrugged: "Is sad, *non?*" And it surprised her how sad she did feel, at this news—as if she'd known the king personally and missed the chance to say goodbye.

Florrie had no friends there. Yet, one day, she crept down into the *salle de séchage* in the basement—a hot, shadowy room in which guests left their boots to dry—and found an ice axe as heavy as a horseshoe. She tested the tip's sharpness; she assessed its weight, as if readying to throw it. And Florrie was so transfixed by this axe that she didn't see or hear its owner—leaning on the doorframe, watching her.

"You climb?" He asked this in English.

"No. I've never climbed anything."

"Then you hike?"

Did she? "Not really, no."

The man was bemused, stepped forward. "Then why are you here, *mademoiselle*?"

This, then, is how they met—in the half dark, an ice axe between them. It was a different sort of meeting, but Gaston was a different sort of man from those she'd met before: quiet, watchful, as taut and contained as a string pulled back. Gaston climbed the Matterhorn every winter; he knew the routes, the dangers. He had reddened cheeks, a peeling nose and he had, too, a strange, unnameable sadness to him which made Florrie feel safer somehow—as if they were similar creatures and could, for a time, be at ease. In Le Bar de Glace, he removed his gloves and showed her missing fingertips. He spoke of the friends he'd lost on Nanga Parbat. ("Frostbite," he told her. "I was nearly dead.") And Florrie was astonished by this world that Gaston inhabited fully—with cornices and sunburn, a need for oxygen tanks. No one had mentioned such things at Miss Catchpole's school.

"Why do you do it? What's it like?"

He'd looked out of the window, considering this. *"Je me rencontre."* I meet myself there.

In the end, Gaston took her on to the Hörnli, from where the Matterhorn began. She'd asked him to: she'd wanted to enter those crystallized heights, to stand where those sepia climbers had stood— and he'd considered this with a smile. *D'accord, Florrie. Ma petite reine.* Their footsteps crunched as they went, but otherwise, there was only a noticeable hush, a sense of enormity around and above. Sometimes Gaston passed sugar to her, punched his own gloved hands for warmth, and he'd ask *Ça va?* But mostly, they'd stand in silence.

Florrie didn't meet herself there. But as she stood, with Zermatt beneath her, she did meet someone. Bobs walked into view. In that cold, sparkling world, Florrie saw her brother as he had been, before the war—smiling, holding a cricket bat. *Fancy a game, Flo?* What, she wondered, was he doing on the Hörnli? Then she saw the other Bobs—Bobs inside his tank, Bobs thumping its sides to get out and yelling and the final blast of fire that scorched his face and hands and lungs so that he'd emerged from the tank like a torch, flailing and screaming for help from his mother or God or anyone. Florrie bent at the waist. *He will never come here. He will never be old.*

"Florrie, *ça va? Qu'est-ce que c'est?*"

Back at the hotel, Florrie managed to call the house on Vicarage Lane. Aunt Pip answered. "He has flu," she murmured. "It's not good, my love. But he'd be so cross if he knew I'd told you. Dr. Winthrop comes daily."

"What of Mother?"

"She's had it, too—but she's pulling through now, and taking soup. The milder weather is coming."

"You?"

"Try not to worry."

Gaston was the only person she had to say goodbye to. She knocked on his hotel door that night and, as they faced each other, she could glance over his shoulder into his room, which she knew, from having cleaned it daily: the folded pyjamas, the book on Schopenhauer, the herb-scented soap in its dish.

He leaned against the doorframe, folded his arms. "When?"

"Tomorrow. At first light. *Mon frère est malade. J'ai peur que . . .*"

Gaston lifted himself from the doorframe. He announced that he'd be leaving himself in the morning, anyway—for Interlaken, for the Eiger—and he kissed her on each cheek in a formal, brief good-bye. Only later, on the bus, did Florrie muse on how she'd seen, in the proprietor's book, that Gaston was booked at L'Hôtel Petit Palais for another twelve nights—and that he had, in fact, extended his stay. There could, she knew, be a thousand reasons why—the least likely of them being her. (She wasn't a climber, after all. Her thigh circumference, she'd noticed, was at least twice his.) But Florrie conceded, as the bus carried her through darkness, there was a tiny chance of it; a tiny chance, too, that he was also feeling sad.

Florrie. Ma petite reine.

In another lifetime, might she have put her own hands on to the table? Offered Gaston her own version of frostbite? *I punched through glass, through wood.* Or held his gaze for longer than it felt proper to? Who knows. But it was this lifetime. She was this Florrie—and her brother was dying on Vicarage Lane, five hundred miles away.

In the old apple store of Babbington Hall, Florrie looks at the postcard. It is an old photograph of Zermatt with snow on its rooftops, but she can still navigate those streets, in her mind, still knows which window had been Gaston Duplantier's. She can imagine herself as she'd been, there—haunted, sorry, trying her best.

On its reverse, he wrote his address. *Trouve-moi, Florrie. G.*

Florrie sets the postcard on her bedside table. In time, she will show this to Renata. She'll speak of how she'd stare at various spaces—doorways, chairs, the hotel reception desk, the *salle de séchage*—and imagine Gaston turning around to find her there. She'll talk of how, with love, one pays far more attention to oneself: one's hair, one's posture, how one says *bonjour.*

Florrie turns out the light. For a while, she imagines taking this postcard—*Zermatt en hiver* printed on its edge—and pressing her love into it; she imagines sending it—*Go!*—into the night. And she'd send it to Gaston, if Gaston were still living. But Florrie knows that, due to an avalanche in the Peruvian Andes ten years later, Gaston is not. So she sends her love down to Oxford instead. *Hold tight, Renata. Don't stop.*

Florrie rolls on to her side and sleeps. Or rather, her mind sinks toward sleep as a penny might sink in water, swaying from side to side. But on the edge of it, a thought comes.

Renata was pushed.

Florrie opens her eyes. It feels like a small, quiet thought; she merely notes it, at first—*There it is*—as if a bird has landed inside her, preens a little, settles and closes its wings. But she continues to stare in the darkness.

Can this be true? Is it possible? And she thinks, *Yes*—for no other reason than it feels easy and right. It feels to *fit*, just so—like a good shoe. And she remembers Sergeant Butterfield at the kitchen table, saying, "A good policeman will listen to *this*, Florrie"—tapping his chest with his middle finger. *"This."*

Pushed. She was pushed.

How simple it seems. How ordinary, even—when Florrie knows it isn't ordinary at all. Someone tried to kill Renata; they pushed her out of a window during a thunderstorm. And, tucked up in bed, Florrie decides (again, very simply, as if there's nothing strange about any of this) that she'll find out who pushed her, and why.

8

The Darker Side of Magda Dabrowski

A t this time of year, the sun rises a little before five. Today (the 23rd of June, a Sunday), Florrie is awake to see this; she notes how her room lightens gradually, how her furniture seems to move forward from the darkness—now her wardrobe, now her green chair. Despite this early hour, she feels rested. And, having visited the bathroom, Florrie wheels herself to her kitchenette where she makes herself a cup of leaf tea in the bone china teacup that Middle Morag bought her years ago. With care, she's able to wheel both herself and the teacup back. One of life's great pleasures is tea in bed.

Florrie sits upright, against the pillows, with her teacup in her lap, and stares at the painted lemons.

The thought, like a bird, has not gone. Indeed, it appears even more detailed now, in its dappled plumage, and it stares back expectantly. Attempted murder: How does Florrie feel about this? Last night, she'd felt perfectly calm with its arrival—*Yes, of course*. But now? As she sips her tea, she wonders whether it feels fanciful, like the plot of a thousand novels or like the musings of a woman who'd had both sedatives and a sizeable single-malt whisky in the same twenty-four hours. But what alternatives are there? It wasn't attempted suicide. And an accident? How does one fall through a tiny dormer window? And if one had wished to sit on a narrow windowsill for any reason, wouldn't one think, firstly, to remove a chutney jar of flowers from it? Before swinging one's legs over the side? Renata would have done so. But the jar had smashed on the floor.

Also, she screamed.

She did! Florrie almost slops her tea at the revelation. How could she have forgotten this? Above the spilling gutters and thundercracks, she'd heard (Florrie *knows* she did) a single, piercing scream that had fallen with Renata, that had only stopped with the single thud. And why might she have screamed if she'd chosen to jump?

Florrie dithers: Should she pull the cord? Tell someone? Possibly— but who? Aubrey Horner would call it nonsense. Georgette would dismiss it in a kinder fashion, calling her sweetheart and fussing like a hen. Dr. Mallory would, no doubt, be summoned back to the old apple store with his embossed leather bag and patronizing air: "Florrie, I'm concerned about your head . . ." And wouldn't the Ellwoods revel in it? Offer this information around, like a bowl of salted peanuts? *Here—have you heard? Poor Florrie . . . Her mind has quite gone.*

As for the police, no. Florrie, being a policeman's daughter, knows perfectly well that the police need evidence—of which she has none, not yet. She has theories only. She has circumstance. *We had a nice chat about Montmartre. We were going to have lemonade.* Even the scream could be dismissed as an issue with her hearing aid, or thunder, or Florrie's imagination being a little *de trop.* None of this is enough for a constable to open his notebook.

No, she thinks. None of that would do. For now, she will keep this thought to herself; she will merely continue to prod at the possibility of attempted murder as one prods at a mango, unsure if it's ripe. Only when she's satisfied will Florrie consider sharing it with someone— although she can't yet imagine who that someone might be.

Sunday morning is a quiet time here. After breakfast, most residents (or those of a Christian leaning and on the ground floor, at least) dress with a slight air of occasion—a tie or pearl earrings, a quick spray of Elnett—before making their way down to St. Mary's Church for the eleven o'clock service with Reverend Joe. Most are diligent in this. Florrie is rather less so. That's not to say she is entirely faithless. She has, all her life, quavered around the notion of God; she has *gone through phases* is how she tends to put it—pious one year and somewhat skeptical the next. Yet, regardless of which phase, she has always loved churches themselves: their hush, their cool, dusty perfume, the tapestry kneelers, the murmured *Let us pray*. Thus, Florrie does go to St. Mary's, sometimes: at Christmas, she went for the carols; there was Arthur's funeral. Sometimes, as with the compost heap, she goes there just to be.

Most Sundays, however, she stays in her room. She'll spend that hour with a novel or the radio or with her own reveries. And, briefly, Florrie considers doing this today. After all, her brain is ticking over like a rattly old boiler and she'd partly like to sit with her thoughts for an hour or two. But today is not like other Sundays. And what comes to mind, at this moment, is Arthur; firstly, because she misses him. But secondly, because whilst Arthur had loved treacle sponge and corduroy and his particular brand of pipe tobacco, his greatest passion had been the horses. Every Wednesday, a copy of the *Racing Post* would arrive at Babbington for him; he'd establish himself somewhere (the terrace, the library) and underline, in pen, the names of runners and riders that he half fancied, checking their recent form and odds. "Bits and Pieces, Florrie! The 2:00 p.m. at Kempton. Fancy a flutter?"— and sometimes, she'd slide pound coins across tables to him whilst he placed bets on his clever little phone. And the reason Florrie thinks of all this, at this moment, is because Arthur had once explained to Florrie about the purpose of the paddock; that is, how, before the race, the horses are paraded in a ring to be assessed by the bookies and punters: Which horse seems particularly lively? Which is moving well? Which is sweating a little too profusely? Which has a glint in its eye?

Inappropriate, perhaps, to compare the congregation of St. Mary's to the paddock at Kempton Park. But the idea is decent enough. For if someone did push Renata Green out of the window, wouldn't they want to seek absolution? Feel a little guilt, at least? And if someone knows something—anything—about it, wouldn't they want to unburden their soul? In short, Florrie decides this: she will pop on her own pearl earrings, powder her nose and wheel herself down to St. Mary's to see who might be sweating or lame or somewhat distracted. It feels like a good place to start.

She opts for her mauve sleeveless dress with its white polka dots and her light, off-white cardigan. On her single foot she pops a lilac shoe. And as she straightens from that shoe, Florrie notices a shadow pass by her window. A second later, she hears the casual, uninterested voice of Magda. "Miss Florrie? Are you there?"

Without waiting for an answer, the carer drifts into the old apple store with her usual accessories: a paper cup of medication, a clipboard, various glinting body adornments and what Marcella Mistry calls *that attitude*. "It is hot again. You think the thunder clears the air, but I say the air is not clearer. Your pills." She offers them. "You sleep okay?"

Florrie takes the paper cup and considers Magda Dabrowski. Alongside the familiar accoutrements, there are new additions: the eye makeup is particularly feline; those fingernails are, today, a deep navy blue—and Florrie detects a thick, peppery fragrance to her. Has she worn perfume before?

"I did," replies Florrie. "Much better."

"No bad dreams? No headaches?"

"Neither."

"Your wrist? Show me." Magda studies the wrist, prods it. "The swelling is less, I think. But . . ." She hisses through her teeth at the colour of this bruise, which is, Florrie admits, surprisingly dark. "It hurts?"

"Only a slight ache, that's all."

"You want pills? I get you pills for it."

"No need, Magda. But thank you."

Magda accepts this with a nod. Then, she assesses Florrie's out-fit with a narrowed eye. "You are going to church?" She doesn't need an answer; rather, she gives a one-shouldered shrug as if to say, *your choice*. "Do you mind, though, if I . . . ?"

Florrie knows exactly what's coming next. Magda doesn't always work on Sundays. But sometimes she has no choice (the timetable tries for fairness)—and, clearly, she resents this. On Sundays, Magda acquires the scuffing, affronted approach of a teenager; she will do what she must, and no more. And thus, on such a day, she tends to linger in the apple store, preferring to spend her time with Florrie—mumbling about the Ellwoods or the political state of the nation—than deal with other residents. She'll talk, too, about Poland—and how she misses it. (Last Sunday, Florrie had asked, *And what exactly goes into your babcia's famous stew?*) Above all, Magda's greatest act of defiance to the concept of Sunday working is to stand in Florrie's doorway and have a cigarette.

And so, at this moment, she does exactly that. Magda reaches into the pocket of her uniform, retrieves a pack of cigarettes with Polish branding, leans against the frame of Florrie's open door with all the disdain and professionalism of an artist's model, sets a cigarette on her plump lower lip and proceeds to light it with the *snap-snap-snap* of a pink plastic lighter. She inhales, holds the smoke in her mouth for a second or two—and exhales with a theatrical sigh.

Only when the pink lighter has been dropped back into the pocket does Florrie adjust her position and ask, "Magda, is there any news?"

"News?"

"I mean, about Renata. How is she? Have you heard?"

"The same. Georgette phones the hospital this morning. They say no change." Magda clicks her tongue. "She will probably die, I think. *Taki smutny . . .* I'm very sad about it."

Yet, as she swallows her first pill, Florrie can't help acknowledging that Magda's delivery of these words of sympathy is rather unemotional—as if she reads them from a notebook; as if, in fact, she *isn't* sad at all. She asks a second question. "The police, Magda. Did they come here?"

"Come?" The carer exhales smoke into the courtyard, glances back to Florrie. "Yes, they come that night. They talked to you. I was with you—you don't remember?"

Florrie does remember, partly. She recalls a policeman with a soft, doughy face kneeling down beside her and enunciating slowly, *Can you hear me, Ms. Butterfield?* "But afterward, I mean. What did they do afterward? Did they go upstairs?"

"Upstairs? You mean, to Renata's home? Yes. I know this because the door was locked, when they find it, so they break it down with I don't know what. Anyway, it's still broken—all splinters, like it was never a door. And they leave the mess for *us*, of course—like we do not have enough work here." She lowers her voice, mutters to the cigarette directly. "Franklin mends it tomorrow. If he's not too busy texting women in his shed."

Florrie takes her second pill. "And what did they find up there, Magda? Do you know?"

"Find? You mean, a suicide note?"

Florrie nods—although she doesn't mean that at all. It was not attempted suicide; so why might there be a note? Rather, she means signs of a struggle—trinkets knocked off shelves and upturned furniture. Or perhaps there were two glasses of wine on the table, not one, or a footprint on the windowsill that was far too large to have been Renata's own. Perhaps there was evidence of a man—say, a jacket on the back of a door or in the bedroom, the rumpled bedsheets, and . . .

You see, I'm in love, Florrie. Me! But she decides not to think of bed-sheets; that feels like a little too much.

"No note. But who needs a note to know what she did? The doctor? He tells the police that Renata is sad for many months now—many, many months."

"But did she seem it to you, Magda? Sad?"

"Me? I did not know her. But I think that I never saw her happy."

It is clear, therefore, what Magda believes. It's what they all seem to, at Babbington—that the withdrawn, solitary, beautiful manager may not have left a suicide note, as such, but no matter: she jumped, all the same. And Florrie hears, too, the past tense in Magda—as if Renata is already dead. *I did not know her.*

With that, Florrie takes her last pill. It's the pink, smooth-shelled one that serves to stop the eerie, flame-hot pain that comes where her left leg used to be. And this pill's cheery appearance brings to mind the various sweets in Mr. Patchett's shop. Pinky preferred sherbet lemons, but she, Florrie, liked everything—the licorice, the acid drops, the slabs of nougat that jammed her teeth together.

"And what of the others?"

"The others?"

"Other residents. The staff. I mean, everyone is sad, of course. But otherwise, is anyone . . . different?"

Magda shrugs with one shoulder. "Reuben cries a lot. Velma—is that her name? With the eyebrows, like . . . ?" Magda gestures. "She keeps talking of it: I can't believe it, oh, isn't it awful—that sort of thing. There is a lady upstairs, too—I don't know which lady—who is pushing tables over and shouting, which she never did before. But how can she know what happened? From the second floor? It is the weather, maybe. Like I say to you: it can make people crazy."

Magda exhales with care; the smoke rolls out into the courtyard in an even, rather beautiful way that they both watch until it's entirely dissipated. How calm Magda seems, how contented; how unbothered she is, when speaking of suicide. But then, Florrie supposes, Magda is a carer. It's her job—to be exposed, daily, to the human body's failings, to its ruptures and ageing, to the sudden and unexplained end of human life; so a colleague falling from a window is, perhaps, not such a tragedy.

Florrie clears her throat. "And Magda, dear, tell me: Is there anyone who needs to be informed? What I mean is, does Renata have any family here? Is there a boyfriend at all?"

At that, Magda grows still. She narrows an eye at Florrie. "Ha. Well. So, I tell you something. She has no family."

"No family? At all?"

"*Nikt*. Georgette? She looks at the form—we all sign forms when we come. You understand?"

"Contracts?"

"Contracts. Yes. They have a part for—how do you say it?—next of kin. But Renata's? Nothing. Empty."

No next of kin? This strikes Florrie as terribly sad. But it doesn't surprise her. Renata had alluded to as much in her office; the fact it was Florrie she wanted to speak to—not a mother or sister or aunt or best friend—rather suggested, too, that she had, like Florrie, no family in her life. "What a perfect sadness," she says—for it is.

Magda, however, seems less convinced. "She chooses it, yes? Like, she goes nowhere. She does nothing. We had staff party at Christmas— did she come? *Nie ma szansy*. Even her shopping: it comes here in a van, like she's too special to go to shop like rest of us. And you know what I see in her shopping bag? Dye—for her hair. Blonde? She is as blonde as I am, Miss Florrie—and I tell you, I am not blonde. But why dye her hair, when she goes nowhere? Sees no one? It makes no sense."

Perhaps she simply likes to be blonde? Just as Magda likes her hair to be bluish-black, like a damson? But instead, Florrie says, "There must be someone, Magda. Wasn't there a man?"

"A man?" She scoffs. "What makes you say that? Because she is thin and pretty? Like I say, she does nothing with her life. And so why might someone say, Oh, I like this person? Oh, this person is for me—this one who works with old people all day and then stays in her room all night, and at weekends? Oh, I love this boring person who doesn't say much and has no friends?" She punctuates this speech with a hard sniff. Then she glances back at Florrie. "When I say old people, I do not mean you."

"That's sweet of you—but I *am* old."

"Only in your body, Florrie. Not"—she taps—"in your head."

Florrie takes this as a lovely compliment and thanks her—but she grapples her way back to the matter of Renata. "Am I right in thinking you don't like her very much?"

"Like her? I do not hate her. But I do not mind that she is gone."

At that, Magda bends down and stubs the cigarette out. In doing so, her pale-green blouse parts from the pale-green waistband of her pale-green skirt—and suddenly, a dark, hollowed eye socket reveals itself on her back. There are teeth, too, and a nasal cavity—and Florrie doesn't understand it whatsoever until she realizes that a tattooed skull is staring back at her—wormy, blackened, enraged.

She exclaims without meaning to.

Magda turns. "You are ill?"

"No, no. It's your"—she points and stutters, trying to find the word—"tattoo, Magda. On your back? It's quite a thing, isn't it?"

The carer knuckles the base of her spine, as if checking it's still there. "Ah. You like it? I get my first when I'm fourteen years old. A rose, my boyfriend's name—normal things. After that, I keep going. It is a good pain, you know?"

"But a skull? It's very . . ." Florrie pauses. She can't think of an adjective.

"My cousin. He did it. He learns to do tattoos for money. So I tell him, whatever he wants to practise on me is okay. He likes skulls so I have many skulls, now. I have one on my leg—with a snake. And I have one"—she turns her back to Florrie, uses both hands to scoop her hair from the nape of her neck to reveal a further, smaller skull with candles placed in its cavities—"here. You like it?"

Florrie can only make a strange throaty noise, like a pigeon. For how can she answer that, in truth, she doesn't really like them at all? They're all artistic, for certain. (The cousin, she concedes, is a talented man.) But these skulls seem so aggressive—not least for being on the skin of Magda Dabrowski, who might be monosyllabic, at times, and dismissive, but is also the woman who cradled Florrie's hand after the police had gone, who made a Christmas card for Florrie with felt-tipped pens and stencils and glitter, as a child might have done. These skulls seem, to Florrie, out of keeping.

"You have one?"

"Me? A tattoo? Heavens, no!"

Magda smiles, narrows an eye. "You seem like you might. There are secrets in you, I think, Miss Florrie—yes, there are." And what a beautiful face she has, when she smiles—despite her efforts to hide it with the kohl and pale powder and blackened brows, the star-shaped stud in her nose. "If you want one, I know a man—in Banbury. He gives me discount so *you* have discount, also."

Florrie composes herself enough to say that this is a very kind offer.

At that, Magda announces she must go. She refastens her hair, pats her pockets as if checking that all is as it should be. But before turning, Magda pauses. "Miss Florrie? How much *did* you see? Of her falling."

"How much?"

"Like, you see her jump? You see her hit the ground?"

It seems a ghoulish question to ask. But it echoes, perhaps, the ghoulish tattoos—and it occurs to Florrie that maybe she's misinterpreted Magda; that her appearance isn't an effort to hide herself but, in fact, a bold manifestation of the real Magda. "Only some of it."

This answer appears to disappoint. The carer stares at Florrie's bedcover for a moment and murmurs Polish to herself before sauntering outside, into the sunlight—leaving cigarette smoke, her peppery scent and shadows in her wake.

Afterward, Florrie studies her lemons. What, she wonders, has she learned from this exchange? That Magda has strange tattoos; that Magda's not fond of Renata. That if Renata does, indeed, have a boyfriend, Magda doesn't know—or won't say—who he is.

What might Herbert Butterfield have advised? He'd kept, she recalls, a notebook. It was slender, with lined pages—stored in the internal pocket of his policeman's coat, which he'd pat, from time to time. In it, he'd write what he needed to remember in his policing life: *Life insurance?* Or *Ask the fishmonger* or *Check size of shoe.* On its front page, it said *Know the victim!*—underlined.

Know the victim.

Florrie supposes that she knows more about Renata than most. But how *little* she knows, even so. What clues might there be, in their conversation? The pinkness of petunias? *Les croissants aux amandes?* These don't feel very helpful.

But Renata is in love. And so all Florrie can think of, at this moment, is that she must discover who Renata Green is in love *with*. This man may not be the would-be murderer, of course, but love is a patchwork of colours and feelings. And, with no friends or next of kin, where else might Florrie begin?

Know the victim. But how?

Florrie pouts, thinking hard. She circles a palm with the pad of her thumb, around and around . . .

All splinters, like it was never a door.

There is no way of Florrie reaching the third floor. There is a lift, yes—but it only reaches the second. To enter Renata Green's quarters, Florrie would have to use her single leg to climb that last part of the staircase—and how might she ever do that? Hop? Drag herself up, step by step, like a wounded soldier in a black-and-white film? How might she squeeze her way between the splintered fragments of Renata's broken front door?

Oh, to have her leg back! Failing that, to have Pinky here—for Pinky would have raced up to the third floor without hesitation. She'd have scrambled up a telegraph pole, if need be—as thin and bendy as a whip, with a healthy disregard for those who shouted, Come down! Once, in their thirties, Pinky had clambered to the top of a rickety unlit bonfire—crates and chairs, old school desks—in order to save the sacrificial teddy bear that had been set on the top. (Pinky's boys had all been distraught at the idea of a teddy in flames; in truth, Pinky and Florrie had been no less upset.) So, up she went—Pinky, a grown woman, risking her life and dignity for the sake of a button-eyed bear.

Butters and Pinks. Pinky had remarked that this sounded like a double act. *Comedians, obviously.*

Obviously.

Florrie looks at her watch: ten-thirty. She has half an hour before church.

I must ask for help. She must ask someone to sneak up the stairs into Renata's quarters for her—but who? Not Magda, clearly, nor Georgette—nor any member of the staff. The Ellwoods? Not a chance. Babs Rosenthal has an adventurous air to her and, with her yoga, would find three floors of stairs no trouble at all, but she's part of the mah-jongg group and would tell everyone, in time. The Lims are both elderly (Kitty Lim is over one hundred years old, or so rumour has it) and might expire in the attempt.

Yet Florrie knows. How taken he'd been with that bumblebee; how earnest, when discussing Shakespeare in the orchard several weeks ago, beneath an early moon. *No, I don't believe it at all, Florrie.* Hadn't he asked, too, if he could help?

The shaving cut. The bright-yellow braces. It can only be him.

9

A Question of Stairs

Stanhope blinks twice, lowers his crossword. "Upstairs?"

She has found him in the library with a newspaper, sitting in a leather Chesterfield armchair that looks out across the lawn. She had wondered, at first, if he might also be preparing for church. After all, Florrie has seen him there before—singing a querulous baritone during the Christmas service and being both a little too late and loud with his *amen*. But there have been other Sunday mornings in which Florrie has found him doing precisely this—sitting with the papers in a patch of Sunday sun.

Today, Stanhope is wearing a shirt of a soft, peach colour; his braces are striped—pink, blue and a thinner line of white so that he resembles one of the deckchairs set out against the south-facing wall in which Velma Rudge has lain for the past few months, tanning herself to the texture of a raisin. The thumbprint's still there, on his left lens. His shaving cut is less.

He doesn't seem fazed by her request. Rather, Stanhope sets down his newspaper and considers her words with no more surprise than if she'd merely asked him to pass her a teaspoon. "To the third floor, you say? To Renata's quarters?"

"The police broke down her door, you see, and it hasn't been mended yet—so it would be perfectly possible to just . . . slip in. I'd go

myself, but the lift only goes to the second floor. And I'm not very . . ."
She gestures at herself. "Would you mind?"

"Mind? Not at all. But can I ask, um . . . why?"

Florrie wonders how frank she should be. They agree, it seems,
that the fall wasn't attempted suicide. But should she offer that she
has a new, deep conviction that Renata was, in fact, pushed? After a
small dither, Florrie opts for a half-truth. "What we said yesterday?
That Renata didn't choose to do this? I just wondered if there might
be something in her quarters to . . . confirm this."

"You think there might be a note of some kind?"

"No note. Magda told me that. Something else."

"I see." Stanhope peers up at the plasterwork ceiling. "Florrie,
it's just a thought, and probably a very foolish one, but last night I
was thinking about all of this—because it's still too hot to sleep, isn't
it?—and I wondered . . . Well, it's all so *unlike* her. Also, those dormer
windows are, I should imagine, extremely hard to just . . . fall out of. I
haven't tried and I'm six-foot-three, so I'm hardly well informed on this.
But it just strikes me that . . . Well, I wondered—I *am* wondering—if
Renata might have been pushed."

"Pushed? Out of the window?"

Stanhope immediately shakes his head. "Oh, heavens! Ignore me,
Florrie. It sounded so much more plausible at four in the morning—
in my head, not said out loud. I suppose I just thought . . . She seemed
so *well* on Friday. So sparky, as I told you. Of course, that isn't proof of
anything—we can all pretend to be fine, can't we? But I also can't help
thinking that if she had tried to take her own life, Renata wouldn't
have done it in such a messy fashion. All that sweeping! You've seen
her office, Florrie: everything is stacked at right angles; pens are
lined up on her desk like sardines. I'm not sure I've ever seen a crease
on that girl. So, to jump out of a third-floor window and . . . It just
doesn't *feel* right. But then, I realize that what I feel isn't proof of anything, either."

"Stanhope?"

"Hmm?"

"She screamed. Renata—that night. I heard it very clearly. I forgot, at first, that I'd heard it, but I remembered this morning."

"A scream? You're sure?"

"Quite sure. I heard it through the thunder."

"A loud scream, then?"

"Very loud."

Florrie and Stanhope blink at each other. And as they blink, Florrie wonders if he may change his mind, if he may decide this is all too fantastical, too intrusive, that Florrie is losing her marbles, and of course he won't go up to the third floor, squeeze through a splintered door and have a peer around the home of a woman in a coma. She worries he'll back away, appalled.

But he says, "You think someone pushed her, too?"

How right this idea had felt to her as it settled beside her last night. "Yes, I do."

"And her door was broken down, you say?"

"By the police. It'll be mended by Franklin tomorrow, apparently, so we don't have long."

"I see. Right. Of course, I wouldn't normally . . ."

"Oh, *I* wouldn't normally."

"But these aren't normal circumstances."

"Definitely not."

"And you say the police have done what they need to? I wouldn't be—what do they say in these sorts of programmes?—contaminating anything?"

"Been and gone."

"Well, then."

His eyes are a butterscotch shade in this light—and she wonders what shade her own eyes might be, at this exact moment. Pewter, or a city pigeon.

"Florrie, what should 1 be looking for, exactly? 1 ought to look at the dormer window itself, 1 suppose. But what else, do you think?"

He isn't appalled. He doesn't think she is certifiably insane. And so, having suggested looking for oddities, breakages or upturned furniture, Florrie decides to go a little further still. "Look, Stanhope, for signs of a man."

"A man?"

"Renata, you see, was *in love*."

His eyes grow as round as two tuppence pieces. "In love? Oh, I say!"

"1 know. She told me this—*she* did, on midsummer's morning. So 1 know that it's true."

"But in love with whom?"

"Exactly, Stanhope. 1 don't know."

"Which is why 1 must look for signs of a man."

"Bunches of flowers. Love notes. Male clothing. A photograph of him pinned on the fridge with a magnet. That sort of thing."

He blinks, absorbing this. "And do we think this fellow pushed her?"

Florrie has no idea, at this stage. "One would like to think that one's beau—lover, gentleman caller—would be the safest person in the world, but it's surprising how often the culprit *is* someone's beloved— say, a cheating husband or a jealous wife, using a dressing-gown cord or a meat tenderiser or just giving"—Florrie mimes this—"a single, sudden *push!* On seeing Stanhope's expression, she explains: "My father was a policeman."

"Ah. I see. Very good."

"In short, 1 just think we should find out who this chap *is*."

Stanhope's eyes gleam; he finds his walking stick and raps the ground twice, preparing to stand. "Now?"

"Yes, 1 was thinking so—*tout de suite*. Whilst everyone else is at church. Less chance of being seen."

"Excellent point. Right-o." And, suddenly aware of Florrie's mauve dress with the white polka dots, he says, "Are you off to church, too?"

"I am. I thought it might be useful."

"Good thinking."

There's an easy, companionable silence. In it, they both smile at each other—albeit rather coyly, sensing that proper smiling wouldn't be right under the circumstances. "Maybe we should reconvene afterward?"

"Yes, lovely. Somewhere cool. Somewhere a carer or an Ellwood can't disturb us—if there is such a place. How about the compost heap? At twelve o'clock?"

"Perfect. And *bonne chance*, Stanhope."

"Ah, yes—thank you. You too."

10

St. Mary's Church, Sunday Morning

Florrie is cutting it close. As she wheels herself between the box hedging, toward St. Mary's, she sees that its clock—a blue-faced thing with rust-coloured numbers—says it's eleven already, and Florrie is not one for lateness. *Faster,* she tells herself. *Go.*

Yet regardless of how she approaches St. Mary's—fast or slow, hatted or unhatted—Florrie is always reminded how much she likes this church. It is, firstly, decidedly squat. Whereas most churches have dreaming spires or high towers, this one is a low, plump creation with a tower and weathervane that barely break the tree line so that one *discovers* St. Mary's, or so it feels, amongst the beeches and yews. She loves, too, its age—how eight or nine hundred years' worth of lives have opened this door with its clunky metal ring, pressed the arch of their boot into its stone step, ducked out of midsummer heat (or hail or wind or a sudden April shower) into the church's gloom and removed their hat, smoothed down their hair. We've all done, she thinks, the same thing. Candles have been lit with a taper. Knees have left their imprints in the embroidered hassocks. Mouths have murmured, *Forgive our sins.* And then everyone has stood and filed back out again.

It is the formality, she thinks. Normally, Florrie would have little care for it—being a creature who'll eat a cream bun straight from its packet, or who has previously popped down to the post box in her bedroom slippers. But she has always liked the orderliness of a church service, the predictability; one knows, she thinks, where one *is*—with the service sheet and hymn books, and the wooden board on which hymn numbers are set. She loves, too, the fact that Reverend Joe meets and greets his congregation—cordially, smiling, and dressed in what Herbert would have called his full regalia. Sunday after Sunday. Month in, month out. And no vicar would, surely, reprimand her for being late.

There he is. As Florrie puffs her way between gravestones, Reverend Joe is nodding gravely at Velma Rudge whilst also trying to usher her into the church. "Yes, quite . . . Yes, this way." Having achieved this, he glances skyward in relief—and he is about to follow Velma into St. Mary's when he looks up and sees Florrie rattling toward him. "Oh, Florrie! Welcome." He fumbles with the hinged, metal wheelchair ramp with a flapping of cassock sleeves. "How's that? Will that do?"

Reverend Joe is not, perhaps, a typical vicar. He arrived in the March gales—blown into Temple Beeches as the elderly Reverend Bligh, with his tortoiseshell cat and cirrhotic liver, had been blown out. And what an arrival: in a faded black T-shirt that said AC/DC on it, with a missing front tooth and a beard so substantial that if a blackbird chose to make its nest in there, one might never know it except for a chirping sound. Naturally, some residents had objected. This man looked, they felt, *unsavoury*; what on earth could *he* know of the synoptic Gospels or the Stations of the Cross? It didn't help matters that in his first service, Reverend Joe had dropped the silver-plated wine jug so that it was dented with a bright *ting!*, and he'd sworn so loudly that the Ellwoods had heard it—(*bollocks*, apparently, so nothing too appalling but still a little too scandalous for St. Mary's Church). For some residents, this sealed their disapproval. But for others (Florrie and Arthur, for example) it had only confirmed that Reverend Joe is as human as the rest of us—which is, surely, what one wants in a vicar. Ever since, Florrie has formed a list of things she likes about him: his slight paunch, his whistling, his insistence on being known by his first name. She loves, too, how he hangs bird feeders from the lowest branches of the ancient yew.

He leans down toward Florrie with an earnest expression. "I'm so pleased you're here. I've been thinking about you, Florrie. What happened with Renata. It's all so . . ."

It was. It is. "I'm glad to see you, too."

He puts his hand on her shoulder. "Well, I hope you'll find a bit of comfort here. And if you ever fancy a chat, there's always a kettle singing in the vicarage."

The beard, the bird feeders, the missing tooth, the fact that he survives (as she does) on tea. But above all, what Florrie likes about Reverend Joe is how kind he'd been about Arthur. For Arthur's service had been so beautifully done. The vicar had spoken with reverence. He'd suggested that what matters is how much one is loved, rather than by how many—which had been so tactful, considering only a handful of people had attended the funeral: Reverend Joe, Renata, Nancy Tapp, Stanhope, Florrie—and yes, the Ellwoods had been there, but out of nosiness rather than any sort of grief. There had been, too, a middle-aged man whom nobody knew but who'd had Arthur's deportment, Arthur's jaw, a little of Arthur around the eyes. He'd left the church before the rest of them. Florrie would have spoken to him, if he'd not left so quickly. As it was, she could only watch him go and think, *I know who you are.*

She parks herself at the back of the church, near the noticeboard and collection box. From here, she has an excellent view. (One sees so much more if one sits at the back of places—buses, schoolrooms, village halls.) St. Mary's was built long before the Babbingtons came along; but they made their mark on it interior—congratulating themselves with carvings and stained-glass windows and numerous plaques that describe their relatives with illustrious words in ornate script. Shafts of coloured light drift down through these windows; they illuminate Bibles, stonework, the polished sides of pews. Under her wheels a dark-red carpet runs the length of the nave, bordered by two wrought-iron grilles beneath which there is pipework, the odd dropped penny, and Florrie can see where decades of feet have worn this carpet down to a paler shade—all those takers of communion, all the mourners and brides.

She notes, too, what's closer at hand. By her side, there is a small trestle table with a Formica top on which there are various things of religious bent: pamphlets on the history of St. Mary's, a few parched crosses left over from Palm Sunday, a plate of leatherette bookmarks for sale with St. Mary's, Temple Beeches embossed on them in gold. Here, too, is the prayer book—rectangular with a red ribbon marker—in which people may write their prayer requests, using a pencil that's attached with string to lessen the risk of inadvertent pencil theft. All those worries and all that gratitude written, anonymously, inside.

But the church isn't, of course, the real reason for her being here. Nor (although she wouldn't say this to Reverend Joe, who is now making his way up the aisle whilst adjusting various parts of his ensemble) is Florrie here for comfort, as such. She's here to watch—and whilst it's hard, from the back of the church, to see actual faces, she can recognize enough of the congregation from their postures or jewelry or various coiffure. The Ellwoods are obvious—side by side, like salt and pepper pots. Aubrey Horner bellows out the first hymn, in baritone. The Professors Lim are here, which surprises Florrie for the Lims have reasoned, long ago, that there is too much evidence against the notion of God for either of them to believe in Him fully; yet here they are, in the front row.

Are there more people here today than usual? Since Florrie only comes to the occasional Sunday service, she can't be sure. But she can, at least, tell who in this church is upset. And with that, Florrie begins to move her attention from person to person with all the smooth, slow intensity of a lighthouse beam. The Ellwoods trill out the hymn with half-closed eyes and apparent heartfelt feeling. Harrold Lim is doing something with a handkerchief. There's a rather distant, superior expression to Marcella Mistry, mouthing the words to the hymn rather than truly singing them—but isn't there a similar expression to Marcella on most days? Nancy Tapp, at the front, is folded over in her wheelchair so that one can't see her expression, as such, but the position of her head suggests that she may be snoozing. And when the hymn ends and Reverend Joe says, "Please be seated," it strikes Florrie that Georgette (still in her uniform) sits a little more heavily than others—as if exhausted or weighted with despair. Is she tearful? Distraught? But when she turns to rummage in her pocket, it's not a tissue but a toffee that Georgette retrieves—wrapped in gold foil that rustles noisily so that Aubrey Horner turns around pointedly, to stare.

Is nobody tearful at all? Not even the Ellwoods, who are known for their theatrics? Not Velma Rudge, who appears to be having trouble with her brassiere, jamming a thumb under her bosom and rummaging so that she isn't paying attention to the reverend at all? Has the apparent attempted suicide of the manageress not shaken them to the core? Florrie pouts, annoyed. Indeed, she could feel quite furious with the whole lot of them—even in church, where fury isn't really permitted. But then Florrie promptly reminds herself that emotions can be hidden, that we can feel something acutely—love, shame, loneliness—and sweep it under an imaginary carpet so that we spend our lives walking over it, pretending it isn't there when it *is* there, very much so. *I'm perfectly fine, thank you*—said so brightly that we could almost believe it. Is this what's happening here?

"It is good," says Reverend Joe, "to see so many of you here after such a sad and turbulent couple of days."

They sing. They pray. There are parish notices. Somebody drops their hymn book; another clears their throat. And then the sermon begins. Reverend Joe mentions a parable, speaks of the metaphorical thunderstorms that can enter our lives; soon, too, he mentions Renata directly—and there is, then, a murmur of compassion in the congregation. There's a faint clucking of tongues, a shaking of heads—and, from someone, an audible *dear, dear.* With this, Florrie's fury starts to dissipate. To continue her carpet metaphor (that one's feelings can be tucked away, out of sight), she supposes that the carpet is now being rolled back; for Aubrey's shoulders seem to drop with sympathy. Marcella lifts her eyes toward the stained glass. And Florrie's disgruntlement is replaced by a sudden rush of fondness for all of them. For aren't we all the same? Weren't we all babies, once? Aren't we all the sons or daughters of people who must have looked in our cribs and imagined how our lives might be—but who'd failed to imagine that we, their children, might ever be in our mid- to late eighties with cataracts or circulatory problems? Didn't *we* fail to imagine it, too? We think, for so long, that old age will never find us. We feel that we, as individuals, might somehow be exempt from it, that we might be given some sort of ticket that allows us to sidestep death, as one might a manhole cover, and carry on, whistling a tune. And then, one day, we find that our knees crack as we descend a staircase or someone offers us a seat on a tube train or we catch sight of ourselves in a shop window and think, *Good God, that can't be me*—so that we realize that no, we aren't exempt. Florrie thinks, *We're in this together. We all have our frustrations and sorrow at being older; we've got regrets and losses and missed opportunities, things said or not said.* And she supposes that every single person in these pews has known moments in their life in which they've felt such tenderness, suddenly—at geese in flight, say, or looking at the hands of a loved one—that they've lacked the language for how they feel. We've all felt longing. We've all felt alone. In short, not showing emotion about Renata's comatose state doesn't mean there's no emotion at all.

And secrets. Here we all are, listening to a sermon with our hands clasped. But Florrie has no doubt that there are secrets inside every single person in St. Mary's, Temple Beeches. Some dark, some even darker. Some as black as tar.

Florrie looks down. She's never quite got used to these scars. At first, they'd been crimson; they were roughly stitched together with a black, bloodied thread that she'd pulled out herself in the end. Now? They are elderly, like the rest of her. They're textured, moon-pale and slightly raised, in parts, so that she could find those scars in the dark, if she had to. They run over her knuckles like lacework. *Florrie, what happened to you?*

There it is. *You.* That old, dark feeling—the pike, with its underbite—drifts back into view.

Not now. Not here.

Rather, Florrie looks up at a stained-glass window. It must depict a saint of some sort, doing something saintly—but she can't be sure which one. He has a kind face, though; there are intricate folds to his clothing and he looks back with an expression she can't quite name: Melancholy? Love?

Stanhope. What is he doing at this very moment? How, exactly, has he climbed the stairs? She imagines his left hand on the polished banister, gaining height in a slow, rhythmical fashion not unlike a metronome. She imagines him fitting himself—all kneecaps and shoulders and walking stick—through the gap in a splintered door. And she wonders how that peach-coloured shirt might look against the dark wood paneling, or in shafts of dusty light.

Florrie dwells on Stanhope for a time. But she also thinks of her parents—of those Bakelite tea trays, the charred Sunday lunch, of Prudence's pliés and pirouettes, performed in the hall. Bobs, too: *Catch it, Flo!* She thinks of Aunt Pip who, in her later years, took to smoking a pipe (because it shocked the neighbours, most likely); she'd smoke on her garden bench in a velvet housecoat, with a dachshund by her feet. Her thoughts, too, move on to Renata—fighting for her life in a room with a cold, antiseptic smell. To be pushed; to have no next of kin; to be newly in love: it's all so much to bear that Florrie closes her eyes very tightly and imagines packing up all her best, deepest, motherly love in . . . what? What will she choose? A box like her Botley and Peeves cheese crate. And then she covers it in a swathe of bubble wrap, adds wrapping paper and string—and it arrives, she decides, with such a heavy, wooden *clonk* that it's heard on the ward below and doctors look up. *What's that?*

And *them.* She thinks of all the residents on the first and second floors. There has never been a visit to St. Mary's when Florrie hasn't sent love to them; but today, her thoughts are a little more specific: she sends love to *her*, to the woman who is, apparently, newly distressed—pushing things over and fighting the staff. Magda hadn't named her. But someone, Florrie knows, is troubled since Renata's fall. So she blows her love toward this person—softly, as if holding a dandelion clock.

The reverend says, "Let us pray."

Florrie is jolted by this. Her eyes open at the exact moment that everyone else closes theirs. The congregation bow their heads; there is, for some, the clasping of palms. Even Joe's eyes are closed as he says, "Heavenly Father, who made heaven and earth . . ."

But someone else's eyes are open.

Nancy Tapp has turned around in her chair. She has twisted as much as her body can and is staring down the aisle, directly at Florrie, with the shiny, anxious gaze of a mouse. *Florrie*, she mouths.

Florrie thinks to look behind her. She mouths back. *Me?*

Yes. You. Meet me outside? Nancy gestures—a forefinger pointing to the door.

Outside?

Yes.

Now?

Afterward.

They nod in secret, satisfied agreement—after which Reverend Joe and the congregation all say an emphatic *Amen.*

11

Nancy's Situation

Florrie feels in a quandary. On one hand, she wants to leave church as soon as possible. It is, after all, nearly midday: Stanhope will already be waiting for her at the compost heap, on the plastic chair with bird droppings on it—and he may have news on Renata's beau. She doesn't want to be late.

But on the other hand, this is Nancy. And the truth is that Nancy Tapp is not quite like the rest of them. There is the matter of *Nancy's situation*—murmured over teapots in a sympathetic tone. There's also the fact that Nancy tends to stay in her quarters. She may come to church, and sometimes make her way down to the dining room, but mostly she prefers to stay in her room, surrounded by cardboard boxes and daytime television, so chances to speak to her are rare. It's even rarer that she might ask specifically for a tête-à-tête.

What to do? The compost heap? In her mind, she's already there. (Does the blackbird rummage? Has the grass snake come?) But she wonders, too, what Nancy wants—for what if it matters? What if she has news that might help Florrie find out what really happened on midsummer's night? Thus Florrie readjusts her skirts, pats her hair and wheels herself out into the sunlight, looking for Nancy Tapp.

Of all the residents—on the ground floor, at least—Nancy has been here for the shortest time. She arrived less than two months ago.

Florrie had been at Babbington for over a year by then; she'd grown used to its routines and voices, its uneven floorboards. She had, too, formed a light friendship with the previous inhabitant of the only other wheelchair-friendly quarters—a gentleman named Dermot Dunn. He'd had a blond toupée and a laugh like a dinner gong, and they'd played draughts together, Dermot and her. But in February, he'd left to join his daughter in County Cork. Thus, his accessible room was scrubbed, dusted and repainted—ready for somebody else.

Nancy came with the first swallows, her handbag perched in her lap. And whilst Florrie tries to greet every new arrival, she'd had a particular wish to welcome one in a wheelchair. (Years ago, Victor Plumley had driven an MG Midget, as silver as the moon, and if he passed another MG Midget, he'd toot his horn and wave. "It's just what one does," he'd explained. "We're in the same club, you see.") So Florrie had knocked on Nancy's door within hours of her arrival, proffering a packet of custard creams.

But they aren't in her room, now. Nancy has pushed herself over to the shadiest part of the churchyard—near the bird feeders, underneath the yew. She has an expectant look, hands folded. "Florrie? Cooee. Over here."

It is impossible to think of Nancy Tapp without thinking of a woodland creature—of a mouse, say, or the hedgehog that Gulliver once found beneath the garden shed and had patted, cautiously, before backing away. Nancy has, firstly, the roundest of eyes. They're dark eyes, too, so dark that the pupil is lost within them; one might see one's own face reflected in their questioning stare. Also, Nancy's voice is higher in pitch than most people's so that it's been remarked upon that only bats or dogs might hear her. Even her mannerisms remind Florrie of rabbits: the occasional flinch or sudden, wide-eyed stillness as if she's in danger and may need to run.

"Dear Florrie. I'm sorry to be so secretive."

"Nancy, are you all right?"

One asks this question instinctively, of course—as younger people say, *How you doing?* Or, *What's up?* But nevertheless, Florrie winces at her question and wishes she'd asked something different; *Nancy's situation* means that Nancy is not, in fact, all right at all. For her, Babbington is a holding pen. She has barely arrived and yet she won't stay much longer because somewhere inside this dainty form, somewhere underneath this grey linen dress with its seed-pearl buttons, underneath Nancy's muscles and skin, there is a ribbon that's curling neatly through her spine. Indeed, it curls so tightly and with such intention (Florrie thinks of bindweed) that no surgeon can extract it. So it stays. It grows. It pinches nerves and spreads into organs. It is this ribbon that has put Nancy in a wheelchair—which she, unlike Florrie, struggles to manoeuvre.

It is a hospice that she needs. Specifically, Nancy needs a room in St. Chad's Hospice—out on the Woodstock road, between the bottle bank and the humpbacked bridge. But no room is available just now. So she waits, here, at Babbington Hall—which is not only the nearest residential home to St. Chad's but also (as Florrie knows) the only place with accessible quarters that don't overlook pylons or have an obligatory colour scheme of dreary bollard-grey. Over those custard creams, Nancy had explained it all: that she'd be here for a month or so, no more. She'd said, *What can be done?*—with a sad, tired smile.

So, no, she isn't all right in the slightest. But Nancy considers the question anyway. "Me? Oh, I'm managing well enough. But listen, Florrie—please. This isn't about me. I want to talk about *you*."

"Me?"

"Yes. I want to hear how you're feeling—after Renata's fall. Because I know what it's like, you understand. Oh, I do, and it's perfectly dreadful."

She does understand—of course. It was Nancy who had witnessed Arthur's fall. His broken spectacles; the single bright crack of bone against stonework: these observations had been Nancy's own and had come from her, firsthand. She'd been returning from St. Mary's early that evening, looked up and seen him—pipe in hand, *put-putting*; she'd thought to call his name, in greeting. But then Arthur had cried out (*Oh!*), started to topple as timber does, and Nancy had pushed and pushed herself through long grass, over tree roots and molehills toward the stone cherub whilst screaming for help from someone, anyone. Reverend Joe had been the first to hear her. (He'd said, later, that he'd thought that Nancy was an injured animal—a rabbit, say, or a bird.)

Nancy hid for a week afterward. Food was taken to her room. And Aubrey Horner said to Florrie, in passing, "Of all people. Of all people to have to see something like *that* . . ."

Here she is now, in dappled light, blinking. "How *do* you feel, Florrie? Please tell me honestly."

What to say? On one hand, Florrie's heart feels half broken by what happened. Part of her is thinking, constantly, about that small, white-skinned body in a hospital room—and it hurts her terribly. But equally, in truth, Florrie feels alive; she feels so very galvanized by the knowledge that this wasn't an attempt at suicide, that somebody pushed Renata Green, that Renata was *in love*; galvanized, too, by the fact that she's engaged in a task of such importance that she hardly recognizes her life. (When, at Babbington, is anything *new*?) But she can't say this to Nancy. She isn't sure she could say it to anyone. "I'm so very sad, Nancy. And I wish I wasn't in this chair—because if I still had both legs, I could have run toward Renata and caught her, or held her hand, perhaps." This answer surprises Florrie—but it's true.

"Ah, yes. For a while, I had dreams of running to Arthur and catching him—me! Catching Arthur, in both arms! I couldn't catch a ping-pong ball these days. But one forgets that, in one's dreams."

It's clear that Nancy is ill. The signs of it are there: the hollowed cheeks, the sallow complexion, the pronounced tendons in her neck. Also, there's a clear distortion of the abdomen over which she rests her hands as an expectant mother might. Yet some things defy her illness: there remains a glint in Nancy's eyes, for example. There's a liveliness in her gestures, in how she glances left and right. What a beauty she must have been, once—and still is, in a way.

"I must tell you, Florrie—come closer. That's better. I must tell you I was surprised to see you in church. It isn't usual for you, I think? But then, these aren't easy times, are they? We must find our comforts where we can. I can't say I'm a steadfast believer; I have my doubts about God, heaven knows. But what harm can it do, to come here and speak to Reverend Joe? He's a good man. And he knows a lot about people, I think; one feels he's gone through troubles of his own. Is this"—she gestures at her abdomen—"all God's plan, do you think? His will? I don't know. But there *is* a little comfort in trying to believe it."

Such remarks take Florrie into new, uncharted territory. (Others have talked of God's will, in the past. Florrie has listened politely, but she's never been wholly convinced. How might He have wanted Bobs to blacken, like toast, in an armoured tank? Or for a carotid artery to redden the snow of an old blacksmith's yard? But she sets such thoughts to one side.)

"Maybe," says Florrie.

Nancy nods, grateful for the answer.

She looks down at her lap. Florrie follows her gaze and notices the skeletal nature of those hands—but also Nancy's jewelry. For on three of her fingers, Nancy Tapp wears three hefty, sparkling rings. The rumour has always been that Nancy has been married three times; also, that she was a socialite in her younger days. And whilst some people at Babbington have felt this unlikely, Florrie can believe it. Seeing her now, she imagines the Nancy of forty years before: elegant, slender, with her tinkling laugh and coyness, slipping between strangers with a champagne glass in her hand. Nancy seems petite, yet if she rose in her chair and walked out of it, Nancy would be a tall woman—not Pinky's height, but taller than Florrie, at any rate—so that the finest of dresses might have looked even finer on her, with no ample bust or bottom for them to catch upon. These rings belong to *that* Nancy—who is still *this* Nancy, of course: a solitaire diamond, a cluster of rubies and, lastly, a single, enormous, sea-green opal, the size of Florrie's own thumb.

Florrie looks down at her own lap. She notes her thighs, the single swollen foot.

"Speaking of good men . . . Well, Dr. Mallory is one, too, don't you think?"

Florrie blinks. Is he? She supposes he must be. A doctor's role, after all, is a kind, well-meaning one; one wouldn't study medicine if one was a miserable sort. It's true that Florrie isn't necessarily fond of the man, but any annoyance she's felt toward Dr. Mallory has largely been because he isn't Dr. Laghari—and he can hardly help that. I should, she thinks, be nicer to him.

"Yes, perhaps he is."

"I'm glad you think so. Oh, I know he seems a little flashy in that sports car and he isn't always tactful, it's true. But he's got a kind heart. One can talk to him. That poor man has listened to me prattle on for goodness *knows* how long! I'm telling you this, Florrie—and the reason I wanted to see you is—because I rather hope that you'll talk to him, too."

"Talk to Dr. Mallory?"

"I know, I know: you'll tell me that you're perfectly fine and don't need to speak to anyone—and you do seem in marvelous form, Florrie. You always do—so cheerful! But what we've *seen*, what we've been through, you and I . . . It is a form of trauma—it *is*. And I don't know much about the world, but I do believe, very much, that trauma can change its form, if one isn't careful. What I mean is, if one doesn't *speak* about one's sadness or anger or shock, if one doesn't express it or acknowledge that pain . . . Well, it turns into something physical—a headache, say, or worse."

"Nancy?"

"I like you, Florrie—very much. Those biscuits? It's the little gestures, like that, that can mean so much to a person. And I suppose I just want you to . . . stay well. To not be too affected by this. That's all."

To stay well. Florrie would rather like that, too. And how she'd love Nancy to be well, also—to shake off that ribbon in her spine like a hula hoop and rise from her chair with a bright *ta-da!* And with that, she reaches for the smaller woman's hand. She sets her own hand down, over it—over the thumb-sized opal and diamond solitaire—and Nancy responds by placing her other hand over Florrie's own so that they are almost playing pat-a-cake in a playground, these two elderly women in their wheelchairs. "Oh, Nancy. It must be so very hard for you."

"I've made my peace, mostly. But some days are harder than others."

Nancy gives a frail smile. But her eyes seem to shimmer, despite her best efforts. As if wishing to hide her tears or prevent them, she suddenly looks up into the branches of the yew tree—and Florrie might have followed her gaze except that she has no need to; she can see, in Nancy's eyes, the reflections of what Nancy is looking at: the church tower, its weathervane, the swifts darting over. Florrie has no need to look anywhere but at these rabbity, watchful eyes. As she looks, she thinks, *This face will be gone, soon. These eyes and these cheekbones and these laughter lines will, in a month or so, no longer exist.* And one should be accustomed to such a thought, by this age; one should be able, at least, to understand it. But it stays, even now, beyond Florrie's understanding. (*Gone,* as Arthur is gone.)

"Promise me? That you'll talk to the doctor, if you need to?"

"I promise."

Nancy and Florrie stay with each other for a little longer— observing the bees passing through the shafts of sunlight, the birds returning to the sunflower seeds. Their hands remain stacked like pancakes so passers-by, if they glanced across, couldn't tell who was comforting who.

On returning from Zermatt, Florrie had found a house of poultices and wintergreen smells, of a restless Prudence. "Bobs," she said, embracing her daughter, "will be so glad you're here."

But Bobs didn't really know anything. He plucked at his bed-clothes, shouted at shadows. His eyes rolled back in their sockets and he was so hot that his skin seemed to hiss when they bathed him. It was Pip who explained the truth of it. "The flu has overwhelmed him. His lungs are . . ."

"Dr. Winthrop?"

"He's coming daily. But, Florrie, if you catch it—"

"Then I catch it."

For the last week of his life, Florrie mopped her brother's brow, lifted his arms to sponge underneath them. His lungs were as laboured as bellows; his skin was leathered, like a pod. And Florrie would watch him sleep and remember who he'd been—the boy who'd stopped traffic to let ducklings cross, who had divided that raspberry tartlet in two and winked as he'd bitten into his half. She studied his face—its pores, its outlines—and thought, *Remember this.*

One night, he mumbled, "Flo?"

"I'm here."

In a faltering breath, Bobs spoke of the life he'd have lived if he hadn't gone to Clervaux, if there had never been a war. He spoke of seeing Mount Everest; of swimming with turtles and seeing southern stars; of coming home to marry Clemency Winthrop and having four children with her, two boys and two girls. He'd have played Test cricket for England—making a double century against India at Lord's. "And we'd have had a dog . . . a very good dog."

She can't recall the exact exchange between them, not now. One might assume Florrie could, since they'd prove to be her brother's last words in this lifetime—although she didn't know they'd be his last words at the time. But there seemed to be an understanding between them: Florrie would live her life for both their sakes. And if she ever thought to tell her brother about Hackney—wanting to be honest with *him*, at least—it was the thinnest of thoughts that vanished, like steam, as soon as it came.

Later, some said that Robert Butterfield's death had been a release for him. After all, he'd been left with a wheezing, lonely, indoors life. His disfigurement had made him smash mirrors. On the long, balmy summer evenings—a time of moths, of watering the garden—he'd lain in bed and listened to the children playing on Vicarage Lane as he'd done once, before the war, and he'd relayed the depth of this sadness to Florrie in a telephone call to her in L'Hôtel Petit Palais. He'd said, "I don't think I can bear it. I just don't think I can." But even so, his death was no consolation—for any of them.

Enough. For Nancy's situation is not the same as Bobs's—and Nancy's concern for Florrie is lovely but not really required. But a promise is a promise, even so. So if Florrie stops sleeping or eating, say, or starts having dreams of Renata's fall from which she wakes with a thumping heart, it's Dr. Mallory she'll call.

12

Dum Spiro Spero

To her dismay, Stanhope is not there. He must have been there recently, though, because the plastic chair is at a different angle, and there's a strange, watchful feeling to the place, as if a person has only just left.

Florrie tries the library. But the maroon Chesterfield chair that he favours is empty. Indeed, the only occupant of the library is Aubrey Horner, who is drowsing—lolling, mouth open, occasionally producing a single, sudden snort for which he mumbles an apology to no one. Florrie has no wish to wake him. (If she did, she'd lose an hour of her day.) So she reverses carefully, carries on.

Stanhope isn't taking coffee in the dining room. Nor is he on the terrace or beneath the apple trees. Florrie hovers near the lavatory for as long as it's engaged, only to find that it's Velma Rudge, not Stanhope, who appears in a cloud of L'Air du Temps. And it's only later, as she wheels herself toward the old apple store, that she finally sees his peach-coloured shirt and striped braces, his smile. He waits on the white-painted bench for her. *Stanhope*, Florrie thinks, *is such a lovely name.*

Inside, he takes the mallard chair, which proves marginally too low for him so that his knees are slightly higher than his seat-bones, and he assesses this unexpected position with mild surprise.

"Tea? Or is it too early for something stronger?"

Stanhope blinks. "Can we?"

"I think we can. It's a Sunday lunchtime. People do. Sherry? Or a little whisky and water?"

He adjusts his collar, delighted. "A whisky would hit the spot, if you're sure?"

As Florrie wheels herself into her kitchenette to pour the two whiskies, she wonders what he's thinking—for he's never been in the old apple store before. What does he make of her painted lemons? Of her pink tasseled lampshade and the saltire flag on her hatstand that she uses, sometimes, as a headscarf? Her Nepalese prayer flags or tribal African mask? What might anyone make of it all?

More important, however, is what he makes of the third floor.

She wheels back with the whiskies wedged between her thighs, offers one to him. "I'm sorry I kept you waiting, Stanhope. I got talking to Nancy Tapp."

"Oh, don't worry. I was late myself. I was rather worried that I'd missed you. That's an uneven staircase, you know—and creaky. Thank goodness for banisters. I felt like I was on board a ship."

With that matter dealt with, Florrie leans forward. "How was it? You got up to her quarters?"

"I did."

"And?

"Oh, let me tell you—it's marvelous up there. Quite marvelous."

"Is it? Oh! *How* is it marvelous? Tell me."

At this, he, too, leans forward. "Everything they say? About Renata? What a quiet life, what a dull life—that sort of thing? They should *see* where she lives! It's not dull at *all*! Her little home is brimming over! I'm not sure I've ever seen so many books in my life! Well, I have in the British Library and bookshops, of course, but not in someone's home. Honestly, Florrie: there are bookshelves on every wall in every room; novels and biographies and non-fiction and travel writing and encyclopedias and poetry anthologies and a great big book"—he holds out his hands—"on Tudor England, of all things. Field guides, too; she has a whole row of them—to British birds and seashells and fungi and the night sky. And she was definitely going to Paris, Florrie. There was a map of it—on the kitchen table. It was folded neatly, but I have to confess that I may, er, have unfolded it a little . . . taken a look. And there were pen marks on it; she'd been making plans. She'd put an asterisk by a place called rue Seveste."

Florrie flexes her toes. "Well *done*, Stanhope! What else?"

In between sips, he lists all his discoveries from the twenty minutes or so he'd spent in Renata's quarters—because there hadn't just been books. There had, too, been art in abundance: in heavy gilt frames or pinned onto corkboards or as postcards set up against the spines of books. There were still lifes, landscapes, a bluish, big-bottomed figure that he assumed was a Picasso, but he wasn't fully sure; seascapes and portraits and a pencil drawing of a sculpture (Venetian, he wondered? Florentine?) that was almost life-size, hanging by the door. There were linocuts and embroidery and a small bronze statue of a howling wolf. There was a snow globe, he said, of the Eiffel Tower, which he'd shaken gently to see Paris in snow. "It was not unlike a proper gallery, to be honest—the sort one would pay for. I could have spent the whole day there."

And he carries on: there were mismatched floral cushions on armchairs, a vintage bedspread on the double bed; also, a radio set to the BBC World Service and a rocking chair and a chest of drawers in a soft, sky-blue colour, painted by hand, and a glass bottle into which had been put some fairy lights that, when turned on, resembled like fireflies in a woodland and would look (he supposed) all the lovelier for being used at night; and there were lavender bags and a bone-china teapot, tealights and a silk dressing gown, and by Renata's bed there was a singular, one-eyed bear that was virtually furless from love and adventure. "A small chap," he explained. "The size of my palm. Oh— and there were some of those . . . sayings. Affirmations."

"Affirmations?"

"Quotes. Cheery things. The sort that tend to be written on drift-wood and hung from a door. TODAY IS A GIFT; THAT'S WHY THEY CALL IT THE PRESENT. *Dum spiro spero.* That kind of thing. This is a splendid whisky, Florrie. Smoky."

It's the best she has. It's a single malt from the island of Islay— thick with the tang of seaweed and peat—and on a different day, she might have told Stanhope about the otter she saw beneath Bowmore distillery as she'd paddled, or about the field of geese that she'd wan-dered through and how, afterward, she had to bang her boots together to free them of clotted goose *messages* (a Prudence term). But there are, today, more important things. *"Dum spiro spero?"*

Stanhope sips again. "Latin. As I breathe, I hope."

What a phrase. It resonates with Florrie—as if, on hearing it, part of her had answered. (Aunt Pip, she knows, would have approved of those three words.) And as she sips her own whisky, Florrie feels such a rush of pleasure and relief—that Renata's quarters are as full as they are; that they are far, far removed from the rumours and prattle of the Babbington residents who've been quite certain that Renata's life has been so drab and insubstantial that any thoughts of suicide were prob-ably *for the best*. The former servants' quarters sound like the home of a woman who wants life and all its wonders—more of it, not less.

"Now. The dormer window. We thought I should look at it—yes?"

"And?"

"Well, I had to be careful because I didn't want anyone to see me up there. But the window is not very big at all. I really don't see how she could have fallen out by accident—even her, as tiny as she is. Also, the curtain was torn."

"Torn?"

"Its fabric—embroidered with flowers, very pretty—had been torn away from its plastic hooks. Only a little, it's true—three hooks out of twenty-odd—but enough for me to notice it."

"Recently, do you think?" But Florrie knows, as she says this, that yes, it must have been recently done. For Renata—she, of the pressed linen blouses and polished shoes—would never have allowed a torn curtain to stay like that. She'd have mended it promptly, sat down with a needle and thread.

"Oh, I should say so. And I'd say, too, it was roughly done, with force—because those three plastic hooks had actually snapped in half. Metal hooks would have been far stronger, but you just don't tend to get them these days. Nothing is made as well as it was."

They both nod at this statement. "And what about men?"

"Men? Ah!" He leans back with a smile and pauses, as if this might be his best bit of news. "Florrie, there were letters."

"Letters? What sort of letters?"

"Love letters! Dozens of them—so many of them that, in fact, I simply couldn't read all of them. Indeed, I didn't read any from beginning to end because that would have felt a bit intrusive; also, frankly, I was running out of time. So I skimmed through them and jotted down the interesting bits. Hang on." He fumbles with a top pocket, retrieves an old receipt on the back of which Florrie can see marks in blue pen. *"I can't sleep for thinking of you. I will wait—however long it takes. I always wondered if I'd ever feel this way—and I do now.* That sort of thing."

Florrie thinks, *My heart.* For it thumps suddenly—like the tail of an old dog that hasn't given up yet, that doesn't know she's old. "Oh, Stanhope. Who wrote these letters? Do you know?"

"Yes, I do. You know him, too."

"Do I?"

"You've met Jay Mistry, haven't you?"

"No!" Or, rather, she means yes—for Florrie knows exactly who he is. *"He* wrote them? *He* did? Marcella's boy?"

"That's the one."

"You're sure?"

"Quite sure. He signs the letters, but one envelope had, too, a return address on it. He lives in Bourton-on-the-Hill, did you know that? Nice place. Steep hill, though. Terrible to park on."

Florrie leans back, amazed. Jay Mistry? Really? She can see his strong jawline; she can see how he'd rolled up his shirtsleeves as far as the muscles of his forearms allowed. Also, she thinks of how he'd opened doors for her and gestured with a flourish: "Please—I insist: after you." *He* loves Renata? This man who whistled jauntily as he crossed the courtyard?

Florrie looks across to her painted lemons and wonders how she feels about this revelation. Is he good enough for Renata? Is he humorous? Kind? And she decides, almost immediately, that, yes, she's very happy at the thought of this pairing; indeed, she'd call Jay Mistry a gentleman (albeit one who wears leather cords and beads around his wrists—but quite a few young people do these days). And he writes letters, too—proper letters! She looks back to Stanhope. "Oh, they'll make quite the couple, don't you think? He's a very handsome chap, and of similar age. Stanhope, this is lovely news."

"Aha! Hold your horses, Florrie." He raises his finger. "Here's the thing: It is perfectly obvious that Jay loves Renata—*I've never loved anyone like this*, et cetera. But I'm afraid I don't think that Renata loves him back."

"What? She must do."

"I'm not so sure. Because these letters go on—they're all dated, you see, and, being Renata, she's kept them in chronological order and in their own little plastic box—to have a rather imploring feel." He returns to his receipt. "*I said I'd wait, I know—but do you feel the same way, even slightly? Am I making a fool of myself?* Also, Florrie— where is it? Ah, here: *Please tell me, either way, for this is getting hard.*"

He glances over the rim of his spectacles. "Unrequited love? It rather sounds that way."

What had felt celebratory (Jay Mistry! An excellent choice) has turned, very quickly, into something so calamitous that Florrie wails. "But she's kept his letters, Stanhope. She's got them in a plastic box. So they must mean something to her."

"True. But perhaps they do in a different way. After all, it can't be very often that one receives such letters—so romantic, so . . . *brave*. They'd be hard to throw away, I'd imagine."

Florrie understands that. Look what she herself has kept in that wooden crate that once held cave-aged cheddar and half a Stilton wheel. "But she told me, Stanhope; she said, 'I'm in love.'"

"No doubt. But not with Jay Mistry, it seems."

Florrie drops back in her chair. Jay—whistling, jovial, broad-chested—loves Renata; but Renata does not love him. It seems peculiar, at first. (How could one *not* love him?) But Florrie supposes that the simplest reason for not returning love is because one's heart is already engaged elsewhere. A soft-natured girl, like Renata, would surely feel sorry for it. Indeed, she might cry on a white-painted bench. But what can be done when you're deeply in love? One is without reason. One can only think of them.

I thought being in love would be easy, Florrie.

"Unrequited love," Stanhope muses, whilst examining something on the side of his glass. "A motive for murder, do you think?"

Thus, in one seamless move, ballet-like, Jay Mistry leaps from one side of the room to the other: from gentlemanly to dastardly; from a hero to a scoundrel. For yes—it is, perhaps, motive enough. To not have love returned: What feelings follow that? Frustration and embarrassment, bitterness and rage. Envy. Grief. Oh, all the darkest sentiments!

"But he seems so . . . nice."

"I know. He's a very likeable fellow. You know, he helped Franklin to get the lawn mower started, back in April? Something had happened to it over the winter. I looked out of the window and there they were, doing things with jerry cans. He didn't have to do that. But this doesn't mean he's not capable of murder, or attempted murder. He's Marcella's offspring, after all."

They sip, allowing for reflection.

"So," says Florrie. "How about this? Jay Mistry has been courting Renata." (*Courting* sounds so old-fashioned now, but she knows no other term for it. *Chatting up*? *Trying it on*? She has no idea.) "But it hasn't worked. Renata doesn't feel the same way—because, most likely, she loves someone else. And Jay Mistry's genial manner gets worn down by all the effort so that suddenly, one evening—midsummer's night, say—he decides to confront her about it. He's had enough! *Why* won't she love him back? So he goes up the stairs and knocks on the door and there's a tussle of some kind—maybe she tells him that she has feelings for someone else and he's so distraught and jealous that he pushes her and out she goes, out of the window—either by mistake or deliberately, we can't be sure, yet—and he shuts Renata's door behind him and darts back down the stairs and no one hears Jay Mistry because of the thunder, and no one sees him because everyone's rushing to Renata. So he gets away with it. Goes back to Bourton-on-the-Hill." Florrie catches her breath. All in all, *un crime passionnel*. "What do you think? Is that possible?"

"It would depend," Stanhope tells her, "on whether he knows the door code."

"The door code?"

"You need it—for the stairs."

The concept of a door code is not new. One is already needed for the back door to Babbington; its keypad hides behind the rhododendron bush, which can grow to twice Florrie's height and must be rummaged through. This door leads from the Hall itself, with all its communal spaces, out toward the various converted outbuildings. It is the only way that she—and the Professors Lim (the stables), the Rosenthals (the barn), Marcella Mistry (the former icehouse, which is more than fitting), Velma Rudge, Aubrey Horner, Bill Blewitt and Stanhope himself (all the former pig sties), Odelle Banks and Sybilla Farr (the two old coach-house buildings—although they're still on their Danube cruise), little Nancy Tapp (the old woodshed) and a handful of others—can actually get into Babbington's main building. It is, therefore, an important door. And the door code exists, Florrie supposes, to ensure that only the residents go in and out—although there's no feasible reason why any member of the public might choose to use Babbington's back door when they have at their disposal the front one, which has no code at all. The front door, too, is far more handsome. It has half-moon steps leading to it; on either side, there are two metal urns filled with lavender. Florrie can imagine the Babbington family striding in and out.

The back door, then, needs a code—a code that changes every fortnight, which is, to be truthful, a proper nuisance, but it is also a good exercise for all their ageing brains. The staircase, too, needs it? She'd had no idea.

"Like the one by the back door?"

"Yes—just the same. Same buttons, same code, same little beep when the code has been accepted. My guess is that it's to keep the residents on the upper floors *in* as much as to keep other people *out*—for their safety." He looks forlorn, sniffs. "Anyway, it's very much there."

"And you entered the code?"

"No, as it happens, because I'd completely forgotten it. And one can't just punch in four numbers at random and hope. I might have set off alarms! The whole thing might have been a disaster except that Georgette came up the stairs behind me and punched in the code. I watched her do it. She then asked what I was climbing the stairs for—so I had to think quickly."

"What did you say?"

"That I was looking for her specifically. That I had mislaid some cufflinks somewhere—my father's cufflinks, which were handed down, heirlooms, and had she seen them? A rotten lie, Florrie. I keep those cufflinks in a pot in the bedroom. But . . ." He shrugs. "It was all I could think of. It turns out that Georgette was there, on the first floor, because of the lady—what is her name? With the long, plaited hair?"

"Tabitha Brimble?"

"Tabitha, that's it. She hasn't been well since the thunder, you know. Fighting the staff, making no sense . . . ah, dear." He looks at the carpet for a moment. "Dr. Mallory has had to sedate her, poor thing. I could see her bed from the landing. She looked so *little*. Did you know that she used to be a concert pianist? Georgette told me. Royal Albert Hall."

There is no adequate response for something so mournful. So they look into their whiskies, say nothing for a while. It is Tabitha Brimble, then, who's unsettled—and this saddens Florrie, although she hardly knows her. Florrie has only been aware of her as one might be aware of the moon's phases, how she sits in the bay window on the first floor and looks out across Oxfordshire like the braced, brave figurehead of a sailing ship.

But Florrie's mind, too, returns to Jay—to his musculature, the slight gap between his front teeth, his hair as dark and glossy as a raven's wing: Could he have known the door code?

"His mother could have told him."

"Yes, that's true. Has he visited Marcella in the past fortnight? We'd need to find that out."

Stanhope has done, Florrie thinks, extremely well. To have returned with all this knowledge: to know of Renata's interests—of her books and textiles and Paris map, her *Dum spiro spero*, and to have copied down parts of Jay's love letters. Her father, she knows, would have been impressed with him.

He looks up from the whisky. "Anyway, Florrie. What about you? Did anything happen in church?"

No wailing. No confessions. No holding up of bloodied hands. Although she does wonder, now, if Marcella Mistry had looked a little more pinched than usual; tighter in features, like a double knot. How much does she know about her son's feelings for Renata? "No front-runners—not that I could see."

"You said you spoke to Nancy?"

"Yes. Just about Arthur, really." No need, she thinks, to say more than that.

"Florrie, should we tell the police?"

"The police?"

"That we think it's attempted murder?"

Florrie ponders. The sensible part of her supposes that yes, they probably should, now. The evidence remains circumstantial, but there is more of it, at least—the torn curtain, these imploring letters, that scream of protest or fear. Any decent constable would now sit down and say, Tell me more. But the other part of Florrie doesn't want to share their thoughts with anyone. She likes that this adventure belongs to him and her. "Not just yet."

He smiles. "Right-o."

That night, whilst drying herself from a shower, Florrie considers the day.

It's not been like other days. But nor was the day before, or the day before that. That Jay Mistry loves Renata? That's new. So is their understanding of Renata's quarters—with all its books, artwork and affirmations, its fairy lights in a bottle. To hear Stanhope talk about it had made Florrie's eyes fill with tears; to think of it now, even (as she pats rose-scented talc under her arms with a powder puff), does the same. That furless bear. That Latin motto—which could, very well, have been a Butterfield expression since carrying on with hope, and good cheer, was always the family way of things. (Those bloody Ell-woods, she thinks—claiming dear Renata has a small, empty life.)

Nancy, too, was new—or rather, her concern was. *Stay well, Florrie.* How rarely, in her life, has she been seen as vulnerable! Or as anything other than stubborn and strong. *A girl that hefty can look after herself*—or so said Mrs. Fortescue, reassuring Prudence over the garden fence.

She wheels herself out of the bathroom, rose-scented.

And *les billets-doux.* Above all, perhaps, they are new. Last night, Florrie could not have conceived of their existence—in a bedside drawer on the third floor, in chronological order. *I always wondered if I'd ever feel this way.*

Florrie parks herself in front of the old cheese crate.

Has she had her own love letters? Ones to show Renata, in due course? Not as such. Those from Edward Silversmith, she burned. The postcard from Zermatt doesn't mention love by name. But there is, yes, a love letter in Florrie's keepsake box—although calling it a letter might be stretching it, given that it only consists of four words and was written on cloth, not paper. But she's kept it, even so.

Florrie fumbles for it. She rummages past her old rag doll, Gulliver's collar, the cocktail menu from the Foreign Correspondents' Club of South Asia—and she finds Jack's note by touch alone, for its texture is like nothing else in there. *You looked beautiful tonight.* He wrote those words on a napkin. He'd slipped that napkin beneath her bedroom door, at the end of the evening—the act of a man who, despite all appearances, couldn't say these words in person, didn't know how. Nor could Florrie speak of the napkin in return. The next morning, she only climbed into Jack's truck, smiled brightly and commented on the heat or whether they had enough water—and neither of them mentioned the dress she'd worn the previous evening, or how he'd touched her, very lightly, in the hollow of her back as she moved through the door ahead of him.

So it is not, perhaps, *un billet-doux.* But a single raw emerald and a white linen napkin are all she has left to prove—to her, to anyone— that, for a time, Florrie was in love with a man who'd stand very still as she approached him, as if she were a creature he hadn't yet encountered, that he couldn't quite gauge or anticipate. ("I didn't expect you," he'd told her.)

Florrie lifts the napkin, breathes. It smells of dust, now— nothingness. But once, she'd believed it smelled of him: soap, diesel, African heat.

She will show this to Renata one day, over pink lemonade. But, for now, it's only Florrie who sees it: She thumbs its corner where, handstitched, is the name of the place where she'd been, briefly, beautiful— in a cream linen dress with a scalloped neckline. (Jack had risen from his chair as she'd crossed the room toward him.) It says THE SUNSHINE HOTEL, LUSAKA—embroidered in red.

13

Jack Luckett and the Sunshine Hotel

Bobs was buried in the leafy grounds of All Saints' Church in Upper Dorbury, next to his father's grave. She remembers it was a windy day. Trees bowed and silvered. The vicar's garments billowed behind him and Aunt Pip's hat (wide-brimmed, ebony with a velvet trim) had taken flight, landed in the chestnut tree. It was Pinky Topham née Underwood who'd retrieved it; she swung into its branches and tossed the hat down like a pancake. Pip had staggered to catch it; Pinky's new husband had remarked, "Good throw!" And Florrie had watched it all, thinking how the old Bobs would have laughed at this.

Prudence took baths and slept.

Pip pedaled away on her sewing machine, made lunch and supper.

As for Florrie, she wandered through the village—the towpath, the old orchards, Paternoster Street—and realized that the men she'd loved were gone, now. Even Edward Silversmith—who wasn't dead, as such, but she could search all her life and still not have him back. Gulliver, too, had breathed his last breath by then. Whilst Florrie had been in France, Prudence had found him—curled up and cooling in the nasturtium patch.

Within weeks of her brother's funeral, Florrie saw the advertisement in the *Daily Telegraph*:

Secretary/assistant required to accompany government miner-
alogist in Northern Rhodesia and environs. Shorthand essential. French an advantage. Eight-month post. Immediate start.

She wrote to the address that morning and heard back the following Thursday. Yes, they said—impressed with her time at the Rue du
Faubourg Saint-Honoré. They assured her there would be a chaperone.

She went to find her mother. Prudence was in the garden shed,
staring at flowerpots—and, having been told, she murmured about
the gardening fork that she hadn't seen for a week now (Where on
earth *was* it?) and drifted out toward the herbaceous border.

Pip, being Pip, was better with the news. She took Florrie down
to the Royal Oak, ordered two beers. "She's afraid, Florrie. You know
that? Any mother would be."

"You think I shouldn't go? Stay here?"

"I didn't say that." Her aunt set down her glass. "Florence. Do you
remember my stories about the Sitwell parrot? The one that we grew
up with?"

"It swore at the vicar."

"Mostly at the vicar. But it swore at anyone, given the chance. And
where do you think it learned to swear? Ours wasn't a happy house. We
married as soon as we could, your mother and I. She chose well—dear
Herbert—whilst I chose a man who'd have an argument for breakfast
and couldn't keep a job, but that's another story. What I'm saying is,
your mother is stronger than she seems—she is. And she knows, as I
do, what it is to feel trapped." Pip sat back. "Also, be careful of the word
should. Women have been controlled by that one word; we've been told
how we should behave, how we should dress, how we should think
and speak and be. Florrie? Tell me: Do you want to go to Africa?"

Florrie looked out of the pub window—at the chestnut tree, at
Mr. Patchett's shop with its newspapers outside. Did she? She was
partly terrified. But she thought, too, of Bobs. She thought of the map

he'd drawn with his finger on a tabletop, of time rushing by—and of what Pip and Prudence didn't know about her, what they must never know. She felt a dark, strange feeling in her belly, like . . . what? Something with teeth. "Yes."

Her aunt raised her beer. "Well, then. Here's to Africa."

On an overcast day in April, Florrie packed a small trunk with clothes, good boots and an Empire Aristocrat typewriter that she'd borrowed from Pinky and boarded the Paddington train. Four days, six trains, three cars, two boats, a horse and a biplane later, she stepped out into the fiery, airless heat of Northern Rhodesia, where a man in dust-coloured clothes was waiting for her under a moringa tree with folded arms, narrowed eyes, and a toothpick resting on his bottom lip. He was fifteen years older than Florrie but not much taller. He was leathered, taciturn—and would say, as his opening words, that he had low expectations of her. "Nobody sane would apply for this job."

Florrie believed this instantly. After all, here she was—Florrie Butterball, twenty-two and grieving and in an impractical sunhat (straw, with floral ribbon), following a man whose shirt was damp under the arms and who wouldn't slow down for her. *I must have lost my mind.* As for the chaperone, there was no such thing. Why on earth was she here? What did she know of this continent? *This is all a terrible mistake.*

But she discovered her own Africa, soon enough—with its goat meat and sunstroke, its spiders as big as side plates, its grassland which crackled like fire to walk through and sliced into her shins. It was music that matched her heartbeat. It was emptying her sore, diseased bowels behind a bush for so long that locals came out to watch her, perplexed by her stance and large, moon-white behind. Her Africa was Jack Luckett's truck, too: how its axles broke on potholes and how Florrie would clasp its roof as the truck bounced down into dried riverbeds, but she'd still bang her head, still knock against

him. It was iodine tablets in water. It was fruit bats and tiny, translucent frogs. And Florrie has never forgotten how, at a long journey's
end, she'd opened the steaming bonnet of the truck to have a black
mamba strike out and miss her by inches so that Jack had yelled and
pulled Florrie against him—against the buttons of his shirt and the
gaps between them. That night, he'd drunk too much. "You were this
close," he'd hissed. "This close."

All this and much more. Making and breaking camp. Singing with
children who fingered her hair, which had lightened to buttermilk
by then. She sees, even now (even now, and in detail), the mechanics of the folding stool she'd sit on whilst recording the dimensions
of prospective mineshafts, the precise compass bearings of emerald
seams. Jack would call out words that she'd write down in shorthand:
*At least ten metres below. Running from north-northwest to northeast.
Superior tonal grade. Minor inclusions on first inspection.* And every night,
by lamplight and with the rustling, absolute darkness outside, Florrie would type up her day's notes a little more neatly to be sent back
to London and read in wood-paneled rooms that overlooked White-
hall. It seemed an impossibility to her that these typed words might
find their way across deserts to a place she could barely believe in
now—with its pigeons and milk floats and Sunday lunches, its steady
English rain.

At first, he seemed furious with her. *He hates me*—for being too young,
too clumsy, for asking too many questions, for her terrible singing
voice. ("God damn it, woman. Get back in the bleeding truck.") But
Jack softened, in time. He'd fill her water flask for her; on the road,
he'd explain the continent—apartheid, minerals, the ivory trade.
When Florrie's shoulders blistered, he made poultices for her and laid
them down so gently that she imagined him as a father. ("How's that?
Try to rest.") Also, one morning, Florrie discovered a thumb-sized hole
in her mosquito net, mentioned it in passing and found, by evening,

that the hole was gone. She studied the stitching by lamplight. It could only have been him.

They'd camp, for weeks at a time, near any rumoured seam. Tribesmen would visit or other prospectors; on the Congolese border, Belgian mineralogists would argue with Jack so that Florrie had to translate loudly for them—back and forth, like a tennis match. Whilst camping, Jack kept a rifle with him—for lions and hyenas, he said, although Florrie sensed this was only half true. He never fired it, in those eight months. But he kept it near and visible; he'd cock it at nocturnal movements, at the singular snap of a twig in the dark. The closest he came to killing something was near Mfuwe late in the day: a blue-black buffalo had squared itself to them, with glittering eyes, and Jack, taking aim, had murmured, "Florrie? I want you to sidestep to your left . . . Do it now." (Later, she decided she wouldn't tell Prudence of this.)

But she and Jack didn't always camp. Twice a month, they would drive to Lusaka to send her typed reports to London and gather sup-plies, and, whilst there, they'd spend the night at the Sunshine Hotel near the Anglican cathedral. It was shabby, at best, to a newcomer's eye, but to Florrie it was luxury. She'd loll in its deep tin baths; she'd sit on its rusty balconies, swatting mosquitos and writing long letters to her mother and aunt on the faded hotel notepaper. In the evenings, she'd descend to the bar in her one good dress and Jack would look up, watch her cross the floor. She liked that bar—with its mahogany furniture, its wooden ceiling fans that chopped the air. The manager, Samson, would open his arms to greet them. *My friends!*

He was, at the Sunshine, a slightly different Jack. He was more relaxed, physically—sitting back in his chair, soap-scented, his hair still wet from his own bath. But here he'd ask more, too, listen closely to her answers; he'd watch Florrie as she spoke. "Why," he asked, "did you come here? I didn't expect you."

"Didn't expect me? But the advertisement said . . ."

"I mean *you*, specifically. What are you—twenty-three? Twenty-four? Most women your age are married by now. What's made you different?"

"Different?" Florrie thought to be offended, that he might be referring to her shortness or her freckled nose. But he didn't, of course, mean those things. And she knew, too, that she *was* different—so she weighed her response to him with care: what to offer, how much to tell. *I'm a bad person. I attacked someone. I might have blinded them. These hands? I punched my way through a wooden door.* She didn't feel able to say this. But nor did Florrie wish to lie to this man, in his laundered shirt with its open neck; this man who could talk in local dialects, who'd breathe the air and announce that rain was four minutes away exactly. Jack Luckett, she knew, would detect a lie. So she spoke of Bobs. She mentioned her father. She said that she'd always been adventurous, always wanted to travel, but that their deaths, too, had changed her view of life and how to live it—and where was the lie in that? Florrie explained that she didn't want the same view from every window for the next sixty years when there were translucent frogs in this world and emerald seams and hotel bars like this one, which overlooked a street of fruit-sellers and car horns. "And anyway. I've had enough of love."

"That sounds like a story."

"Maybe. Yes."

He looked down into his beer. "Enough of love . . . Well, I'm sorry to hear that. For Samson, I mean."

"Samson?

"He worships you, Florrie. You hadn't noticed?"

"Worships? Like . . . a goddess?"

He smiled. "Steady, now."

Was it friendship? Perhaps—but a strange, charged kind of it, in which both were aware of the movements of the other, of what the other had touched or worn. And friends, she supposed, didn't hold each other's gaze across markets; they didn't place their hand on the chair that the other had just risen from to feel their residual warmth. One night, as Florrie's eight months drew to an end, Jack turned off the truck's engine and didn't get out immediately. Instead, he thumbed the steering wheel. Twice, he cleared his throat. And he spoke of his estranged wife, how she'd left him years ago for a more temperate climate and an old family friend—and Jack turned to Florrie, then; he said, very simply, "Stay." And Florrie might have stayed—if she hadn't wanted to; if, on finding the darned corner of her mosquito net, she hadn't felt such tenderness for this man who rinsed his shirts in a bucket each night and hung them from low branches so that she'd watch them stirring in the dark, like ghosts of himself. She might have stayed if she'd been a different Florrie, one who felt deserving; one who was not so terribly afraid. But she was *this* Florrie—and she knew she couldn't stay.

On her last night in Africa, she walked out to join him as he looked into the dark. "Why do you love it here?"

"Here?"

"Africa. Tell me."

Florrie wanted to know. She wanted to have his answer so that for the rest of her life, when asked about this continent, she could give Jack's answer as her own. And as Florrie waited, she supposed he'd speak of tribes or grasslands, of fruit bats or elephants or his dilapidated truck whose dashboard he'd pat at a journey's end, as if to thank it. She supposed he'd speak of gemstones.

But he turned toward Florrie. He came so close that she could feel his own warmth. "You think I love it?"

"You must do. Look how well you know it. How you've been here for years and haven't left."

"I've tried to leave. Believe me. I've been back to London. I went to Spain. They have emeralds in South America, too—better ones, they say. But this place, Florrie . . . It enters your blood. You stay here long enough and . . . that's it. You can't be without it. Is that love? Tell me. You're the one who knows."

He studied her mouth, her cheekbones.

You can't be without it. Yes, it sounded like love. And she had a sudden wish to slap him, to grapple, or to tell him that she had been ruined by love, torn open by it, and how dare he look at her like that? *Lions*, she thought, *do not scare me; rifles and mambas and spiders do not.*

"Florrie, what happened to your hands?"

He would not look away. Florrie, too, would not—and so they stood, nose to nose, like rivals, assessing each other's strength. She knew Jack wanted the truth. Perhaps he already half knew it, having known her for eight months, but wanted to hear her say the words. And could she? Could she speak of it? To this wise, tired, weathered man who had his own scars—two, on his abdomen, which looked to Florrie's mind like a blade's doing? Nothing would shock him.

Hackney. How a woman called Euphemia had saved Florrie's life, in a manner of speaking; she'd lifted her, bloodied and broken, from a metal-framed bed. She thought to say the word *empty*, or *joyless*. But Florrie said nothing to him.

Jack nodded once, stepped back. He bade her good night. Then he carried the lantern into his tent and left its flaps unfastened.

Florrie stood in the dark. She looked at his drying shirt. She noted the breeze, the overhead branches, and wanted, suddenly, to stand boldly with her feet apart and to roar into the darkness, to bellow like the buffalo they'd found, once, thrashing and foaming in the last stages of birth—a birth that was breech, that would not come. Jack had touched Florrie's forearm: "We can't help her. Come on."

But Florrie didn't roar. She only knew, calmly, that she'd remember this exact moment all her life—and that each time she'd wonder, *What if?* What if, beside those drying shirts, she'd told Jack about what had happened with Teddy Silversmith? What if she'd walked into his tent with her hands held out toward him? *Look. Feel them. I'll tell you all of it.* What if she'd stayed in Northern Rhodesia for one month more, or two, or six?

All these other lifetimes. All these different choices that she could have made and which, in the years to come, Florrie would imagine— all the different outcomes, all with Jack in them (Jack kissing her forehead, Jack by her side).

Over her shoulder, Florrie could see him in his tent, his silhouette on the canvas sides—a man standing still, looking down. Listening for a footfall, a single word from her.

I love him. This man who'd written *beautiful* on a hotel napkin, who'd secretly mended a mosquito net. She did not have to spend her life alone. But there was, too, what was safer, what she could and couldn't do.

She sent her love for Jack Luckett through the canvas.

Then she walked past his tent, back to her own.

14

A Most Beloved Son

Everybody knows when Jay Mistry first appeared at Babbington Hall. There'd been a gathering of some kind in the dining room—a talk on local history, perhaps, or a recital—and a young man (in his early forties, which is unquestionably young in Florrie's eyes) had sauntered past the French windows, unaware of the audience to the left of him. He'd whistled as he went, hands in pockets; the autumn light had caught his cheekbones and made his dark hair shine. And this man had paused briefly—to see the view down to the orchard—which had been long enough for the Ellwoods to detect his broad shoulders, for Velma Rudge to note the circumference of his upper arms so that she'd adjusted her position and murmured to the room, "Who is *that*?"

Nobody was entirely sure. Was he even meant to be here? Had he taken a wrong turning on the Woodstock road? But then he came a second time, and a third; he began to acknowledge the staff with a cheery wave across the courtyard, conversed with carers, remarked on the weather to Aubrey Horner—and they realized that he must be visiting someone. But who? Who did he resemble? Was it someone upstairs, on the first or second floor? "I wouldn't mind," chuckled Velma over a bowl of soup, "if that handsome young man chose to visit *me!*" At which point, Marcella Mistry set down her spoon and narrowed her eyes, as a serpent might. "That handsome young man is my son."

To Florrie's knowledge, Marcella Mistry had never actually wanted to come to Babbington Hall. One could, of course, reason that nobody ever *wants* to enter assisted living; by doing so, one is acknowledging that one's body can't do what it used to, that one is moving one step closer along the path of life, with all its potholes and inclines. But even so, Marcella had been particularly bitter about the whole business. Even as she'd risen from her taxi, she'd radiated anger like a lump of glowing coal.

For weeks, this fury remained. She—Marcella, with her silk scarves, Chanel No. 5 and firm, raised jawline—had damned the food as dismal, the staff as wholly inept. The décor was, she claimed, dated; the floorboards were uneven. Last summer, in the dining room, she'd declared that she was nothing like *you lot*, waving her hand as one might wave at a persistent stench, which had been one step too far for Alan Rosenthal, who'd risen in his chair like scaffolding and set his palms down on the table. "It's not a prison," he'd replied. "Leave, if you want to, and give us all some peace." That quieted Marcella. She set down her sweeping condemnations. But she retains a certain sour tang. She will say "You there" when seeking a carer's attention; she addresses the Ellwood sisters as *Number One* and *Number Two* and calls Velma Rudge *the chubby one.* As for Magda, there is an enmity between them. "That woman," Magda states, "is the rudest person I know in my whole lifetime."

Perhaps. But Florrie learned, long ago, that the prickliest bushes grow where fires have been; they're prickly for their own protection, that's all. By this logic, she suspects that Marcella's been burned to a crisp. Three times now, out of sympathy, Florrie has tried to make friends with her. Three times she's knocked on the low, solid door of the former icehouse, announced herself perkily through cupped hands. Two of those times, Marcella had dismissed Florrie curtly, as if she'd been a salesman—"Not today, thank you!"—before closing the door. But on the third time, Marcella had conceded defeat and allowed Florrie into her quarters, where she'd made tea by adding cold milk first (that is, milk straight onto the teabag), which had caused Florrie to physically stifle her dismay with a fingertip to the lips. But they'd sat together, at least. They'd exchanged pleasantries—on a radio programme or the view of the beechwoods from Marcella's window—before sitting in slightly awkward silence. Florrie thought afterward, *At least I've tried.*

This is, therefore, her fourth time knocking.

"Oh, God." Marcella peers around her door with all the warmth and hospitality of a hermit crab. "I suppose you want to come in?"

Marcella Mistry's quarters are darker than most. Icehouses, of course, have no windows, but a handful of small, square ones and a skylight were added during the Hall's renovations so there is some natural light, at least. She has, too, a radiator that runs the length of her sitting room—switched off, in such weather, yet still imposing. But otherwise, her home is tastefully done. If their Babbington rooms are a glimpse of how they all lived before, the Mistry home must have been impressive. Marcella's walls are an ivory shade. Her artwork (landscapes, mostly) hangs in heavy gold frames. And there are antique items in these quarters: a grandfather clock with a painted face, a sandalwood chest, a corner cabinet in which Florrie can see champagne flutes and silverware. There are porcelain figurines on her windowsill—ladies with skirts and parasols, with tiny waists and hands.

Marcella, too, is well presented; she wafts ahead of Florrie in dark-red trousers, the colour of raspberry jam, with a long cream tunic with a dipped hem. Her hair—grey, but still with traces of the blonde she'd been, in her younger days—is twisted into a *chignon du cou*. When Marcella turns, Florrie sees an array of sparkling adornments: there

are several gold chains around her neck, a circular brooch with diamante on it, and so many gold bangles—a dozen, perhaps—that they
slide up and down her pale, slender arm with any gesture, tinkling
like bells. All in all, Florrie feels newly embarrassed at her own out-
fit which, until now, she'd been rather fond of: a matching skirt and
blouse of a soft hazelnut colour with pink piping, pink buttons and a
pink underskirt.

"Tea?" This is said so flatly that it sounds like a statement, rather
than a question.

Florrie declines with gratitude.

Marcella lowers herself into an armchair and raises an eyebrow.
"So. Why are you here, Florrie? If you don't mind my asking?"

"No, I don't mind. Quite right—to ask, I mean. Thank you. Yes."
There's such a haughty quality to Marcella that Florrie feels like a
schoolgirl; she half expects *oafish* to come.

"Well?"

Florrie settles herself. (She practised this last night in her rose-
scented bed.) "I only wondered how you *are*, Marcella. This business
with Renata. It's shaken all of us, hasn't it? And I thought you looked
particularly sad in church yesterday."

"Shaken? Not really. These things happen. People cut their wrists
or climb down onto train tracks. We've been doing those sorts of
things since the start of time. As for being sad, that woman chose to
do it. She knew very well what she was doing. It's a shame she felt so
desperate that this became her choice, perhaps, but if I feel any sadness, it's in that she failed in the act. She knew what she wanted—and
yet she hasn't achieved it. Or rather, she hasn't achieved it *yet*. A coma,
apparently—so she may still succeed."

Florrie sits, slack-jawed. Even for Marcella, this is quite a display—
like being presented with a row of kitchen knives. Florrie assesses her
options: she could gasp or scold; she could lift off her brakes, pivot

sharply and leave the room in wordless disapproval. Or she could swallow her feelings and carry on. "You aren't particularly fond of her?"

"Renata? Fond? God, no. I didn't mind her in the beginning, I suppose—although she was always rather insipid, in my view. Airs and graces. Weak in her leadership. And far too thin."

Florrie shifts position. Making judgements about someone's shape is not something she agrees with, but now's not the time to say so. "I think she does well as a manager. It can't be an easy job."

"No? There are harder ones."

They sit, without tea, in their chairs. Marcella lifts her wrist; she examines the bangles, turning each one around in a full revolution before moving on to the next one. (One, Florrie notes, is a bejeweled snake, its tail clasped in its mouth; its eyes appear to be rubies, furious in their stare.)

Florrie clears her throat. "Actually, I rather had your son in mind. Jay, is it? I wondered how he was managing. Because I heard that *he*, at least, is rather fond of Renata."

Marcella drops her wrist. Several expressions pass over her face: a pout, a sigh, a narrowing of her eyes, a flash of anger, a fleeting smile that has both anger and sarcasm in it. "The Ellwoods, I assume? There's no stopping them, is there? We could plug their mouths with a cork and they'd still find a way to prattle on. Mind you, I can't say they're wrong—not this time. Fond? Yes. Oh, Jay has been quite smitten. I'm at a loss as to why, frankly; she was pretty enough, I suppose, but what else was there *to* her? She had nothing to say for herself. If one cracked that brain open, what would one have found there? Not a lot, I shouldn't think."

Florrie hears the past tense. "She's still with us, Marcella. She may yet wake up, and—"

"Wake up? Ah, you're quite the optimist, Florrie. Is it true that you talk to that potted hosta? It can't actually hear you, you know. A machine breathes for Renata, as I understand it—a machine. *You* may be hopeful but that sounds like death to me."

Florrie tightens her grasp on her armrests. Remember, she tells herself, those prickly bushes; think nice thoughts, Florence. "Anyway, Marcella—how *has* he been? He must be ever so upset. We all are, of course, but if he has feelings for Renata, it's all the more—"

"Are we? Upset? All of us?" Marcella adjusts her position so that her bangles clink against each other. "I imagine he would be, yes—if he knew."

"He doesn't know?"

"That Renata tried to kill herself?" With this, there is the slightest softening of Marcella's features; she glances out of the window. "Not yet. Let's wait for the machine to be turned off first—until we have a proper outcome. Because he will be upset, I know he will. I like to think Jay might be over her now that his heart has mended in the past few months. Because he's stayed away—did you know that? He's kept away from Babbington since early April, which seems unfair to me, frankly. He's my only child: don't I have a right to see him? We speak on the phone but it's hardly the same. Still, he said he needed that—to be away from here, to try to move on." Marcella's eyes glisten. "He's got a soft heart, my boy. He enters everything with all of himself and no caution. But his father was the same way." She nods. "There he is."

Florrie follows her gaze. At first, she thinks she's meant to be looking at the Mistry wedding photograph, in its heavy frame: a twenty-something Marcella with her dashing new husband, arm in arm, standing in front of a scarlet hibiscus. There is a sense, in this picture, of the Indian heat and closeness; she thinks, too, how happy they both look. But Florrie realizes, then, this is not the photograph she's meant to be looking at. Rather, it's the one to its side. This one is of Jay, looking back at her. It's a lovely photograph, and taken recently by her estimation, for he looks exactly as she remembers him. His eyes are shining. His forearms are defined, strong. He wears a white shirt with sunglasses hooked through a buttonhole and a silver pendant (a coin? a piece of shell, even?) hangs from a leather cord, like a shoelace, bright against the quadrant of skin. And he is smiling a broad, easy smile—natural, as if caught laughing. All in all, it is a handsome face. But good looks, she knows, do not mean that they know only good deeds.

Marcella fumbles with the picture frame. She curses her arthritic hands, their maladroitness, and Florrie looks away and pretends she doesn't see. "Here, Florrie: take it. He's quite something, isn't he? Let me tell you, he had his pick of the girls when he was younger. I've seen girl after girl fall in love with my boy. You should have seen some of the Valentine's cards! The swooning! The blushes. Look at that wretched woman—the Russian?"

"Russian?"

"Tattoos. Piercings. That attitude."

"Magda," Florrie tells her, "is Polish."

"Oh, I hardly care where she's from. I only care that she's mooned after my boy in such a shameful manner. See? They all love my Jay. Yet it's been *Renata*, of all people—our bony, dull manageress—who really opened him up, who made *him* blush and send her flowers. And I've never understood it. Jay called her *the one*—the one! Her? The manager of a care home? With all the charisma and warmth of a block of wood? Yet how on earth might I have persuaded him otherwise? Boys don't listen to their mothers—or not past the age of twenty, anyway. Of course, we know now that she was quite mad—jumping out of windows—so I should have some sort of compassion toward her, I suppose. But I won't forgive her for breaking my boy's heart, Florrie, for turning him down—I won't."

At that, Marcella looks down. She smooths her trousers.

Florrie turns back to the photograph. *Jay called her the one. He enters everything with all of himself.* "He lives in Bourton-on-the-Hill, doesn't he?"

"He does."

In her head, Florrie is wheeled into the Babbington minibus and is driven north, between verges of yarrow and cow parsley, over crossroads and underneath horse chestnut trees to the sign that says WELCOME TO BOURTON-ON-THE-HILL and the Olde Worlde Tearoom where they serve proper teacakes—and how long does that take? Half an hour, no more. Jay could drive here and back quite easily—even in a thunderstorm.

"He's not been here since . . . April, you say?"

"April, yes. He came to see me on my birthday. What news to be given as a present!"

"News?" This throws Florrie. She was preparing to ask about door codes. "What news?"

"That he was off! Her fault, of course."

"Off? Like curdled milk?"

Marcella rolls her eyes as if Florrie is being endured, at best. "To Nepal! Didn't you know? Didn't the Ellwoods deal *that* out to everyone, like a deck of playing cards? I'm surprised they missed that one. They watch that reception hall like a pair of nosey old crows . . . They take it in turns to peer through the keyholes—I've seen them do it. Vile women, both."

"Nepal?"

"To build a school, apparently. When he said he wanted to get away for a bit, I thought he meant a week by the sea or with friends in London. But no, not Jay. To mend his broken heart, he's decided to be charitable. Somewhere with yaks and altitude sickness. I might have minded less if he'd thought to visit his father's family whilst he was out that way—he still has cousins and an elderly aunt. But no, he just wants to *help* people."

"Nepal? Are you quite sure?"

Marcella scoffs. "Am I sure? What sort of question is that? Yes, I'm sure, thank you, Florrie. He went a month ago. And if you need proof . . ." She reaches to the side table, retrieves a postcard between two twisted fingers and offers it to Florrie with a small shake of insistence as if to say, *See?*

Phulping Katti. Florrie knows it. Or rather, she knows *of* it, having trekked near it many years ago. It's in the Himalayan foothills; it's where snow creaks and rumbles, where yes, there are yaks, and to push one's hand into their fleece is to find a deep, extraordinary warmth and a smell that she's never found again. It's where prayer flags snap in the wind, like socks on a washing line. And looking at this card, Florrie's not entirely sure of her feelings: for here, in her hands, is the proof that no, Jay Mistry couldn't have tried to kill Renata out of lust or desperation. He's gone to Nepal to find peace. And Nepal is a little too far to come back from, just for a night.

Dear Mum. He speaks of the night skies, of snowmelt. It is signed *Your loving J xxx.*

The stamp is a Nepalese stamp. Its date is from a week ago.

"Why, Marcella, do you think Renata doesn't love him back?"

"Why?" She shrugs. "Because she's mad? Because she thinks she can find someone better? I'm not sure that I care. What I do care about is my boy—and I say that it would be best for everyone if they turned off that machine tomorrow and the doctors use it for someone who *wants* to live. That's what I hope for."

"Oh, Marcella."

"You think I'm wrong to say so? That I'm cold-hearted? Well, I dare say I am—but I tell you this: Babbington will be a better place without her—for all of us. Reuben will stop being moon-eyed and useless; Renata's plan to move the Ellwoods to a different room—well, that's obviously done with, now; Georgette can finally manage this place properly, which will benefit us all—even you." She narrows an eye at Florrie. "You don't have any family, do you? Then let me tell you this, too. When one's children are small, one worries that they'll hurt themselves physically; they'll bang their head or get stung by bees. And as a parent one does everything one can: one teaches them about road safety and one tells them to never, ever dive into shallow water. But as they grow, it's the other hurts that cause the worry. Heartbreak, disappointment. Because one can't prevent those or make them better." Marcella looks back at the postcard. "You can't know, Florrie, what mothers would do for their children. We become she-wolves—even at eighty-two. We may seem sweet and good-natured, but we'd all fight for our child's sake, claw out the eyes of someone who'd hurt them. I'd die for my boy—do you understand? I'd unplug that bloody machine myself if it meant he lived a happier life."

15

Five Minutes in the Lavatory

T he nearest accessible lavatory to Marcella Mistry's quarters is back in Babbington Hall itself—along the corridor, left, left again and in the far corner with a bronze w.c. screwed into its door. Technically, it's for visitors—but it's a nearer harbour for Florrie than the compost heap. For a harbour is what she's after; a place to catch her breath after Marcella's violent storm.

Florrie locks the door and exhales. The sounds of her arrival—the clattering of wheels, the single click of the door lock—all fade away. The lavatory is quiet. Indeed, she half imagines that it's watching her—the taps, the loo itself, the soap dispenser. What, they ask themselves, is about to happen? Is this person about to cry?

Florrie isn't sure, either. Her eyes prick; she notes, in her hands, a slight tremble—and closes them into fists. But then a certain crossness follows so that she wants to bang those fists on her armrests, to mutter uncharitable things about Marcella to the stack of turquoise paper hand towels, which isn't Florrie's way but sometimes she can't help it.

You don't have family, do you? Then let me tell you this.

So it's always been. Florrie wears no wedding ring; there are no children or grandchildren or great-grandchildren who visit her. (The Topham boys send Christmas cards, dear creatures, but she can hardly expect them to visit her when they live so many miles away and have such busy lives.) She is, therefore, somehow viewed as *less*. Less what? Less substantial. Less important. Less womanly—or so Babs Rosenthal would have it, believing that having children is a woman's raison d'être. (Indeed, Babs Rosenthal talks of her offspring and nothing else so that poor Alan Rosenthal rolls his eyes in exasperation when she starts with any tale about school nativities or clarinet exams. "Oh God," he groans. "Not this again.") "No children? At *all*? Ah, *what* a pity . . ."—as if Florrie had missed a train she'd run for whilst shouting, "Wait for me."

We become she-wolves.

Is this true? Is this how Prudence Butterfield née Sitwell had been? Prudence had never seemed wolf-like—admiring the scent of an orange, or standing at the till in Mr. Patchett's shop in such a daydream that Mr. Patchett would say her name twice or three times. Yet who knows how she'd been, beneath it all? Knowing that her son was fighting in a war? Or that, later, her last surviving child— her only daughter—was sleeping in tents in Northern Rhodesia with who-knows-what or -who outside? Her airy, girlish nature had been real enough—and a form of protection, or so Pip said. But, yes, Florrie thinks: her mother would have unsheathed her claws, if she'd had to. She'd have set down her trowel, rolled up her sleeves and fought for both her children until there was blood on the floor.

And Pinky? She'd have done the same. She poured love over those boys as one might empty a watering can—freely, messily, marveling at what was sprouting up in front of her. *Where have they come from, Butters?*—as if Pinky herself had played no part in it. But equally, Pinks would have marched into various London schools to *have a word* with teachers when having a word with anyone wasn't Pinky's way. And it never lessened—that fire, that love. Even in Pinky's final days, lying in her hospice bed, it had been her sons (all married, by then) she'd thought of. "Keep an eye on them, Butters?"

"Yes. Always."

Look, too, at Magda Dabrowski: she has bolts and skulls and inked roses, but she has, too, a child. Magda told her this at Christmas, when she'd started to cry over her Sunday cigarette: "Her name is Ula, Miss Florrie; it means *my little bear*." And it is this little bear who makes Magda work in a foreign country where the weather is worse but the money is better, that makes Magda send her wages back to southeast Poland so that she might not seem to be a she-wolf, at first glance, but in truth, she is a she-wolf in every waking moment. "I only tell *you* this," she'd murmured. "The others? They are not good enough to know of Ula-bear."

Florrie turns on the tap. She dabs cool water on her wrists, presses a damp paper towel around her eyes.

Magda: She has her own feelings for the wandering, heartsore Jay Mistry. Her dismissive *taki smutny* makes sense now. She's jealous, disappointed, tired of hoping. She'd love to be the recipient of those *billets-doux*.

But it isn't just mothers, of course. A father's love is no less. Look at Herbert, who pressed such firm kisses onto his daughter's forehead that Florrie would feel their pressure afterward; for ten minutes or more, his love spread out like a star. Look at Dougal Henderson; what might he not have done for Jimmy? His boy with the glue-thick spectacles that magnified his eyes, and whose habit of clapping his hands with excitement would cause his father to make an injured sound, as if the enormity of his love was almost too much to bear? ("I worry for him, Florrie. I worry all the time.") And Arthur. Oh, dear Arthur—who had been so wholly misunderstood by this place. Clownish, disheveled, with a penchant for gambling and *put-putting* on the pipe; people assumed there had been no marriage for Arthur, no children ("Because who on earth," remarked Sybilla, "*would*?"). But once, Florrie had found Arthur crying in the churchyard. "I have a child," he'd confessed, "that I've never seen. A boy—a man, now. He is fifty years old and I've never even seen him . . . What a *waste*, Florrie! Oh, what a terrible waste." And when Florrie had suggested that it wasn't too late—that there's still so much more to come, that there's always joy in the world and all the other familiar platitudes—he'd shaken his head. "*Look* at me. Who'd want to discover that *this* was their father?" And Florrie's heart had spilled over with feeling so that she had cried with him on that bench. They'd shared a hanky and a bag of crystallized ginger. And they had been dearer friends after that.

Florrie, I've uncovered something. About someone here.

She turns off the tap. "Right."

Back to the matter in hand. For if it wasn't Jay Mistry who climbed those stairs, who did? And if it isn't Jay Mistry Renata loves, who is it? And if one wishes to hear all the gossip of Babbington Hall—its comings and goings, who loves who, whose teeth are real and whose are not—isn't there really only one person worth speaking to? Or, rather, two?

16

Enter the Ellwoods

lorrie has always enjoyed her own company. This isn't to say she doesn't enjoy people, too: people can be the most wonderful things—passionate, learned, well traveled, gentle, generous, imperfect and so full of stories that Florrie can spend a whole day with her chin in cupped hands, listening to them with a smile. The right people are a joy. But she also needs her silence. She tries to avoid overly peopled, clattering places—not least because of her hearing aids.

Thus it is with a degree of reluctance that, after having had a sandwich back in the old apple store, Florrie wheels herself toward the dining hall as lunchtime comes to an end. Most of the residents of Babbington do not share Florrie's enjoyment of solitude. Most thrive on the quiz nights or bingo or the monthly movie nights in the library when Franklin brings in a projector that lights up the wall on which, normally, there's a portrait of Her Majesty. But they thrive on mealtimes most of all. The dining room, at this hour, will be full of noise.

Nevertheless, she goes. Florrie punches in the door code, passes through the back door, wheels herself up the ramp and into the reception hall where she bears right for the dining room. There's the residual smell of breakfast—the lingering waft of bacon and eggs. She smells, too, strong coffee, which she rarely drinks now because it makes her heart thrum, but, oh, she loves the taste and smell. It reminds her of the coffeehouses in Cairo or the metal espresso pot that rattled on Middle Morag's stove before she poured it, held at a height.

Florrie enters the room. And on entering it, she immediately hears the sound she is expecting—which is her name, trilled out in two soprano voices, and the clatter of teacups being abandoned in surprise. They rise from their chairs, arms open. "Oh, Florrie! Look, it's Florrie. *Do* join us. We've made a space—just here!"

Emily and Edith are not actually sisters. They're related through marriage only, having each married one half of a set of twin brothers (now deceased, both having succumbed to the same heart complaint in their fifties). But one could be forgiven for thinking that they, in fact, were the identical ones. They're of the same tall, slender build; they have the same features—which include prominent noses, sparkling eyes and small, pinkish, puckered mouths as if invisible drawstrings have tightened them and might, at any moment, be loosened so that words can pour out like water, flooding the room. Both have steel-grey hair. One (Edith? Florrie can never remember which Ellwood is which and it's far too late to ask them now) wears hers twisted and looped at her nape, not unlike a pastry; the other's hair, in contrast, is as straight as a poker and worn loose, to her shoulders, save for a section that's kept from her face with a girlish, sparkly comb. They have the same mannerisms, turns of phrase; they can often be found walking arm in arm or sitting primly like bookends. They even wear the same clothing, at times—the same watches on their wrists with mother-of-pearl faces, matching bejeweled brooches shaped like a fleur-de-lis. So yes, it's understandable why some people think they're twin sisters. The Ellwoods have never seemed to mind the misunderstanding. The only protestation comes from Emily (is it Emily?), who reinforces that *she* (Edith?) is a full year older than her.

Florrie slots her lap under their table.

The Ellwoods glow at her arrival. They settle back down in their chairs without taking their eyes off Florrie, retaining their beatific smiles. One of them (she decides that, from now on, the pastry-haired Ellwood will always be Edith) leans forward, palms on the tablecloth. "Well . . . *what* a surprise. You hardly ever come into the dining room, Florrie! It is quite lovely to see you. We have been thinking of you lately—haven't we?"

Emily nods. "Oh, we have. Very much so." She, too, leans closer. "Tell us—how *are* you, dear? We heard that you saw *everything* . . ."

"I am," Florrie assures them, "quite well."

"Oh, but you can't be. To *see* it! Was it so very dreadful?"

"Did you see her step out of the window?"

"Did you see her land?"

"How shocked you must be!"

"*So* shocked!"

They stop, heads tilted to the same side. They're studying Florrie so intently that they bring Gulliver to mind and how transfixed he'd be on detecting mackerel. "It was very dark," Florrie reminds them.

"Of course. And such rain! Wasn't the rain something, Em?"

"*Wasn't* it? Torrential! And the thunder, too! We couldn't sleep, could we, you and I? We could barely hear ourselves *think* with it! We made ourselves cocoa and looked out at the rain. Perhaps you, Florrie, couldn't sleep, either? Is that why you looked out of your window?"

"And that's how you saw her? Is that how it happened?"

"*Was* there very much blood?"

Florrie feels the quiver of irritation. "I'd quite like," she decides, "some tea."

Instantly, Edith throws her left arm into the air like a schoolgirl, straightens her back in her chair. "Clive? I say—Clive? Could you bring a fresh pot over here, please? A little more milk, too, if we may."

Clive is nowhere to be seen. He is probably in the kitchen, scrubbing pans of bacon fat, but this doesn't stop Edith from thanking him

and lowering her hand with a satisfied air. She knows that Clive will
have heard her. After all, the Ellwood voices have a certain reverberat-
ing quality, like the *ting* of a tuning fork. "You know, dear Florrie, you
can tell us *anything*."

It's true—Florrie could. But she also knows that, having murmured it, it would be rolled through the whole of Oxfordshire like
a bowling ball. That's why she's here, after all. The Ellwoods like to
think they know everything. And perhaps they do: their quarters
(shared, with twin beds) are within Babbington Hall itself, within its
oldest, wood-paneled part. Their door leads directly onto reception;
their bedroom wall adjoins that of the manager's office. Also, their
sitting-room window is marginally curved, with a cushioned window
seat, which allows them to look directly on to the half-moon steps
and the lavender urns that stand beside Babbington's main door. Of
course, when sitting there, they pretend to be reading. But nobody
believes, for a moment, that they are. In short, their quarters are at the
heart of Babbington; there could be no better place in all of Oxfordshire from which to eavesdrop, study or peer.

So it is that the Ellwoods are *informed* (their chosen term—
instead of *nosey* or *bloody interfering*, which others would probably
opt for). And they pass on what they know with a lick of the lips.
These are the women who will sidle up to any new arrival, smiling
with purpose, as pickpockets might. They're the ones who learned
of Nancy Tapp's three marriages, Reuben's dieting attempts, of
Georgette's failed fertility treatment ("which is," they murmured,
"such a *very* costly business"), of how Stanhope Jones has been
divorced for nearly twenty years now ("and his ex-wife was *Dutch*, of
all things!"). They've been so desperate to learn precisely how Florrie
lost her leg that she has refused to say a word about that, just to frus-
trate them—claiming it's all too upsetting to speak of. ("Of course,
dear Florrie! We *quite* understand . . . a car accident, perhaps?") But
if one is to be generous to the Ellwoods (and Florrie tries to be), they

also tried to match Aubrey Horner to that toothy, curly-haired artist who offered lessons at Babbington for a while, in the hope of a Babbington engagement. They noticed the slight yellow tinge to the previous vicar long before anyone else did, which surely saved his life. And they'd welcomed his replacement, Reverend Joe, with a warbled song of welcome outside the vicarage and a round of applause. By and large, they mean well.

They are showing a form of benevolence now. For Emily is leaning forward, one palm pressed to her collarbone, and saying, "Florrie? You look rather peaky. Are you sleeping? Eating properly? I swear by a pint of stout once a week—for iron."

Edith tuts. "It isn't iron, Em. It's the shock of the thing! The distress! Do you remember what happened to Fergus?" She returns to Florrie. "Fergus, our nephew, lost his job—something in finance—and promptly took ill with whooping cough—"

"It was pneumonia, Edie."

"—with pneumonia; we were all quite shaken for weeks and weeks. We were preparing for the worst, you see. But he rallied far sooner than we did—and just in time for Christmas, which was a blessing." Edith leans forward conspiratorially. "The Ellwoods were a sickly bunch, is the truth of the matter. Hearts, mostly. Although it was kidneys, too, with your Gordon, wasn't it?"

"Kidneys." Emily nods. "We should have known. He was urinating *far* too much."

At that, Clive arrives with the teapot. His rubber shoes squeak on the laminate flooring; he sets down the pot in a blunt, disgruntled fashion so that a drop of tea jumps out of the spout. "Enjoy," he says, as people do now—but in a tone suggesting that he has no interest at all in whether they enjoy it or not.

In his wake, the Ellwoods fuss with three new teacups. They pour, stir and offer one to Florrie as if it's gold-plated. "*Here.*"

"Thank you."

They watch as she sips.

"*Such* a terrible thing. Although, of course," Edith offers, "these things do happen. There's no accounting for it. We knew a man in Islington who drank rat poison—who knows why? He had such a lovely house—didn't he, Em? A roof terrace! In Islington! Heaven knows how much *that* cost him. And who was that woman at your book club? With the hosepipe and the car?"

"Oh, her. Gosh, I can't remember her name. Made excellent meringues. Good cheekbones. Heavens, what *was* her name?" They both stare at the tablecloth before conceding that, no, her name has gone. "And do you remember," Emily adds, "that politician? Stepped onto the line at Belsize Park. He had a saintly name. Saint-something. St. Clair?"

"Quite a saintly face, in fact, as I remember. He reminded me of Gordon but slightly darker hair."

"And better kidneys. Yes, that was such a sadness. Hadn't his daughter . . . ?"

"She *had*. And he'd never recovered."

"Oh, my!"

Briefly, Florrie imagines taking both the Ellwood heads and banging them together like a pair of cymbals. *Take that!* But that's not a kind way of thinking. Instead, she fixes her smile. "I'd had no idea at all about Jay Mistry. But one doesn't hear much from the old apple store."

It's like dropping a crumb on a pond's surface: life rushes up to grab it. Down go the teacups. "You didn't? About Jay? Oh, *we* knew—didn't we?"

"We *did*, Edie. Before anyone else! Of course, technically he came here to see his mother so, in the beginning, we thought nothing of it. But then we started to notice that he'd . . . linger."

"Linger?"

"Linger. Outside our door, near the manager's office. That's how we knew—that he must have liked Renata; that he wasn't just visiting

Babbington to be the dutiful son. Oh, it was all rather endearing, wasn't it? We'd see him checking his reflection in the glass of the portraits—moving his hair this side or that. And we'd hear him, too."

"Hear him?"

"Not on purpose, Florrie, you understand. Heavens, no! We'd never pry. But with Renata's office being so close to our quarters . . . Well, the acoustics of the place: sometimes one just *happens* to hear things. He'd ask her out to the pictures, to restaurants. And he bought her flowers! Do you remember those tulips, Edie? Tied in raffia?"

"Half of Holland, I should think!"

All this is in keeping with what Florrie already knows: Jay Mistry (poor dear man—in Nepal, and therefore categorically not an attempted murderer) loves Renata yet she, alas, does not love him. But somewhere, there's a man with whom Renata *is* in love. And so Florrie adjusts her skirts, preparing to ask the Ellwoods (who are now quibbling between themselves over who should pour the milk) a more pressing question. "Do you have any thoughts on why?"

"On why?"

"Yes—*why* Renata refused Jay. After all, he seems a splendid chap."

The sisters-in-law cluck in agreement. "How he might be Marcella's son is *quite* the mystery. Must take after his father, although none of us know much about him. Terribly handsome, by all accounts. And rich, I should think! Have you seen those gold bangles she wears? How much must *they* be worth?"

"Just going back to Renata—"

"Ah, yes! Well, we did wonder if she might be a little like Sybilla Farr? In that she"—Emily glances left and right, as if checking for traffic—"prefers female company. I mean, anything is allowed these days!"

As it should be, Florrie thinks rather sourly. And Florrie realizes that subtlety is no good with the Ellwoods; she needs to take control of this conversation because it appears to be pinging about like the ball in a game of bagatelle. "Right. Well, I've been wondering, personally, if Renata is in love with someone else. That's my offering. Any thoughts on that?"

The Ellwoods sit bolt upright. "In love? With someone else? Who? *Who*, Florrie?"

"I have no idea who. But Renata having a secret boyfriend . . . It seems the likeliest reason to turn poor Jay down."

Instantly, the sisters-in-law are adamant: "No, no, no. Quite impossible. Renata did not have a boyfriend—secret or otherwise. Absolutely not."

"How can you be sure?"

"Because we'd know! We'd see! Our quarters, Florrie: we don't *want* to hear and see so much; we don't *like* that we can hear most conversations in the reception hall. But it simply can't be helped. And we can both tell you—can't we, Em?—that Renata has never had a romantic visitor. She's had building contractors and ambulance drivers and that chap who came to unblock the drains; and she's had potential residents, of course—like you, Florrie. Oh, we remember you coming here! You arrived in a rusty old Fiesta and we thought, Surely *she* can't afford Babbington's fees!" The Ellwoods titter in unison. "But boyfriends? Certainly not."

Florrie shifts her jaw. "You might have missed something."

At that, Edith and Emily burst into a chorus of indignation— clucking like hens when a fox comes by. "Missed something? *Missed* something?" Edith is so affronted that she sets down her teacup and Emily pats her forearm and there's a brief muttering between themselves. *She knows no better, Edie. Patience, now.*

"All I'm saying," Florrie reasons, "is that you can't be in your quarters all the time. Sometimes you're at church. Sometimes you're walking around the grounds or here, in the dining room—as you are now. And sometimes, of course, you are sleeping. What if a boyfriend came at one of those times? Or what if he came . . . at night?"

The idea has only just come to her. And how right it sounds; how pleased she is with herself for thinking it! For wouldn't a boyfriend come in the evening? After the working day, at least? He might stay the night, even, creeping downstairs before daybreak . . . *How* things have changed since Florrie's girlhood—and she is half inclinded to say this when Emily Ellwood gives a sudden, loose, exasperated sigh, as a bored horse makes in its stable. "Oh, for heaven's sake! Of *course* they don't come at night, Florrie! No one comes after eight o'clock."

"But how do you *know* that?" Again, she thinks of cymbals.

"Because, Florrie—"

"Because *what?*"

"Because that's when Babbington Hall is locked!"

Locked? Florrie blinks. It stops her in her tracks, like a five-barred gate. She had no idea. Why hadn't it ever occurred to her that Babbington would, sometimes, be locked? Because, she realizes, it's something that she's never needed to know. Florrie doesn't go out in the evenings for dinner with children, or any old friends; nor does anyone ever really come to see her. So the opening hours of Babbington have never mattered to her. How horribly foolish she feels. "That's true?"

"Yes, it's true! The front door is locked at eight o'clock when the day-shift nurses and carers go home. Of course, all the outbuildings are still accessible at all hours—we aren't captives! But the Hall itself? One could lean on the front door's buzzer all one wanted at one minute past eight: no one's going to let you in. And even if someone *did*—say, Renata had let some fellow through reception at one in the morning—they'd have to disable the alarm before doing so, which makes a frightful noise. Doesn't it, Em?"

"Oh, it's far too loud! Louder than the alarm itself, I shouldn't wonder. It wakes us at six in the morning, when the door's unlocked again for the day. Ghastly, really."

"But there's the back door." That, she knows, is never locked. It doesn't need to be, with its door code. "Surely someone could creep in that way, after dark?"

"They could—theoretically. But he would still have to walk through the reception hall, wouldn't he? He'd still have to walk past our quarters. And those wooden floors are as creaky as a barrel, are they not? The whole reception hall groans and grumbles with the slightest weight upon it. Even Nancy Tapp sounds like an elephant and she's like a thimble on wheels! So, Florrie, I'm afraid we can be perfectly certain: there's been no boyfriend here."

It is done. It is over. There's a triumphant air to the Ellwoods—as if a game's been played and they, the Ellwoods, have won by a good margin. They beam at each other, victorious; then they turn to Florrie, consider her with angled heads as if she deserves their sympathy. "Florrie, you are *such* a funny little thing!"

Florrie has, of course, been called worse. But there's a certain bite to how the Ellwoods are laughing at her now—side by side and back and forth, like children in a swing. *Isn't she funny? Oh, so very funny!* Pinky, she knows, would have seethed darkly through her heavy fringe and said, with a raised finger, You leave Butters alone.

Florrie looks out of the window to her left. From here, she can see the orchard. She sees its ripening fruit and, beneath it, the mismatched collection of deckchairs that were carried there, for the shade. It was there, in the orchard, that she'd talked with Stanhope all those weeks ago. How lovely that had been—an early summer's evening, and a lively conversation with such a mild-mannered, thoughtful man. What could have been nicer? ("I do," he'd offered, "find *Othello* tricky because it's all such a waste, isn't it? All that sadness—and for what?") *I'd rather be there*, she thinks. *I'd rather be with him.*

"Florrie? Florrie? There you are. You must forgive us. We can both be a dreadful tease. Now, everything we've told you *is* true. But . . ." The Ellwoods glance at each other, bright-eyed. In the short time that

Florrie has been daydreaming, a silent agreement has clearly been made between them, for Emily leans forward conspiratorially. "Well, there is something else, you see. What you said—about her loving somebody . . . Now, Renata doesn't have a boyfriend *as such*."

"As such? You just said that no one visits her!"

"And they don't! But . . ." Emily gestures to her sister-in-law, as if to say, *You tell her*—so that Edith pats her pastry hairdo, preparing herself. "Edie? Don't keep dear Florrie waiting, now."

Edith stops with the pretence, drops her hand. "Renata had *post*. That morning!"

"Post?" Florrie leans forward across the table so suddenly that her bosom knocks over the sugar bowl. She'd normally apologize profusely to anyone in earshot, tidy up the sugar, but instead she says, "What kind of post?"

"It was a *card*."

"A card?"

"A greetings card."

The Ellwoods shine like stars. How pleased they are to have this knowledge; how thrilled they are, evidently, to have Florrie's full attention. Emily comes closer, rolls up imaginary sleeves. "It arrived that morning—the day that she jumped. Edith and I were just setting off for breakfast, along the corridor—about nine o'clock, or thereabouts—and as we approached the manager's office, there she was, standing in the doorway, wearing navy, which is really too harsh on her colouring, to my mind. A lighter blue would have been kinder; something to match her eyes. But anyway, there she was. And she, Renata, was opening something—a card or a letter, we couldn't quite tell at first. And her *face* when she saw it, Florrie . . . The expression! Well, she was flushing to the colour of a peony, I should say—one of those very dark peonies, not the light, sugar-pink ones that one usually gets. She's pale, isn't she? Most of the time? But I tell you—she wasn't then."

"It was definitely a card? You saw it?"

"Oh, we did! A card with a bird on it—although it was hard to tell what kind of bird because Renata dropped the card as she saw us approaching, and she became quite flustered in picking it back up. She was *very* secretive."

"The envelope matched her blushes! A deep pink—wasn't it, Em?"

"Oh, yes. Very deep. I had a heavenly cardigan in that colour once—cashmere. The blasted moths got it."

"What," Florrie urges, "did the card say?"

"How can we know *that,* Florrie? Without rootling through her drawers? Which is, of course, something we'd *never* do—and never have. Just as we haven't sifted through the glove compartment of a car or checked our husbands' pockets. Not once."

Edith shoots a glance at her sister-in-law. "Quite. But I would add, Florrie, that we did see the handwriting from a distance, and it was rather ornate."

"Oh, very! Curly. Formal. It said *For Renata Green*—and the *F,* Florrie, was like one of those squiggles in music. You know—at the start of things."

"A treble clef."

"Exactly! A treble clef. Which isn't how Jay Mistry writes, because we've seen his letters—quite by chance, you understand; he'd push them under the office door. Anyway, Florrie, we didn't see the actual message, no. But to have chosen an envelope in that colour! And to have created such a blush in our pallid, underfed Renata! It must have been quite the declaration of love."

"Not," remarks Emily, a little tartly, "that it made any difference. She still . . ."—and using a teaspoon, she mimes Renata's nocturnal fall, landing with a thud on the tablecloth.

The Ellwoods sit back. Edith mouths something at Emily—regarding, no doubt, the mention of glove compartments. As for Florrie, she feels less inclined to bang their heads together; indeed, she is refreshed and ready as a houseplant that's been watered. A card!

Ornate handwriting! Here, surely, is the man Renata loves. And thus, thank goodness for these bored, beady-eyed gossips with nothing better to do than to peep through keyholes and loiter in doorways; for the location of their home allows them to see everything that comes in, goes out or stays.

"Your quarters really *are* in the centre of things. How handy for you. But didn't I hear rumours that you were leaving them? That Renata had plans for that?" So Marcella had said.

Is there a sudden *froideur* from the Ellwoods? A twitch, and a fixed smile? "Oh, that was nothing. There *was* a little talk of Renata wanting to turn our rooms into some sort of visitors' lounge—whatever that means! I do dislike that word—*lounge*."

Emily leans forward. "There was even talk of a coffee machine! A place for visitors to wait, I suppose—a place for prospective residents to look through brochures, that sort of thing. Our rooms are the loveliest of all, it's true. But where were *we* meant to go?"

"Anyway, it hardly matters, now. Georgette's taken over Babbington Hall and she's excellent—isn't she?"

"Oh, she is, Edie. *Much* better. I imagine there's been quite the pay rise for her."

"So that's that." Edith smiles sweetly. "There'll be no visitors' lounge now."

Afterward, Florrie moves herself along to the reception hall, where she stops beneath a Babbington portrait and puts on her brakes. She isn't sure which Babbington she's looking at. The inventor? The gambler? Even the pig farmer? Usually, she'd deliberate on this—but she has far more important matters at hand.

As if she's just come back from a coastal walk, Florrie feels that she has pockets to empty and sift through—keeping the pearls and seashells, discarding the plastic and weeds. What has she learned from speaking to the Ellwoods?

Firstly, that Renata has had no personal visitors. Jay Mistry had been the only one—and even then, it had been during working hours, their conversations conducted in the reception hall or in corridors. And whilst there must, surely, have been moments in which the Ellwoods weren't peering through keyholes or turning up their hearing aids, Florrie has to concede that they are quite remarkable in what they see and hear. If they were able to spot Reverend Bligh's cirrhosis from twenty paces, or to learn (who knows how?) that Georgette's latest fertility treatment hasn't worked again, then they'd have sniffed out a boyfriend in no time.

The second discovery, however, is better: Renata has had mail. And if Florrie's to extend her seashore analogy, this is a particularly impressive part of her haul: the still-hinged cockle, the oil-blue mussel, the oyster shell or the razor clam. Here, surely, is who Renata loves: this man with ornate penmanship, whose words made her blush like a peony.

You see, I'm in love, Florrie.

There is so much more than Oxfordshire.

And her third discovery? That Babbington's front door is locked from eight o'clock every night, that no one can enter or leave without setting off the alarm or disarming it. Fine, Florrie thinks: no one used the front door. But the back door *is* possible. And yes, on a normal evening he might have woken the Ellwoods, with their swiveling, bat-like ears, as he crept up the stairs that creak like a ship in a stormy sea. But that night? Midsummer's night? It had a storm of its own. *We could barely hear ourselves think with it—could we, Edie?*

Whoever pushed Renata used the back door. There is, she sees, no other way of it. Which means that he—the pusher, the would-be murderer—must be close to Babbington, working or living in it. He must know the four-digit code.

17

By the Compost Heap—Part Two

I t is Stanhope she wants to speak to. All she wants, after seeing the Ellwoods, is to share her thoughts with someone—and, specifically, with him.

It makes sense that she does. During his investigations, her father, Sergeant Butterfield, had had colleagues to speak to. Over a cup of tea and a currant bun, they'd sit down heavily and assess the evidence, the new lines of enquiry: a possible fraud or mistaken identity. "Sarge, how about . . . ?" Herbert had shared his thoughts with his own children, too—on the sofa, in the evenings—although it had largely been Bobs who, being older, had proved the more helpful. Might the suspect have used the towpath to escape on, undetected? And did it rain at all, on the night in question? Their father would clap a thigh in approval: "Excellent, Bobs! Well done."

To share, then; to have a partner, as it were. Yet Stanhope is nowhere to be found. It's only as she's wheeling herself, gingerly, toward the old pig sties (one of which, she knows, belongs to Stanhope) that she learns he's gone out for the day. The Professors Lim tell her this. They are walking, arm in arm, as crooked as a pair of croquet hoops; on seeing Florrie, Harrold pauses so that his wife, Kitty, comes to a standstill also. "Stanhope? He's gone to Oxford, Florrie. Took the minibus. Something about needing to buy something for someone. Back by six,

I should think." Seeing that Florrie is a little crestfallen, Harrold adds: "Nothing we can help you with?"

There isn't. It is only Stanhope she can speak to about Renata's secret correspondence, the Ellwoods' prattle or Marcella's maternal fury. She thanks the professors, anyway.

So it is that Florrie finds herself sitting by the compost heap a little after five o'clock on a late June afternoon, staring at the grass cuttings with her hands in her lap. There are midges, dancing in columns; she can see a flattened place amongst the vegetable peelings where the grass snake might have been. She is here because if she can't speak to Stanhope directly, she can, at least, speak to an imaginary version of him—and so she pretends he's sitting beside her, on the cracked plastic chair.

How beautiful it all is, she thinks—greenish-gold, in the fading light.

Love, then—and being in love. Is it possible to have such feelings for someone you've not actually met? Not seen in person? Who one knows through greetings cards alone?

It is, Florrie admits, quite baffling to her—that someone can be in love with a person they haven't sat in a room with, haven't examined under the stark, unflattering lighting of a corner shop. Surely one needs to be *with* them? She is reasonably confident that she would never have loved Victor Plumley based solely on his letters, and she only came to love Dougal Henderson when physically close to him—on *Damsel*, in fact, with the rain coming down so hard that they'd squinted, noses wrinkled, beneath their anorak hoods, and Florrie had considered his face and decided she adored it for all its lines and bristles, for all its weathering. And Jack Luckett? Heaven knows, she'd have run a hundred miles from a written account of him: divorced, sullen, abdominal wounds from a bar brawl, fifteen years older and of no fixed abode. Who might read that and think, *Oh, how lovely*? Yet Jack was more than lovely, in the end.

So, yes, it's a strange concept—falling in love without really meeting. But she's aware that time moves on. In her mother's era, there were still debutantes; in her own time, one was courted or wooed. Then the sixties happened (during which time Florrie was largely in airless, equatorial countries)—and so much changed after that. These days? The young (and even the not-so-young) seem to find *l'amour* through computers or mobile phones, from profiles (is that the word?) and photographs alone. It isn't something Florrie understands. But nor does she understand the space-time continuum or neurolinguistics or how hydrangeas can turn from pink to blue—and that doesn't stop these things from being real, and true, and good.

There it is. The dark, sharp feeling—that pike, which lingers down in her belly—passing through a shaft of light as if to say, *I'm still here.*

She looks down, smooths her skirt.

Back to Renata. Her card. Being in love. And if Stanhope were, in fact, sitting beside her at this exact moment, she'd probably announce to him that the sender of this card—this suitor, he of the ornate handwriting—might not necessarily live so far away. Easy to think, of course, that he must: in Florrie's day, one only went to the trouble of writing a letter and buying a stamp when someone was physically out of reach. But times have changed; the word *remote* has altered its meaning—and online love isn't, she supposes, just for those who live miles apart.

But the pusher, she's sure, lives nearby. And so, perhaps, does the sender of the card. And whilst this doesn't mean that these two individuals are, in fact, one person, Florrie is suddenly convinced that they are. She stares at the cracked plastic chair. "Whoever sent this card to Renata also pushed her, wanted her dead." Does this sound foolish, spoken out loud? Yes—even to her. But nevertheless, Florrie has such a strong inkling about it. She has this curious, hard certainty—low down, like a swallowed cherry stone—that she and Stanhope are looking for just one person, not two. Of course, it makes no sense.

But sometimes in this life, one just *knows* a thing. Sometimes—despite all reason and common sense, despite one's better judgement—the human heart is quite convinced that something will happen, or something is right, and then it *is* right or *does* happen. Look at Florrie's first sighting of the little house in Scotland; look at how, with the arrival of Pinky Underwood, Florrie had thought, *She's going to be my best friend forever.* Look at the name *Temple Beeches* and how Florrie had felt on hearing it, in Mrs. Pringle's Book Bazaar: *That's where I'll go.* Even look at how Florrie had woken, one morning, in an attic room off Holywell Street in the heart of Oxford, aged sixteen, and *known* she had the right feelings; this, she'd been certain, was love.

The chair stares back at her.

Herbert would call it instinct. Prudence would have mentioned something about the universe whispering to her, through cupped hands. And Pinky? She, too, had a habit of setting down wisdom—albeit casually, with a shrug, as if she'd found this truth in the street and it was, most likely, inconsequential. *You'll change your mind tomorrow* or *He'll write within the week.*

"We are looking for one person."

Arthur, too, comes to mind. There he is, turning the pages of the *Racing Post.* Or rather, there he is, carrying his tray of peach cobbler and custard and glancing from left to right, as if somebody might hear him.

She looks at her watch. It's nearly quarter to six now. Time for cheese and biscuits, a little whisky, perhaps.

Florrie takes the brakes off her chair. But with that small mechanical click, a strange sensation comes. What? She isn't sure. Is she being watched? It suddenly feels like she might be. Or it feels like that click of the brakes has caught the attention of something so that it's holding its breath, listening for more. *What?* It's like something approaches. She waits.

She waits . . .

There! A realization lands in front of her, like a leaf.

The magenta envelope. Florrie has also seen it. She saw it with her own eyes—its colour, its squareness, the *F* like a treble clef. For it was in Renata's wastepaper bin, on midsummer's morning; it had been with them, watching in the shadows, as they'd talked about love and Paris and pink lemonade, about making the most of one's life.

18

An *F* Like a Treble Clef

It does not feel like three days since Florrie last went to the manager's office. On one hand, nothing has really changed in that time: the lawn is still thirsty as she hurries past it; the various floorboards still clonk beneath her as she enters through the back door and heads toward the reception hall. But on the other hand, everything is different. *She* is different.

Florrie expects, on arrival, to find that the office itself is also unchanged—the same dark-red curtains tied back with the same faded tasseled cords, the same filing cabinet and the same black leatherette chair on castors and the same trapped smell. She expects there to be no change at all except for a lack of the manager herself.

But when she finds the open door and peeps inside, Florrie makes a bright "Oh, I say!" For there are changes everywhere. None of the furniture is positioned as it was: the desk has been dragged to the window; the filing cabinet is in the far corner; chairs and potted plants and even the threadbare rug have all been hauled from this side to that, from left to right. The curtains (which are still the same curtains) are no longer half drawn in a casual loop but pulled back in their entirety, allowing the early evening light to pour into the room as if a sluice gate has been opened. The Virginia creeper has been cut away. And there are new additions to the room—including a fruit bowl, a hatstand, a framed print of the Birmingham skyline, a teddy bear with a

T-shirt that says HUG ME on it and a large aloe vera in a scarlet pot. She notices, too, that there is paperwork everywhere—on every surface, spilling onto the floor. (Is this even the same room? Florrie wonders. Has she wheeled herself into a different office?)

The greatest change of all, however, is Georgette. Not only is she *not* Renata, but she is so far removed from Renata—in character, voice, movement—that Florrie stares momentarily. She knows Georgette, of course. Yet she is newly struck by her height, which must be six foot, at least. Even in her pumps, Georgette must duck under beams in the oldest part of the building; she's changed the lightbulb in Florrie's kitchen by merely reaching up. And this height is matched by Georgette's physique: her bust, like Florrie's, is ample; her bottom, too, is wide; yet, unlike Florrie, Georgette has poise and a certain regal magnificence, sailing through the corridors of Babbington like a flagship so that residents can't help but lower their teacups and gaze. She stands, at this moment, like a statue. Her left hand holds the phone to her ear; her right hand sits on her hip. Her hair—which is pulled back tightly into a knot—has both an iridescence to it and has (Florrie knows) a creamy vanilla smell. She looks up, sees her visitor. She nods as if to say, *Come in.*

"I see. Well, yes, Doctor. I see . . ."

Florrie parks herself by the hatstand. Three days—that's all. And yet even in the smallest of corners, there is Georgette in some way or form: a spare pair of shoes with the heels flattened down; a mug on a shelf that says WORLD'S BEST AUNT.

No Parisian calendar.

Nothing is at right angles that Florrie can see.

"All right, lovey. Yes, I agree."

This, too, is a difference between Renata and Georgette: Whereas the former is deemed aloof and reserved, by some, there's no possibility of saying the latter is so. Affection pours out of Georgette. In her thick Midlands accent, she will scatter out terms of endearment like seed: the postman has been called *sweetheart*, Aubrey Horner has been *my duck*. There have been *darlings* and *lovebugs* and *my lovelys*, and a surplus of the good, affectionate Birmingham term of *bab*. Once, in her early days here, Florrie had knocked into a fire extinguisher and was clumsy in reversing back from it and Georgette had helped, saying, "Let me help you with that, sugarplum"—which Florrie had been quite taken with. (In nearly ninety years of life, she'd never been called a sugarplum before.)

"Quite, Doctor. Yes, I understand that. All right-y. You too, my love. Goodbye, now."

Georgette hangs up, sets her left hand on her other hip. Briefly, she stares at the telephone as if something's written on it.

"I can come back . . . ?"

"Florrie. Ah, no—you're all right. I'd normally shut the door with those sorts of calls but there's still no air in here, is there? Can you feel it? Ever so stuffy. Anyway, I'm off at six. So it's now or tomorrow, my lovely."

"Is it Tabitha Brimble? On the second floor?" She wheels forward.

"You've heard? Yes, it is, bless her. She's usually so calm and gracious; honestly, sometimes you'd never know she was ill. But she seems so frustrated lately. Keeps calling us all liars, striking out . . . Reverend Joe popped up to see her—you know how nice he is. But even then . . ."

Florrie's heart clenches. She sends out love like an arrow—hasty, instinctive, strong.

"Anyway, I'm sure Dr. Mallory will manage it. He's working so hard—what with Dr Laghari being off on maternity leave . . ." Her attention drifts, momentarily. "Actually, I'm meant to be keeping an eye on you, Florrie. No headaches? No blurred vision? Because you know what that might mean." She raises a finger with this last sentence, as if any concussion or internal bleeding would be Florrie's fault entirely.

"No headaches, no. And my vision is only blurred when I've taken off my spectacles."

Georgette ignores the joke. "And your wrist? How's that, now?"

Florrie proffers it. "Coming along. Is there any further news? From the hospital?"

"No news, I'm afraid." She sighs. "All such a shame."

Florrie likes Georgette—she does. (She warms to anyone who is naturally jovial, who, on being thanked, will say, "Don't mention it, flower.") But as the new acting manager discusses what a shock it's all been, how terribly sad, and as she bestows all her finest terms of endearment on Renata (*poor darling, the angel*), Florrie finds herself feeling a slight disgruntlement. And she knows exactly why. Three days is no time at all. Renata is still the manager of Babbington Hall; Georgette is only acting manager—a temporary post until Renata's well again. Yet there's no hint of Renata in this room whatsoever. There are no Post-it Notes or highlighted timetable, no terracotta pot with pens in. There's no expectation that Renata will return. She— Renata—has been swept out of here like a cobweb; she's been scrubbed out, painted over, and yet this is still, surely, *her* office; this desk is surely still *her* desk. And Florrie rather feels like making some sort of objection, of announcing, *Stop right there!*

Instead, she adjusts her elastic waistband. "You must be very busy, Georgette."

"Oh, you don't know the half of it, treacle. Bills to pay, paperwork to sort out, brochures to send, medication to order, insurance to renew, staff appraisals to plan. The bloody jackdaws are still there. And the plasterwork in the west wing is crumbling in places so we'll need to get a builder in because that's beyond what Franklin can do. And Reuben has handed in his notice, which means we need to find someone else, and quickly, because we're low on staff as it is." The words are, in a way, a complaint. Yet Georgette's tone is as cheery as if she's listing her holiday plans.

"Reuben's leaving?"

Georgette sighs. "He gave his week's notice. He's ever so upset, you see. I think he was fond of her—possibly too fond. But it *is* upsetting, isn't it? Knowing that someone you work with wanted to kill herself? Anyway, Florrie. What can I do for you?"

"Yes. Thank you. Of course. Well, I was here a few days ago—on midsummer's day, actually—and I think I dropped a shopping list."

"A shopping list?"

"It sounds dreadfully foolish, I know, but I'd been keeping it for several weeks—jotting things down so I wouldn't forget. And having lost it, I have no idea at all what was on there. None! It was on the back of an envelope—bright pink. Magenta. I don't suppose . . ."

Georgette raises her brows. "That I've found it? No, Florrie. As you can see, I've had a bit of a tidy—things needed sorting out. Renata collected everything! A pink envelope?"

"Yes. And my handwriting, if it helps, is a very loopy business. Very dramatic. Perhaps Renata found it and popped it in the wastepaper bin?"

Georgette bends down, rummages under her desk and reemerges. "It might have been in there, bab, but it isn't there now, I can tell you that much. It's empty—see? It's been taken out."

"Taken out? Where to?" She feels her pulse quicken.

"To the blue bin, Florrie. By the kitchen door?" Georgette says this with a smile, as if Florrie amuses her with her lack of knowledge about the life span of wastepaper. "Tomorrow's recycling day."

The recycling bin, then. But it is late in the day—and whilst there's still enough light to wheel herself around in, Florrie knows, with a heavy heart, that she needs more than that. She needs, ideally, her left leg. She needs to be younger and taller than she is. Or she needs Pinky—for whom delving into a recycling bin would be the easiest, simplest thing in the world. She'd have done it without hesitation—head down, bottom up.

Pinky. Who'd eat an apple in its entirety—core and pips together. *Can't waste it, Butters.*

I will, Florrie decides, speak of her, too—when the time comes. All right and proper, of course, to tell Renata of those six men in her life (a list she could chant, if asked to: Gaston, Jack, Victor, Hassan, Dougal and Teddy Silversmith); that love is the kind one finds in poetry or romance novels or in Hollywood films. But what of friendship? What of the deep, unshakeable love of friends? Isn't that just as wonderful? And worth the same celebration? In her final hours, Pinky Topham née Underwood had turned her head on her pillow to find Florrie's gaze and smiled slowly at her—and that smile had had everything in it, every laugh and adventure and secret, every wrong turn. *What a time we've had—you and I.* And hadn't they? Hadn't they had their own love story—two awkward schoolfriends, one short and one tall? Who'd tumbled through life in their own different ways but never far from each other? Like a pair of mismatched shoes with their laces tied together. Like a pair of odd socks in the wash.

So, yes, Florrie will talk of friendship. She will, at some point, move those glasses of pink lemonade to one side, lean forward across the table toward Renata Green and say, *Love? Magic? The proper, lasting kind? Then let me tell you all about the girl from Pepper Street.*

19

The Gift of Pinky Underwood

Most of Florrie's closest friendships in this life have been with men. Through Bobs and her father, she learned how to place bets at the bookmaker's, how to change a tire and a host of other skills that were, in those days, deemed solely of male interest or capability. It followed, therefore, that the male sex never really fazed her. Indeed, Florrie often startled men with her view on England's batting order or the Attlee government. Such views led to conversations; conversations led to friendships—and so she's been blessed with the company of some marvelous men in her life. She never lost touch with Emmanuel from the Sorbonne, exchanging letters in French for fifty years or more; after he lost his wife, Jeremy Topham continued to meet Florrie for afternoon tea, to exchange Christmas cards until six years ago when his heart slowed to a gentle stop in his sleep. The Topham boys (still boys to her, despite all being in their sixties now) have always seemed to enjoy Florrie's company, rather than endure it. And there was Victor, of course—darling, wonderful Victor with whom Florrie has had her greatest adventures: he'd share secrets with her, at four in the morning, that he could only share with someone to whom he'd entrust his life.

But Florrie's best friend was always Pinky Underwood.

They met on their first day at Miss Catchpole's school in Upper Dorbury when they were seven years old. Florrie remembers the day even now: the chalk dust, the splintery desks, a multicoloured alphabet pinned to the wall and the fact that she, Florrie, seemed both shorter and plumper than everybody else. Miss Catchpole had been hard to warm to. She had a narrow, pointed nose as if somebody had pinched it; she'd express her disapproval by clearing her throat.

It was this sound—the clearing of Miss Catchpole's throat—which announced Pinky's arrival into Florrie's world. It was the final September before the war. She—the new girl—turned up ten minutes late. On hearing the door creak open, Miss Catchpole had looked up, folded her arms, cleared her throat for far longer than required and said, "Ah. The latecomer. Children, take a good look at her: look at the girl who thinks that punctuality doesn't matter—nor appearance, seemingly. Well, don't just *stand* there . . ."

The stranger was a skinny, mute, moon-eyed creature who made no sound as she crossed the room and sat down at the empty desk beside Florrie. She slipped in without touching anything. She hunched, staring at the floor. And when Miss Catchpole announced, "Children! Bring out your pencils, please!," Florrie saw how the new girl's eyes widened in horror as she peered at all the pencils being lifted out of pockets or bags. This girl had no pencil of her own. (She'd had nothing, in fact—not even a packed lunch.) And a deep, crimson blush appeared, like nettle rash, on her neck.

Miss Catchpole had delighted at this. "Is the girl who was late *also* the girl who forgets to bring what she's *asked* to bring?"

The late girl's blush deepened further. It rose over her jawline and up to her ears.

"Answer me, child. Do you have a pencil? *Do* you?"

"Yes, she does!" Florrie emerged, breathless, from under her desk, proffering a pencil with a little rubber tip. For Florrie (having been warned by her brother about the pedantry and sadness of Miss Cecily Catchpole) had brought two pencils of her own, just in case; and here she was, setting one of them down on the desk of the girl who resembled a damson in colour by now. "She must have dropped it, Miss Catchpole." To the new girl, she whispered, "There you are."

So it began. That pencil announced the start of a friendship that would last for sixty-seven years. At breaktime, they played hopscotch in the yard; at lunchtime, they shared a slice of pork pie; at three-thirty, they wandered out of the school gates together discussing which type of bun was best: currant or iced? (Currant, they agreed.) It all felt so easy.

Her proper name was Margaret Underwood. But there were three other Margarets in Miss Catchpole's class that year—and they'd not seemed amenable to sharing their name with the scrawny girl from Pepper Street whose clothes were far too big. What, then, to call her? That blush was not forgotten. Indeed, the blush would come back with any wrong answer—on her cheeks, her forehead, her ears, her neck.

The nickname was introduced by Miss Catchpole herself—and not kindly. "But it's better," the girl reasoned, "than what my father calls me. And I like pink—don't you? Some pink things are ever so nice. Jelly. Ballet shoes."

As far as Florrie knows, no one ever called her Margaret again.

She lived five streets away, near the railway station. This was near enough for Pinky and Florrie to meet after school or on weekends—to hunt for conkers or find newts in the pond, to pick apples from the tree that drooped over the towpath, to spy on Clemency Winthrop with envious sighs. It was near enough, too, for Pinky to appear at Vicarage Lane without warning. She'd press her nose against glass, peep through the letterbox or simply stand on the lawn, expressionless, with sleeves pulled down over her hands. "The Underwood girl," Herbert would observe, unsure, "is standing by the woodshed again." Pinky was, perhaps, a human form of Gulliver: she'd slip through the door, eat Butterfield food, drink Butterfield milk, warm herself by the Butterfield fire and blink lovingly at them—and no one ever minded. After all, there was a sense that—also like Gulliver—she had a dark, private history that could only be guessed at. They all saw the clues: how Pinky would jump at a slammed door, how she'd gather bacon fat from the bird table and gnaw it on the way home. "That girl," Prudence said, under her breath, "knows sad things, I think."

What a strange, fractured start to life. On one hand, Pinky had the Butterfield house—with its laughter and music and charred Sunday lunches, its Bakelite tea trays and cosy fireside; she had Florrie—half her height and twice as wide—with whom she could cartwheel or read *Schoolgirl* magazine or emulate Clemency's physique with two pairs of balled-up socks down their tops. On the other hand, she had Pepper Street.

Years later, after the war, Pinky confided that she owed her life to the Butterfields. "I mean it, Florrie." And a few years later still, it would be Florrie who'd murmur these same words back to Pinky Underwood (or Pinky Topham, as she was by then); it was Florrie who'd be indebted, speaking of life and death. *What would I have done without you? Where would I have gone?*

It's what friends do. Florrie knows that now. The most loving of friends will do anything. They will guard one's secret with knives and sticks and stones. They will lie. They will steal. They will visit that friend in a cold, grey building with barred windows and clutch their scarred, bleeding hands and say, *It will be all right, I will get you out of here.* They won't mind when that friend sinks down on the floor of Paddington Station at rush hour saying, *Oh God, oh God*, as Florrie had done. Pinky had settled down beside her, taken Florrie's hand. They'd sat there, on Paddington concourse, with commuters moving around them like water, whilst Pinky said, over and over, "Don't worry, Butters. We'll be all right. I'm here."

On Florrie's return from Africa, she went straight to Vicarage Lane. She hadn't confirmed her return: she took a train to Oxford, a bus to

Upper Dorbury, found the spare key to the front door under the geraniums and entered a house that seemed smaller somehow. Prudence emerged from the kitchen, astounded. "It *is* you! Oh, my! Oh!"

For five days, Florrie stayed there—sleeping in her childhood bed with an emerald in her hand. She watched the autumn leaves unpin themselves by the railway embankment, remembered the baobab trees. "How *was* it, Flo?" So she told stories, to her mother and aunt— of drums and mosquitos, of the night that elephants came into the camp and munched on marula fruit. She unfolded a map: "Here, I surprised a rhino. Here, the wet season came." But she couldn't speak of Jack Luckett—at least, not to them.

Pinky—who had been married for over a year by then, and was living in a townhouse in Kew Green—was adamant. "Come and see me. Come tomorrow." So Florrie caught the train down. She and Pinky walked arm in arm through Kew Gardens or sat in tearooms with condensation on the windows, and Florrie would pour all of it out to her—his drying shirts, his absent wife, his thumbed field guide to African flora, which he'd read, like a novel, by lamplight in his tent. "Sounds like he was in love with you."

"With me? Of course not."

"Why not? Why couldn't he be? And you," asked Pinky, buttering her teacake, "were in love with him?"

Not really. Maybe. Yes, she had been. Maybe she still was.

"So why did you come back? Why didn't you stay a while longer and . . ." But Pinky knew. She realized perfectly—and let the sentence roll, unfinished, into the dust. "How's Upper Dorbury, now?"

Florrie knew the real meaning of this question. And she examined the back of a teaspoon as she worked out what to replace a proper, truthful answer with; for she didn't feel able to say, in this café, that six years had passed since Teddy Silversmith and Hackney and the gouging of that poor nurse's eyes, those leather restraints on a metal bed—six whole years—yet the village of Upper Dorbury couldn't go back to how it was before, just as Florrie could never be the former Florrie. "He asked about my hands—Jack did. And I couldn't tell him."

"Why not?"

"Because I can't tell anyone." It would break her—the grief and the shame.

Pinky considered this. She finished the rest of her teacake before rolling up the sleeve of her gingham blouse as far as the elbow. She held her arm out. "See that?" There was discoloration there. On the soft skin on the underside of her friend's forearm, Florrie saw a reddish mark of old, damaged skin that she'd never noticed before. "I used to tell people it was my fault. That I'd knocked a saucepan over, that I'd been running through the house and caught its handle. Soup—or that's what I'd say. And I told that story so often that I came to believe it myself. When it hurt me—because it still did, to press it—I'd think, *Oh, me and that soup!*"

"But it wasn't soup?"

"It was a poker—the end bit. Father held it in the fire first. And I never thought I'd tell anyone that—except then I met Jeremy. And when he asked me, I told him the truth, that it wasn't soup at all. And I told him because I wanted him to know *me*—the real me—even if it made him like me less for it. But he married me two months later so he can't have liked me less. Anyway, the funny part? The mark stopped hurting after that. See?" She prodded herself to demonstrate. "Listen, can't you talk to someone—anyone—about the London thing?"

Could she? Find a stranger, say, or a doctor of some kind and tell them what happened the first day of April, six years ago? And if she did, what difference would it make? It would change nothing. It would not undo what she had done.

"I'm so sorry," she said, "about the poker."

Pinky smiled. "You made it hurt less, too, you know." And with that, she reached for Florrie's hand. Her fringe was still long at this point; by Christmas, she would have started to wear it pinned to one side, revealing her face as the removal of ivy will reveal the lovely brickwork that one had, perhaps, always sensed might be hiding beneath but now there was proof of it. "Come and live with us—with Jeremy and me. No arguing. He'd love it. He believes you're a good influence on me. Clearly he's wrong, but let's let him think it."

"I can't . . ."

"You can, Butters."

She'd be in the way. She'd be a burden.

"Don't be so bloody stubborn. And didn't I basically live for free at Vicarage Lane? Come back down to London. Stay with your best friend."

It was settled, then. Florrie came to live at the Topham residence—in the spare room that was wallpapered with pansies of blue, purple and gold. Here, she slept and cried. From here, too, she'd walk for miles—through Kew Gardens or Mortlake Cemetery, down to Richmond Park—trying to forget Jack and trying, too, to find a few tentative words about *It* and Teddy Silversmith that she might be able to whisper without falling down. (*Love. Blood loss. My broken knuckles.*) But all these words were too much for her—too much, and not enough.

Those were quiet days. There was nothing monumental, nothing new to challenge her. She drifted, sat on benches—and all the local shopkeepers came to know her. The florist would offer chrysanthemum stems; the baker would call out—*Florenzia!*—and wave with a huge, fleshy paw. She loved, too, the cheese shop called Botley and Peeves—a fragrant cave of a place in which they sliced through cheese with two-handled knives or wires, and where she'd declare their little cubed samples quite delicious. In the antiques shop on Kew Green, the elderly Mr. Aksoy would offer Florrie sweetened mint tea in the tiniest cups without handles. She felt she was drinking from a thimble. He, too, was almost as small.

In the autumn, Florrie bought a pendant from there—garnets in a cluster on a gold chain. "It's a thank-you."

Pinky wrinkled her nose, bemused. "What for?"

"You know."

"Don't be silly."

"You got me out, Pinks. You and your great-aunt."

"You got *me* out, too. You saved my life. Listen, we love each other, don't we? Presents and thank-yous aren't needed. Having said that, I'm definitely accepting this. Help me put it on?"

Pinky wore that pendant all the time—even to do the housework, even when she slept. It was, she announced, the second-best present that Florrie had ever given her, a rubber-topped pencil having been the best.

Tonight, in her old apple store—and in a freshly laundered night-dress with the shipping forecast burbling on her bedside radio—it's this pendant that Florrie's looking at. It's a battered thing, now. It was lost and found a dozen times, or more; Pinky's boys, in their infancy, would grapple at its chain or jam it into their drooling mouths. Some-one even tried to barter for it, once, in Cairo's central market, which had scandalized Pinky; she'd slapped her palm across the pendant as if guarding it with her life. *Sell* it? This?

Florrie peers at it more closely. She thinks, *Oh, my darling friend.*

They knew and shared everything, every part of their lives: mar-riages, births and funerals, sherbet lemons and bottles of wine. They shared dancing to Elvis in Pinky's kitchen, swimming in a midnight loch, the cancer diagnosis that brought Florrie down from Scotland to that same spare room with its pansy wallpaper to be near the best friend she'd had in all the world. All the wild laughter. All those gifted days.

In the garden at Kew Green, on a particular day in April and in their late twenties, Pinky had turned beneath the apple tree. "What happened. Hackney. I feel it's left a hole in you—a big, sad, echoing thing. Butters, I want you to be happier than this."

She'd been wearing this pendant, then. And they'd hugged beneath that tree, snuffling into each other's shoulders until they broke away to dry their eyes and blow their noses. "I know," Florrie answered. It *had* left a hole. It had set a feeling inside that hole, too—sharp-toothed and sly, like a pike. But what could be done, beyond what she was doing? Which was carrying on, breathing in and out? And repeating the old family sayings, like *Something good is coming to you? Joy is out there, remember?* Somewhere, somewhere.

The postcard from Zermatt. The linen napkin from the Sunshine Hotel. But Florrie will also take this garnet pendant to her meeting with Renata, lay it down.

Be in love, certainly. Have romantic feelings. Have your *billets-doux* and magenta envelopes. But at this exact moment, it isn't that sort of love that Florrie wishes for Renata: Above all, she thinks, have a best friend. Have someone who'll keep your secret for fifty years or more and love you no less for knowing it; who'll stand outside a building in Hackney in the rain for hours, if need be, just to give a single wave. Have someone who'll say, *We're in this together.* Have a Pinky of your own.

20

In Which They Visit the Blue Recycling Bin

Stanhope blinks twice, lowers his crossword. "The bin?"

The following morning, after breakfast, Florrie finds him sitting on the veranda with his walking stick propped against his knee. It's lovely to see him. He has today's crossword on his lap. His shirt and braces are a medley of various greens—moss, emerald, lime. As she'd approached him, she'd noted that his pose was contemplative: three fingertips resting on his lips with the fourth one tapping, lightly, against his trimmed moustache.

Now she has his full attention.

"You'd like me to help you to retrieve something from the recycling bin?"

"Yes, please. The blue one by the kitchen door. And it needs to be done this morning before the binmen come."

Stanhope considers this. "That's a sizeable bin. I'm not sure I've seen a bigger one. I mean, heaven knows what they actually put in it."

"That's why I need your help, Stanhope. I'd do it myself, but . . ." She gestures, once more, at her missing leg, her bosom, her general width and height. "You wouldn't mind?"

"Mind? Not at all. But what's happened since Sunday, Florrie? What are we looking for?"

A wren provides a long, bright warble of notes from the ivy as Florrie gives her account of yesterday. It is not a short account: she had encountered the heady Chanel No. 5 of Marcella Mistry, and a Nepalese postcard with a date from the previous week; she'd experienced the clacking of the Ellwoods, as busy and monotonous as knitting needles, the disdain of Clive as he set down the teapot; how Georgette has seemingly planted herself into the role of manager with all the pride and permanence of a summit flag. She tells him about Babbington's front door being locked at eight o'clock, about the curious acoustics of wood paneling; she even remarks on the abandoned notion of a visitors' lounge, which has nothing, really, to do with the matter in hand—but Florrie tells him anyway because she finds herself wanting to; these brown eyes and patient, saintly expression rather encourage one to divulge. She even considers speaking of Pinky, for a moment—because Pinky had been on her mind last night. But Florrie stops herself, breathless. She wonders if she's said too much.

"Goodness me. That's a lot."

"It *is* a lot. But this card, Stanhope. We need to know who sent it. Look for a postmark, perhaps."

"Magenta, you said? A magenta envelope?"

"I saw it—I *know* I did. In the wastepaper bin. But it isn't there, now."

"Because the bin has since been emptied? Into the recycling?"

"Exactly."

He looks up to the top of the beech hedge; he nods slowly, in assessment, as a chef may when tasting a sauce. And Stanhope is about to say more when he pauses, head cocked—for whistling comes. Both Florrie and Stanhope turn in their seats and peer between the beech hedges as Franklin, the groundsman, comes into view. He is pushing a wheelbarrow. He walks with the slow, bouncy tread that young men seem to now; equally, his trousers—despite being belted—seem oddly low-slung, as is the fashion, and there have been grumblings about this from other residents. ("One sees," said Sybilla Farr, "his *undergarments*"—said as if the word itself had an unsavoury taste.) But

Florrie is only intrigued by it all: How do those trousers stay up? How might Franklin run, if he needed to? He'd look like a man in a sack race. And isn't it draughty like that?

He doesn't seem to notice them. Instead, he lollops on, out of view.

Stanhope and Florrie continue to gaze in that direction. "A good word," he says, "isn't it? *Magenta.* Named after a battle, did you know that?"

Florrie didn't know that.

"Somewhere in Italy, I believe. So"—he turns back to face her—"she's in love with someone who she only writes to? Who never comes here? Who she never actually *sees*?"

"It could happen. There's all that online business now."

"Ah. So there is. Virtual—isn't that the word for it? But the would-be murderer would need to do it *in person*, not virtually at all. He'd need to know the door code."

Florrie wonders if she should explain her inkling to him: that these two men may, in fact, be just one. But she won't do so now—for who knows exactly what time on a Tuesday the binmen come? They can't sit and ponder.

"You know, the penmanship was ever so fancy—with an *F* like a treble clef."

"A treble clef? That *is* fancy." And they consider each other with light, appreciative expressions before Stanhope takes hold of his walking stick and prepares to hoist himself into the air. "Right! Shall we? Florrie, lead the way."

"Latin," he tells her, as they go. "To badly behaved teenaged boys. The same school for forty-three years—on the south coast, near the sea. Not the same classroom, though; after twenty years I moved to an upstairs room and that was much better. It was nearer the staff room, for one thing."

"Ah. *Dum spiro spero.*"

"Quite. It's a marvelous language—the father of so many, of course. Although those teenaged boys never seemed to think so."

This feels an entirely fitting role for him. Stanhope stoops now, but Florrie can imagine the upright teacher he must have been, standing behind a mahogany desk with chalk in his hand and saying, rather wearily, Quiet at the back. To have taught—and to have, therefore, an interest in learning—is in keeping with his knowledge of Shakespearean tragedies and how he'd suddenly quoted Wordsworth as the daffodils appeared. And there is, too (how can she put it?), a slight air of disarray to Stanhope. Effort is made, certainly—the trimmed moustache, the citrusy smell, the carefully considered braces and shirt, and all these things are lovely. But if Florrie looks more closely, she sees the creases; she notes that the gold clips on the braces—left and right— aren't evenly positioned, and there's a button working itself loose on his cuff so that Florrie can see him forgetting the names of pupils or patting his top pocket for a mislaid pen; he has the air of a man who can pass a whole day with his nose in a Latin text, who can navigate the British Library perfectly but is less sure of the public transport to get there. None of this, of course, is thought unkindly. After all, this slight disarray is something of a Sitwell feature—for if there was any sort of liquid in an unsealed container, Prudence would knock it over; if she popped on a clean apron, there'd be a tomato squirt within the hour. This combination of trying one's best against a natural dispensation to fall into a pothole is familiar to Florrie. Indeed, she probably has it herself. ("You'd tripped over your own *feet*, Miss Butterfield?" The Ellwoods, she vows, must never know this.)

"Why Latin, in particular?"

They pass beside the ivied wall of the west wing, past Nancy Tapp's room and a Grecian urn. "Because I enjoyed it as a child. I understood its worth. My father was an archaeologist, you see—well, an amateur one. But he was a true amateur—from *amare*, to love—so most of my school holidays were spent scrambling over Roman ruins with him, trying to read inscriptions before the heavens opened. We went to Northumberland, mostly, so the heavens opened a lot." Stanhope sighs fondly. "He would have loved to have been a proper archaeologist—pryng open sarcophagi or raising Viking longboats . . ."

"What did he do instead?"

"He sold life insurance. But he was at his most alive in his anorak, fumbling over lichen—much to my mother's frustration, I'm sure. She preferred an indoors life. And she never came with us on those trips. Too far, she said—which it was back then, I suppose: Kent to Northumberland, before a motorway? I spent half my childhood sleeping in the back of a Hillman Minx. What of your parents, may I ask? Were they well matched?"

"Mine?" Where might she start with how much she loved them? Or how different they were? One had dreams of being a ballerina, apologized to her own elbow if she knocked it on something; the other kept an orderly to-do list in his pocket, used the speaking clock. "They worked very well together. My mother lost a bread roll once, and my father found it in the woodshed."

"Why was it in the woodshed?"

"Heaven only knows."

"They sound like a fine pair. Lovely."

"They were," she replies—feeling proud of them.

They turn the corner of the kitchen—and stop. The recycling bin stands before them. It's a bold, electric blue with a black lid. It has a sticker on it, detailing what can and cannot be deposited in it: newspapers, cartons and plastic bottles are fine; damp cardboard and bubble wrap are not.

"Here it is," Stanhope says.

Florrie glances around, wide-eyed. She's suddenly profoundly embarrassed, as if all the detritus from this bin, and others—bin bags, potato peelings, sodden copies of the *Oxford Mail* lying on the ground—is her fault somehow. She feels she should apologize for not having tidied first. Flies hum and stop. On the ground, a wasp creeps into an aluminum can.

"Magenta, yes? An envelope?"

"Yes. Square. With black handwriting on it. Stanhope, I can't possibly ask you to do this."

"Forty-three years of teenaged boys, remember. Nothing can faze me."

Stanhope appears to steel himself. He sets his walking stick against the brick wall, flexes his fingers, seizes the lid—and his expression appears to change with every inch that the lid lifts up, from trepidation to relief to considerable interest. "Drinks cans," he announces. "Blue paper towel. A cardboard box that held"—he tilts his head—"a dozen bottles of toilet cleaner." Then he takes his walking stick, holds it by the shaft, not the handle, and proceeds to stab at the contents of the wheelie bin as if unblocking a drain. As he does this, Stanhope lists his finds: tuna cans, newspapers, boxes that held one thousand sterile wipes, junk mail, an ice cream tub. ("Vanilla," he adds over his shoulder.) And this all feels rather pointless until he performs a final jab and suddenly freezes. "Hang on."

"What is it?"

Stanhope peers in. "It's definitely pink, or pinkish."

"A magenta-ish pink?"

"I'd say so."

"And an envelope?"

"I can't quite tell." He passes his stick to her. "Hold this for a moment?"

With that, Stanhope inches himself onto the balls of his feet, places one hand on the plastic rim and reaches, precariously, into the dark depths of Babbington Hall's recycling bin. For a moment, he's half lost to it. He folds at the waist so that his head, shoulders and pale-green shirt disappear into the bin itself; his lower half stays with Florrie so that she is momentarily flustered and thinks to reach for his ankles in case he overbalances and disappears entirely—and what then?

"Aha!"

But Stanhope does not tip over. Instead, he retrieves himself from the bin. He's acquired a damp blotch on his sleeve and his hair has raised itself a little from his scalp in the effort—but it's his right hand that Florrie looks at. For in it—and held out, like a sacrifice—there is a square object, deep pink in colour. It is stained, in places, and wet, but there's no mistaking it or its letter *F*.

"Well *done*, Stanhope!" She bursts into sudden, short applause.

They smile at each other—triumphant, a little breathless, as archaeologists might smile on discovering a Saxon hoard. How good, she thinks, his smile is; how well it suits him, too. But Stanhope's smile doesn't last; it wilts at the edges and a frown appears as he thumbs the edge of the envelope.

"There's something in it, Florrie."

"In it?"

"A card."

"*The* card? It's still in there?"

There should not, she supposes, be any pleasure taken in solving a crime. They are trying to find a would-be murderer; Renata, dear thing, stands (or lies) on the very margins of life. It isn't right to feel happy or such a thrill that one balls one's hands into fists and strikes the armrests of one's wheelchair, just once, in excitement. They should be acting in solemnity. Yet here they both are, shiny-eyed; her pulse, she notes, is a little faster.

"How about a pot of tea?" Stanhope offers. "I did a little shopping in Oxford yesterday—and can offer you leaf, not bag."

21

The Little Brown Bird

They head to the old pig sties as quickly as they can. Yet, as is often the way when one's in a hurry, they seem to encounter half of Babbington as they go. The Ellwoods wave with a synchronized *Yoo-hoo*; Velma Rudge turns a corner so quickly that she almost collides with Stanhope and simpers—before regarding Florrie with a cool raised brow. Also, there is Dr. Mallory: he crosses the courtyard to meet them, saying, "Hold on a moment, you two!"

On reaching them, the doctor sets down his leather bag. "There you are. Florrie, you're a hard one to get hold of. Never in your quarters!"

"Aren't I? Well, I like to be out and about."

"Then you're feeling well, I take it? No headaches or flashbacks? And your wrist?"

She reassures him—a little curtly, perhaps—that she's perfectly fine.

In the end, it's Stanhope who has the longer conversation with the doctor—regarding his light sleeping, a tendency to indigestion, and various minor complaints that make Dr. Mallory smile to himself, as if he finds Stanhope amusing. "All part of getting older, I'm afraid." He claps a hand on Stanhope's shoulder. "It's to be expected at your age, Stanhope. I suggest just getting on with it!"

They watch him leave, swinging his bag.

"I think I prefer Dr. Laghari."

Good at heart. So Nancy Tapp had called Dr. Mallory. But Dr. Laghari has never once been condescending; she has never left a patient feeling decidedly worse about their age or body than they did before she came—and can the same be said for Dr. Mallory? "Yes," murmurs Florrie, "so do I."

And lastly, there's no escape from Aubrey Horner, who sits outside his quarters (also part of the old pig sties), remarking on the swifts that swing down between the outbuildings as effortlessly as conkers on string. "Splendid," he booms, gesturing. "To think they've come from Africa! When I was out there, in fifty-four . . ." Yes, Florrie nods; yes, quite marvelous—whilst all the time thinking of the magenta square that she's wedged between her thighs.

Once inside, Stanhope closes the door and rests himself against it. "Heavens. Do you think we need a barricade?" Then his eyes widen at his surroundings. "I do hope you don't mind a certain . . . disarray."

Florrie doesn't mind disarray at all. Life is, in her opinion, too short for dusting a skirting board or minding the odd cobweb in a corner. In fact, as she looks around, it is her own quarters that she thinks of. For just as hers have a slightly ramshackle quality, so there are books everywhere here—filling shelves in both a vertical and horizontal fashion, on tables and chairs, stacked on the floor. There is, too, a gentle oddness to so many of his possessions: intricate silver trinkets, an antique globe with a lightbulb in it, a crooked taxidermied wading bird. She notes a lump of terracotta under a glass dome (a Roman floor tile, he explains, with a pawprint on it). Also, above the doorway into his kitchenette, Florrie finds a map, several metres long, of all the forts and points of interest on Hadrian's Wall—and she dwells on this for a time, recognizing names from books. There is only one armchair—tartan, well used and somewhat misshapen. (His version, she thinks, of her mallard chair.)

Stanhope opens and closes his hands nervously, as a child might. "I suppose some would say it *is* a pig sty, of sorts. But I just find I run out of space for things. I seem to . . . accumulate."

"It's lovely," Florrie tells him, meaning it.

Within a few minutes, Florrie and Stanhope are sitting at his kitchen table with a pot of leaf tea, two mugs, two shortbread fingers and the magenta envelope lying between them with all the portentousness of a casket. It's looking far grubbier than it had four days before. Its top-left corner is heavily discoloured from the contents of the recycling bin and the black-inked handwriting has, in places, run. But she can still read every word written on it.

> *For Renata Green*
> *Manager*
> *Babbington Residential Home*
> *Temple Beeches*

"Remind me," Stanhope says. "She received this on midsummer's morning? The day she fell?"

"Before nine o'clock. That's when the Ellwoods saw her with it."

"And she'd blushed?"

"To the colour of a peony, according to them."

They look at the envelope, look at each other. Look at the envelope again.

"You do it, Florrie."

From the depths of the envelope, Florrie retrieves the card. It, too, is square. It has a glossy feel to it, and a firmness that suggests it's a card of good quality. On the back, it is perfectly blank—no writing at all, either printed or handwritten. But the Ellwoods, she sees, were right: here, on the front, is a bird.

"What is it, Florrie?"

The bird is depicted in an illustration—in coloured pencil, with a rather faded, Victorian aesthetic, as if taken from a vintage guide to ornithology. She has seen such illustrations before. Yet this bird, to Florrie, is new. She is familiar with most birds of garden and hedge; after a lifetime's enjoyment of pottering in gardens or woodland, she has become able to identify most British birds by sight or sound alone— from Oxford's iridescent starlings to the eagle that wheeled high up above her Scottish home. But this illustrated bird with its dappled plumage is not one that Florrie's ever seen—not in books, not with her own eyes. "It *is* a bird, Stanhope—but I can't say that I know what kind."

She shows it to Stanhope.

"Golly. What *is* that?"

The first adjective that comes to mind, as she considers it, is *adorable*—followed by *sweet* and *charming* and *button-eyed*. For this bird is not unlike a mouse. Its feathers seem fur-soft; it appears to be lying down, hunkering, as if feeling shy today; its expression (if a bird can have an expression; Florrie suspects she will dwell on this later) seems a little bashful, unsure and apologetic, which is how Florrie has always thought most mice to be. And the bird's colouring, too, is beautiful—consisting of various browns, from chestnut to blackish to gold to *café au lait*. She thinks, *Hello there.*

"Ground-nesting, I should think," Stanhope offers. "Mottled plumage."

"You know birds?"

"Me? Not in the slightest. But it looks a little like tree bark, don't you think? Or leaf mold. And that pose . . . as flat as a pancake, really. Which means it would look flush against the ground."

She pushes the card toward Stanhope. "Your turn. You open it."

"It feels ever so intrusive."

"I know. But we've come this far, Stanhope, and it might matter terribly. And we're only trying to help her."

"You know her best. It's better that it's you."

So Florrie opens the card. Inside, it is equally stained; whatever juices might have dripped onto the envelope in the recycling bin have seeped into its contents and turned its whiteness to a mottled brown. But its words are still quite legible:

I NEVER STOPPED HOPING I'D FIND YOU.

There it is, she thinks. The song of this little, sweet-eyed, watchful brown bird is one of hope and love. And these words do not come from Jay Mistry—but from someone else who is in love with Renata and for whom that love (at last!) is returned. *Keep going*, she thinks. *Wake up soon.*

"May I?" Stanhope takes the card, reads the words himself. "Gosh. The Ellwoods were right, then—it *is* a love note. I must say that I don't trust them, as a rule. They exaggerate, for one thing. Also, they are often wrong: they think my ex-wife was Dutch for some reason, and I don't think she'd even been to Amsterdam for the weekend—not in her whole life. But they're right about this note, it seems. It's ever so romantic. And it makes sense, doesn't it?"

It does. For Renata is in her forties now. This language—of hope, of having not lost it, of having kept a candle burning in the long, long quest for love—feels wholly fitting for someone of middle age. And this card suggests, too, that somewhere a man—also middle-aged—has found love, at long last, in the slender, white-blonde manager of a residential home. *Dum spiro spero.*

"There's so much, isn't there, in those seven words?"

There is. There is longing. There's passion and relief. The smaller, lowercase *f* in *find* has the same treble-clef qualities as the *F* in *For*. And beneath these words, Florrie also detects the evident reason for Renata's hankering for newness. *I thought it would be enough*, she'd said, holding the chutney jar of blooms. *But lately . . . Oh, lately, it's not been enough at all.* Isn't that what love does? It alters how one sees the world. It makes one look at one's reflection or one's village or the view from one's childhood bedroom window with quiet amazement—as if all these things have changed somehow, or never been looked at before. *I was illuminated*, she thinks, *by Teddy Silversmith. I wasn't oafish with him in his attic room on Holywell Street.*

For a short time, they sit in silence. She stares at the envelope without seeing it—lost, or becoming so, in her reverie. But Stanhope, it seems, sees the envelope perfectly clearly.

"Look. No stamp. See? It was hand-delivered. Pushed under her door first thing that morning." He smiles as if this is only a trifling matter. "Must live locally."

At that, they set the conversation down. Their brains feel full, stretched with thoughts and worries; they decide that, for now, enough's enough. Outside, the day rolls on. Outside, too, are all manner of obstacles, some of them in human form—carers, sisters-in-law, uneven floorboards, gathering heat and a patronizing doctor—that neither can quite find the energy to face. "Stay for a while," he says, "if you like."

She would like to, yes. And with a cheerful nod, Stanhope starts to prepare a form of lunch: he opens a pre-packed sandwich, which they share at the kitchen table, locates a box of miniature lemon sponges. He boils the kettle for a second time.

He doesn't seem embarrassed by his slight untidiness anymore. When they move into the sitting room, he doesn't brush the crumbs from the armchair; he doesn't seem to notice the lone sock on the floor. He seems, in short, more comfortable—and whilst he makes his way to his armchair, Florrie considers these trinkets of his life. For here, on these shelves, is *him*. Here—amongst the dusty tomes and terracotta tiles, the well-tended succulents in coloured pots—is the character and life of this rather lovely man. She asks him about this book or that. She remarks on a sepia photograph of a boyish Stanhope with his father, trowels in hand. And they—Stanhope and Florrie—talk for a long time that afternoon; they talk with the same familiarity and ease with which they'd discussed Shakespeare in the dusky orchard, and whether his tragedies—not his comedies or histories—were, in fact, the *forte* of his *oeuvre*. They discuss a whole night-sky of matters: from milecastles and hypocausts to her lifelong wish to play the trumpet; from Nietzsche to ice cream flavours; from the undeniable horrors of global warming and what is coming ("I think of my grandchildren and I can hardly bear it, Florrie") to Sergeant Butterfield's unshakeable belief that people are, essentially, kind and good. And when the teapot is emptied for the second time, Stanhope discovers an elderly bottle of amontillado sherry, which he pours into mismatched glasses—and on they go: with the names and descriptions of childhood pets, of dreams they've had, of how Stanhope broke his arm as a boy by jumping from a treehouse, of how much they both love the Olympic Games and which sport they would do, if they had their time again. (Tennis for Stanhope—with that double-handed backhand; pole vault for Florrie, or gymnastics, perhaps.) He offers his thoughts on the current state of Westminster, which Florrie agrees with wholeheartedly—*Yes!*—and this requires a further drop of amontillado so Stanhope goes to the kitchen and brings the bottle back with him.

"A chess set?" she remarks as he tops her glass up. For it sits in the corner, with pieces as intricately carved as scrimshaw, waiting for their moment.

"Yes. It was my father's. Do you play, Florrie?"

"Aunt Pip taught me. She taught me all sorts—how to rack up a billiard table or whistle so loudly that it stops traffic. I do love chess very much. But I've not played a game in some time now."

"Well, there's a board here. If you ever . . . you know."

This is how she spends her Tuesday afternoon. And there's a moment in which Florrie chastises herself for it (*Should she be solving an attempted murder? Searching for clues with a magnifying glass?*), but also, she is aware of how rare such an afternoon *is* these days. Sherry, and chattering? With a new, dear friend? And as the hours move on, as the sherry bottle empties, Florrie finds that their conversation becomes more reflective. Stanhope tells her, apropos of nothing, how much he misses the sea. Also, he isn't quite sure he really wished to be a teacher—"It just rather . . . happened." He admits to having been lonely as a child, and that he can't believe—can't understand it, even—how he's suddenly become an old man when surely he wasn't five minutes ago. "My word," he says, with a distant expression. "Life *is* a funny business."

And then it's Florrie's turn to be wistful—so that she ruminates on Gulliver and secretarial courses, on her time at Miss Catchpole's school with its chalk dust and discipline, the limewash on the walls. ("Florrie *what*?" Stanhope asks, incredulous. She repeats it sheepishly: "Florrie Butterball.") And, feeling unfettered by the amontillado, she brings Bobs forward and presents him to Stanhope: the thatch of hair, the traveling dreams, how he'd carry his sister home under one arm like a camping mat or a rugby ball. How he'd ask every Christmas for a copy of *Wisdens Cricketer's Almanack*.

"A brother?" He smiles a little sadly. "I always rather fancied one of those—older or younger, it wouldn't have mattered. *Butterball* . . . Golly. My schooldays weren't always fun, either, I must say. I've always been tall, you see. *Flagpole*, they'd called me. Flagpole Jones. I decided it was better to laugh with them—because what else can one do? Do you know, in the school nativity play, they dressed me in black, put a star on my head and made me stand in the corner? Everyone had to look up at me and say, 'Lo!'"

Oh, this story! Florrie spills over with—what? Fondness. Sympathy. (She imagines Stanhope, exactly as he was.) "The star, though—that's an important part. No one could have found the stable without you."

"True—yes. Thank you."

She looks down at her sherry. Stanhope must have seen her scars—
or he's seeing them, now. And in the companionable silence between
them—in which he assesses the near-empty bottle, holds it up to the
light—Florrie thinks, *Don't ask me, don't ask me.* For in this softened
state, she does not trust herself not to pour *It* and *the Hackney thing*
out of herself. "Stanhope?"

"Hmm?"

"How I lost my leg. What have you heard?"

"Heard? I've not heard a thing—although the Ellwoods have
pressed me on the matter. Asked me if I know how it happened—
which I don't, of course, and there's no need to tell me."

"Mulled wine," she offers. "The church choir was singing 'Silent
Night' outside my door and I dropped my pan of mulled wine and it
gave me a nasty burn and my circulation is so bad these days . . ." She
shrugs. "It's not my best story."

"I won't tell a soul. I'm so sorry to hear it."

"Ah. Well. Look at poor Nancy. Arthur."

She is so fond of his face. The old masters, she feels, painted
faces like these—in their depictions of saints or the Magi; she has
seen a face like his in the National Gallery, the Louvre. His eyes are
tea-brown with wrinkles beside them. There is a scent, too—clean
and bright like a chopped-up lime—and she wonders if this is soap
or cologne, or some sort of wax that he might use on his moustache.

"You were married? You mentioned your wife who wasn't Dutch."

"Gretchen. Yes. Some German blood in her, actually—but for heav-
en's sake, don't tell the Ellwoods that. We met on the Bakerloo line. I
rode an extra seven stops, just to keep talking to her. We were happy,
for a time. At least, I thought we were—but afterward I wondered if
we ever really had been, whether we'd just convinced ourselves of it.
But we had Peter—our boy. He's sixty now, and a grandfather! I'm a
great-grandfather! How did that happen? He phones twice a week and
comes when he can. Or I might stay with him, of course. It's why I've

moved to Babbington—to be nearer to him, in Princes Risborough. But they live busy lives, don't they? All these young people. I don't expect them to find the time where there's so much else to do. And Peter needs to see his mother, as well, which is a lot of driving. She moved to Devon, you see, married a dentist." He smiles as if to say, *What can we do?*

Florrie hears all the sadness in this. Also, the love. But she hears, too, what is coming—which is that Stanhope, having taken a sip of sherry, is turning the conversation around like a tanker in a harbour and now asks, "What about you? Have you been married, Florrie? Any children? Grandchildren?"

She sits perfectly still. Perhaps she should have predicted this, prepared herself for it. But, in truth, it's rare that she's asked such questions these days. The assumption was made long ago—before Babbington, before her cottage with its view of the Malverns—that a short, jovial, bosomy woman in an array of pastel colours and a fondness for talking to inanimate objects could never have been married. And yet here Stanhope is, asking with an attentive expression. He hasn't assumed this at all.

What do I say? How much does she share with him? How much does she offer this kind, patient, bespectacled man in his lime-green braces and mint-green shirt, in an old pig sty on a June afternoon? *Gaston. Jack Luckett. Hassan. Dougal Henderson. Edward Silversmith.*

"Yes," she says. "I've been married. To Victor. We were married for nearly thirty years. Nobody knows that, Stanhope, because nobody asks, I suppose. And he died a few years back—in a hammock in St. Lucia, actually, which strikes me as a fine way of going—so he never had the chance to visit me here. But he was a wonderful man. We traveled the world together—he was a diplomat, you see—and we had the most marvelous time. We stayed friends after the divorce—right until he died." She misses his voice on the telephone: "Greetings, *la mia Firenze!*"

"A diplomat?"

She drains the last of her sherry. "He loved Cairo the best, I think. He said the pyramids were ours—his and mine."

A realization seems to be rising in Stanhope, like a tide. "The prayer flags in your room. The African mask. And you mentioned Delhi in passing—I remember that. Gosh. Well, this all makes sense now."

Florrie waits. She allows this discovery to find, in him, its high-tide line—and she wonders if, in fact, he *had* made the assumption that she'd never married but was just being thoughtful in asking her. Somewhere, in the distance, she can hear a strimmer; she can hear, too, the voice of Aubrey Horner and here, in Stanhope's sitting room, Florrie feels her own small sadness—as if, somehow, she's disappointed him.

"Renata," she announces. "What shall we do now?"

He seems grateful for this change of subject. "Yes, quite right. Renata. Good. Florrie, I'm not entirely sure."

Nor is she. Her brain feels heavy, like a wet sponge (for which she blames the sherry). Yet even so, she leans forward in her chair, sets the glass down and tells Stanhope about her inkling. "This"—she points at the little brown bird—"was sent by the would-be murderer, I'm sure of it. He knows the code—he must. He used the back door, climbed those stairs—and no, he wasn't seen or heard by the Ellwoods because who might have heard anything during that thunderstorm? And this was hand-delivered, Stanhope—before nine that morning— which tells me that he is *known* here, that he either works here or lives here because nobody batted an eyelid at him pushing a card under the manager's door." She adjusts her waistband, looks for his answer. "Sometimes one just *knows* things—don't you find?"

He doesn't protest or frown. "Yes. Yes, I do. Also—"

"Yes?"

"Well, there's something else. The bin."

"The bin?"

"Are we back with poor Jay Mistry? I mean, it's not *him*—obviously. What I mean is, are we back with unrequited love? Because I don't think this fellow—the writer of this note—is the person Renata was in love with."

"What?" She is crestfallen. "Why not?"

"Because look where we found this little brown bird. Renata had thrown it in the wastepaper bin."

Of course. He's right—dear Stanhope is right. One doesn't throw a note from one's beloved in the bin. But that doesn't change Florrie's conviction: This is *him*. *He* pushed her—he did. Never mind, then, who Renata is in love with. What matters far more is who Renata does *not* love. What matters is who she is loved *by*—a man who sends a message of yearning and a lovely, dappled bird, who is so enamoured and jealous and enraged by his unrequited feelings that he pushed Renata from a third-floor window. It is who and why—and how.

Florrie looks back at the bird. *Are you a clue, little thing?* She imagines it gives a blink in reply.

"Meet me tomorrow? I've got an idea."

"Right-o. Where?"

The usual place, she tells him—at half past nine.

22

Friday-Night Daiquiris at Alphonso's Place

As Florrie wheels herself home, it's Gretchen who comes to mind. Gretchen Jones, a woman she's never met. How had she been, as she'd traveled on the Bakerloo line? Tall, surely. In a long summer dress that accentuated her waist, perhaps; the sort of woman who could be encircled by a single arm, or carried over a threshold without risk of embarrassment, without the carrier sweating profusely or slipping a disc. And Florrie wonders, then, how Stanhope might envisage Victor Plumley. That is, if Stanhope is indeed envisaging her former husband, or trying to—which he probably isn't. But if he *did* envisage, what might he see? It makes her smile—because no one could ever envisage such a wonderful man. So many times during their marriage she'd looked up to see him—crossing a lawn or laughing at a party or meticulously drying between his toes after a hot bath—and smiled in amazement at her own good fortune. She'd think, *There he is.*

Having returned from Africa, she'd been wary of outstaying her welcome in Kew Green. After all, there can't have been many young husbands who'd be content with a third (plump, distracted) person living in their marital home. But Jeremy chided her for this. "We're delighted to have you. You regale us with stories, you cook an excellent *coq au vin* and you put a spring in my beloved's step. In fact, we may forbid you from ever leaving. Isn't that right, Pinks?"

"Absolutely. Do as you're told, Butters."

How much Jeremy knew about Florrie's past, Florrie was never quite sure. Pinky would never have told him the truth of what had happened to his wife's friend's hands—but she must have told him something because of his kindness to her, and the fact he didn't pry. But, equally, Florrie felt that Jeremy genuinely liked her company. It can't have been false delight when she taught him how to bat in the garden; he can't have been pretending when he laughed so hard at her joke about the African village that came out to observe her, squatting in a bush, that he sprayed sauvignon blanc through his nose and had to lie down on the chaise longue. "You're doing us both good," he assured her in the kitchen. "Pinky can find things . . . hard."

What was hard for Pinky—for both of the Tophams—was trying to conceive. Eighteen months of marriage and no children. "The fault," Pinky sniffed, "must be mine." So this, too, was a reason why the Tophams seemed so grateful for the duck *à l'orange* set down on the table, the evenings of Scrabble, Florrie's tales of chasing away that dog from the steps of L'Hôtel Petit Palais, a broom in her hand, at which Pinky hooted, hands in the air. Jeremy Topham's eyes would shine with love when he saw his wife laugh like that.

Nor could it have been forced kindness when Jeremy came home one evening, set his briefcase on the sideboard and informed Florrie that there was a secretarial post at the Foreign and Commonwealth Office. "Fancy it?"

She worried that she wouldn't be good enough. She typed well, yes—but so did a thousand other girls. And wouldn't they prefer someone a little younger and prettier? With a slightly smaller behind? That, she'd come to realize, was the way of things.

"Nonsense!" cried Pinky.

"Nonsense, indeed. Who wouldn't be lucky to have *you* type their notes? And, if my wife might forgive me, there's nothing wrong with your behind. Anyway, Victor's not that sort of chap. Old-fashioned. Thoroughly decent." With that, he planted a kiss on his wife with a flourish and left to run a bath, calling over his shoulder: "Ten-thirty tomorrow, Florrie? I may have said you'd pop along . . ."

This was how she met her future husband: in an office off White-hall with a clock that was governed by a tarnished pendulum, which she watched swinging back and forth. Victor Plumley—a returned commercial attaché who'd been saddled with interviews because somebody else had a head cold—was twenty minutes late. Florrie—a reasonable timekeeper herself—was marginally disgruntled by this. She sat in her best dress, ankles crossed, mulling over this slight dis-courtesy, when the door was thrown open and in he came—adjusting his cuffs, pouring out apologies and smelling of heady eau de cologne. "I am *so* sorry . . . Please forgive me. Or rather, *don't* forgive me because I don't deserve it and it would be far better for us both if you gave me a dreadful time of it, for a day or two, at least. I might learn to be more punctual then, because"—he checked the clock—"being twenty-three minutes late is not what gentlemen do. Not what future ambassadors or high commissioners do. *Don't* forgive me, do you understand? Not on any account."

Florrie nodded, not understanding at all.

He beamed, breathless. He didn't assess her dress or physique. Rather, he just beamed at her face. "Jeremy Topham tells me you know cricket."

"Yes. And shorthand, and my typing speed is eighty-two words a minute, and—"

"Best English batsman?"

"Easy—Len Hutton."

"Bowler?"

"Trueman, by a country mile."

"The job is yours, Miss Butterfield. How does Monday sound?"

There were so many things she liked about Victor. The first was his appearance. He was not handsome in the same way that Florrie wasn't beautiful. (He, too, tended to be plumpish; he was only an inch or so taller than Florrie, which meant he was shorter than everyone else.) But nevertheless, Victor took pride in himself: he was ironed, pressed, polished, and he had a *penchant* for the cravat, which gave him a slightly eccentric air. He pronounced words beautifully, like a radio announcer; he took his time in choosing adjectives—so that colleagues were *truculent*, coffee was *exquisite* and the shade of Florrie's cardigan was *pistachio*. She liked, too, his joie de vivre: Victor never seemed in a bad mood. An inclement day was excellent for the garden; a delayed train was merely on the slower side. He'd greet everyone as if he were delighted to see them—regardless of who they were. "Come on *in*, High Commissioner! How *are* you, Colonel?" To the postman, he'd clap his hands together: "Tell me, Ernest, how *is* your lovely wife?"

That's a good sign, her aunt Pip told her. Watch how they speak to the coalman or to the boys who polish their shoes.

But, above all, Florrie liked this: that for all his bonhomie, there was a sadness in him, too.

She didn't need glasses back then. She had perfect vision with which to admire the various colours of petrol in a puddle or how the wisteria at the Tophams' bloomed against the wall. These eyes saw, too, Victor's secret. And he must, in turn, have seen hers—for Florrie was not like the others in the typing pool. They were younger than her, flighty and excitable; at five-thirty, they appeared to rise from their chairs with a squeal and rush out into the sunshine, arm in arm, in their white cotton gloves. Florrie, in contrast, would water the potted plants in the entrance hall. She'd saunter out with a book tucked under her arm.

"I realize," he said as she put on her coat, "that it's Friday afternoon and I'm sure you have plans. But, if not, how about a daiquiri
at Alphonso's Place? The bar with the awnings on Beak Street? They
do more than daiquiris, of course, but honestly, Florrie—those things
are sublime." And Florrie accepted—knowing, with certainty, that he
wanted nothing from her, that she had no reason to fear him because
there was no chance of love in this suggestion—or not the dangerous kind.

How alike they were, Victor Plumley and her. Over lurid cocktails
in impractical glasses, they talked about everything and nothing: the
Queen, space travel, the Cuban revolution, whether pineapples were
better than grapefruits, how they both felt about jazz. Their childhoods
had had their differences—not least because of money, and because
Victor referred to his mother as *that sour old bat*. But they'd both
waved their brothers off to war. They'd both had fathers who died too
soon. And in their teens, they had both experienced something that
had changed the way they walked through the world, which they still
felt tender from. (He didn't say what, at that time. But he talked of
wanting to die, of feeling unable to rise from his bed—and Florrie had
nodded, understanding this.)

Friday daiquiris became commonplace. And, after the fourth such
evening—and having established that they somehow fitted together,
like a pair of gloves at the lost and found—Victor and Florrie started
going on excursions: to Hampton Court Palace or Box Hill, to drool
over oysters at Whitstable. On these days out, they discussed what
they wanted from this life—this brief, single dance in the sunlight of
life. "Adventures," she told him, whilst eating a crumpet in the grounds
of Osterley House. "I've always wanted them." From the first moment
that Bobs drew the world with his finger on a kitchen tabletop, this
had been the truth.

"Not to be married with children? Don't most women want that?"

"Not me," she replied. "Not these days."

In return, Victor spoke of his single childhood dream in life: of being a British ambassador, of traveling overseas. "Perhaps it's the fault of being thoroughly miserable at boarding school and always hankering for escape. But as soon as I heard of the job—and I was seven years old, Florrie, I remember that day—I fell in love with the thought of it. Representing one's country in other countries . . . Helping nationals, making friends, thwarting coups and dining with princes. I understand now that it's not quite like that, of course. But to be an ambassador . . . It's still what I want."

"Will it happen?"

"I'm ready. I joined the Foreign and Commonwealth Office as soon as I left university. Since then . . . well, I was the postboy, at first. But for over a decade now I've been climbing the ladder—part of the consular staff in Dublin and Jakarta, third and second secretaries in Muscat and Istanbul. Commercial attaché in Riyadh last year, which was a busy job, I can tell you. And it's all been marvelous—a joy. But I'm tired of waiting for the big one, Florrie."

"Why the wait?"

He chewed, considering this. Having swallowed, he said, "I wonder if it's the lack of a wife. Looks odd to foreign countries. Looks odd to *this* country, maybe. I'll be forty in March, you see. And wives are integral to the role—vital; one does a better job, they say, with a wife. But let me tell you this: as ambassador, I'd be splendid."

She never doubted it. Charming, attentive, persuasive Victor, with conversational ability in six different languages, a knowledge of all the main religious holidays and such a talent of being with people. He dazzled the Tophams when he came for dinner; he bewitched Prudence and Pip when, one Saturday, at Victor's suggestion, they drove to Upper Dorbury in his silver MG Midget—and it had been a glorious afternoon of strawberries on the lawn, of tales of London, of admiring Pip's latest creations of taffeta and lace. ("Do you, by chance, make cravats, Philippa?") With Prudence, they mused on whether the delphinium was a little too blue—and what colour might one call it? (He'd offered lapis lazuli.) "You know," said Prudence, taking his arm, "that she's named for a city?"

"I do. The finest of cities, no less."

"And that she's my little baby girl? Even now?"

He turned to face Prudence with a serious expression. "I'll look after her. I promise I will." He kissed her knuckles in reassurance, closed his hands over her own.

And one afternoon in late May—a scorching day, as Florrie remembers—they drove down to Brighton, the wing mirrors smacking against cow parsley and dog rose, reciting poetry over the sound of the engine. On arrival, they paddled in the sea. And at the day's end, they sat in companionable silence on the end of the pier with the English Channel glinting before them, with France beyond. "I find the questions so hard. No wish to settle down, old chap? That sort of thing. And I should think you've had it worse than me."

Florrie nodded. *You'll be left on the shelf, dear.* Jeremy's mother had, not long before, peered over her teacup at Florrie and said, bright-eyed, "Tick-tock!"

Victor glanced across. "But you've known it, I think? Love, I mean—the proper sort?"

She looked down at her bare, sandy feet. "Edward Silversmith. I met him in our local shop when I was nearly seventeen. I loved him. I loved him ever so much, Victor, but he didn't love me. Or maybe he did love me for a while but then he started to love someone else—and he loved them much more. So that was that." How simple that sounded, how small.

Victor squeezed her arm. "Nobody since?"

She shook her head. Too afraid, by far; she knew this absolutely. "Not really. You?"

"Me? Oh, my heart has been broken so many times I'm amazed it's even still beating. The man I loved most went to prison for it. He went to prison for *me*, I suppose. Afterward, he ignored me in the street—as if I was nothing to him."

There, at the end of Brighton pier, she squeezed his arm in return.

He'd proposed in the spring of 1959. Florrie and Victor had been sitting in the window of the Fat Cat Bar in Great Pulteney Street—he drinking a rum punch, she with a pint of stout which left a line of froth on her lip. There were daffodils on the bar top that she'd been admiring from her window seat when Victor set down his glass with such emphasis that she flinched, stopped talking.

"Florrie, I have a suggestion. We get married."

"Who gets married?"

"We do."

"We do?"

"Yes—me and you. Now, I know it sounds like utter lunacy. But also, I'm wondering if it isn't the sanest thing we could possibly *do* in our situations. That is, wanting what we want in life, and feeling as we do. Now, I'd like to do this properly, to set out my stall, as it were. May I?"

She nodded, licked the foam from her lip.

"Good. Right. Florence, I think you're splendid. You are humorous and kind and strong and utterly charming, and I adore our conversations, and when I arrive at your table—any table, anywhere—you greet me with a smile that is so entirely beguiling that I feel quite weak with it and consider myself obscenely fortunate to be the gentleman who might be about to share a teapot or carafe of Côtes du Rhône with you. Every other man in every room turns green with envy."

"They do not."

"They do. You don't notice it because you're normally admiring a tablecloth or investigating a hole in your stockings—but it's true. In short, I love your company. I am proud, indeed, to be in it. And I will never tire of it or take it for granted.

"Secondly, I'm rich. I realize that this isn't any particular interest of yours—but I am, even so. Not disgustingly rich but enough to feel queasy. Now, knowing you as I do, Florrie, I can't believe for a moment that you'd wish for diamonds or furs or a box at Royal Ascot or any of the normal foolishness that people spend their money on. But there's money enough for whatever it is you *would* like: an area of woodland, say, or your own library with ladders on wheels that you can move back and forth to reach the upper shelves. I'd buy you the very finest trumpet. Whatever you'd like. And if you were ill, I'd make sure you received the very best care. Indeed, I'd do the same for your mother and aunt, Florrie: they'd never have to worry on that account. They're both as adorable, lively and slightly mad as you are—and I'd never let them struggle. What I'm saying, Florrie, is that I would look after you. I'd care for you from the top of your head to the tip of your toes for all your life—and yet I'd never control you or clip your bright wings. You could still have your freedoms, I promise you that. You'd never have to type another letter again, unless you wanted to. Queasily rich, remember?

"And thirdly," Victor paused, leaned forward a little and fixed Florrie with his serious eyes. "I could show you the world."

"The world?"

"With you on my arm, I'd become ambassador—within weeks. I know I would. And I have no idea where that title might take us, Florrie. All I know is that each posting would be for three years, no longer, and so we'd never have any permanent home in the world, as such. It would be a rather transient life, I'm afraid. But oh, imagine it! We'd live in all sorts of cities—with minarets or monsoon season or a risk of communist insurrection or with polar bears in the distance! We'd meet armies and artists and we'd be useful; we'd guard and promote British interests, of course, but we'd also *help* people. I've always wanted that life—and I want *you* to live it with me." He paused to calm himself. "You loved Africa, didn't you? Nice? Don't you think we'd have a splendid time, *mi Firenze*—you and me?"

They sat for a moment. Victor's words sank down onto the table. "What would you need from me?"

Such a question did not, perhaps, seem fitting for a marriage proposal. But not many proposals were ever like this. And Florrie wanted to know; before saying yes, she wished to be sure what he'd need from her, in the coming years. She wanted to be clear on this.

Victor inhaled slowly. When the exhalation came, it was measured, through pursed lips, as though there was a candle in the middle distance. Then he reached for her hand. "Darling Flo . . ."

In short, Victor hoped that Florrie wouldn't mind his *preferences*. (This was his choice of word.) That is to say, he hoped that she wouldn't be upset when Victor's heart—as full, heavy and cumbersome as a bucket from a well—would, invariably, start to spill over or be poured elsewhere; when he would empty it onto someone who categorically did not have Florrie's silhouette or scent or body parts and who did not have the liberty to kiss him in the street. Would she mind? If Victor fell horribly in love? "Because I do," he explained. "I have a wretched tendency to fall desperately in love with entirely inappropriate people—or rather, for wholly appropriate, wonderful men who love me back and yet who I simply can't *be* with because of their wives or laws or God's rules or public bloody decency, or whatever else. In any case, it all goes wrong and I'm left in a terrible way, for a time. Until it all happens again, of course." Could Florrie bear this?

She turned, looked out of the window. She watched pedestrians wandering down Great Pulteney Street in their skirts and matching jackets. She looked up at the guttering, the hunched pigeons, the watery blue sky of London in spring. Could she? Bear it? For the rest of her life?

"Of course," added Victor, with a slight blush to his cheek, "I could bear it, too. That is, I could never expect you to remain . . . unfulfilled. The love I can't give you: I would never want you to live without it, so that if you found it elsewhere . . . If *you* fell horribly in love . . . Even if there was a child with someone, you and I could—"

Florrie tightened her grasp on his hand, silencing him. She didn't want these words. "No."

"No? Your answer is no?"

"No, it isn't no. It's yes."

"No, it's yes?"

"Yes—I'll marry you." He was safe. He made her laugh. She could imagine herself—now, and for the next fifty years—leaning her head against his shoulder on buses or in cinemas and being able to sleep there, against him, without fear or pretence. He'd put his arm around her. He'd carry her home, if need be.

"Yes? You're sure?"

"Yes."

He kissed her on the cheek with gusto—and they both cried and laughed into their handkerchiefs.

Pinky had not been convinced. In her kitchen in Kew Green, holding a wooden spoon, she narrowed an eye. "I mean, he's wonderful, Butters. He's such a gentleman—and he laughs at Jeremy's jokes, which always helps me to like someone. But are you in love with him?"

"In love with him? No."

"Is he in love with you?"

"Not in the slightest. He's in love with the world, with living— and I suspect he might be partly in love with the delivery boy from Whiteleys."

"The one with the squeaky bicycle? Redheaded?"

"That's the one. But Pinky, it doesn't matter. I do *love* him, and very deeply—isn't that the important thing?"

"Yes. It *is* important. But what about . . . ?"

Pinky left the sentence unfinished. Like a fishing rod in the water, all manner of words swam toward the tip of it: *The bedroom?*

Tenderness? Children? What Pinky's great-aunt Euphemia had called "conjugal rights"? Then she reached forward, took her friend's wrist. "Listen. Let me say this once. I'm going to say it because I'm your best friend and best friends say such things and you can't hate me afterward because those are the rules. Florrie, what happened with Edward . . . It wasn't your fault."

"Then whose fault was it?"

"His—Teddy's. Or no one's. Not yours, anyway. Please, Butters: stop hiding from life."

"Hiding from life? I'm not hiding."

"Fine—not from life. But from love, at least."

"I'm not doing that, either."

"That man in Africa? Yes, you bloody are."

At that, Florrie had a cry. All of this was true. But she knew, too, that Victor Plumley was a kind, decent man she could trust with her life—and wasn't that what mattered? "Please don't shout. Maybe you're right. But he's lovely, and he's offering me a wonderful life—and we're like peas in a pod, he and I. Is that so bad?"

Pinky watched her. "Does he know about it?"

"Hackney? No. He knows there was *something*—that's all."

"Oh, Butters. You still think of her, don't you?"

Every day. Every hour. "Of course I do."

At that, her best friend acquiesced. She wrapped herself around Florrie like a dark, angular cat and exhaled dreamily. "*Florence Plumley* sounds so *regal*. And please marry before September."

Florrie frowned. September was still five months away. "Why before September?"

Pinky smiled, turned a brand-new shade of pink. "Because there'll be another Topham in the house by then."

Thus, Florrie was engaged to Victor Plumley.

The happy couple announced the news to Pip and Prudence in person, who clapped and cried beneath the quince tree and clasped

Victor as if he'd surfaced from water. They announced it, too—as one did, to be proper—in the *Telegraph* and the *Times* for everyone to see.

It *was* right. Florrie could never say otherwise when that decision—that acceptance of hers, in the Fat Cat—led to such extraordinary people and places; when she found herself saying thank you, out loud, to whatever might hear her—the walls of the temple, the leafless trees. She has seen the pyramids because of her decision. She has stood on a promontory, pinched her nose and jumped into a black, bottomless lake from which she emerged like a silvery fish, gasping with joy. *Look where I am.* She has danced with Victor on terraces or in empty, night-time market squares to no music at all—just the wind in the trees. And she remembers, too (even now, on the edge of sleep in the old apple store at Babbington Hall), the stray kitten that found her in a sun-baked church in the town of Sancti Spiritus in deepest Cuba— and how, together, they'd discussed the virgin birth and what religion really meant. Florrie had stroked the nape of its bony neck, felt such tenderness for that kitten and the world and everything she loved. And she felt so grateful to Victor Plumley for finding her and loving her, for offering her safety, for lessening the hurt—although she didn't quite forget.

She sent packages of love from every single place—wrapped in goat hide or sealskin, fragranced with cinnamon or greened with herbs. And whilst she was sometimes sad or lonely, at least Florrie was never afraid of being hurt again. And there was never a day—not one, in nearly thirty years—when she didn't look forward to Victor, her husband, in his paisley pyjamas, climbing into bed at the end of the day with the bedsprings creaking. "*What* a day it's been, Mrs. P . . ."

Mrs. P. For nearly thirty years Victor called her this—amongst all his other names for her. She, in return, would call him *Mr. P.*

23

Tea with the Vicar

The birdsong seems particularly noticeable today. As Florrie approaches the compost heap, she is certain the sparrows in the beech hedge are louder than usual, that the song thrush that favours the old orchard is a little more melodious than it was the day before. Even the jackdaws' squabbling seems a little kinder on the ear. These are, of course, troubling times. (This morning, Magda informed Florrie that there was still no news from the hospital; the manager still breathes by machine—and Magda had moved her palms back and forth, as if squeezing a bladder: *like this*.) Yet it doesn't mean that birdsong isn't still lovely. It's lovelier, maybe.

Stanhope is already there. "Good morning, Florrie"—lifting an invisible hat. He's in a powder-blue shirt with lemon-yellow braces; his right trouser leg is slightly higher than the left. "You look charming, if I may say so."

She wears a dress with a lace-edged neckline in the hue of an over-ripe peach. "Thank you. So do you. I like those braces."

They smile at each other. "Shall we?"

On this bright June morning, Stanhope and Florrie are heading for church. This is not to offer up prayers for Renata or to light a tealight on the metal stand: it's the vicar they seek.

It had been Florrie's idea. Having finished the amontillado, she'd decided that it was necessary to identify the bird. Perhaps the bird means nothing. But there's no denying that for all its sweet-eyed expression and velvety appearance, it's an unusual picture to send to someone you've waited for all your life. Does it have meaning? Is it a clue? She feels (and Stanhope has, since, agreed) that it would be good to find out.

They could go to Babbington's library—where there are reference books and field guides. Also, the Babbington computer is there (for those residents who don't have their own little screens or clever mobile phones); it's tucked into an alcove with ASK BEFORE USING taped to it, as if an ignorant octogenarian finger might set the keyboard on fire. But Babbington Hall has changed for them in the past twenty-four hours; cupboards and alcoves and locked doors that have, previously, seemed quite harmless now seem shadowy. For if the sender of this card knows the door code, he could be anywhere. And there's the risk, always, that an Ellwood might turn up, peer over a shoulder; Aubrey Horner might join them, tell an hour-long tale. What's more, computers can (according to Stanhope) actually store what people have used them for, remembering pages and data, so that anyone could, if they pressed the right buttons, discover what they'd been looking at ten minutes before. "The vicar," he suggested, "might he be able to help us. After all, he knows his birds—and he seems a decent sort."

He *is* decent. Florrie can't say she knows Reverend Joe very well, but what she knows, she likes. As well as his commendable beard, his occasional swearing, his kindness about Arthur and his decision to let the borders of the graveyard grow wild to encourage butterflies, she likes the fact that he doesn't appear to amend himself at all. He is entirely who he is—take it or leave it. Nor is Joe without humour—which feels essential in a profession like his. Florrie detected this humour early; he'd been hanging those bird feeders into the yew and, seeing Florrie, had quipped that, yes, our heavenly Father may, indeed, feedeth the fowls of the air—but the odd worm or beetle didn't really cut it. "I like," he'd said, "to give the Big Guy a helping hand."

The Big Guy. The Boss Man. Him Upstairs.

They pass those feeders now. Here, beneath the yew, are blue tits and great tits, robins, finches, a single grey squirrel who has been known to hang perpendicular to the ground, head down, but who is currently eyeing them from a branch, disgruntled. How used to people these birds have become. In the beginning, they'd have darted away from a single footfall; now they barely notice the going back and forth of the faithful and not-so-faithful.

"Lovely," says Stanhope. "Hasn't the reverend done well?"

Florrie could sit here, birdwatching, for hours. But then a clattering comes. The sound sends a blackbird squawking into the far corner; the blue tits spin into the yew.

A figure emerges from the church. Or rather, she is trying to emerge; her wheels have caught and dislodged the metal boot-scraper and she's trying to move it out of her way. Having done so, Nancy looks up. She doesn't wave but there's a visible pleasure at seeing them—and she calls out, as she makes her way. "Florrie! Stanhope! Hello."

Stanhope, once more, lifts his invisible hat. "Good morning, Nancy. Another fine day."

She heaves herself toward them until, puffed, she puts on her brakes. "Yes. I hear it'll reach thirty degrees, or so they said on the radio. Not quite as hot as last week but even so—it's a little too much for me. Tell me. Has there been any news?"

"Of Renata?" Florrie shakes her head.

"Oh, it's so hard to bear. And yet, do you know that I almost forget? I wake up and know that something has happened—but I can't immediately remember what. For a few seconds every day, I forget I'm unwell and I forget that Renata has fallen." Those rabbity eyes glance across the churchyard. "Dear, dear. Anyway, I'm glad that I've run into both of you. *I* have a little news, at least."

"News?"

"A room has become free—in St. Chad's. I'll be leaving on Sunday—in four days' time. I'm not telling everyone—most won't even know I've gone, let's be honest. But I wanted to tell *you*."

What is the right response? Does one congratulate? Is this good news? It partly feels it; after all, this is what Nancy has been waiting for. Yet it also feels very much *not* good news at all. Perhaps Nancy herself isn't sure, either—for she shrugs, raising her palms upward so that her various rings catch the light. "I am not entirely sure how I feel. Relieved, I think—but frightened, too. Grateful. And sad—I can't deny that. But I suppose that most people feel this way."

Had Pinky? Toward the end of her life, she'd seemed accepting of what was coming; outwardly, at least, she hadn't seemed to mind the London hospice, the roses in vases, the chance to look out of windows at trees and watch them blowing back and forth. In her last days, her three strapping sons had been able to sleep in a neighbouring room; Jeremy had slept beside her, in a chair. And she, Pinky, had whispered, "Isn't this lovely? It's like the old days—all under one roof." But she can't have truly felt this way—or not only this way, at least.

"We'll miss you, Nancy," Stanhope offers. He says this with gravitas, as if underlining the words.

"You're very kind. I've not been here long, I know. But I've felt very welcomed—by both of you, and others—and the setting is so peaceful. It will be hard to leave."

Florrie is unsure what to say. She can only think of how their hands had been—stacked up like pancakes. "Nancy, is there anything we can do to help?"

There's the tiniest shrug, a half smile. "If only you could perform magic, Florrie, dear—although I rather think that if anyone at Babbington can, it's you. No, I don't think so. There's nothing to pack or *do*, as such. I only wish Arthur was here, still. And I'd love it if Renata could wake before I leave; I'd love to go to St. Chad's knowing she was better. But I think that's asking a little too much of you."

They all smile awkwardly.

"You've seen the reverend today?"

"Joe? Yes. About ten minutes ago. He's out and about—doing vicarly bits and bobs." Nancy flexes her fingers, studies them—and there's a sense, momentarily, that she has something more to say so that Florrie thinks, *What is it?* But nothing more comes.

"You won't leave without saying goodbye, will you?"

Nancy's smile is tired, genuine. "Of course not, Florrie—thank you. Both of you."

They watch her roll away.

"Oh, golly."

"I know." It all seems so unfair. But then, wouldn't such an illness be unfair for anyone? No one deserves a tumour which threads out through the body like an exploratory vine or an electric cable—just as no one deserves to be blown up in a tank, or stabbed in the snow in a blacksmith's yard off Paternoster Street, or to have a bubble pop in one's brain in the middle of a post office queue, as happened with Aunt Pip in the end. *Let us all fall asleep,* Florrie thinks, *in a Caribbean hammock, à la Victor.* Or in a cosy bed, preferably with fresh linen and a hot-water bottle, with the soft murmur of conversation around us— friends or loved ones discussing fripperies so that we can slip away, unnoticed, as if into the next room.

If only you could perform magic, Florrie.

"Stanhope? Let's solve this by Sunday."

He blinks his penny-brown eyes. "By Sunday? Really? Do you think that's possible?"

Possibly not. But they can't pull out Nancy's cancer; they can't turn back the clock so that all of them are twenty again—with all the appropriate health and energy and unwrinkled foreheads. Nor can they force Renata's eyes to open, on command. They can't do any of these things that Nancy Tapp is asking them to do (indeed, only the Big Guy can, if He's listening, or in a benevolent mood). But they can do *this*, at least—can't they? With a fair wind? With luck on their side?

"Let's give it a try, anyway."

The church's interior feels beautifully cool. Also, it is quiet: there is no one else here. There's no rustling of gold toffee wrappers, no sudden sneezes, no *Let us pray.*

"Hello?" calls Stanhope. But nobody answers.

It is just them. And whilst that might be reason enough for Florrie to reverse back out of the building, it makes her want to linger instead. It suits her far better—a church outside working hours. It has a deeper peace; there is a better sense of its age, of all the services and acts that have happened here: the christenings and marriages, the heartbroken farewells, the prayers that have been offered out of thanks or love or fear. Do such things leave something in the air? Or in St. Mary's stone-work? In its wooden rafters?

She wheels herself down the aisle. Dust motes float in diagonal shafts. The pews look expectant, empty. Looking back, Florrie sees the place where she'd parked herself on Sunday, next to the trestle table with its pamphlets and bookmarks, the maroon-and-gold book of prayer requests. *How little*, she thinks, *I knew then*. And Stanhope, too, is there—at the far end of the aisle. He's standing in an oddly simple way and looking up at the stained-glass windows, at their dusty rays of coloured light, with a kind, wistful expression so that Florrie knows he's in St. Mary's physically, but he's thinking of another place or time.

"A strange business, isn't it—faith? I've never been quite sure what I believe. All these years, and I'm still not certain. I have some days when I think we just . . . die. End. Grow cold and stop—and afterward, know nothing about it. After all, so many people have died before us; we can't *all* go somewhere else, can we? Think of the crowds. But other days, I will have a quiet conviction that there really *must* be something going on. I'll be in a certain place—a nice woodland, maybe, or just sitting quietly in my room—and I'll feel a presence, very strongly, so that I'm minded to speak out loud to it. Yes, a strange business."

There really must be something going on. It is a good way of putting it. (How dignified, too, he looks as he stands there, in this shaft of light.) And Florrie opens her mouth to reply when she hears, in the distance, a whistling. It's faint and tuneless: a bird of some kind? But the whistling becomes louder, more distinctive; the whistler is human and is approaching the church. Florrie meets Stanhope's gaze.

"Ready?" she asks.

"Ready."

The vicar invites them for tea. Neither Stanhope nor Florrie had expected this—but, on being asked if he had five minutes to spare, Reverend Joe had looked at his watch, dropped his arm, smiled brightly and suggested it. "What do you say? The vicarage is less than a minute's walk from here. It's not exactly the Ritz, I'm afraid—but it's certainly comfier than a wooden pew."

This is how they find themselves following him up and down the metal ramp, into the sunshine and away from the yew. They head for the southwest corner where the main gate to the church leads onto the road. And all the while, Reverend Joe is talking: Is it hot enough for them? Have they heard that peregrine falcons are nesting in Leamington Spa again? "And do mind that tree root, won't you? I trip on that thing all the bloody time."

They let two cars and a bicycle pass. Then they cross the road toward a detached, plain, redbrick bungalow with double-glazed windows and a broken drainpipe. "Not much," he smiles, "but it's home."

He's right: the vicarage is unremarkable. It is neither tidy nor disordered, neither modern nor out-of-date. And whereas other homes (Stanhope's, Renata's, Middle Morag's from her Scottish life) have offered insights into their inhabitants—their character and interests, heritage and quirks—this one doesn't seem to offer much at all. It says very little about the man who is, at this moment, filling up the kettle from a vigorous tap whilst calling over his shoulder, "Do move things about, if you need to!" Florrie looks around. All that needs to be moved, in truth, are books. A dozen or more are laid across the kitchen table, between old mugs of tea and biscuit crumbs—and all are religious in nature. A book about the Gospels lies open on its pages; a weighty tome called *A Prayer for Every Day* has been bookmarked with a torn corner of paper. *How to Write a Sermon* has a cracked, fraying spine and Post-it Notes protrude from its pages like small piano keys. And there are notepads, too—with tight, hurried handwriting on them and intricate doodles. That he's a man with religious interest is evident. But otherwise, there's not much to speak of *him*.

They settle themselves at the table whilst the vicar hunts for mugs. When he opens cupboards, Florrie sees that they're mostly empty; when he pulls out the cutlery drawer, there's only one spoon.

"It's lovely of you to have us here."

Joe pours hot water from the kettle into three mugs. "Pleasure, Stanhope. Chatting with people is one of the best parts of the job, I reckon. The main part, even. Biscuit?"

He may have a colourless kitchen with empty cupboards but Reverend Joe is an attentive host. His tea is bag, not leaf, but an excellent strength; he shakes the digestive biscuits onto a chipped, off-white plate. And when he offers milk, he apologizes that it's coming straight from the carton—although it's precisely how Florrie would have offered it and she tells him so. "Saves washing up." They all raise their mugs in a wordless salute.

So they sip. They chew. Florrie wonders how long it's taken Reverend Joe to grow a beard like that. And why do men who otherwise appear to have no redness in their colouring at all often have a little redness in their facial hair? So it was with Jeremy Topham. In later life, Victor lived with a foreign correspondent called Roly (a doting, laughing delight of a man), and his moustache had been copper-bright. As for Dougal Henderson, his hair was virtually white when she knew him, yet his stubble retained a strong ginger hue so that Florrie had asked, once, if he'd been redheaded in his younger days. "Oh, aye," he told her. "Redder than yours. Red as a fox, as a rusty nail."

But she can't think of Dougal now.

Reverend Joe Poppleton chatters away through a mouthful of biscuits—about hoovering, about hymns, the recent thunder. But soon, the chattering slows.

"So." The reverend sets his mug down. "Now. How can I help you, folks?"

He is good, Florrie thinks, at this. He has the right tone of voice—informal, gentle, with a slightly beckoning feel—so that one could, quite easily, confide or confess.

She and Stanhope exchange glances.

Joe fills the silence. "How are you both doing? After Renata's . . . fall, I mean."

"We are well enough."

"Well enough." He nods at this, seems to set down his role as vicar and be, instead, just a regular man in a Pink Floyd T-shirt. "Yes, perhaps that's my answer, too. The whole thing is just . . . I should be comforting you—and everyone. But I'm not sure I know how to. I keep thinking, could I have done more? Were there clues that I missed?" Briefly, he seems quite lost—this middle-aged, bear-like man.

Stanhope gestures with a half-eaten biscuit. "You're writing next Sunday's sermon? Florrie told me that the last one went very well."

"You did? Oh, that's good to know—thanks, Florrie. I did try to talk about what happened—but where do you start? And I had so little time to *do* it in. She fell on Friday night; I only had a day to write the sermon—but even then I had to see people, be with them. Georgette asked me up to the first floor, too—to sit with some of the residents there. Mind you, I'm not sure I made much of a difference to Mrs. Brimble . . . Anyway, it was nearly midnight before I could pick up my pen and have a go at writing the sodding thing." He takes another biscuit. "Sermons are bloody hard to write, you know. And it doesn't help that Reverend Bligh was apparently a whiz at them . . ."

It is tempting for Florrie to say that Reverend Bligh could drone on and on like a bee at the window and everyone knew he kept cans of warm lager in the vestry. But instead she says, "I think you're much better. More natural."

"Natural? Is that a nice way of saying I swear more? I know . . . I do try not to. But that's twelve years of being a doorman, I'm afraid. I said *crap* in front of Velma Rudge the other day and that really pissed her off."

"A doorman?" They say this in unison.

Joe smiles. "That's what everyone says. But, honestly, it's not really that different from what I do now. Most of that job was talking to people about their troubles—loss or despair. Loneliness, quite often. I'd sit on the pavement with them. Get them a taxi or a strong coffee. Listen as they talked about the kids they didn't see, or the spouses they lost. I've had grown men cry on my shoulder outside nightclubs at two in the morning, and, a month later, they've come back to thank me. Changed men, sober men. New jobs, or better husbands and fathers. Often with a new haircut, too, I noticed. Anyway." He claps his hands on his thighs. "What about *you*?"

Florrie brings her thoughts back from nightclubs and taxis. "As it happens, we've come to talk about birds."

"Birds? I wasn't expecting that. Any particular ones?"

She dips down between the folds of her skirt, lifts the magenta envelope from between her thighs. Then she pushes it across the table. "This one. Do you know what it is?"

Does he flinch? There's the briefest change in atmosphere, as if someone has passed by the window. But then he rouses, pushes the last of his biscuit into his mouth and smacks his palms free of crumbs in a business-like fashion before lifting the card as if it were hardly of any importance at all. "I do, Florrie. And what a bird. They're not much to look at, it's true—little brown things. But they're migratory—coming all the way from Africa for just a month or two. They're not common now, but few birds are, I suppose, except feral pigeons and those bloody jackdaws that raid my sunflower seeds—although everything must live." He looks back up. *"Caprimulgus europaeus."*

Stanhope lowers his mug. *"Caprimulgus?"*

"You know Latin?"

"I do, yes. But *caprimulgus?*"

"I know. Very odd. One can't take *caprimulgus* literally, of course."

"No, I wouldn't have thought so."

Florrie—bewildered, quite at a loss as to what *caprimulgus* means—takes Stanhope's wrist and shakes it lightly, as a toddler might seek attention. "Excuse me, but what are you talking about?"

"Capri, from *goat.* And *mulgus*: to drink milk . . . to suckle." Stanhope looks back to the vicar. "Why on earth is it called that, do you suppose?"

The reverend strokes his beard in one long, smooth action; then he does it again. In doing so, the beard visibly narrows—and he looks, she thinks, like an ancient chieftain. "Fear? That's what I reckon. These little birds have been prone to folklore and superstitions and all sorts of bad treatment—as owls have, too, poor sods. They're nocturnal and camouflaged, so you rarely see them. But their call is . . . How do I put it? Eerie, otherworldly—like a low, electrical hum. Churring, it's called. And I guess we're frightened—aren't we?—of weird nocturnal sounds. We always think the worst—like a *clonk* downstairs in the middle of the night is always a burglar, never the central heating coming on. That's my thinking, anyway. People heard this call, felt afraid—and so the rumours started. That this bird suckled livestock or brought bad luck. An omen."

"An omen?"

"That death was coming. That sort of thing." Joe looks down at the picture with fondness. "That's a nightjar."

A nightjar. The name swoops down in front of them, settles on top of *Gospels for All*. And it feels familiar to Florrie, instantly (How? Where?)—so that she fumbles through her brain to find its hiding place. A feather! She has the feather of a nightjar in her keepsake box—brown, as soft as air. It was given to her by someone (Who? She fumbles again). By Bembe, that's who—their handyman in Uganda who believed it was proof that evil spirits had passed by. He'd stood on the back doorstep of their sun-baked house and offered it, insistent. "See? We must be afraid." But Florrie hadn't been afraid in the slightest—for how could any bird mean trouble? And a bird with such beautiful feathers, too? So she'd kept it in the end: an *aide-mémoire* of Kampala, and of being there.

"I've never heard of it," says Stanhope. "But then, I've not been very good with birds. Florrie?"

Bembe, who'd swept the yard with a slow, mechanical rhythm. "Yes. I think so. When I was in Africa. Are they here now?"

"Here? In Britain, yes—the summer's their time. But not near Temple Beeches, I'm afraid. They prefer heathland, coastlines . . . Folks, can I ask—what *is* this card? Why do you have it?"

One ought, of course, to be able to trust a vicar. Florrie ought to be able to entrust him with the scream, the *billets-doux*, the fact they believe Renata was pushed—and that it would go no further. But this empty kitchen unnerves her; something about *him* is different, since she laid down the card amongst the biscuit crumbs. So she only offers some of it: "It was sent to Renata—this card. She received it on midsummer's morning, a few hours before she fell."

"It's Renata's—and yet *you* have it?" There's a new, brief sharpness in the vicar's tone.

"Oh, we didn't steal it, Reverend. There's been no breaking of commandments here—no, no. We found it, that's all—Florrie and me.

We found it and we wondered who sent it, because—" Stanhope stops. Because? And his kind, open face has panic blowing all over it.

"Because," says Florrie, taking over, "of what's inside. We think someone has feelings for Renata. They may even love her, you see— from the words? And we are worried that this person might not know she's fallen—and wouldn't they *want* to know? So that they can be at her bedside, holding her hand and talking to her? We don't like to think she's lying there alone. So we're trying to find out who sent this. So that we can let them know."

It seems, to her, that Joe is uneasy. Under his beard there's movement—the working of his lips, or shifting of his jaw. He asks, "Who's it from?" But without waiting for an answer, he suddenly leans forward, scoops the card back across the table toward him and opens it up.

"I never stopped hoping I'd find you."

How different it sounds, in the vicar's voice. At first, Florrie had thought these to be such romantic words, but now she hears the obsessional edge to them—the darker side of love. That talk of omens, too, hasn't helped the mood. Reverend Joe looks up. "So . . . An admirer?"

Stanhope—who seems quite oblivious to the tension in the room—chips in brightly. "Well, we think so. Possibly. A very impassioned one, perhaps. And why not? I've always thought Renata lovely. Nothing wrong with being quiet or keeping oneself to oneself. But *who* is the admirer? That's the question. And *where*?"

The vicar thumbs the edge of the card in thought. He reads the words a second time—softer, to himself—then closes the card and passes it back to Florrie. "I know nothing about an admirer, I'm afraid. She's certainly never mentioned one."

"You speak with her? Know her?"

Joe's expression changes again; the dark cloud blows through to leave something quieter. He picks up his mug but doesn't drink from it. "Sometimes I've found her sitting in church. Once, she came here—sat where you're sitting now, Stanhope. We'd chat." He studies the mug. "Know her? I thought I did a little, at least. But I had no idea that she'd try to . . ."

At that, he leans back in his chair, into a shaft of sunlight that falls across the draining board and catches him; it illuminates his left side, as sunlight might illuminate a tree. And in this light, Joe suddenly seems older; Florrie sees, in more detail, the greyness at his temples and an old scar on his brow, and she wonders how it must truly feel for him, to have exchanged a life of breaking up fights outside nightclubs for one of offering sermons in a small, squat Oxfordshire church where most of his parishioners are in their late eighties. She wonders, too, *Why choose it? Why come to such a quiet place?*

"Renata isn't on her own, if that helps. In hospital. I've gone there twice, sat with her."

"You have?"

"As her vicar, yes. As a friend. Yesterday I was there for three hours, praying at her bedside. So, if the reason you're trying to find its sender is for Renata's sake—well, there's no need. She has me—and Him. The Big Fella. What I'm saying to you both is, don't worry too much about this card. Better, I reckon, to let the matter go."

Joe Poppleton—very much himself again, bear-like and talkative—accompanies them back to the church. They cross the road together, talking of various, unrelated matters: the beechwoods, politics, the alcohol content of the communion wine. When Florrie asks about owls, the vicar lists all the owls of his lifetime—including the pale, heart-shaped one that would quarter the scrubland near his childhood home.

Near the bird feeders, they pause.

"Reverend? Tabitha Brimble. You said you'd seen her. *How* is she upset? How does it show itself?"

"Agitation. Anger. It can happen with dementia, I know, but it's come on so suddenly with her. She's usually so gentle. I'm not allowed favourites, but if I was . . . She pushed someone over yesterday. I could have done with her in Soho!" But he quickly regrets the joke. "I don't understand it—the change in her, I mean."

They make their goodbyes. But, having turned away from them, the reverend pauses and turns back. "For what it's worth, she asked about nightjars, too."

"Tabitha?"

"Renata. Not long after I came here in March. She saw the bird feeders and asked me: had I seen a nightjar or heard one—that sort of thing. A coincidence, that's all. Anyway, you know where I am if you need me." He gives a single nod, punctuating his sentence—and sets off through the greenish light, toward St. Mary's Church.

Stanhope watches, blows out his cheeks.

"Lordy. Do you think this is another one in love with her?"

Florrie isn't sure. There'd been shadows in Joe, without question—moving, like those on a riverbed. But what had been the cause of them? Those seven words? The nightjar? The possibility of love? It would seem a little un-vicar-like—to be obsessively in love. But then, aren't vicars still humans? With beating hearts? "I suppose he'd know the door code. And his kitchen is rather . . ."

"I know. I wonder if our reverend's planning on leaving soon. In a hurry, even."

Bembe comes back to her again. That sweeping back and forth, like a metronome; that soft, soft feather which he'd offered with a straight, insistent arm. "Burn it. Evil is coming." One might not have thought that such a serious, expressionless, monosyllabic man (did he smile even once in their time in Uganda?) could have such passions in him, such strong beliefs. But she couldn't have guessed that Renata had *Dum spiro spero* on her wall, or that Reverend Joe had wrestled drunks to the ground. We all have our secrets.

"Either way, Florrie, the vicar's not our man. In the kitchen? I glanced across at his sermon. Rather haphazard handwriting, admittedly, but far better than mine—but I paid particular attention to how he'd written *Our Father*. The *F*?"

"Not a treble clef?"

"I can't say I trust him fully. But no, Florrie: not a treble clef."

24

The Sitwell Parrot Is Remembered

Their journey back through the churchyard is a quiet one.

"What are you thinking, Florrie?"

Victor used to ask her this. He'd claim she had a quizzical expression that would come upon her like a passing cloud and her lips would purse, child-like. He asked it in temples or in the back of taxis and, once, on the terrace of the Hotel Continental in Saigon, not long before the war—("What's going *on* in there, Mrs. P?")—to which she'd answered, "I'm sending love, Victor; hang on a moment." And he'd nodded, sipped his beer, waited till it was done.

But she isn't sending love now. "I'm not quite sure." On one hand, there's a levity to her. They have, after all, made progress: the bird is a nightjar—tiny, misunderstood; Joe, for all his curious behaviour, did not write that card. But on the other hand, troublesome thoughts are rattling inside Florrie like seeds in a pod. There's so much to untangle in all of this. And it doesn't help that this is a hot, airless morning; a cooler Florrie would think far better, she's sure. So she asks Stanhope if he'd like a Rose's lime cordial in a shady spot on the terrace.

"I'd like that very much."

"Right. Let's look at what we know. Early on midsummer's morning, someone hand-delivered a card to Renata, a card with a nightjar on

it; they pushed it under her door—so they must be familiar with Babbington Hall. And later that night, someone else—or, we think, the
same person—tried to kill Renata by pushing her out of the window.
Broken curtain hooks, her scream, the chutney jar of flowers falling
with her, et cetera. And for the latter, at least, they'd have had to know
the door code—because they could only have used the back door at
that hour. Is that right?"

"I think so."

"One of us, then. Gosh."

Florrie sips through a paper straw. Stanhope, in contrast, is trying to drink his cordial in the normal fashion, yet the straw remains
in the glass so that it prods against his spectacles, pokes him in the
nose. In the end, he removes the straw and peers at it. "And," he adds,
"the nightjar must have meaning. Because Renata had asked the vicar
about it—and why would she do that otherwise? This little brown bird
like a piece of tree bark? It means something to Renata—and it must
mean something to *him*."

This is all true. People don't send pictures of nightjars to each
other without reason. Certainly, it wouldn't be a typical choice for a
love note. Hearts or flowers or teddy bears, maybe, but not a dappled,
secretive, beady-eyed bird that's had an unfair reputation.

Stanhope looks, she thinks, like a king. He (having no actual,
physical hat, despite pretending to raise one in greeting to people) sits
in the shadier seat; it's a slatted wooden chair with reclining capabili-
ties, armrests, cushions and a stool for his feet—not unlike a throne.
His forearms are laid on the two armrests. A slight breeze moves the
hazel tree so the light moves, as if he's being fanned. He lifts his glass,
prepares to sip again. "Love, I mean. It's a funny old thing. And I can't
say I'm an expert, Florrie. Gretchen would testify to that. But what
we thought sounded romantic . . . When the vicar was reading those
words, they didn't sound romantic at all to me. Perhaps it was *how* he
was reading it. Or perhaps I was still adjusting to the fact that Reverend

Joe was a doorman before this—a bouncer! At nightclubs! There's a thought. Mind you, he's got the physique for it. I'd like to see the man who can beat Joe in a fight! Next time I see him at the church door, in his Sunday outfit, I'll half expect him to say, 'One in, one out!'" He pauses for Florrie's smile and then carries on. "Anyway, I listened to him reading those words and . . . well, they felt different to me. Too much. Obsessive, even. They didn't sound like proper love to me."

Florrie agrees with this. *I never stopped hoping I'd find you.* Certainly, those words could be romantic if they were gently said, and wanted. But Renata hadn't wanted them.

"We saw—*you* saw—the card in a wastepaper bin. A wastepaper bin! I'd offer that this means"—Stanhope raises a finger for emphasis—"the Ellwoods were wrong. That blush? Which they think was of desire, of bashfulness? I propose that it was actually a blush of anger, Florrie—or frustration. To be pestered like that . . . It doesn't really seem like a loving act."

Florrie looks to her left, toward the dining-room window. Through it, she can see the brown curtains tied back with their yellow tasseled rope; she can see the plastic tablecloths, the jugs of water, the salt and pepper pots. It is approaching midday. Soon, the church clock will chime twelve times—and, soon after, others will come. Residents will drift in—from their rooms or elsewhere in the grounds—and they'll murmur about Renata or their grandchildren or last night's television.

Stanhope, she knows, is right. Everything he's just said—under the hazel, holding a glass that's clinking with ice—is, without question, the truth. These words are not of love. These words are those of infatuation. They're the words of a person who's lost all sense of reason in how much they love (or *think* they love) poor Renata Green. And it occurs to Florrie that she isn't really surprised. After all, she's always known that there are some women in this world who inspire exactly that sort of devotion, whom men will see and talk to—just once— and be quite undone by, believe themselves in love with before the day is out. Renata is, clearly, one of them. Jay Mistry had fallen for her entirely—so much so that he's in the Himalayan foothills now, drinking snowmelt and breathing the thin, strange air in an effort to mend and be free of his feelings. Even Stanhope, to a point, has been wholly charmed. And this man, too: *this* one—who wrote the nightjar card—may have felt such passion that murder was possible. But Renata is not the only woman who can cause a *crise d'amour*. In Florrie's Highland life, there was Isobel Boyle—the great beauty, patchouli-scented, who'd be followed out of a room by ten pairs of eyes, all sorry for her leaving. Nancy Tapp has it, in her way—dainty, girlish, quizzical, with that delicate voice and dark, perceptive eyes. She married three times, or so it's rumoured: three men had wished to marry her, which is three times more than many. And there was Clemency. Above all, perhaps, there was her: Clemency Winthrop, the doctor's daughter, with her dark-blonde hair that curled just so, her not-too-big bosom and dimpled smile. Her laugh, too, like a bicycle bell. Florrie and Pinky had spied through the keyhole of the sitting-room door as Aunt Pip had measured her for a tea dress, and afterward they'd sulked, kicked a pebble down the road between them, back and forth, because even they—eight-year-old girls, one short and one tall—had understood that there are some people in this world who have what is required, who will never have trouble in being liked, or loved.

Nor had Butters and Pinks been the only ones to think it. Catches were dropped when Clemency wandered past the cricket pitch. Bobs would stutter out his compliments to her—about anything, everything: her hair, her smile, the tiny size of her feet. She has played, Florrie thinks, such a role in my life—Clemency Winthrop—without even knowing it.

Stanhope leans forward. "But then, what if it's more than that?"

"More?"

"More than pestering? Like *stalking*, I mean. Like this man is obsessed with her. What if Renata blushed and stuttered at the

Ellwoods out of fear, more than anything else? It sounds rather dramatic, I know. But perhaps she'd already refused this man—several times, who knows? And she was even hiding from him these days—up in the eaves, with all her books and fairy lights. What do you think? Of course, it makes no sense to me—trying to persuade someone, like that, badgering them into submission. Heavens, you can't make someone love you back. You can't"—he pauses, searches for the word— "clobber them with love, in the hope they'll also feel it. In fact, I've always rather thought that the opposite is true: if you give something the space to grow—as you would when potting-on—it's far more likely to."

When potting-on. Stanhope, the gardener: she hadn't known this. And it is Victor, then, whom she thinks of: all that freedom he'd offered her; all those days in which Florrie explored and danced and caught local buses before returning to him, sunburned and radiant. He never minded once: he'd say, "Tell me all about it, Mrs. P." Hers was, yes, a different marriage from most. But even so, wasn't it a fine example of one? They shared the same surname, but she wasn't owned by Victor Plumley; this made her feel, conversely, so much closer to him. And what comes to mind, at this moment (rather strangely, she admits), is the parrot of her childhood—or, specifically, of Prudence and Philippa Sitwell's childhood: that white cockatoo with a pale-blue tongue who'd sit in the corner of the Sitwell drawing room and shriek, "Damn you all" or "Bugger off!"—and who was prone to snapping at a forefinger if you came too close. That parrot can't have always been that way. It had learned its ill manners from its owners, no doubt. But perhaps it had also grown sour from being chained to a perch all its days and nights, from being prodded into language, woken from its sleep. It nipped and squawked and cowered sometimes, rolling its wise eyes to the ceiling; and, as Florrie sips her own lime cordial, she wonders how it might have been if they'd unchained that poor bird, opened the living-room window and said, Go! Be free! What might its nature have been if the dreary, monosyllabic Sitwells had allowed that bird to stretch its wings to full, dazzling capacity? It wouldn't have sworn, Florrie's certain. It might, instead, have quoted poetry. It might have perched in a horse chestnut tree and bid a bright good morning to all who'd wandered past it.

Poor parrot. It had deserved better.

And poor Renata, too. Because this possibility—that she's been hounded, stalked, pressured into love—sounds so very plausible. For hasn't it seemed like she's been hiding? Tucked away on the third floor? Hasn't she grown much thinner lately? Didn't she weep, privately, on the white-painted bench a few nights ago—where nobody could find her except Florrie and the wren? All this whilst still being newly in love—with somebody else.

I thought being in love would be easy.

"Florrie?" Stanhope had retrieved his paper straw and been prodding his ice cubes with it, frowning in concentration. But now, he's looking at her. "We need a pen and paper."

"Do we?"

"I propose that we make a list of all the men at Babbington who might love Renata—or who might *think* they love her when, in fact, they don't at all. Would-be murderers who know the four-digit code."

That afternoon, on the terrace, Stanhope writes the names down. By their calculations, on Babbington's ground floor—its assisted-living quarters—there are only five male residents. (One fewer, since Arthur died.) Of those five, two are married—and whilst both Florrie and Stanhope agree that married men can have their passions elsewhere (as married women can), they consider it unlikely that the nonagenarian Harrold Lim would have the physical strength to push a woman out of a third-floor window, or that Alan Rosenthal might be allowed even five minutes away from Babs. Both men are swiftly discounted.

"Who does that leave?"

Of the three single, male residents, two can be swiftly set aside, as neither was actually here, in Babbington, on the night in question. Bill Blewitt—being keen on both narrow-gauge steam trains and seaside resorts—was holidaying on the south coast (and still *is*, as far as anyone knows). As for a certain Stanhope Jones, he spent midsummer's night sleeping on a too-hard mattress at his son's house, in Princes Risborough, only to return the following morning. "As my son, his wife, my grandson and two unruly great-grandsons could all testify, if they had to," he offers cheerily.

There is, by their calculations, only one resident left.

"Aubrey?" Stanhope scratches his head. "Really? Do you think?"

It's a strange thought, certainly. But Aubrey had been quite captured by the painting tutor with the corkscrew hair. He'd had no interest in painting at all until she turned up—and after that, he'd bought his own easel, his own sable brushes. Florrie nods. "It's possible."

There are staff, too, to consider. And whilst there's no doubting that the carer's role is largely a female one, Stanhope calculates that there are three further candidates at Babbington; three men who could have grown obsessive over the days and months, entered the back door and slipped upstairs.

"Three?"

Stanhope counts on his fingers: Franklin, Reuben and Clive. "We'll need to see their handwriting," he says. "I'm not sure how we'll do that. But I'll think of a plan. I'll come up with something. Florrie?"

Florrie looks down at her hands, with their intricate scarring. Once, she thought they looked like cracks on a dry riverbed, or the veins on a fallen leaf; she tried not to mind them, to accept them as part of herself. And they *are* a part of her, it's true. She can hardly remember a time before them; when she'd look at these hands and not see their damage.

"Are you all right? You're being very quiet, if you don't mind my saying so. You have been since the vicar. Florrie, is it me? Have I said the wrong thing?"

How could it be him? Sitting there with his butterscotch eyes and slightly raised brows, the thumbprint on the left lens of his spectacles which has been there for nearly a week now? It isn't him. But, yes, she is quiet. Florrie knows she is. She'd started the day with a certain joie de vivre, aware of the birdsong and shafts of light, and yet now she's sitting here, on the terrace, musing on her damaged hands and with a new, heavy sadness in her chest. Is it the aftermath of that amontillado sherry? Or the sudden return of Clemency Winthrop?

And it's the pike, too—always the pike. It turns in its peat-brown water.

Florrie knows that love—the proper, deep, extraordinary kind—is not about *you*. So many people think it is. But real love is all about *them*, always—about the person you love above all others, whose happiness you long for above all other things. With love, you want the best for them. You want their contentment, their safety. You want them to laugh freely, to dance, to live a long, healthy life of joy and gratitude—even if this happens away from you, even if your beloved never knows your name. For that person, you'd walk through deserts. You'd light candles in churches. You'd deny yourself a thousand things in your own life if it meant they had just one of them—just one. You'd lie to your parents. You'd walk past the open flaps of a tent hoping that *they* might have that chance for love, instead of you; you'd shake your head at the marriage proposal of a good, kind man on a Scottish lochside because you'd rather *they* had this moment. For one has, with love, the curious notion that you can pass on your own allowance of happiness to them, in some fashion—as if bequeathing pennies that you'd rather *they* spent, not you. *Joy? Here. Have all of mine.*

Teddy taught her this. And there he is, suddenly, in front of her—aged eighteen, holding a milkshake in Cadena Café and speaking of

Plato. Love, he'd explained, is thinking of *them*, not of one's own self. He taught her (with Plato's help) the true meaning of love. And then he'd set down his milkshake, reached for her hands, which she wasn't yet ashamed of.

Florence Butterfield, I will love you all my life.

How tired she feels, suddenly. All this yearning for someone; all this longing to hold a person who can't even be touched or seen.

"I want Renata to wake up, Stanhope."

He fumbles for her nearest arm, her left one. Having found it, he moves down to her wrist, then her hand—and as he does this, he only keeps looking at her face with his wise, saintly gaze. "I know. But I think we're nearly there, now. We'll find out what happened—we will. And Renata *will* wake up."

Florrie herself had said this, a few days ago. She'd announced it in her kitchenette: "Renata will survive"—as if the words themselves would be enough to open those blue eyes. But how old and foolish she feels now. "By Sunday? I don't think so."

Stanhope leans closer, tightens his grasp on her hand. "*Non desistas*, Florrie. Leave it all to me."

25

Mrs. Victor Plumley: A Life

(including turtles, plumbago, a woman called Gladness, the
nocturnal silence of Everest base camp, *stroopwafels* and Hassan
abu Zahra)

Wh> hat a life she had with him—with Victor, man of cravats
and half a dozen languages, who'd kiss Florrie's hand
without warning.

Even now, she's amazed that it happened at all. They'd married
on a cloudy Thursday afternoon in St. Marylebone Church with his sea-
green cravat matching the sash on her powder-blue, Pip-made dress.
She'd had sugar-pink roses as her bouquet. The organist had attempted
Pachelbel's *Canon in D* as they left the church, as husband and wife.
And Prudence—delighted, tearful, overcome—had thrown a handful
of rice so badly that it rained down on her own head and shoulders,
not theirs, and Victor's uncle Bernard, a widower, had found this such
a charming sight that he'd introduced himself to her.

"Here's to our married adventures," Victor declared. That night,
they drank champagne in the double bed of the honeymoon suite of
the Landmark Hotel, looking over the chimneypots of Marylebone
and Baker Street. Most brides, Florrie supposed, would be in their silk
knickers by now, shaking with nerves. Yet here she was in her favourite

cotton nightdress and ribboned bed socks, slurping champagne, discussing the chimney sweeps of old (How did they actually get *up* the
chimneys? Did they climb, like monkeys? Or use ropes?) and hiccup-
ping, once in a while. Victor beamed, in his pyjamas, whilst providing
the occasional hiccup of his own. No, there were no silk knickers. But
there was laughter and a pillow fight, and dreams of the future, the
sharing of a whole box of peppermint creams—which, all in all, must
have been lovelier than many other wedding nights.

Before turning out the light, Victor thanked her.

But she had reason to thank him, too.

For the next twenty-nine years, they slept as they did that first
night—side by side in their marital bed, keeping to their halves of it.
But occasionally, in the depths of night, Victor's foot might wander
across to find her or Florrie might lift her head from the pillow to
check that Victor was still there, still snoring in the dark. If one was
ill, the other came with flannels. If Victor's heart got broken (as he'd
predicted it would), Florrie would sit beside him on the bed, with one
arm around his shoulders and say, "Maybe next time."

A strange marriage? Certainly. They never saw the naked body of
the other. Kisses were on the forehead or cheek, never on the mouth.
But what a world they saw, as husband and wife. What stories they
forged between them—involving fruit bats or sandstorms or funeral
pyres or formal dinners in which there'd be some small catastrophe
which they discussed later ("Did you *see* his face?") from their two
separate sides of the bed, the headboard rattling from laughter. Their
love was not the proper, conjugal kind. Yet Florrie loved her husband
unreservedly. And he, Victor, loved her—calling her *mi reina* or
mariposa or *my fragrant English rose*. He'd haul her over his shoulder in floodwater; he'd ask her to dance at ambassadors' balls with a
flourish—"Might I have the pleasure?"—and if Florrie ever had nightmares, as she sometimes still did, Victor would clamber across to her

side and wrap his arms around her and say, in time, "Shall I make some tea?" So yes, it was a curious thing, but also, it brimmed with love.

Victor had been right: within two months of their wedding day, he finally received his promotion. Their first marital posting was in the Netherlands: civilized, close, with no poisonous spiders in alcoves or immediate risk of a coup. "We're going in at the shallow end, Florrie."

The Hague was the perfect starting place. Every morning, Victor would polish his shoes, add eau de cologne and leave their house in the Scheveningen district to catch the tram to the embassy on Lange Voorhout; Florrie, instead, explored. She dipped through the archways of the city, felt the stonework of churches and the plinths of monuments; at the harbour, she watched the fisherwomen with their white lace caps. And on sunny days, Florrie might venture up to Amsterdam, where, aged twenty-seven, she finally learned to ride a bicycle. She wobbled through Amsterdam's streets, over its bridges; she marveled at the Vondelpark, befriended an elderly prostitute on Stoofsteeg called Lieke with whom she'd share *stroopwafels* from a shop near Centraal. *Would Lieke like to work in the embassy?* she pondered. There were jobs there, after all. But Lieke shook her head. All those big rooms? Those corridors? "Anyway," she shrugged, "I'm good at what I do."

Florrie loved those days. And she could easily have spent each one of them on her own with a packed lunch and no proper agenda, but she had certain obligations, too. As Mrs. Victor Plumley, the British ambassador's wife, she was always invited to the weekly women's lunches hosted by other ambassadors' wives who, as a group, reminded Florrie of buttons in a jar, for how varied they were: the pearlescent, the hardy, the skittish, the bold. One day, the most dominant button in the Netherlands circle—Augustina Bott, the American ambassador's wife—leaned across a tablecloth during the pudding course, and said, "You *are* trying, aren't you, Florence? For a family? I mean, what else *is* there in life?" And Florrie had set down her spoon and smiled with all her might. She thought of galleries and music, of the glitter of the canals on full-moon nights, of laughing with Lieke on the front steps of her workplace about a particular uncastrated cat who'd climb through Lieke's windows at an inopportune moment. (Florrie had laughed till she'd cried, at that.) *What else is there?* She could have written a list for Augustina.

"She said *what*?" Victor said, brushing his teeth that night. "That woman. I wonder who came first—the pert Dutch secretary or the nosey old wife."

Florrie was kinder to Augustina Bott after that.

Nevertheless, she understood quickly who she needed to be, for Victor's sake. Of course, she wanted to ride the water taxis all day or play gin rummy with the Stoofsteeg girls, to run barefoot into the Dutch tulip fields. But she was, also, a diplomat's wife—and had no wish to let Victor down. So Florrie bought an elegant grey dress with a white lace collar. She no longer sat on the front steps of the brothel on Stoofsteeg (choosing, instead, to sit around the back). And, on a stroll near the Peace Palace, Florrie murmured to Augustina that yes, a family would be lovely if the good Lord was so inclined.

"Quite right, Florence. Quite right."

The Hague, Havana, Lisbon, Kampala, two visits to Delhi, Kingston, a brief spell in Nairobi, a longer one in Cairo, and eighteen months in Kathmandu. There was a time when Florrie could rattle off every posting in sequence, give the street names and house numbers—but now? She's less sure of the order of things. Sometimes, she can hardly believe that any of it happened at all. How did she find herself at Everest base camp? Or playing cards with strangers in a nighttime café lit by the headlights of an old Ford Cortina? Moths of all sizes had come to those headlights. Owls would come down for the moths.

But they did happen. They had not been dreams. And whereas some marriages might be undone by rat infestations or typhoid outbreaks—or, indeed, by men staring unapologetically at Florrie's bosom on public transport, which felt de rigueur in certain places— the Plumley marriage thrived. They never failed to laugh. They'd enter holy places together, hand in hand. And sometimes they'd catch the eye of the other, across a crowded room, and think, *Look where we are, you and I.*

Florrie remembers this, too, of their married life: there were always people. There were cooks, maids, drivers, travelers, other diplomats, deputy chiefs of mission, charity workers, writers, botanists, politicians, army officials, rebel leaders, hawkers in markets, squabbling children, street cleaners and gardeners and financiers and priests, tourists without passports, tourists in need. There were always Britons to soothe or explain to, to track down in jungles, or young British bodies to repatriate. And, once in a while, Victor would enter prisons—hellish, dangerous places—to speak to British backpackers who'd arrived in the country with drugs in their shoes or lower intestinal tract with no idea how those drugs had got there, and Victor would work tirelessly, tactfully, to save them from a lifetime's imprisonment or, in one instance, the noose. Sultans came for dinner. Nobel Prize winners stayed in the guest room. The attaché to the Philippines (a sweet-natured man) asked for Victor's gold cravat.

How happy he seemed. Victor's enthusiasm for life was far more, in these countries, not less. To increase the happiness of others: this was, for Victor, his purpose. But he could love too much at times—or too recklessly, at least. In Delhi, there were rumours of Victor and a businessman. In Cuba, he declared he loved the cook. In Kenya, he lost his heart entirely—and his financial senses—to a fisherman in Mombasa who would bring red snapper to their house, as an excuse, and leave the cold, radiant bodies on the kitchen table. "Doesn't Yaro have," Victor sighed, "the loveliest smile in the world?" Yes, Yaro did— but Yaro also had nine children and a furious wife who threw stones at their car one afternoon. "Dear Florrie," he murmured that night. "I'm so sorry. How can you bear it?"

There was no need to be sorry. She had so little to bear, compared to him—and she kissed her husband's hairline, murmured, "Oh, my darling Mr. P." . . . She wished (Oh, how she wished) that the world were better for him—this beloved, gentle, generous person. Perhaps, one day, it would be.

"Tell me, Florrie? What of you?"

He meant, she supposed, was she lonely? But how could Florrie be that? She'd learned that she was good at making friends. Lieke, in Amsterdam, had only been her first. In Lisbon, she'd had Benedita. On a balcony in Cuba, Camilo—in his eighties, at least—taught Florrie to salsa, despite having no real language between them. In Kampala, Bembe the handyman told Florrie, very solemnly, that writing *no* in salt on the ground would keep the snakes away—and it proved right, for the entirety of her time there: not a single snake was seen in or near the Plumley house. It was there, too, that Florrie befriended the cook—Gladness, with permanently floury hands and a laugh like an outboard motor—to such an extent that they'd sit in the shady part of the garden eating papaya and discussing parents or menstruation or how to shuck an oyster, and all the other great questions of life. Being of a similar physique, they shared dresses; they peered approvingly, every Tuesday, at the gardener next door. And they listened to the moon landings together in the kitchen, after which Gladness reasoned that, yes, it was all very clever—but Mr. Armstrong and his friends hadn't pushed out a ten-pound baby in breech position with nothing but a bottle of rum for distraction and *that*, she felt, was worth higher praise than standing on the moon.

And always, there was Pinky—as constant as a star. She made it to The Hague in the beginning—having left Jeremy at home with a pair of toddlers. ("They'll burn the house down. London will go up in flames, I'm telling you.") Much later, too—when her boys were all grown—she and Jeremy met the Plumleys in Cairo, sucking dates from their fingertips and marveling at souks. But for the rest of the time, Pinky was the calm voice on the telephone, the sender of cards and letters, which often contained peculiar, childish creations for Auntie Florrie—made of crayon, dried pasta or wool. "Don't you be replacing me with Gladness," she'd teased, her mouth full of something, from her home in Kew Green. "Or there'll be trouble. I mean it, Butters."

But Victor had meant more than friends. He'd meant, was Florrie in love somewhere? Was there, for his wife, another man?

Mostly, no. She wasn't looking.

But then, in her forties, Florrie met Hassan. Officially, he was her driver and interpreter, but unofficially, he was so much more than that. Florrie, having very little spoken Arabic and with no understanding of its windblown script, was offered a guide in this slight, immaculate man whose eyes were like resin in transparency and hue. Every morning, Hassan would collect her in his car and say, "Where may I take you?"—as if the whole world were possible, not just Cairo. He took her to functions, other embassies; he drove her as Mrs. Plumley, the British ambassador's wife. But he'd drive her, too, as Florrie—just her, as she was; and how delighted he always seemed when she asked to truly *see* his city—not merely the Sphinx or the feluccas on the Nile but the spice markets, the cemeteries, the botanical gardens, the mosques, where she'd cover her head, remove her shoes and spend an hour or more inside, almost sleeping. She asked him for recommendations: *his* favourite café, *his* best view of the Nile.

Soon, their conversations drifted away from Egyptian geography into one's regrets and dreams, one's private losses. On the steps of the Hanging Church, they shared secrets as others might share a hookah pipe, back and forth between them. Also, once, Hassan sang for her. On the edge of the desert, beneath a new moon, he'd set his hand to his chest and sung an old, mournful Bedouin song that stirred Florrie's heart; she, in exchange, had attempted a quavering version of "Silent

Night" (she could think of nothing else at that time), which she sang with closed eyes, arms held wide. And she'd felt such a sudden rush of tenderness at certain words that she'd had to stop and turn away. Hassan only sat, watching.

"We've become good friends, haven't we?" So Florrie said in the market, over her shoulder. Hassan had replied, "Yes, we have." But sometimes, in the rear-view mirror of his Toyota Corolla, Florrie noticed a look in Hassan's eyes that suggested something else, something deeper.

"Your husband. He is . . ."

"He is?" Florrie waited. But she knew that Hassan's resin eyes had seen it all.

"You are sad, I think? Mrs. Plumley?"

Sad? She thought to say no. For what might she be sad about? Sitting here, in a café by Zuwayla Gate with date palms outside? With Prudence and Pinky and adventure in her life? With Victor—who, in Egypt, called her *Hatshepsut, my Florence of Arabia*? But she nodded at Hassan. "Sometimes."

At that, he took her hand. He reached across the Formica tabletop, took her left hand with both of his and unfolded her palm. Then, very gently, Hassan traced her scars; he studied them intensely, followed their rise and fall as if she were a map—over her knuckles, under her thumb. And then he kneaded her—her wrists and forearm, the crease of her elbow; he felt her musculature and bone, her deep freckled softness; he traced the regal blue veins of her, at her thinnest point. And Florrie allowed it, realizing that she hadn't been touched like this in decades, that no one had ever drawn a slow line, from joint to joint, with their fingertip. She closed her eyes to feel it better.

All this in a café on an overcast Tuesday afternoon. Outside, there were car horns so that Hassan leaned closer to be fully heard. "If you were not Mrs. Plumley but . . . Who were you before? Your name?"

"It was Butterfield."

"Butterfield? If you were not Mrs. Plumley but Miss Butterfield, and if I was me, as I am now, I would tell you that I'd never let you be sad in all my life. I would make sure you never were."

No one could keep such a promise, of course. Nor could Florrie reply in the way he hoped she would. Yet she knew that Hassan meant well by this, that he was speaking bravely. "But I am Mrs. Plumley," she murmured as she retrieved her left arm.

She wrote about all of it. In those twenty-nine years of marriage, Florrie kept a diary. She didn't write daily, or even weekly. But she'd make notes of what she saw or heard in each place that could never have been found in a guidebook or on a map: the geckos on the walls in Havana, the tangerine hue of the monks' robes in Nepal, the size and weight of the avocados that grew in the gardens of all the Caribbean countries. She noted how crowds of ten thousand people could move and think like one single creature, how taxis would, sometimes, strap coffins to their roofs. And she recorded, too, the astounding plumbago, the *citron pressés*, the slack, pale haunches of Indian cattle that set themselves down in the middle of the street so that traffic had to part like a river around a rock. She learned of the Kennedy assassination whilst drinking iced tea with the Memsahib Lunch Club and they'd all clutched their chests or each other, beneath the ceiling fan. All these things would be written down, in Florrie's diary: *Birds open their mouths here, pant.*

She boarded trains and buses, took carts pulled by mules, rode bicycles and walked. She entered foothills. She traveled down the coastal road, with the sea glittering. She climbed down from buses at quiet, dusty settlements where people stepped out from their houses to see her buttermilk hair, to eye her with suspicion. She could have been afraid. Sometimes she was. But mostly, there was only kindness offered to her—a bed in a corner, a bowl of food, gestured directions to a church on a hillside which looked abandoned, at first sight, but in which Florrie found a swallow's nest and a ceiling painted with moons and stars. And in that church, she wrote it all down. *I can hear goats as I'm writing this.* And she sent love to all her loved people—starry, goat-scented love.

What else did she see? And write of?

She remembers a rhino passing by her—so close that she could hear its brittle gauze of flies, could have touched its spine. She remembers the bananaquit birds. On swimming off the Cuban coast, she'd been startled by a pop of air to find a turtle surfacing next to her; it had stared at her with outrage before sinking back down like a dustbin lid—and she'd written of this in her letters, knowing that Pinky's boys would be thrilled to hear of a turtle's appearance in Auntie Florrie's life. She remembers, too, standing on the equator with Victor. He'd taken a photograph—Florrie astride a painted white line, one foot in the northern hemisphere and one in the south, with her hands on her hips in a defiant, happy pose and covered in so much dust that she looked like brickwork. That night, he'd raised a glass of beer: "To you and me, Mrs. P."

And cricket: How could she not write of that, every time she saw a version of it? Even if only in passing, through the window of a train? There was cricket on the beach at Mombasa; cricket in the dusty alleyways of Delhi where stray dogs would lift their legs against the stumps. In Bombay, she spent a whole day—from sunrise to sunset—at the Oval Maidan. The palm trees swayed, monkeys scratched their underarms, fruit-sellers approached her with lychees or sweet limes—yet it was her childhood garden that Florrie saw, as she sat there: trellises and hydrangeas, with Gulliver as umpire. *Butterfield wins it! A six!*

This, too: toward the end of their married, traveling life, Florrie—in her fifties by then—saw Mount Everest. She didn't climb it, of course. But she'd trekked for six days to its base camp and, on arriving, had broken down. She'd knelt on the bleached, shingled ground and wept—for the beauty, the peace, the steaming yaks, for Victor and Pinky and Pinky's boys. She wept for Bobs and her parents. She wept with gratitude. And she cried, too, for having known joy (oh, that small, lovely word)—joy, in the truest meaning of it—for a handful of minutes when she was seventeen years old. Florrie cried until it hurt her. Then she quieted—and sat, listening to her surroundings: the gentle clinking of camping equipment and small, watery sounds.

Who might ever know that Florrie has lived in such places? That this dumpling of a woman with a chopped-off leg had, in Cairo, lain in the dark bedroom, stared at the shuttered windows and imagined the sand and fellucas and date palms and bony, homeless cats slinking through the dark? She'd imagined Hassan abu Zahra—in his linen *jellabiya*, reading underneath a single filament. In another life, Florrie might have kindled the spark in her heart for Hassan; she might have blown on it, like embers, as he'd kneaded her forearms across the Formica tabletop. *Habibi*, he'd told her, means "beloved one."

Tonight, she sits in her mallard chair with her diary on her lap. And, as she sits—surrounded by the deep nocturnal silence and the occasional chime from the church—Florrie has a better understanding of herself. How she feels. This new, sudden sadness that came to her today? Perhaps it isn't new at all. It is Hackney. It is *what happened*. It is the night above all other nights. Above all, it is love: because for all those six men have meant to her, for all that she's loved her parents and Bobs and Pinky and Gladness and Emmanuel explaining poetry on the Pont des Arts and Gulliver, even, who'd blink his love with a satisfied mew, there's a love that surpasses all of them—all of them, combined. The pike? It's the pain of having that love but with nowhere to put it; it throbs all the time, like her missing leg.

The London business. It. The thing with Great-Aunt Euphemia.

The dark-stoned building on Lower Clapton Road.

The doctors had talked of psychosis. "Electric shock treatment, Sister Mary. That's the thing for this one."

How determined Florrie had been—aged seventeen, on fire with grief—that she'd never say a word of it. How certain she'd been that saying nothing whatsoever would be the only way to survive. But here she is now—in a room with Nepalese prayer flags and tartans and a framed print of plumbago and an eighty-eighth birthday on its way— and she finds that yes, yes, she wants to speak of it. She *needs* to—as a rattling kettle on a stove must be lifted to one side, or the heat turned down. "I've got," she whispers to the painted lemons, "to tell someone about it all."

Wise Pinks. Lovely Pinky Topham, who'd never grown too old for pulling faces across a crowded room or pressing her best friend's nose like a doorbell. *Hello in there.* If she were here now, she'd say to Florrie, *Oh, thank goodness! At* last.

Florrie sniffs.

She'll speak of it, then—*It.* But to whom? Renata would be the obvious choice. But what Florrie sees, at this moment (staring at the discarded conch shell that she herself had dived for, off the coast of Tanganyika), is that it's someone else she wants to tell this story to. She's had so many good, lovely people in her life. But only now, at Babbington, has she found the person it's worth being honest with, the person who would not (she's reasonably certain) be appalled or back away. Rather, he'd look kindly at her. He'd murmur, *Gosh* or *Right-o.*

Not yet, she thinks—but soon. When all this is over.

Florrie makes her way to bed, turns out the light.

In the dark, she thinks of surprises. There have, of course, been many in her life. Some have been her very worst moments (Herbert's death, the news of Pinky's lump—and her second lump, and her third). But haven't there been some wonderful ones, too? And haven't those been far greater in number than the bad? No one could have imagined those tiny translucent frogs in Northern Rhodesia whose internal organs could be seen through the skin, like the busy mechanics of a carriage clock. Middle Morag, too; how did she appear, with her Gaelic tales and friendship with corvids, her passion for single malts? And how surprised Florrie had been when Pinky had phoned her in Cuba to speak of Far End.

"Far what?"

"Far End. It's a cottage. In Shropshire. She's left it to you. Do you know, she was one hundred and four? Died in her sleep in the grounds of Windsor Castle; friends with the Duke of Edinburgh, apparently, which I never knew. Anyway, she's left it to you."

In Havana, Florrie lowered herself down to the tiled flooring. *Why me?* But they both knew the answer: because Euphemia had understood. Because she'd lifted Florrie from a metal, bloodied bed and tended to Florrie's wounds, in the days that followed—and one does not forget such deeds, or hushed exchanges. "Butters. Just accept that she was fond of you."

All these kind people. All these surprises she's had in her life—and here, now, is one more: in her cosy bed in an old apple store, Florrie thinks of those braces, how he'd folded himself into a deckchair and struggled to get back out. How lucky I am, Florrie thinks, to have found such a new, dear friend! And so *late* in life, too—when one does not really expect new friendships. She wonders if this (if he, Stanhope) is not the best surprise of all.

26

Florrie and Stanhope Visit Four People

Florrie has never been entirely sure what Franklin's job title is. As she understands it, he came to Babbington to mend taps, sweep leaves and generally assist the gardener, Norman, who'd been an affable, creaking man not much younger than most of the residents here. But after his retirement, no new gardener arrived. Franklin merely seemed to move into the role, learning about the pruning of roses via the internet and taking photos of fungi or birds' eggs on his phone. So perhaps he is, technically, the gardener now. (No one else tends to the grounds, after all.) But he's also the man who unblocks lavatories or fiddles with the fire alarm, who salts the steps in frosty weather. It was Franklin who ascended a rickety ladder last spring to pop wire cages over the chimneypots to thwart the jackdaws (and failed). It will, Florrie knows, have been Franklin who swept up the shattered chutney jar of flowers. So, no, she's not quite sure what his official title is.

Nevertheless, he must be spoken to. And thus it is toward Franklin's shed that she and Stanhope are heading. Florrie feels marginally better today. Stanhope, she knows, has noticed this—although he hasn't said as much. He's only glanced over at her, once in a while, with a benign, relieved expression, as she's chatted about nightjars and Bembe's feather. She decides to broach the matter.

"I'm sorry for being blue yesterday. It was the heat, I think. And there are so many feelings, at the moment—aren't there?"

"Feelings?"

"I worry for Renata, and I'm sad for Nancy. Even for Tabitha Brimble upstairs. I still miss Arthur. And on top of that, there's somebody here at Babbington Hall who's not what they seem, Stanhope—dangerous, even—which isn't nice to think of. How quickly it's all happened, too." This is perfectly true. Only six days ago, she'd been out in the grounds with her floppy hat and secateurs, snipping away at buttercups with no thoughts beyond wishing to try to cheer up Renata. Who could have imagined all that's come since then?

"Ah," he says, in his kindly manner. "There's no need to explain. I'm only glad you're feeling a little better. These are strange times, Florrie. Yes, very strange."

So here they are, making their way along the gravel path on a brand-new, sun-bright Thursday morning. Stanhope is making his *dab-shush-shush*; there's a rhythmic squeak to her wheels—and over the top of these noises Stanhope explains that last night, in bed, he devised a plan. "I thought it all through. We need to see their handwriting, yes? Of all four of them? See if any of these people write in a swirly, fancy way—treble clefs and whatnot? Well, I've worked out how to get it—four ways, one for each of them."

"Lovely. What do you need me to do?"

"Would you be kind enough to look after this for me?" He produces a spiral notebook with a pen tucked into its spine; Florrie takes it and pops it between her thighs as if putting bread in a toaster.

Franklin's shed appears—a rectangular building of red brick and ivy, with a blue plastic barrel underneath its downpipe. But their attention is caught by the half-open door. Through that door, Florrie can see a pair of legs—in black canvas trousers with reinforced knees—stretched out. As they come nearer, more is revealed: Franklin is sitting in a camping chair with his feet on an upturned bucket. He is virtually parallel to the concrete floor; he lies, rather than sits. In one hand, he is holding a coffee mug; it rests on his chest, on his grubby T-shirt. In the other, he holds a mobile phone, the screen of which he is stroking vertically with the pad of his thumb. His position is such that his lower half is almost off the chair entirely, and his trousers, Florrie notes, are so low this morning that most of his behind (mercifully clad in greying cotton underpants) is hanging down, above the waistband, and is a mere inch or two from the floor.

They both pause, for a moment, unconvinced. It's somewhat of a stretch, she admits, to imagine that this individual might be capable of obsessive love and declarations. But who knows what our own selves are capable of? And can't so much be hidden from view?

Stanhope says, "Knock-knock?"

A single noise follows—*Yup?*—which Stanhope takes as permission to push the door wide. In doing so, Franklin—Babbington's groundsman, maintenance worker and odd-job man, the man who was once overheard by Magda to break wind so loudly that she scolded him in hissed, furious Polish—comes into clearer view. Florrie notes the Thermos flask, the empty packet of crisps. Franklin looks marginally surprised but doesn't move. He glances up once before looking back at his phone. "All right?"

There's a scent of coffee, of earth and diesel—and a slightly darker animal scent which Florrie suspects might be Franklin's boots, for the laces are untied, the tongues loosened. "Forgive the intrusion," says Stanhope.

Franklin shrugs, continues to scroll. "S'okay. I'm not busy. What's up?"

It's a question that Stanhope's not used to. She can see him dithering, internally, on what, precisely, it means: What *is* up? He chooses to reply with a question of his own. "All fine in here?"

"Fine?" Franklin sniffs. It's a damp, purposeful sniff after which he swallows. "Yeah, I guess. I mean, the ground's still like bloody concrete and I'm not a fan of this weather. Heatstroke's a real thing, you know?"

"After Renata, I mean. We mean."

"Oh, right. Yeah, it's weird, isn't it? I'm not, like, distraught. I mean, she's my boss and it's definitely sad, you know? But I'm not, like, friends with her or anything."

Stanhope blinks twice and rearranges his expression into something neutral. "But you swept where she fell, I think? That must have been a very difficult thing to do."

At that, the younger man sets down his mug, removes his feet from the upturned bucket, inches himself into an upright position and pushes his phone into a back pocket. He scratches his bristly jaw. "It was all right. You couldn't see much. The bricks looked the same; I mean, if you fall onto bricks, you're the one who'll be damaged, right? Not bricks that have been there for three hundred years or something. If there was any blood, I didn't see it. The rain must have washed most of it away. Listen, I can't say the whole thing is nice because it isn't, is it? But I've had worse to clear up in my time. I've worked in pubs. Do you know the Black Bull on Cleaver Street?"

There's a general consensus that, no, they don't know the Black Bull, and Franklin says they're lucky, starts to mutter about the landlord who's got it coming to him if he doesn't mind his manners, and, sensing the conversation is running away from what matters, Stanhope raises a hand to gently interrupt him. "Franklin? Sorry. Yes. We were wondering, Florrie and I—there's a rose."

"A rose?"

"Apricot, in colour. With a pinkish hue to its outer petals. Very pretty. It grows near the lavender bed on the south side, toward the church. We were wondering if you knew its name?"

Franklin's face adopts a thinking expression: he twists his jaw, as if something's stuck in his teeth and he's using his tongue to remove it. "Apricot rose . . . not sure. Norman planted most of the roses, not me. Is it, like, this high? With pinky-orangey bits?"

"Exactly that one."

"Golden Sunset, maybe? Something like that."

"Lovely. Thank you. Well, could I ask that you write that down for us? So we remember? I have a sister who adores roses and I think she'd quite love that one. Florrie, I believe you have a notebook and pen? May I?"

Franklin's baffled. "You want me to write it down for you?"

"My hands aren't what they were, Franklin—you wait till you get to our age, young man! Anyway, we'll probably forget its name as soon as we're out the door!" He laughs at his own joke; Florrie laughs, in support.

Franklin writes the name down, returns the pen and notebook.

Once around the corner, they open the notebook. *GOLDEN SUN-SET.* The handwriting is tiny, evenly spaced in a gradual slanting down the page. The letters are all capitalized; they aren't joined up at any point, as if printed. In short, it's not the handwriting they're looking for.

"Well, I think we probably knew it wouldn't be. Obsession takes effort, after all."

She tends to the pleats in her pink gingham dress. "You have a sister, Stanhope?" He hadn't mentioned this on the sherry afternoon.

"Me? No, I'm afraid not. Only child. This sister is a complete fabrication of mine—but just for today, I hope a jolly useful one."

The kitchen at Babbington Hall is seen as private land. Despite several doors leading into it—all swinging both ways, all with little round windows in them—there's a definite sense of the kitchen being out of bounds to residents, a point beyond which one must never go. No sign actually says this. But everyone knows, even the staff, that beyond these doors it is the kingdom of Clive.

Stanhope, being tall enough, is able to peer through one of the windows. In fact, he must stoop to do so. "He's in there, Florrie. He's seen me—but I think he's pretending that he hasn't. He's doing something with a spoon."

Beyond the doors, Florrie hears a clatter. There's the low rumble of commercial radio, the hum of the chest freezer and the single, hard sound of Clive clearing his throat. A tap bursts on, smashes water in the sink, then stops. There is no point in knocking or calling out.

Florrie pushes the door with her foot and they enter. He—Clive— remains impassive. There's no acknowledgement of them beyond a slight twitch of an eyebrow; he stirs a pan of boiling water. "I follow orders, I'm on a budget and I don't do birthday cakes."

Imagine, she thinks, the life he must have had—a chef in the navy, slicing and dicing for ravenous sailors, peering out of portholes at passing icebergs or tropical coastlines. It feels a partly familiar life to Florrie, and in recent months she has rather wanted to sit down with Clive and ask him about it: Did they ever dock in Mombasa? Has he ever eaten durian fruit? But Clive does not radiate any proper bonhomie. She has never felt brave enough to ask such questions—and here they are, having wandered into this kitchen without warning. Florrie beams. "No, no—we aren't here for a birthday cake."

"A complaint? Because let me tell you this: I always do yolks runny. It's how a yolk should be. And if I have one more moan from those bloody sisters . . ."

Clive is not a small man. Underneath his apron, there is a rather solid mound of abdomen—a belly that, if prodded, would surely offer a springy resistance (unlike the Butterfield mound). She guesses that he's well into his fifties but he may be younger; the general air of Clive is that he's lived a challenging life. His forehead is permanently bunched. His hair is almost gone entirely. And Clive's forearms are tattooed, scarred and surprisingly hairy things, with the girth of an average thigh. Moreover, his tattoos are not like Magda's. Whilst hers are still a vivid green and have their own strange beauty, Clive's are faded. They're mostly words—blurred, as if they've run in the rain.

"Gosh, no," says Stanhope. "Not a complaint. Rather, we're here to compliment you. Do you remember how much I liked the rhubarb crumble? I told you a few weeks ago. We were wondering—Florrie and I—if we might have the recipe?"

These words cause Clive to set his spoon down. He wrinkles his forehead further, suspicious. "The recipe? For crumble?"

"For *your* crumble. There was a secret ingredient, surely? I've been telling Florrie all about it. She missed out on it, didn't you?"

"I did, sadly. My mistake."

"Perhaps you used cinnamon? There was a definite spice to it."

Clive hesitates. He glances between the two of them as if assessing their worthiness, as if their whole lives are being weighed up in his two broad hands, to see if they're deserving of his crumble recipe. "Ginger," he says. "Fresh ginger root, grated—not powdered, understand? My mother swore by it. A touch of ginger brings a bit of heat to the sharpness. You need less sugar if you use ginger. And I might add a touch of allspice, depending on my mood."

"Ginger in the crumble mix, too?"

"Not in the crumble. But I use ground almonds in it. My invention, that. Works in any crumble—apple, plum. The lads used to love it, at sea. Said mine was the best crumble they'd ever tasted and they weren't just being nice, those boys." His eyes seem to glisten; he looks away.

Stanhope asks if Clive might be willing to pop this information down, on paper. "It's for my sister. She'd adore the recipe. I know she would. She loves rhubarb, you see, but it's a fickle vegetable, isn't it? Only a few ways to truly enjoy it."

"Marvelous vegetable," Clive corrects him sternly, finger raised. "Overlooked, to my mind. People who don't like it just don't understand it. Now, I don't normally give out the recipe, Mr. Jones. But on this occasion, I am willing. Just make sure your sister knows that it comes from me, that it's *my* recipe. Got it?"

"Clive's crumble. Got it—yes, absolutely."

"And fresh grated ginger, not powdered. That's the key. Tell her?"

"I will."

Thus Clive writes it down. And as he writes, Florrie eyes the movement of his pen: is it erratic, angular? Is there a flourish on the *g*? But when he slides the paper back across the worktop, she sees how flat the handwriting is—squashed, as if a weight had been laid down on it, so that his *a*'s and *d*'s are virtually the same. The *f* of fresh ginger is a plain business—as all his other letters are.

"Not him, either," says Stanhope afterward.

"Not him."

Reuben—dearest, portly, self-conscious Reuben—is far harder to find. Stanhope knows he's at work today, having heard his voice through an open window. "But that was just after breakfast. So I'm not sure where he might be now."

Rather than wandering the corridors, they decide it might be prudent to try the staff room first. This, not unlike the kitchen, has an air of mystery to it. The room is located in the heart of the Hall—near the central staircase and the Babbington portraits—and is hidden from the world by an elderly, studded door that wouldn't be amiss in a Tudor castle. Who knows what lies behind it? Sofas, kettles, postcards from foreign holidays, a biscuit tin? But Florrie has never been inside it. No resident has, to her knowledge.

It's Magda who opens the door. She opens it in a Magda-like fashion—languid, uninterested, with a heavy sigh. But her expression softens when she sees Florrie. She props open the door with her hipbone. "Reuben?" She ponders. "I am not sure. Earlier, I know the Mistry woman had him." *Had him*—as if Marcella might have thrown open a trapdoor, grasped poor Reuben and dragged him inside, spider-like. "But maybe he is with Georgette now—in the office?"

Away from the staff room, Stanhope and Florrie agree that they will take themselves to the reception hall and wait underneath the Babbingtons for Reuben's reappearance; when he leaves the manager's office, he has no choice except to wander past them, toward the lifts and the external door. "That's when we'll ask him, Stanhope."

"Right-o."

So they sit—Florrie in her chair, Stanhope on the leatherette arm-chair with tweedy armrests. And, by sitting next to each other, the height difference between Stanhope and Florrie is no longer quite so marked. Just as it had been by the compost heap, a few days before, she can see him with more clarity—the tortoiseshell rims to his spectacles, the various shades of grey in his neatly trimmed moustache. She looks at his hand, how it's close to her own.

"A rakish look, don't you think? Like he's up to no good?"

Momentarily, Florrie thinks he's referring to himself. But then she realizes that Stanhope's considering the largest of the Babbington portraits—of a shrewd, smirking, bearded gent in a vast coat that comes down to the ground, one hand on his hip. In the background, there are distant smoking chimneys rising from the landscape. "I suppose he's the one that did something with mineshafts. Ventilation?"

"Ventilation, yes. Or that's what Renata told me, anyway—on my first day here."

They contemplate the Babbington features. They pass a few more gentle remarks on such matters as how the lampshades need a light dusting, or how this reception hall really does have the most wonderful view—and then they hear, in the distance, a familiar rhythmic sound, like a pair of knitting needles. The sound grows louder; Stanhope murmurs, "Oh please, no . . . ," and Edith and Emily Ellwood come into reception with their arms linked, their heads down, their feet moving in a curious scurry. They are engaged in some sort of furious, clackety disagreement. ("That's *not* what you said, Edie." "It is *exactly* what I said!" "I'm afraid it absolutely *isn't* what you said *and*, Edith Ellwood, I don't care for your tone." "*My* tone? *Mine?* How *very dare* you!") They barrel past the reception desk.

But then, of course, they stop. On seeing Stanhope and Florrie, they skitter to a halt and straighten in unison. A half second of blinking is followed by simpering smiles. "Oh, how lovely to see you both! Florrie! And Stanhope! What are you both doing just . . . sitting here?"

Between them, they manage to bluster an answer: taking a rest, admiring the Babbingtons. Florrie wonders loudly if she's acquired a stone in her shoe. "Also, it occurred to me," offers Stanhope, "that I've never actually sat in this chair before! Not in the whole six months I've been here! So I just thought that I'd sit here. See what it's like."

Emily's unconvinced. "And what *is* it like?"

"Very nice. Yes. Comfy. I might sit here again."

The Ellwoods are clearly disappointed. They'd hoped for better answers than this; their smiles droop at the edges and they glance at one another as if to say, Dear, dear . . . With no scent of gossip in the air, they make their excuses—"Do come and sit with us again, Florrie, won't you? We *did* enjoy tea the other day . . ."—and file into their quarters, close the door.

"Golly," Stanhope says under his breath. "I thought they'd find us out."

A moment later, a door opens and closes. The floorboards creak. And Reuben comes into view with that slow, endearing lollop of his, his shoulders hunched as if this will somehow lessen his height or make him disappear entirely. His skin looks particularly raw today— as red as a berry, down by his chin. He glances down at his clipboard as he goes, which means he fails to see the edge of the rug, catches his toe, and although he rights himself he blushes at the brief indignity and at the large shudder and boom that it makes. Even Florrie can feel the reverberation, under her wheels.

Stanhope has already risen. "Young sir! May we have a brief word?"

This declaration startles him.

"You aren't in any trouble," Stanhope assures him. "Far from it. It's merely a question that we were hoping you might answer. A strange question, possibly."

How old is he? Twenty? Just, perhaps. He partly seems older—but Reuben is, Florrie thinks, a boy who has happened to grow into this strapping, physically adult body before he's ready for it; he's not yet at ease with his hormones and limbs and facial hair, or his slight speech impediment.

"Is there any news?" Stanhope keeps his left hand on his chest, as if pressing his imaginary hat to it. "On Renata, I mean."

The carer looks back to the clipboard, as if the answer is written there. "Um, no. Not really. They say that even if she wakes up, she might not be able to talk very well, or move like she used to. She might not remember anything."

"But there's no change, as such—that you know of?"

Reuben shakes his head. "I thought she was happy here. I mean, she's quiet, I know. But I'm quiet, too—and she said that it was all right to be quiet; it's just some people's way of it. I didn't know she felt so . . ."

"You're fond of her, I see." Stanhope nods sympathetically. "As am I, I might add. Lovely girl."

Reuben looks back at the clipboard. "You, um, said you had a question? If you need Dr. Mallory, he's here, at the moment. I could—"

"The question," says Stanhope. "Yes. No need to bother the good doctor. It's regarding my morning pills, Reuben. I believe we all get a multivitamin—all of us. You get it too, don't you, Florrie?"

"Do I? Yes, yes, I do. The oval one? Yellowish?"

"Yellowish. That's it—isn't it?"

Reuben nods.

"Lovely. Good. Now, do you happen to know the brand name?"

The poor boy is baffled. "The brand name? Um . . . We get it from the surgery. Fortissimo, I think? I can check with Georgette."

"Fortissimo. Marvelous. I only ask because I feel so much *better* for it and I'd like to tell my sister about it. Could you write the name down?"

He does so, hands the notebook back. And in the slightly awkward silence that follows, Stanhope says, "We're sorry to hear you'll be leaving us, Reuben."

"Thursday," he answers—and then nods once, as if reinforcing this notion to himself. "I just can't . . . I mean, it's . . ."

They smile at him, as grandparents might. *Ah, Reuben. We know.*

This, then, is how they acquire the handwriting of Reuben, which, Florrie notes, is not what she expected it to be. What had she imagined? That it might be ungainly, small—as if ashamed to be written on paper at all? But how delighted she is to see that his handwriting is, in fact, a thing of beauty: italicized and even, placed centrally on the paper with quiet confidence. It's the kind of writing one might find on a scroll or decree, but it's not fancy enough, she decides, for a magenta envelope.

After Reuben's departure, Stanhope turns to her. "I'd say he loves her, Florrie. There was something in his sadness that made me think so. Perhaps it's why he's given his notice, do you think? Young love can be terribly strong, can't it?"

"It can."

"But he didn't send a card with a nightjar on it."

No, Reuben did not. And as they leave the reception hall, a little downhearted, Florrie glances back to the door in its far corner. Are they there? The Ellwoods? On the far side of that door with their palms pressed against it, holding their breath to hear every word? Are they watching her now, through the keyhole? What they've seen and heard, in their time . . . Florrie imagines their eyes, as bright as candles—like those in the sockets of Magda's inky, watching skull.

There is a final name on the list. Since it's approaching lunchtime, Florrie wonders if refreshments aren't in order—a pot of tea or a gin and tonic—before finding Aubrey Horner. But there's a firm set to Stanhope's jaw when he considers Aubrey's name. "Right," he says, rotating a shoulder as if preparing for something physical. "Let's get this over with."

Just as it would be both fair and rather unkind to declare the Ellwoods gossiping sorts, so it would be to call the retired army major a bore and a tedious flirt. For whereas Reuben is clearly uncomfortable being himself, Aubrey Horner is so delighted to be Aubrey Horner that it seems he wishes to speak about himself whenever he can. He will pause in the corridor to speak of the Falklands conflict; he'll hear a word, any word—*aspirin, tree, custard, November*—and say, "Ah, that reminds me of the time when I was . . ." This doesn't mean that Florrie doesn't *like* Aubrey. Nor does it mean that he doesn't have a generous heart, that his feelings can't be hurt or that he can't have lonely days. But, simply put, Aubrey is not a gentleman from whom it's easy to slip away. Once a story's started, an hour can be lost. Florrie has heard many accounts of battle formations, of Aubrey's narrow escapes.

He prefers, too, a female audience. Aubrey is known for the ease with which he feels able to sit himself down on a sofa next to someone—an Ellwood or Velma Rudge—without warning, so closely that their knees and elbows touch, and say, "Have I ever told you about my experience at Goose Green?" Some residents have literally hidden on seeing him—behind a hedge or a drawn curtain—or locked the door of the accessible loo. Marcella Mistry—who suffers no fools—has swatted Aubrey away like a wasp, snapping, "Away! Away!"

"I don't mind him, on the whole," Florrie replies.

"Nor do I, I suppose. But I'm afraid I found myself sitting beside him at lunch a few days ago."

"Ah."

"Quite. Something to do with a bombed frigate. But we can do this, Florrie—we can."

Aubrey's quarters are part of the old pig sties. But whereas Stanhope's home is at one end of the terrace, Aubrey's is at the other. He's made that corner of Babbington his own—with his easel, deckchair and footstool, a metal wheelbarrow planted with geraniums. He's sitting there now—wearing a straw hat, with a small glass of beer beside him. He's gazing across to the tower of St. Mary's with a paintbrush in his hand.

He turns, sees them approach. "There he is! Stanhope Jones! And the ravishing Florrie with her . . ."—he gestures, admiringly, at her upper abdomen. "How are you today? Pull up a pew, won't you?"

"We can't stay, I'm afraid. We've got . . . commitments. But we would love the quickest of words with you, Aubrey."

He sets down his paintbrush, narrows an eye. "We had a good chat, you and I—didn't we, Stanhope? Two men chatting about the old days? I told him, Florrie, about a lad I knew during my Falkland years. It's a good story. He was only a nipper—eighteen, nineteen—and a Yorkshireman, of all things. And we were on patrol one day, when I noticed the most enormous—"

"Aubrey? Forgive me. That's why we're here. That story—yes. You mentioned a frigate, I think. Would you believe I've entirely forgotten the name of it?"

"Frigate? Which one? I've known many frigates in my time."

"It sank something . . . And you saw an albatross from it."

"Aha!" He raises a finger. "You're thinking of HMS *Alacrity*. Gorgeous, she was—one of the best of her type. Took out an Argentine transport ship, which they weren't happy about, I can tell you. That was our girl, though. She knew how to handle her menfolk, she did.

Or rather, she let *us* handle *her*! How about that, Stanhope? Eh?" And he laughs with his whole body, shaking in his chair.

Stanhope adjusts his walking stick, unsure how to answer. "Very good. Right—*Alacrity*. Thank you. Could I ask you to write its name down?"

"Write its name? Down, on paper? What on earth for, Stanhope? You aren't a journalist, are you? Trying to write my life story without paying a penny for it?"

There's an uneasy laugh. "Gosh, no. It's simply that . . ."

Florrie waits. Aubrey waits. They both look at Stanhope, waiting for the reason.

". . . I believe it's a crossword answer. A crossword. Today's. And by the time I get back home, I'm sure I'll have forgotten the word. *Alarm?*"

"Alacrity." Aubrey remains unconvinced but he reaches to the side of him, into the metal box, and retrieves an artist's pencil; whilst searching for it, he mutters, "Pencil, pencil . . ."

They watch him write the word.

He hands the notebook back. "I tell you this, Stanhope: the day my memoirs are written—not by me, because I'm too busy for that— they'll sell straight off the shelves. Bestseller, film rights—the lot. I was there for the end of poor HMS *Ardent*—have I told you that story? Oh, I've got tales." He glances across to Florrie. "Of course, there are some things a gentleman couldn't possibly tell . . . The women in Ascension were—"

Stanhope announces a task he'd forgotten about—"You know the one, Florrie? That thing you said you'd help me with?"—and for a moment, she's entirely nonplussed before saying, "Ah, yes—that."

Aubrey salutes at their departure. As they leave, Florrie glances back and thinks how contented he seems—in the deckchair, on this warm summer's day with its woodpigeon sounds. He watches them, salutes again. But if he woos every woman who passes and talks of himself so frequently, how content can he truly be? How lonely might

he feel inside? She thinks she should spend more time with Aubrey—
both she and Stanhope should, perhaps, when all of this is over, when
Renata is well.

HMS *Alacrity*, Fortissimo, GOLDEN SUNSET, and a recipe for rhubarb crumble. All the writing is different. All of it has its own merits
and quirks—but none of it's Gothic or looped.

"Drat," he says. "What now?"

Florrie has no idea.

She looks up. There's a crunching ahead. Dr. Mallory is making
his way over the gravel toward his car. He is in his shirtsleeves with his
jacket folded over a forearm, the other arm carrying his black medical
bag. Florrie considers him—confident, broad-shouldered. He presses
something that unlocks his car (which is as red as a glacé cherry) and
opens the door, puts his bag and jacket inside—and Florrie wonders
who he's been visiting here. She supposes it's poor Tabitha Brimble
again, restless and unhappy. Or it's the doddery Kitty Lim. Or it's
Nancy Tapp—waiting in her sparse little room, surrounded by boxes
she never unpacked. (How long now till she leaves for St. Chad's?
Three days? Two?)

"By the way, Florrie—it wasn't him, either. He prescribed me
sleeping pills recently and I watched him write the prescription. Have
you even seen how he writes? I'm amazed the chemists can decipher it.
It's fortunate I didn't receive suppositories or contraception tablets by
mistake. Anyway, the Ellwoods tell me he's seeing a married woman
down near Woodstock—although who knows where they got that
rumour from. They started it themselves, perhaps." He sighs, watching the doctor drive away. "That reminds me: Florrie, I have something to confess."

Confess? The sun is behind Stanhope so that she can't read
his expression.

"Yesterday? After our lime cordials on the terrace? The Ellwoods joined me, I'm afraid. Asked if I knew anymore about your missing leg. And I shouldn't really have said anything, I know, but I couldn't help feeling irritated that they were still asking such things; it's your business, not theirs. So I told them you lost it in a motorcycle accident in the Peruvian Andes. Forgive me."

Forgive him? There's nothing to forgive. Florrie never made it to South America. Now, realistically, she probably never will. But how lovely to think that the Ellwoods believe otherwise—that they will whisper now of the leather-wearing Florrie, the Florrie who rode through high mountain passes, who fired up her Ducati with a single downward push of the heel before adjusting her goggles and setting forth. A far better story, she thinks, than tripping over one's feet in the kitchen.

"Thank you, Stanhope."

"Anytime."

What now? What is left? Who can they speak to? Stanhope suggests a pot of tea in his quarters and considering it over an almond slice—but Florrie declines. It has been a curious day. She'd started it feeling hopeful; now, she is less so. Even the shiny, fictional Ducati and her Andean adventure can't lift her spirits back up.

She has always been aware of that strong, inner voice that says yes—the instinct one has when something is right (like Tigh Beag or marrying Victor or taking her job in L'Hôtel Petit Palais). But sometimes there is, too, the other little voice—which tells you when something's not right at all. And whilst it's easier, by far, to ignore this voice, to send it to the corner like a misbehaving dog, that doesn't stop it from saying (or shouting, even), *No, it's not right* or *Florence, you stupid girl.*

It was Mrs. Fortescue, their neighbour, who'd first used that adjective. Miss Cecily Catchpole, too, favoured it; to her, Florrie was

stupid—as well as *cumbersome, oafish* and *on the chubby side.* It didn't
stop from Florrie putting her hand up in class. "Come *on*, Florence.
We're all waiting . . ." But so often she'd give an answer to which Miss
Catchpole, delighted, would trill out, "Wrong!"

She was never called such names on Vicarage Lane. There, Florrie
was *cheery* and *button-bright* and *our lovely little Flo*—and she preferred
to believe this, at first. But then she moved into her teenaged years and
onward—and so came all the other moments of wrongness: knocking
over a line of skis outside Le Bar de Glace; popping the seams of a pencil
skirt from the act of bending down; misunderstanding the mechanics
of the little folding stool she was handed, in Africa, so that it collapsed
underneath her on her first morning and Jack Luckett said, "Jesus
Christ, woman"—and strained like a rope as he'd tried to haul her up.

Getting it wrong in France—with absinthe and Gaston. Getting it
wrong by being in France at all—and this feeling of horror, and failure, this voice of *What were you thinking of?* which accompanied her as
she rushed home from Zermatt to be with Bobs before he died. Getting it wrong at ambassadorial parties by undercooking the lobster or
forgetting the name of the French president's wife. Getting it wrong
with her own feet, on the infamous night of the dropped mulled wine.
Getting it wrong with Arthur—for *she* should have gone to see *him*,
perhaps, to find out what he'd uncovered on the night he fell. (Would
he still be living, if she'd done so? Tied his laces differently, in a tighter
knot?) Getting it wrong with Edward Silversmith by believing that
she, Florrie Butterfield, might be enough for him, that he meant it
when he said he'd love her all his life; that he wouldn't see women like
Clemency Winthrop and drop Florrie's hand, without hesitation. Getting it wrong by having not spoken of *It* for so long.

"Florrie? You look quite pale."

Has she got it wrong again? Dumpy, girlish, one-legged Florrie.
(In Montmartre, she'd had enough French to understand the meaning

of *Elle est une petite boulette . . .*) "Stanhope? Am I a fool? Have we got
this wrong?"

"Wrong?"

"Maybe she did jump. Maybe she did want to die."

"Renata? No. She is in love, remember? She *loves* someone—and
for the first time. And she wanted to go to Paris, to watch Wimbledon
fortnight—to *live*, remember? She didn't jump, Florrie, and you are not
a fool." He's as stern as he must have been in his schoolteacher days.
Put that away. Quiet down.

But even so, the voice inside Florrie has woken; it swims, she
knows, with the yellow-eyed pike. *Stupid and clumsy and wrong.*

Back in her room, she thinks that she got it wrong with her family,
too. *I should have told Prudence. I should have found her*—rootling
through the coal bunker or practising an arabesque or sitting on the
bench at the end of the garden with Pip—and said, There's something
you should know. For what would she have done? Or Bobs, or any of
them? No one would have disowned her. They'd have been shocked,
certainly, and would have felt it best that the neighbours didn't know;
but they wouldn't have loved Florrie any less. And if she'd confessed
everything, there would have been no distances. For the rest of her
life, Florrie could have slotted her fingers through her mother's own
without feeling the lie, the secret inside her. *I'm not who you think I am.*
I should have told her.

But Florrie never did. And so, when the news reached Florrie that
Prudence Butterfield née Sitwell had died (having had a stroke at the
kitchen table, with a burnt apple pie cooling on the side), it was regret
that rushed into Florrie, along with shock and grief and rage and a
deluge of love—as if she were empty, and all this was thundering, fast-
flowing water that filled her entirely. Florrie had been in Kathmandu.
She'd been preparing for dinner with the chef de mission, squeezing

herself into a crêpe burgundy dress, when Victor had knocked on the bedroom door. "Florrie? Oh, my darling Flo . . ."

I should have told her. I should have told her. She thought this over and over—as they flew home on various aircraft, as flowers were ordered and hymns were sung, as Florrie stared at the coffin, which seemed too small for all that gentleness and care. She shook hands with other mourners, nodded and thanked them until Victor put his arm around his wife and said, "Enough, now. Come away." He led Florrie to the weathered bench by the war memorial where he rocked back and forth with her in his arms. "There, now."

Dear Victor. Within days, he had to return to Kathmandu. And it was on that bench that he told Florrie that their next posting would be Buenos Aires, of all places—and did Florrie want to learn the tango there, or try *dulce de leche*? But he knew. Florrie knew it, too—that she couldn't go to Argentina, or abroad at all. With this vast, echoing loss, she'd entered a new chapter in her life; there could be no return to how it was before. To be still. To be *here*, in her homeland—that was all she could manage now, whilst knowing Victor (darling Victor) could not be still at all.

He wrapped her back in his arms. "Oh, how I love you, Mrs. P"— said with an emphasis on every single word so that she understood its second meaning. And that evening, under the quince tree on Vicarage Lane, Mr. and Mrs. Plumley reminisced till nightfall: of embassies and people, of night skies, of swimming in the shallows of Lake Nyasa until they noticed the blink of a crocodile's eye; of the mishap with the ceremonial cutlass, of the temple to Krishna where, at dusk, bats rolled out like ribbons from every window and door. *My Helen of Troy. My Hatshepsut.* And, like this, they laid the Plumley marriage down between them—very gently, full of love, as if it had earned its sleep.

27

Tigh Beag *or* Florrie's Revelation

I n the aftermath, Florrie would lie in various rooms of her child-hood house without moving. Or she'd stand in her parents' bed-room, looking out of the window at the rooftops and trees. The memories Florrie had—of Christmas mornings and summer evenings, of Prudence weeding, bottom-up, in the flowerbeds, of Gulliver's affectionate head butting against her own—all seemed as thin as gossamer, too thin to have ever happened. She'd stare at the copper-stained bathtub. She'd sit on the floor for hours.

But her aunt was still there. Pip would come, a little stooped now, with tea; or she'd shake Florrie's wrists very lightly to rouse her. "Florrie? There you are. We need to do something."

"Yes. Of course."

"Only when you're ready."

The house needed to be sold. So, gradually, Florrie and Pip emp-tied drawers and wardrobes, climbed into the attic with its card-board boxes; they had to make decisions about everything they found in them—letters, earrings, lace-edged linen, the brown envelopes in which Prudence had saved her children's milk teeth. What to throw or keep? What to take to the charity shop? There were photographs of her parents in their younger days with people Florrie didn't recognize. She thought, *I never asked enough.*

It was more than hard, more than lonely. Even with Pip, she felt on her own. At night, Florrie would stare at corners; she'd open a bottle of wine and finish it, sleep fully clothed on the sitting-room floor. She'd ring Pinky at strange, unsociable hours; and Pinky, understanding what was needed, would listen, nod, share her own memories of Prudence ("She gave the best hugs, Butters. I mean it—the best"), which made the house seem less empty, for a while. But nevertheless, it still echoed. Hallways stood, unsure.

The house was sold within the week. Pip would move, she explained, to a small flat less than a mile away, with a view of the graveyard and its cedar tree. "There's room," she promised, "for two." Pinky, too, was adamant: Florrie should come back to the house at Kew Green, as she had done once before. But Florrie, standing on Vicarage Lane with its SOLD sign in front of her, had only wanted to run from all of it—no pretence, no lies, no having to explain. She'd wanted to go where nobody knew her, somewhere small and far away. Far End? In Shropshire? No, she wasn't ready; it was tenanted—and anyway, it was the north that she craved. (Go north, she thought, without knowing why.) And therefore, at the start of her fifty-eighth year (too late in her life, surely, to be starting again), Florrie Butterfield took a train to Glasgow, walked across to its bus station, caught the first departure and stayed on to its final stop, nearly three hours to the north. This is how she discovered Achnacross: a small town of pitched roofs and gables, running the length of a west-facing shoreline at the end of a steep, dark glen. Its river carried snowmelt into the Atlantic; red deer trod down its streets at night. She stepped off that bus, breathed its air, set down her suitcase and cried.

Florrie spent five days and six nights at the Achnacross Inn. By night, she slept or stared at the ceiling. But by day, she summoned the strength to walk out into the Scottish landscape, to fill her internal spaces with these blustery, outer ones. She used her hands to haul her bulk to the summits of every peak she could see from her window and, from those tops, she'd see peninsulas and islands, the angled Nevis range.

It was through these wanderings that she found it: a small, white single-story house, a mile from Achnacross, on the road to Kinlochardour, where they'd once mined for aluminium. She saw it from above—how it sat in its own cove, surrounded by pine trees. Having descended to it, Florrie circumnavigated the house, feeling its roughened walls; she saw its missing tiles, its exposed concrete and breeze block, the blooming moss in its guttering. There was no romance to the place. But there was something about it that Florrie recognized and, seeing its FOR ALL sign, she asked herself, *Why not? Where else might she go?* She cupped her hands, peered through its salty windows: there was an open fireplace, a dusty iron bedstead; the bath suite was a curious orangey-pink. The house had land, too—a garden of weeds and animal tracks led down to a dark-sand beach. To stand there, at low tide, felt like standing on glass.

Tigh Beag. *Little House.* Florrie bought it for the asking price. All her worldly possessions were driven up in a van. And she disinfected the kitchen cupboards and bathroom; she painted the walls a pale grey, pulled up the questionable carpet to find half a shilling and a flagstone floor. She unfolded her bed linen of Egyptian cotton and broderie anglaise and pulled the bed to the window so that, in the mornings, she could watch the tides, the sun's trajectory from dawn to dusk over the loch. Some days, she'd sleep without any movement. But there were nights, too, when she'd rise, dress and go walking— without a torch or moon to see by, governed only by tree lines and running water—and she'd hoped Prudence might appear, from the shadows. (She'd whisper, "Mother, are you there?") And Florrie knew how the locals must have whispered and wondered who was living at the old MacFarlane place; who, exactly, *was* this middle-aged, big-bottomed creature with tangled hair and a solitary air, who'd crouch to marvel at lichen? Who was seen crying on the pier? (*Where is she from? Is she married? What's her name—do we know?*) In time, she'd befriend these people. But in the first ten months of her life there, Florrie tucked herself away.

It was grief, of course. But she understood, too, that she grieved for far more than Prudence or her father, for Bobs or married life. Look, she'd think, at what I've lost. Look at what I do not have. It was no use that she'd seen elephants feasting on a marula tree, danced the salsa on a Cuban balcony, or that she'd spent her life trying to be generous and good; this was not how a woman's life was measured by the world. (Where was the husband? The children? The house?) And, in Tigh Beag, she thought of Jack Luckett's profile in his dusty truck; she saw Hassan abu Zahra glancing up, bright-eyed, from a glass of mint tea and saying, "Where may I take you?" She thought of the fellow traveler she'd met on a bus to Eldoret, who'd written his number on the back of his ticket and said, "Call? Please?" But she'd never called.

And Ted. Teddy. Edward Silversmith. It was at Achnacross that Florrie finally allowed herself to go back to Teddy, to unfold their story like a map. She went back to his attic room on Holywell Street, in Oxford; to his owlish spectacles and how he removed them; to the busker outside who'd played "Blue Moon" as he'd kissed her collarbone. It was there, too, in Tigh Beag that, for the first time in her life, Florrie returned to that tall, red-brick house in Hackney, walked through its door, ascended its stairwell, looked out of its window on to Lower Clapton Road to see Pinky standing there, looking back. She remembered the nuns. *You only have yourself to blame, Miss Butterfield.* Florrie was both fifty-seven and seventeen, standing on the wet sand.

Pinky sensed all of this. On the phone, she said, "Right. I'm coming up"—and arrived three days later, descending from the bus as if she'd only come from a mile away. She cooked and ironed. She walked, arm in arm, with her best friend through all the lush, damp, earthy smells of a Scottish springtime. And one night, as they faced each other on the sofa—sharing a tartan blanket—Florrie said, "Do you know what today is? The date?"

The first day of April. "Forty years today."

"Forty, Pinks—forty. Where has the time gone? Every single day, I've . . ."

"I know. Oh, poor Butters."

"Do you think Teddy ever loved me? I mean, really?"

"Yes," said Pinky, without hesitation. "But not nearly as much as someone else is going to."

Florrie! She rouses herself. It is late evening now. She's in her night-dress and bed sock, in her mallard chair. She must have been dozing, for the ice has melted in her glass, diluting the whisky, and the glass has tilted and spilled. Her half dream—of "Blue Moon," of the beach at Tigh Beag—skitters away, like a leaf.

What stays, though, is the date. The first day of April: that day, every year, is Florrie's hardest day—and Pinky Topham née Underwood was the only one who'd ever known that. She'd mark the date, too—as if *It* was something that happened to her, which, of course, it did, in a way. Every year, without necessarily speaking of it, Pinky would mark the anniversary with a crackling transatlantic phone call or an unexpected package from London—a book or a bookmark, a painted handprint from one of the Topham children, a trinket from Mr. Aksoy's shop, a box of gingerbread, a newspaper article that might remind Florrie of Englishness, a packet of flower seeds. If Florrie was in England, they'd make sure they met on that day—for a woodland walk or fish and chips or a browse in an art gallery followed by a pot of tea and cake. Once, they bought an excessive amount of cheese from Botley and Peeves and ate it in the garden at Kew Green and neither of them mentioned the date's particular meaning, but they knew—they both knew. "How are you, Butters?" That question was everything. That was Pinky's way of saying, I know what day it is.

One time, she sent a card. In fact, Pinky probably sent numerous cards, over her adult lifetime, but there's only one that Florrie has saved, with the passing years, and which sits in her old cheese crate, even now. It was sent on the thirtieth anniversary. It arrived at the Plumley house in Delhi: a painting of a London sunrise, as seen from an upper window—a fourth floor, or a fifth—and this picture had unbuckled Florrie, as she'd stood on a raffia floormat, aware of the car horns and donkeys and the delicate scent of the laburnum tree. This card had sent her back to London. It had made her three decades younger, bleeding and afraid. *Where is she? How could you? No, no, no.* It made her long for her childhood bed—and she felt her way to a chair.

Inside the card, Pinky had written: *Sending love, today and always. But you know that. P x*

In her old apple store, Florrie looks to her left.

The nightjar card sits on the table beside her. This little brown bird meets her gaze: it looks at her with fondness, with mild concern. Florrie whispers to it, "Help me, little thing"—as if the bird can hear. For she is growing old and tired; and she's tried her best, heaven knows. But she doesn't want to give up now—for Renata's sake. For the dying Nancy Tapp.

And maybe the bird does hear. For an idea comes to her then.

Midsummer's day. Hadn't Renata—dressed in navy, still holding that chutney jar with both hands—said, "Today is a hard day for me"? Florrie's lost the precise wording but wasn't there something like that? "I'll be feeling more myself tomorrow, I'm sure."

The date, then. *The date.* She reaches for the card. She studies the nightjar once more—as if it's sentient, not an image on a card but a proper living bird. She looks at those seven black words inside it. Then Florrie returns to the magenta envelope with all its stains and creases, the slightly putrid smell it has retained from its time in the recycling bin. She studies the *F* like a treble clef.

There is nothing new here.

But then Florrie looks again. She touches the back of the envelope; it was torn open in a hurried way. In being torn this way, the paper has become ragged, feather-like; when she tries to seal the envelope again, she can't—its lines don't quite meet up. But in trying, something appears.

A second treble clef appears.

It is far, far smaller than the first. It is written, too, in a different pen with a finer nib so that Florrie must bring it all closer to her reading light and squint through her bifocals in order to be sure. Is it? Yes. There is a word here.

On the back of the envelope, there is the word *For.*

For what? And Florrie flattens the flap of the envelope, forcing it down; she tries to make it look as it must have done when Renata first received it—before it was opened, and torn. And there it is: amongst the pulp and adhesive and undefinable stains, it says, *For 21st.*

She presses one hand to her mouth, to her growing smile. She makes the noise that a child might make in its sleep, turning over—*Oh!* And Florrie has never been sure of what's going on in this world—that is, if there's a god or goddess, if there are ghosts or angels or an afterlife, if there are human souls which survive the bodily death or ten thousand other secrets that are mostly disbelieved but at this exact moment, she feels that Pinky is right here, in this room, helping her. She thinks that Arthur himself is not far behind—and that they've made friends, without her, so that they're both cheering her on like she's a tired horse. *Keep going, girl! You're nearly there!* And perhaps they are all here—her parents and Bobs and Prudence and Victor and even Gladness, applauding so that there's flour everywhere. "Look," says Florrie—to a room that's both empty and yet not empty at all. "*What a thing!*"

Stanhope. She wants Stanhope's company. So Florrie grapples for her dressing gown and manoeuvres herself into her wheelchair; she puts the card in its envelope, wedges the envelope in the usual place, takes off her brakes, pushes herself outside into the cool nocturnal air and wheels herself quickly, with determination, along the back of the pig sties, through a darkness that's broken evenly by the pooled, golden light of bedroom windows and the flickering blue of television screens.

She knocks three times, breathless.

He opens his door, confused. He, too, is in his dressing gown. And when he sees Florrie, this expression deepens further—for she knows she's pink-cheeked and puffing, proffering the stained magenta envelope like a winning lottery ticket, with a knitted yellow bed sock on her one remaining foot.

"Florrie?"

"The date! Midsummer. It was an anniversary."

"Of what?"

She *knows*; she is certain. "Something terrible."

28

In Their Dressing Gowns

They sit facing each other—Florrie in her wheelchair, Stanhope in his faded tartan armchair with its fraying edges.

"So . . . not a lover at all?"

His quarters are different at this hour. What had seemed a little ramshackle during the day takes on a different air at night—softer, even cosier. The warm, coppery glow of his globe catches the edges of things—his stacked books, his antique maps, his replica Roman pottery, his collection of walking sticks and television set.

"No," says Florrie, "I don't think so."

"Not a stalker? We thought a stalker."

"Not as such."

He adjusts his spectacles. "Then . . . it doesn't have to have been a man? Who sent the card, or pushed her?"

Stanhope's right. The nightjar has nothing to do with love—or not romantic love, at least. *I never stopped hoping I'd find you.* True, no doubt, but this person with the *F* like a treble clef had looked and hoped and dreamed of Renata in a way that hadn't been passionate. The nightjar is no token of *l'amour*. No one was *in love*. Rather, something had happened (One? Ten? Twenty years ago?) and this person has never forgotten it; they've had their own pike, in their own dark waters. And the sender of this card could, therefore, be anyone—of any sex or preference, any age. Indeed, the four gentlemen Florrie and

Stanhope saw yesterday are the only ones at Babbington who could *not* be the would-be murderer (along with both Florrie and Stanhope, of course). So who does that leave? Literally everyone else: the Professors Lim or Marcella Mistry or the Ellwoods or Velma Rudge or dear, sullen Magda or the magnificent Georgette. It could be the Rosenthals in their matching lambswool cardigans. It could be any staff member. All it takes, she thinks, is the ability to walk up three flights of stairs unnoticed; all it takes is the ability to knock on Renata's door in a storm and push her out of the dormer window—without dislocating a knee-cap or incurring a bruise—and creep back down again, as quietly as a mouse. All it takes is the ability to lie afterward.

"No, it doesn't have to be a man."

How, she thinks, did Stanhope appear in her life? She knows when he arrived. She recalls his appearance in the dining room, with his unclouded, uncomplicated face—and she could list every conversation with him since, if she was asked to. But it's *before* that amazes her. Florrie thinks of all the tiny decisions—instinctive or considered—that both she and Stanhope have made in their lives which have led them to this moment, to sitting here. What if she'd turned left, not right? What if she'd married Dougal Henderson? What if she hadn't sung "Silent Night" to Hassan abu Zahra but chosen a different carol instead, so that she hadn't gasped, heartsore, to hear it being sung outside her door forty years later—and sixteen months before? She would not have dropped her mulled wine; she wouldn't have lost her leg; she wouldn't have come to Babbington Hall in the village of Temple Beeches. And there have been, no doubt, ten thousand other moments in her life that, if she'd lived them slightly differently, would have meant she wouldn't be sitting here—here, with him, at this very moment, in a room that's the colour of firelight and in her toweling dressing gown.

Flagpole Jones and Florrie Butterball.

In this half-light, like candlelight, they regard each other.

"I didn't expect this," he says. "I could never have imagined any of this."

Florrie does not reply. What words is she able to offer in return?

Stanhope goes to speak further. "Florrie, I want to say—"

But then, somewhere behind him, a carriage clock begins to ping so that Florrie says, "Oh, the time!"—and she takes off her brakes, makes her apologies, prattles about the benefits of sleep and what would people say if they could see her here? In her fraying dressing gown with nothing structural underneath? And she turns toward the door as Stanhope tells her that it's a very nice dressing gown, and it's not late at all. But Florrie is already through the door. "Tomorrow?" she calls over her shoulder.

Behind her, she hears his quiet good night.

29

The Nightjar Explains Itself

There is only one computer at Babbington for the use of residents. Others exist, no doubt—in the manager's office, for example, or the staff room; and Florrie is certain that there are computers of various sizes and ages in people's homes. (The Professors Lim have something so large it looks like they could land spacecraft; Marcella, she knows, has a screen the size of her handbag which she taps at, briskly, with a painted nail.) But in terms of a computer for residents who don't have such devices, this is the only one.

"Do you know what to do with it, exactly?"

"Possibly," Stanhope answers. "I don't know."

It is, in effect, a large television with a grey plastic block beside it that whirrs softly to itself and which, haphazardly, flashes a green light. There is a keyboard, an oval contraption on a fabric pad (which is, Stanhope offers, known as a mouse) and a chipped mug with pens in. She tries to tell herself that it's just a fancy typewriter, but typewriters never required passwords or had a low, fuzzy, electronic buzz. They never linked you to the whole wide world, as computers do.

There is also that laminated sign: ASK BEFORE USING.

"I think we should, shouldn't we?"

Florrie thinks to say that it's probably best that they keep this to themselves and not ask—but at that moment, the floorboards creak out in the corridor. Georgette appears, pauses in the doorway. "Hello, lovelies. You okay? Need any help with that?"

They widen their eyes at each other, unsure. But this hesitancy brings Georgette into the room. She crosses and sets a hand on the back of Florrie's chair, as if for balance. "You'll need the password first. Let me." And she leans forward, across Florrie—one bosom perilously close to the other—and prods at the keyboard. "There—you see? *Bab-Hall*. Then you click, type in whatever you want to know—and click again. And if you want to print anything, it's that button—see? But maybe only print a page or two, lovebug. The cost of printer ink these days is criminal." She straightens back up, sets her hands on her hips. "What is it you're after, anyway?"

There can't be any sharing of what they know, or suspect—not even with Georgette, with her vanilla scent and *lovelies*—so Florrie and Stanhope reassure the acting manager of Babbington Hall that they only wish to look at bus timetables or remind themselves of the capital of Luxembourg or to have a look for birthday presents for Stanhope's (non-existent) sister until Georgette shrugs, accepting it all. "No worries. But shout if you need me, won't you, sweets?"

They watch her departure.

"Right," says Stanhope. He has lowered himself into the desk chair and sits gingerly on it, not quite trusting its wheels. "Do we start with her name?"

Florrie pulls her chair alongside him, slots herself under the desk and brings the keyboard closer. Her hands are different hands these days—they are stiffer, as well as discoloured and knobbly—but she has not forgotten how to type from her Parisian job, or from the Empire Aristocrat which she'd balance on her knees at the mouth of a mineshaft; thus the name *Renata Green* appears on the screen in reasonably quick time. She clicks, as instructed, with the furless mouse. And she and Stanhope both make the same exclamation when row upon row of stories appear in which Renata's name features. "Goodness," says Stanhope. "This is marvelous." They are newspaper articles, mostly— mentioning Renata's arrival at Babbington, or last year's summer fete, which had raised funds for a local charity, and there, in a photograph, is Renata shaking hands with the local mayor. *New manager at residential home.* There are several stories on Arthur Potts. But there is nothing useful here.

"It's nothing we don't already know," Stanhope says. "Should we add the date?"

Florrie adds the date—*21st June*—and clicks. But the list of stories looks, by and large, the same—as if the date itself has no link at all to Renata. She tries *Renata Green Midsummer's Day*, but that, too, proves hopeless—so much so that the computer questions her typing. *Did you mean Midsummer's Day in Sweden?* "No, I did not," she replies.

Renata Green nightjar. But that, too, offers nothing.

They consider the cursor. It flashes rhythmically. It has an air of expectation, as the nightjar does, as if it knows something that they do not.

Florrie stares. It feels like they're facing a brick wall, but there must be a way of scaling it. The anniversary of what? Nothing good, surely, or nothing easy, at least. And what comes to her now is the memory of having to give her name, when she arrived at that red-brick building in London; of being asked in a blunt, officious way, as if she were due to be handcuffed and sentenced. ("Are you a first offender?" And she'd nodded, afraid: *yes*.) And she hadn't said Butterfield, there. She'd felt entirely unable to say that loved, lovely word in such a place—as if to do so would be a betrayal of all her beloved ones. So she said Silversmith. She offered, in a trembling voice, that she was Florence Silversmith—who was, she tried to believe, not quite the same as Florence Butterfield.

She'd wanted to change, in there—to leave her old self behind. And, knowing this, more thoughts come to Florrie, as the computer whirrs: the thick, heavy curtains in the manager's office at Babbington, how they were only ever half drawn; the private, high-up quarters on the third floor; the shopping deliveries that Magda had scorned ("like she is better than the rest of us") and the colourant that Renata uses to turn her hair white-blonde; how she never goes anywhere—to cinemas or outings. How she said no to Jay Mistry's suggestions of dinner together when anyone else would have said yes, please. And even these photographs—these, on the computer screen now—suggest that she, too, is in hiding: for, yes, Renata is smiling beside the mayor or at St. Mary's autumn festival with the rickety Reverend Bligh—but each time, the smile is watery and thin. In each, Renata is slightly turned away, as if suspicious of the camera or the person behind it.

This time, Florrie does not type Renata's name.

Rather, she only types *21st June* and *nightjar*—and what appears, at first, is what she expects: namely, a list of articles about this little brown bird, its churring, its heathland preferences and African wintering. She scrolls down, and more comes: nightjar walks, followed by supper; how to help protect the nightjar; how to listen for them; how to spot them in flight, which seems, by all accounts, very hard to do. *Whilst the nightjar will begin to return to Britain in late June, the best time to hear it is in July, when its churring can be heard over southern uplands and ...*

"Stop." Stanhope grasps her shoulder. "My God. Look."

Florrie moves the cursor, clicks.

What she sees on the computer screen is a photograph of a woman. She is young, in her teens; she has dark, straight hair with a heavy fringe and her figure is fuller, much stronger; she wears thick mascara that rounds her deadened eyes. The photograph has been taken hurriedly, from an awkward angle—as a professional photographer might snap a movie star as she hurries from a theatre, or into a waiting car. But it's not a movie star. She looks so very different; she looks so different that, if Florrie hadn't been looking, she'd have seen no resemblance at all and thought nothing of it, scrolled on. But she *is* looking—and there's no doubting that this is a younger Renata; this is Renata from many years ago.

"Oh no," says Stanhope. "Oh, heavens. Look what it says beneath."

The headline of the article reads:

NIGHTJAR KILLER GOES FREE

30

Bannerman, Trott and St. Clair

They print what they can. They fumble with the paperwork, secrete it about themselves (under Florrie's cardigan, against Stanhope's chest, in and under her pink-chiffon lap) and hurry to his quarters. And on getting there, Stanhope draws the curtain despite it not being eleven o'clock in the morning yet and snaps the kettle on and clears away the books and crosswords and plate on which there are crumbs of chocolate cake and looks at her, breathless. "What do we need?"

Tea, they agree, and good lighting. Having found both, they set out the printed pages on the kitchen table as if setting out plates for a formal occasion.

"This one," she says. "Let's start with this one."

It's from the *Daily Telegraph*, twenty-five years ago.

There were emotional scenes at the Central Criminal Court yesterday when the sentencing was made in the case of Maeve Bannerman, who had previously been found guilty of the manslaughter of her two friends. The judge, having spent fourteen hours deliberating, ruled that, despite the conviction, Bannerman should escape jail time due to both her remorse and her age at the time.

The case made national headlines in the summer due
to the nature of the deaths, and their political connections.
In the early hours of 21 June, the car in which Bannerman,
Meredith Trott and Polly St. Clair had been traveling was
found submerged in the River Ember near Molesey, having left
the road at the approaching bend. The women—aged sixteen
and seventeen at the time—had been drinking in the Nightjar
nightclub on the King's Road in Chelsea, owned by the property
tycoon and Conservative party donor Milos Castellanos. Trott
and St. Clair both died in the accident. Bannerman survived
and raised the alarm by flagging down a passing taxi. Both
bodies were retrieved, downstream.

Judge Bingham ruled that, whilst Bannerman had by
admission been driving carelessly, she had neither drugs nor
alcohol in her system and had not previously been known to
the police—therefore he saw no benefit in sentencing her
to a jail term. "The purpose of jail," he stated, "is to punish the
criminal, protect the public and act as a deterrent for any
future misconduct. In this case—a tragic accident which will,
most likely, haunt the accused for the rest of her life, and for
which she is evidently remorseful—I see no purpose in ruin-
ing a third young life." Bannerman has been sentenced to five
years' community service and a lifetime driving ban, and has
been ordered to pay all court costs.

The apparent leniency of this sentencing has caused outrage amongst the families of St. Clair and Trott. Max St. Clair,
the Conservative MP for East Chilterns and the father of Polly
St. Clair, has declared it to be "shambolic and immoral"—and
has lodged an official complaint with the Crown Prosecution
Service. In an emotional response delivered from the steps of
the Old Bailey, he vowed that he would continue to fight for
justice for his daughter and Trott, disputing the testimonies in

favour of Bannerman. He maintained that Bannerman had a coercive, controlling nature and that she remains a danger to the public. He claimed that, in the months before their deaths, both girls had changed considerably in temperament—and that his daughter had expressed a fear of Bannerman.

An enquiry is also under way into the running of the Nightjar, from which multiple claims have since arisen of underage drinking, sexual misconduct and drug dealing. Castellanos was charged last month and awaits trial.

Stanhope looks up from the article. He blinks at Florrie with a pained, sorrowful expression. "I can't believe it. I just can't. Renata?"

"Except she wasn't Renata. Not back then."

He has grown quite pale. His hands have a tremor which he attempts to hide by searching for his handkerchief and dabbing his nose. But Florrie finds herself feeling strangely calm. All this feels, to her, unsurprising. She can't explain it—for she never imagined this, of all things; she'd had no idea. But part of her also thinks, *Of course*—as if she should have known this all along.

How curious it is—to see Renata with dark hair, to see her stepping through journalists in a beige belted coat, with hooped earrings, a darkly painted mouth, a hardened expression and a raised hand against the camera that's photographing her. Strange, too, to see *more* of her, for she has a softness to her body, a voluptuousness to her that she lacks entirely in her Babbington life. She is the same yet wholly different. Or she's different but wholly the same. And, tentatively, Florrie tries out her proper name.

"Maeve Bannerman."

"You know," says Stanhope, "I remember this. I do—I'm sure I do. Or the politician, at least. Let me see . . . Twenty-five years ago. We were still living in Kent; Peter got married that year. Yes, I remember seeing the news—the father speaking on the courthouse steps and

everyone shouting. He was furious. Do you remember, Florrie? And
didn't he die in the end?"

"Die?" She can't recall. Twenty-five years ago, Florrie had been in
Achnacross. She would have been wading out into the sea, or lying
on her side for hours without moving. Latterly, she might have found
herself watching Dougal Henderson's boat as it came back to harbour.
She wouldn't have been watching television at all. "I have no idea."

"You don't remember any of it? Oh, yes, he died. He killed
himself—the father. Max St. Clair. He stepped down onto the train
tracks at rush hour. Somewhere in London. Belsize Park? He'd been
awaiting trial himself, I think."

"Himself?"

"He burned the Nightjar down. Arson. Someone was in there—a
cleaner, or waitress. I can't recall now. They didn't die, I don't think,
but it was quite a business."

Stanhope is still, for a while. Then he takes a forefinger and moves
it, very carefully, over the face of Maeve Bannerman, as if the printer
ink might remove itself to show the Renata he knows. "Well. We've
talked of motive, haven't we? Or why someone might want to kill her?
I believe we have it, Florrie. I like to think I'm a gentle chap. I've never
been in a physical fight in all my life, I'm happy to say, and I've not
raised my voice since my teaching days. But if someone was to hurt
Peter . . . Well, I'm not sure I'd recognize myself."

We become she-wolves. I'd unplug that bloody machine myself. "Do
you think a parent did this, Stanhope? Do you think it is revenge?"

How long ago it seems—their conversation in the orchard. In it,
they had discussed Shakespearean tragedies—revenge and unchecked
anger, the follies and whims of mankind. And whilst they'd marveled
at the plays' intricacies and humanness ("that chap knew all our foi-
bles," Stanhope had said), they'd conceded that revenge feels rather
outdated now, as a motive for any sort of mischief. And yet had they

been wrong to think so? Wrong to suppose that the human heart, four hundred years later, can't feel the same fire and unfairness, the same hunger for justice? For one's children, it seems, it can.

He makes a strange, tender sound—as if he's moved in a way that's hurt him. "Oh . . . Of course. Oh, gosh."

"Stanhope?"

"Renata. In Latin, her name means 'reborn.' From the verb *renascor* . . . She's tried to have a second life."

And has she managed it? To have a second life? Florrie looks into her teacup. It's hard for her to know, sitting here in Stanhope's quarters whilst she, Renata, is wired to a machine. But she's minded to think, *Not really.* A quarter of a century has passed since the Nightjar; twenty-five years in which Renata has, yes, made a living trying to help people; she's dyed her hair and changed her name. But she's also lived a quiet, private, unpeopled life with no friends or acquaintances; with no travels or adventures, no bright-pink dresses—and no belief that she's deserving of having such things. And this has never struck Florrie, or anyone, frankly, as being a rich, content or rewarding way to live. But Renata also knew that; she had stood, in that office, and spoken of wanting to change her life—of *les croissants aux amandes* and feeling awake. *I thought being in love would be easy.*

She has not, Florrie thinks, let go. She has a different name but her heart is the same. And she still lives, daily, with the fact that she killed two friends on a summer's evening; that she killed, perhaps, a third person a year later—under a train at Belsize Park. No wonder Renata cried on the white-painted bench, outside Florrie's window, the night before the anniversary—for how does one escape something one did? That can't be undone, now? She must have thought, too, *How on earth do I tell him? This man I love?*

All that hiding. All that learning of life through books and art and calendars, not through living itself. Partly, Renata felt she deserved no better than that. But partly, too, she must have been afraid of being discovered—of someone turning around and asking, Maeve? Is that you?

"She didn't want anyone to know—who she was, what she'd done." Stanhope sighs like a father. "But someone *does* know—don't they?"

All day, they stay in his room. When they are hungry, he feeds them—rummaging in his cupboards, finding cheese and water biscuits and tinned peaches, celery, cans of tonic water, a bag of salted peanuts. All afternoon, they sift through the printed pages and think of the lives that were ruined or lost.

Stanhope takes a water biscuit. "You knew nothing about the St. Clair case?"

No, and Florrie tells him why. She tells him that after her mother, Prudence, had died, she had sold the family home. "Then I went to Scotland, to a place called Achnacross. I lived there for nine years, in the end. I had no television so I've probably missed out on much more than that."

He flinches. "Achnacross? I know it."

He can't possibly. It has been two decades since Florrie left there and, in all that time, she is yet to meet a single soul who's been to the village or knows of it.

"A quayside, stacked with lobster pots? A hotel, I think—painted pink? We took Peter there as a little one. But then we went back for years and years—long after Peter was fully grown. The days were so lovely and slow at Achnacross—or so it seemed to me. A peaceful place."

It was. And as she stares at Stanhope, as he cracks the water biscuit with a particular care, she thinks, *He has stood on the quayside. He knows of the westerly winds that blew in, of the otter population and the bluebells in the churchyard.* "Did you see a white cottage in the trees? Right on the lochside? On the road out to Kinlochardour?"

He pauses to think. "Did it have a washing line?"

Of course he knows it, she thinks. "Yes. That was it. That was mine."

The frailty of it all. The frailty of life, by which she doesn't just mean the way in which a life can be over, quite suddenly—from an untied shoelace, say, or a car leaving a road on a midsummer's evening. Rather, she thinks of how, sometimes, this life has seemed to be bordered by the thinnest of cloths—a gauze, a veil—through which one can see the other lives that one might have lived, if one had chosen differently. Renata, she thinks—or, rather, Maeve: What if she'd driven a little more slowly? Left the Nightjar a little sooner, or not driven at all? What if she'd never met those two girls? Or woken up that morning with a headache so that she'd decided to stay in bed? There are so many other lives that could have been had.

Florrie looks across at him. Stanhope Jones is drowsing in his armchair. His head has dropped forward toward his chest; his hands still hold the empty teacup and, as he breathes quietly, Florrie takes off her brakes and gently removes the cup from Stanhope's tilting hands. She worries that he might be cold—for summer afternoons can have their chill, not least when bones are getting old. What can she do? She finds his coat. She wheels herself back toward him, lays it over his knees, trying not to wake him—and Stanhope stirs at this. He makes a sound like a dreaming dog so that Florrie wonders what he sees, in this dream, and if he is happy in it. She smiles to watch him sleeping. Then, soundlessly, she wheels herself away.

31

The Man with a Boat Called *Damsel*

Ten months after her arrival, Florrie woke to find heavy snow in Achnacross. There was an absolute stillness, drifts that reached her windowsill and later, down on the shoreline, she found the shallow water had thickened and slowed, like glue. It was as Florrie trudged back toward the house—bed-haired, braless, wrapped in a blanket, pyjama bottoms tucked into her Wellington boots—that she found a couple waiting on her doorstep, in sheepskin jackets and gloves. "Logs," the man shouted, pointing. "We thought you might not have enough!"

So Florrie met the MacLeods. Later, she thanked them for their kindness (and apologized, too) by forcing herself to dress properly and carry a Sitwell fruitcake through the drifts to their gabled house by the inn. "Oh, come in, come in!" they said, flinging cats to one side—and like this, Florrie met others: their sons and cousins and half brother, a great-aunt and a sister-in-law, their oldest friends and neighbours, old Bruce who ran the petrol station (You'll be the mysterious lass at Mac-Farlane's old place?) and blind Tuppence the dog. At the MacLeods' Christmas party she met more—the Kerrs, the Hendersons, Isobel Boyle with her pentagram earrings, Barney McCabe with his two bad knees. And it was here, too, that Florrie met the Morags—three small, elderly women who lived in a row of three fishermen's cottages and were known, for ease, by their positioning: Left Morag, Middle and Right.

"They've been guessing," Middle Morag said. "About your story."

"Who?"

She gestured vaguely at the rowdy kitchen as if to say *all of them*. "But I tell you this: your business is your business. I don't care for prying. There's not a creature on this earth who doesn't have their woe."

Florrie stared, assessing how it felt—to be recognized as haunted, to be seen as sad. She hadn't been seen this way, before. She'd always been capable Florrie—physical, cheery, the girl who'd wave with both hands, as children do. But here, at Achnacross, she was being seen for what she was: thinned like a garment that's been boiled and tumbled and pressed so much that, in parts, it has become transparent. And did she mind it? It felt better. It felt like an honest and better way to be.

It was a tentative Florrie who started to work at the Achnacross Inn. Four times a week, she served ale and whisky and venison steaks in the wood-paneled bar. Fiddlers played on a Saturday night; wet woolen socks and bobble hats were hung on the woodburning stove to dry; and all the dancing and card games and kissing and sleeping in corners was surveyed by a mounted stag's head that Florrie would greet as she passed underneath. She'd polish its glass eyes sometimes. The staff were all far younger than her—in their teens or twenties—and this daunted Florrie at first. *What do I say to them?* But she'd been an ambassador's wife; she knew how to bridge distances, hold hands with ages and nations—so it didn't take long before these young, shining creatures would gather at closing time and listen, round-eyed, to Florrie's stories of Everest base camp or emerald mines, or Cairo by moonlight. She advised on how to slice a mango. "You've seen," they breathed, "a *yak*?"

"Are you married?" The Henderson boy asked her this.

It was nearly May. Florrie had popped some bluebells in a pewter tankard, set them on the counter and was stepping back to admire them when Jimmy came into the bar. She wiped her hands on a tea towel. "Married? Me? No, not now."

"How long?"

"How long was I married for?"

"No—since you stopped being married."

Florrie considered this. She'd been divorced from Victor for over a year by then.

"And"—the boy picked at the skin on his hand—"are you still sad about it?"

"About not being married?" Florrie smiled. What curious questions these were—all the more so for coming from the shy, bespectacled, buck-toothed lad who washed the pots on Fridays and Saturdays. But she liked Jimmy's shyness, his unbrushed hair. So she answered candidly: no, she wasn't sad; yes, she still loved her former husband— but only as she loved her other, dearest friends. "Jimmy, why are you asking this?"

He thanked her, left the bar. And, through the bar window, Florrie watched him cross the road, pass the petrol station and break into a run along the old shepherd's track, toward the Henderson place.

She'd known of *Damsel* all the while. She was a navy-blue boat with an off-white cabin; her fenders had been scoured by salt and rain to the palest shade of pinks. Florrie knew that she bobbed by the jetty. She knew, too, that *Damsel* sometimes puttered past her house in the evenings, from lobster pot to lobster pot.

"If you ever fancy a trip . . ." The first time Dougal Henderson made this offer had been at the MacLeod Christmas party—in the MacLeods' hallway, as Florrie was putting on her coat. He'd followed her out with a mince pie, saying, "Aye, granted—it's a bit cold, the now. But in the spring, maybe? If you like?"

In April, he'd asked again. He'd entered the bar on a Saturday night, drunk with the Kerrs in the farthest corner and had glanced up whenever Florrie went by. At the bar, he'd had to shout. He'd leaned forward, cupped his hands to his mouth: "Three pints and a dram of Speyside, please!" And he'd added, still shouting, "The boat? Remember? I mean, only if you fancy it . . . ?"

The third time had been at midsummer. The evening had been dusky, still warm; there'd been no midges, for once, so Florrie was sitting on the quayside with a book, eating raspberries straight from a punnet. She'd glanced up as *Damsel* approached her. She watched as Dougal moored up. "How are the lobsters?" she asked. "You know, Florrie," he answered, climbing ashore, "it would be no bother to . . ."

Only when he asked a fourth time, in the autumn, did Florrie fully realize that Dougal had, in fact, asked her three times before. Under the oak trees, she stared at him. "I thought you were just being nice," she said.

"Nice? Florrie, I don't take people out on my boat."

"But . . . You've just asked me if—"

"Aye! I've asked *you*. I'm asking *you* to come out on my boat with me. You—nobody else." And with that—in the woods, with twigs in her hair—it dawned on Florrie that Dougal Henderson wasn't just being nice.

She thought, briefly, to refuse. The thought of the trip itself excited her, that was true—pulling ropes up from the depths, looking back to the coastal lights as the day faded and having such depths beneath her; but she feared that Dougal (whom she had, in truth, noticed for some time now) would make some gesture—an offered hand as she boarded the boat or a gentle word as they passed Tigh Beag—to which Florrie would respond instinctively. Because she knew she was tired of hiding. She was a different Florrie these days—or she was trying to be.

In the end, they rattled along the coastline in cool October air. Looking back, Florrie saw the coppery hues of bracken and woods;

from the water, Dougal pulled lobsters too small to be kept so showed them to Florrie, explained their parts, turning them over before dropping them back. "The best shade of blue in the world, I reckon"—and Florrie agreed that it was. For a while, too, they dropped anchor. On turning off the engine, a silence rushed in—and Florrie closed her eyes to hear it, to feel the roll and lift of the boat so that Dougal had to say her name twice to rouse her. "Florrie? Florrie? Here. Take this." She turned, expecting a lobster or rope. But he'd brought a flask of tea with two cups: "I hear you like leaf, not bag."

Slowly, Florrie found herself looking for Dougal—for his shoulders in a queue, his profile on his passing boat, for his waterproof jacket on the hatstand as she entered the Achnacross Inn. If she saw it—moss-green, with his handknitted scarf stuffed in a pocket—she'd hide in the ladies' loo, for a while. On hearing his name in passing, she'd blame her age for the sudden flush. *What now?* she wondered. *What do I do?*

"I don't think I can," Florrie answered. He'd asked her to dinner at the Henderson place.

Dougal teased. "You can't . . . what? Eat? It's easy enough."

She'd smiled back. "Yes, I can eat—heaven knows. But . . ."

He understood. "It's just a meal—that's all. Food on a plate."

Food on a plate, trips on the boat and long walks in the glen during which he'd remark on deer prints, give the Gaelic names for things. Florrie learned far more about Scotland this way, but mostly, she learned about him—about this contemplative, generous man, his hair as white as snowfall but which had once (so he said) been fox-red. She learned of his childhood self—stammering, always too tall for his age. And Florrie learned, too, that the joints in his hands ached in cold weather; that he preferred the smoother single malts; that the love of his life was his son and the finest, brightest moment of all had been Jimmy's birth. She learned that, once, on *Damsel*, he'd seen the eye of a cresting whale—"and that whale," Dougal told her, "saw mine. It looked right at me, *saw* me."

Florrie learned that Left Morag was his aunt, that the handknitted scarf had come from her; also, that Dougal had converted the barn himself to make the Henderson home, that its skylights could blow wide in sudden, gusty weather and fill the rooms with Atlantic air. She saw, too, that his hands were huge, like chalices, and so careful in how they touched her collarbone or wrist or felt the weight of her hair, which was buttermilk through age by then, not sun. And Florrie discovered that Dougal had nursed his wife through eight years of cancer, had scattered her ashes off the promontory—and how, he asked, does one ever accept that a body one has loved is reduced to powder? Gone?

In turn, Dougal asked about her. He wanted to learn—and this surprised Florrie. "I hear you lived in Africa?" Or "Tell me about . . ." He'd ask about her brother, the books she loved, if she believed in the human soul. Sometimes he'd reach—across a table, or a gear stick— and take Florrie's hand without speaking. He'd rub her thumb with his thumb.

"Did this hurt?" Which wasn't the same as saying to her, What happened to them? No one had been this thoughtful in how they considered her scars.

"Yes." For it had. "But they don't hurt, now."

How patient he was with her. This, above all, is what she learned about Dougal Henderson: he never hurried. He took his time. He knew—they all knew, in Achnacross—that Florrie had been broken or burned, somehow. Dougal seemed to understand that if he moved too quickly, Florrie might duck under his arm with a nervous laugh, say, My goodness, is that the time?—and that he'd be left with only a still-warm, Florrie-shaped space. When, at last, the kiss came—under a chestnut tree, a whole year since she'd boarded *Damsel*—one of them trembled, or both did.

That Christmas, he bought her an atlas. She, in turn, found a whale in a gallery in Arisaig, carved from driftwood, a knot for its eye. And later, Florrie watched Dougal stacking the pots on the jetty in sleet, punching his gloved hands for warmth, and understood that yes, she loved this man. This could, she knew, be a good, happy life. And wasn't she ready now? Hadn't enough time passed?

She tried. She did. But, in the end, Dougal rubbed his eyes as if tired. "Is it something I've done? Is it me?"

"No." How could it be him? "I promise, Dougal—it's not you."

"Your husband, then? He hurt you, or—"

"Victor? No. He was kind."

"Is there someone else?"

"Another man? No."

"Then . . . who? What happened? Florrie, please."

How close she came to offering it all. On the sagging sofa in the Henderson place, hand in hand, Florrie nearly told the story of Teddy and bandstands, of "Blue Moon" drifting from a busker in an Oxford street, of joy and loss and guilt and her cavernous, echoing enormity of love that hadn't diminished in any conceivable way in the years (forty-four by then) that had passed since *It, the Hackney thing*, how she still thought of what happened every single day. How she needed more stitches than anyone could guess at; how the police had thought, for a time, to be involved. And she started to cry, as her answer—so that Dougal enveloped her, kissed, smoothed back her hair. "Florrie, listen to me: it doesn't matter what it is." And this tenderness had, suddenly, felt like too much to bear. She wanted, at that moment, for this depth of love—from a patient, wise, honest man who marveled at lobsters, who locked and unlocked the Achnacross church every dawn and dusk—to go to someone else. So she pulled away, smoothed her own hair back. She breathed in to calm herself. "I think . . . we should be friends."

"Friends? Really? Florrie, you can't mean that."

"I think it's for the best."

Back in her room, she looks at a Scottish thistle—pressed, dried. She stares, eye to eye, at all the wasted love. There was the slow, considered kneading of her wrist in a café in Cairo; there was Jack Luckett smiling up at her, from the mouth of a mineshaft, adjusting his hat so that he could see Florrie better; there had been Gaston's single, slow scratch of his jawline with his thumb before he said "*Je me rencontre*," and there'd been Dougal, too, stamping his feet for warmth on the quayside in a hard, sideways sleet. Florrie remembers these moments for a reason. They were the moments in which she understood her feelings; with that adjustment of Jack's hat or with Hassan sitting opposite her with those wanting, resin eyes, she'd thought, *I am in love with this man*—suddenly, like a struck match. And tonight, she'd also been struck. As he'd drowsed in his armchair, with his chest rising and falling, Florrie had had the hard, clear understanding that she has come to love Stanhope, too.

She sits with this thought for a while.

From her mallard chair, she imagines how it might have been if she'd chosen to wake him gently. Or if she'd waited until Stanhope had awakened, apologetically, of his own accord. Neither of these things happened, of course; she removed herself, as she's always done.

Florrie will not, therefore, see Stanhope again. Or rather, she will *see* him, naturally—across the grounds or in corridors—and exchange pleasantries, and she will like that very much. But it would be better, she thinks, if she doesn't see him in any prolonged, meaningful way. She can't wheel herself across the courtyard in her dressing gown, for example. She can't talk with him, in an orchard at twilight, of Shakespearean plays.

Pinky, of course, would disagree. She'd say, Butters, for the love of God. Aunt Pip would remind Florrie that this is a too-short life, that a sensible woman is quite the tragedy—and frankly, both would be right. But neither Pinky nor Pip is here. And Florrie must decide for herself—as, perhaps, she's always done. So she decides that she will set the matter of Stanhope down, like an unfinished book. She will not speak of the pike, not now or in the future. Rather, she will solve the mystery of who tried to kill Renata Green—once and for all, and all by herself.

32

Florrie Proceeds on Her Own

Florrie tries to sleep—but can't. Her mind and her heart are too full. One o'clock comes, then two. She turns on the radio, thinking this might help her: there are documentaries on oligarchs and an exiled poet; she listens to the hourly news. She rearranges her pillows, tries lying on her side. But none of this helps at all.

In the end, she switches on her light. It's 3:41 on a Saturday morning; it is, she supposes, the deepest part of night, in which only the mouse and the owl might be moving. No one else, she's sure, will be awake—or not on the ground floor. She reaches for her hearing aids, manoeuvres herself to the edge of her bed—for if she can't sleep, she must do *something*. And Florrie knows exactly what she wants to do.

There's a cool, earthy scent to the courtyard at this hour. It is impossibly quiet—not even a breath of wind in the trees—and Florrie winces at her own small noises: the squeak and crunch of gravel, the clanking of her wheelchair. ("*Shh*," she tells it, as if it might obey.) Ahead, on the first and second floors of Babbington Hall, she can see the electric glow of the nurses' stations, from which they drift in and out of residents' rooms. But downstairs, on the ground floor, Babbington's in complete darkness.

Florrie reaches the back door, pushes her hand through the rhododendron leaves and enters the four-digit code. With it, the door

unclicks and swings back automatically, bonks against its hinges—
and these noises seem loud enough to wake the whole of Oxfordshire,
so that she imagines lights snapping on or windows being thrown
open with a barked *Who goes there?*—and even when she's pushed herself inside the Hall and heard the door close behind her, Florrie continues to hold her breath.

Did anyone hear this? See her?

But there's no sound at all. The silence is absolute. Florrie looks
straight ahead, down the corridor—and, in doing so, she sees that
the ground floor is not, in fact, in proper darkness. In the distance,
there's a soft, greenish light. As she wheels herself, cautiously, toward
it, she's aware of the noises beneath her—the floorboards' creak, the
clonk of a ramp as she rolls both up and down it, and despite her slow
movements she thinks, *They will hear.* For don't the Ellwoods hear
everything? The single *ting* of a teaspoon against china? A dropped
penny? A lone, muffled sob?

The green light is coming from the plastic box above an emergency exit. It is the hard, bleached lighting of a laboratory or an
operating theatre—too stark to look at directly, or to stay beneath.
So Florrie backs away, down the corridor. But then she finds another
light, too: down to her right, in the main entrance of the Hall, there's
a table lamp on the reception desk. Is that always lit at night? It
seems odd, that it might be. And, creeping toward it, Florrie sees
how its sweep of light reflects in Babbington's windows, bounces
back from the worn leather armchairs and illuminates, too, the satisfied face of the Babbington inventor with his collar and lace cuffs.
This lamp has a pleated shade, a brass stand, and it's switched on and
off by a small brass chain that is, at this moment, moving a little—as
if it's only just been touched.

Just a draught, Florrie thinks. Or it's her own imagination—which
has, she knows, its wayward tendencies.

But all this is a distraction. It is the library that Florrie has come for. So she pivots slowly, away from the reception hall, and makes her way toward the library door. It's ajar; she can move through it with ease. But inside, the room is completely black: there's no light source at all and, being wood-paneled, with bookshelves and thick, elderly curtains, there's no chance of reflections or a chink of starlight. Florrie can't even see a yard in front of her. She can't even see her lap. And to put on the overhead light? Such a sudden brightness would surely be detected by an Ellwood so that they'd lift their head from their pillow and say, What is that?

All she can do is inch forward into this wall of dark. Her remaining foot bumps against objects that she has to decipher by touch or sound—a table, a sofa, the wicker basket for discarded copies of magazines. She can smell the clothbound books. She can sense, too, the nearness of them, as if these bookshelves are standing people, holding their breath. It's only as she reaches the alcove (which she gropes for, feels the sides of) that Florrie knows she's where, at last, she needs to be.

Her hands find the keyboard, the monitor.

She fumbles for the button—and *click*! There's an immediate whirring. There's a beep, a buzz and the sudden phosphorescence of the entire computer screen so that Florrie shields her eyes against its brightness and thinks, momentarily, of turning it all off again because the noisiness of it all surely will bring the Ellwoods winging in, scrabbling and ungainly, like seagulls fighting for bread. But still, there are no footsteps. No one comes.

Florrie exhales.

She allows her eyes to adjust.

Four o'clock in the morning. When did she last see that hour? But Florrie is wide awake—and sets to work. She types and clicks; she clicks and scrolls. She dismisses articles. What she's after is

photographs: she wants images of what happened to Renata Green—
not words. And there are, Florrie discovers, hundreds of them: of
the Nightjar itself, with its wrought-iron railings; of flowers in cel-
lophane tied to those railings; of a pink neon sign that reads COCK-
TAILS 'TIL LATE! Later, too, she finds images of the charred shell of
the Nightjar, still smouldering. Also, there are pictures of the place
in better, happier times—seemingly famous people with their arms
around each other, musicians and models, actors and writers. Even
minor royals, it seems, had partied there. But these aren't the photographs that Florrie's looking for. Nor does she dwell on the grainy
police photographs of an upturned Volkswagen Corrado in a swollen
river, or the police cordon—with its white tents and divers—that followed the crash. Rather, Florrie wants people. She wants scenes from
outside the courthouse—that is, Maeve Bannerman (as she was) in
her belted coat, one hand raised against a camera's flash. But also,
Florrie wants to see the bereaved; to see the faces of the parents of
the two girls who died that night, to study the profiles and gestures
of those who heckled from the gallery and who, later, gave their terse,
tearful responses on the court steps.

Max St. Clair is easy to find. There are some images of him as
a minister: smart, broad-chested, cutting ribbons or shaking hands,
giving a speech at a lectern in a time when he didn't know the name
Maeve Bannerman. In fact, Florrie half recognizes him. But mostly,
the photos show a raging Max St. Clair, post-Nightjar: He has a raised
fist and a florid complexion. Sinews in his neck that stand proud and
tense, like rigging on a ship.

But what of the Trotts? Or Mrs. St. Clair?

Florrie carries on. Leaning forward in her chair, lit by the screen,
she scans every photograph of the gathered crowds. Is there anyone
here she knows? Any jawline or profile or knotted brow? Any slope of
the shoulders that she might recognize from St. Mary's congregation

or the dining room? Is that an Ellwood, twenty-five years younger? Are those the Professors Lim? Could that woolen beret be Velma Rudge's from two and a half decades ago? Is that policeman's profile a little like Reverend Joe's?

But she recognizes nothing. When, at last, she finds the Trotts—John Trott, a chartered accountant, and Charlotte, his wife—they're brand-new faces to her. But Florrie wonders if they might also be new faces to those who *did*, in fact, know them; if their faces had changed instantly with the news of their daughter's sudden, watery death. For they look almost featureless, erased; they are withdrawing into their winter coats, staring blankly through the crowds and camera flashes. They are there, she thinks—but also not there.

John and Charlotte Trott and Max St. Clair. None of these people are at Babbington Hall.

But isn't there one more parent? Still unaccounted for?

At that, Florrie hears a noise.

It comes from the corridor. She is motionless, as taut as a bow string. A person? A breeze? Have there been any stories of a Babbington ghost?

Maybe it was nothing.

But, no, it comes again. It's the floorboards: one creak and then another. Someone is approaching, slowly, along the corridor. They stop outside this room.

Florrie's thought, girlishly, is to try to hide—as if she isn't this age, isn't one-legged. (*Behind the sofa?* she thinks. *Or the curtain, perhaps?*) But the footsteps are coming nearer still and there is a light (A torch? A moving light, at least) scanning the walls of the library now, and the bookshelves and armchairs. *A burglar,* she thinks.

A voice calls out: "Who is that?"

The woman enters the library as she enters all rooms—slowly, nonchalantly, as if she were merely passing by at quarter past four in the morning and has better things to do. Having entered, she stops.

And she turns toward Florrie in a smooth, single motion as though she's mechanical, on some sort of automated plinth. "Florrie?"

"Yes. Yes, it's me." They study each other in near darkness.

"What are you doing here?" Magda delivers this in her flat, monotone voice, as if she's reading the words from a blackboard.

"Researching things. I couldn't sleep."

The carer approaches at the same unbothered pace. There's a pause, a click—and a single bulb is illuminated, suddenly, above Florrie's head. It reveals the alcove, spills out to show Florrie's dressing gown and the immediate carpet, the bare feet of Magda Dabrowski, the loose velour tracksuit bottoms, the midriff with its silver stud, the T-shirt on which there's an image of a cartoon bear and, above all of this, Magda's face as it has never seemed to Florrie; for a moment, she's unsure if it's Magda at all. For Magda wears no makeup. There's no kohl, no heavy brows. Her hair is undone to her shoulders. "Florrie, you know the time?"

"Yes. But Magda, what are you doing here? You live in Oxford."

"Normally. But since Renata fell . . ." She shrugs. "They need someone here, yes? On site. An insurance thing—I don't know what. There is more money in it so I say yes."

"You're staying on the third floor?"

"In Renata's place? No, thank you. In the staff room. It's not so bad. There is a sofa and I watch television on my phone. Smoke out of the window. But tonight, I hear noises, so . . ."

How beautiful she is. Take away the thick, blackened eyebrows; wipe off the kohl and thickly daubed cheekbones; pull those false eyelashes away from the corners of her eyes and you have, in front of you, an ethereal, beautiful creature whose features are far more clearly defined than they were when filled or ringed with black.

"So. Tell me. Researching what?"

What to say? How to explain this? Florrie wonders how much she should say. Or rather, she wonders how much she can trust Magda—for it's true that the carer wasn't born when the Nightjar deaths happened; true, too, that she's from southeast Poland and not the English home counties. But even so, couldn't Magda still be involved in some way? Know something? The carer stands there, arms folded, with a firm, dark expression.

Florrie decides to partly trust her. "It's complicated. But could you help me? Magda, is there anyone at Babbington called St. Clair?"

The carer purses her lips. She is suspicious of this question but doesn't challenge it. She only takes a strand of hair and feels her way down the length of it; on reaching its end, she examines the tip. "St. Clair? How do you spell this?"

Florrie explains.

"Why do you ask?"

"Oh dear. Well, I'm not sure I can say too much, Magda—or not at the moment, anyway. I'm so sorry."

"Is it illegal?"

"Illegal? Heavens, no!"

Magda, again, gives the one-shouldered shrug. "It might have been. It wouldn't matter to me. Florrie, I help you anyway. St. Clair? Like, *Saint* Clair?"

"Yes. Here on the ground floor—or upstairs, too. Do you know?"

"I will check. I can look at records."

"Would you? Oh, thank you, Magda."

"But Florrie—let me say this. It is past 4:30 now, and those sisters who aren't sisters? The nosey old crows? My *babcia* would call them *stara ryba*—like two old fish with their mouths like this?" She gulps, to demonstrate. "They wake early. And if they see you in here in your dressing gown like that, I think they tell a thousand stories to other people—yes?"

"I should go?"

"Yes. You know them—what they are like."

She does. "May I print something before I go?"

"Sure. It is expensive, but it's not my money. I find out about the St. Clairs for you now, and then I find you."

She touches Florrie once, very lightly, on the shoulder—a flinch of her fingers, no more than that. Then off she goes, swaying like an empress in her tracksuit bottoms and teddy-bear top.

Back in her quarters, Florrie boils her kettle—and settles herself in her mallard chair. Outside, day is breaking. There's an apricot glow in the east and she can hear the wren in the ivied wall—preparing itself, starting to bustle.

"Right."

Using her magnifying glass (bought from an antiques market in Bombay, as she remembers it), Florrie moves through further photographs, paying attention to everyone in the crowd: every seam and button and buckle; every gesture or turn of the head; every handbag and glove and scarf; every shade of colour; every shadow on the ground. Nothing. "But there must be something," she declares to her lemons on the wall.

And so she comes to the last photograph.

Florrie hadn't, in fact, meant to print it. For it isn't a picture of the Nightjar or courthouse—nor any part of the Bannerman case. It's a picture of Max St. Clair from a few years before. It is election night. He has won his seat (the caption beneath this photograph is *Max St. Clair takes East Chilterns seat with narrow majority of 78*), and he's giving his acceptance speech. And whilst he is at the photo's heart, there are others on the periphery—dejected candidates from other parties, the returning officer, enthusiastic supporters with clasped hands listening to St. Clair make his promises. But also, in the crowd, there's an arm.

In fact (she peers closer) there are two arms—both raised a little, with hands facing each other. This person is applauding the victorious Max St. Clair.

And what Florrie is staring at is not the arms themselves, nor the hands, but what's *on* them. What's been added. What is adorning them.

She leans back in her chair.

No. But she checks again, through her magnifying glass: there is no mistaking it. Twenty-five years later and it looks exactly the same.

Later, after breakfast, Florrie takes herself back outside. She rolls down between the topiary trees, the Grecian urns; she can hear birdsong and the rattling of trolleys, a sense of life and new beginnings that wasn't there three hours before. And she moves through the church gate, past the ancient yew, heaves herself up the metal ramp toward the church door, which is propped open and drops down into the church with all its restfulness and hush.

How often has Florrie prayed, truly, in her life? In the proper sense of it? Kneeling, and with hands pressed together? Not often, it's true. There has been the expectation of it—so that, on entering churches or cathedrals, mosques or synagogues, or even when standing in a stone circle in her anorak, in the rain, she has found herself wanting to murmur something to someone, to whatever might hear her: Thank you or Sorry—or, most often, Please. Have those been prayers, or a form of them? And what of sending love? For Florrie has sent love, in the Sitwell fashion, nearly every day of her life. She's imagined packing her big, beating heart with all its love and longing, wrapping it in crêpe paper, securing it with adhesive or ribbons or raffia or brown, glossy parcel tape, and labeling it with the address of its recipient—and she's imagined sending it out, into the world, as one might stand on a rooftop and release a racing pigeon. *Go! Go! Find them!* And isn't that a form of prayer?

But to write a prayer down, on paper? She can't recall having done it—not once. Nor has she ever read the written prayers of others, which feels, to Florrie, an intrusive thing to do. But she parks herself in front of the trestle table. She reaches across the embossed-leather bookmarks and pamphlets on the history of St. Mary's, Temple Beeches, and lifts, with both hands, the prayer request book. She sets it in her lap.

It is bound in maroon cardboard. Attached to its spine is a blunted pencil, tied to the binding with a length of string.

Behind her, at Babbington, people are breakfasting. Mail is being opened. Tea is being poured. But here, in the half-dark hush of St. Mary's Church, Florrie Butterfield is turning the pages of the prayer request book; she does so with care and reverence, as if the prayers were sleeping and must not be disturbed. She makes her way through the months and years, through the written, secret worries of so many human lives. *Please be with my husband during his operation. Please pray for Roger with his diagnosis. Pray for my grandsons as they start university. Pray for Della, whose heart is hurting her. Please don't let there be a war.* There are hundreds of them—prayers for bereavement and illness and exams and heartbreak, for courage and patience and for a good night's sleep; for hope against financial destitution; for hope that a child might soon be conceived; to give thanks for the safe arrival of twins or for a much-loved cat being found; to ask for governmental wisdom; to express relief that a breast lump has been pronounced benign.

All these human worries. All these written words that mean, mostly, *help*. And it's only when Florrie reaches the last three pages of the prayer request book that she catches her breath.

On the morning of midsummer's day, it says this:

Pray for my Polly.

That's all. But the pencil has been pressed deeply into the paper; the lettering is jagged, like a mountain range—and the *f*? It's elaborate, considered: a tiny treble clef.

Afterward, Florrie sleeps. She returns to the old apple store and—in full daylight, fully dressed—fumbles her way into bed and brings

the sheets about her. For she can hardly bear the weight of her tiredness now.

Nor can she bear the grief. *Pray for my Polly.* Those words seem so
small until one understands them. And, in understanding them, Florrie now considers Nancy's dignity and quietness, her fear of going to
St. Chad's and how terribly hard it must be to know that that ribbon
is curling its way through her vertebrae. Yet, in that prayer book, she
did not write for her own sake. She did not pray for herself. She prayed
only for her daughter, who is long dead.

She has carried on. She—Nancy Tapp—has kept going, or tried
to; she has woken up every morning, stared at the ceiling and decided
that, yes, she'll try to make it through the day. Pip had said this, once:
after Herbert's death, Florrie had hovered on the landing and overheard her aunt saying, "Prue, listen to me: we have to make it through."
And isn't that true? All we can hope for? One step, then another. One
hour, and one more.

But it can be so hard—so terribly, desperately hard—that we arm
ourselves with whatever we can to help us: *Dum spiro spero* or daydreams of Paris, pentagram earrings or a prayer request book. Or
we marry someone who can't hurt us and we travel from country to
country, filling our losses with small, bright adventures, with people
who make us smile with their own way of surviving (*write* no *in salt,
Mrs. Plumley; it will keep the snakes away*)—and, like this, we do carry
on. We do find ourselves a year older, or two, or twenty, so that what
had felt unbearable, at first, seems a little fainter, harder to believe
in. We have set so much life between that loss and now that it seems
like it happened to somebody else—except that it didn't. It happened
to us. And Florrie's pain can, at least, be tempered by knowing that
there hadn't been a death in Hackney. But Nancy? Her pain cannot be
tempered or set down. And if Florrie had the strength, she'd pack up
her heart—all her love and sympathy—and wrap it in black paper. *I'm
so sorry. I didn't know.*

But she doesn't have the strength.

Instead, Florrie closes her eyes. Oh, to be eight years old again—in her childhood bed on a summer's evening, with the curtain drifting in and out. With Herbert and Prudence in the kitchen; with Bobs whistling on the staircase, pausing to converse with the fat, talkative Butterfield cat—and for nothing to be damaged yet, or broken. To not yet understand how much life can hurt.

She drifts, drifts toward sleep . . .

On its edges, she hears a sound: small and rough, as if trying not to be heard.

A square of paper has been pushed under Florrie's door. She does not reach for her glasses; she is too tired to retrieve this note—and only wants to sleep. But Florrie is glad to know it's there—and, as she closes her eyes, she likes to think of him writing it, uncertain of the wording; of him bending down to post the note through to her with all the curious, angular slowness of a giraffe at a watering hole.

Stanhope. She lets him go—and she lets go, too, of the afternoon light, of the distant sound of a woodpigeon's call and voices. Florrie enters a cave-like sleep—dark, with no awareness of anything beyond it, with no dreams at all.

33

Edward Silversmith

She was three weeks off her seventeenth birthday when she met Edward Silversmith. She'd been at the village shop. Mr. Patchett kept the vegetables at the back and so it was here, as Florrie rummaged through the potato sack, that he must have first seen her; bottom-up in her corduroy pinafore, commenting to herself about the potatoes' sprouting, greenish quality. She'd dropped one. It had rolled across the Patchett floor, stopped against a man's boot. He'd offered it, bemused. "Yours, I believe."

Later, she'd dream of being asked by people, So, how did you meet? She wanted to say, He handed me a potato. She wanted to explain how she'd risen from her crouching position, seen his tortoiseshell spectacles and the hole in his jumper and his small, lopsided smile and had known, with certainty, as people did in books. *Ah, that potato . . . That's when I knew.*

He was a student at Brasenose College—physics, he told her, as if the word had magic in it. He'd been living in Oxford for three years, by then—in a room on Holywell Street opposite New College and a permanent line of bicycles. Florrie was amazed: firstly, that she was only meeting him now. But also because it felt like she had, somehow, met him before. There was both a familiarity to him and a newness that entirely thrilled her. (When had she ever had conversations about physics before?) In cafés, she'd cup her chin in her hands and ask about the laws of thermodynamics or what absolute zero was. On a bench in Christ Church Meadow, she swiveled to see and hear him better, one leg beneath her—no matter that it was an undignified pose.

"It's the basis of everything," he'd tell her—and list the possibilities of atomic analysis, the wonder of calculus. Sometimes Florrie returned to Vicarage Lane with a sense that her brain was physically stretching, like a waistband, adjusting itself to so much news; she'd look at her bedroom ceiling and think of all the galaxies beyond.

One morning, she sat down heavily at the kitchen table with a restless, wondering sigh.

Aunt Pip, cracking eggs in a basin, looked up. "Are you ill?"

She twisted a strand of hair. "No, not ill. Just . . ."

What did she seem? She lacked the words herself. She had never been so taken with one person before. With hindsight, some people must have known. Some—Dr. Winthrop or Mrs. Fortescue, say—must have seen this new, permanent flush in Florrie's cheeks or her tendency to gaze out of windows and wondered if such changes were caused by a boy. Pinky Underwood certainly did. "What's his name?" She asked this sitting under the footbridge, eating a plum.

"Who? What do you mean?" Florrie had denied it, at first. But soon she took Pinky's wrist and confessed. "Edward. Teddy. Ted. He handed me a potato."

"He did what?"

Yet her family never spotted this. They may have done, if life had been calmer, if they'd had more opportunities to look and see. But Prudence still mourned her husband. Also, Bobs's nightmares were worsening by then; they'd started to enter his waking mind, to seize his daytime thoughts so that he'd throw ornaments, kick doors. Once, Aunt Pip found him stamping on the laundry basket and raging—"You bastard! Get away from me!"—and, in trying to help him, she came away with bruises for which, afterward, Bobs was so desperately sorry that he punished himself by banging his head on the iron bedstead and bled and lost teeth and had to be sedated with drops in a water glass, and Prudence and Pip both cried in the bathroom, hoping Florrie couldn't hear. Dr. Winthrop was visiting daily. So, no, perhaps they— Pip and Prudence—didn't have time to spot the shine to Florrie's eyes.

Teddy would wait for her at the bandstand in Upper Dorbury's park. Always, he was there first. Sometimes he'd watch her approach, smiling, with his hands in his pockets; other times, Florrie came from a different direction and could see how Teddy acted when believing himself to be unwatched. He might take out a comb. He'd clean his glasses on a little white cloth or refasten the buttons on his woolen coat and Florrie would think, *Look*. She was no great beauty, she knew that—and yet here he was, combing his hair for her.

Teddy was no great beauty himself, in truth. His face—its reddish cheeks, its crooked incisor, its prominent nose down which his spectacles could slide so that he'd push them back up with the heel of his hand—was not classically lovely. No sculptures would come of it. But Florrie loved this face, all the same. She loved it for its quizzical expression, its patchy attempts at a beard. She loved, even, the slight lisp he had on certain words when he became excited with his talk of electromagnetism or Newton's laws. But above all, Florrie loved his face because it was *his*; because underneath it was Ted's mind and all it contained. Yes, he knew about physics. But he also knew Yeats and Gandhi and the songs of Sinatra; he'd quote his own father, who'd been (and he confessed this guiltily, in a whisper) a Cambridge man. And Florrie remembers how, in a café called Cadena with a view of the ruined castle, over a toasted teacake, he'd spoken of Plato's musings on romantic love. "We should want," he said, "our loved one to be their best selves, to live their best life. It's a selfless thing—true love."

Yet it wasn't just his mind that she loved. Florrie noted everything: his scent, a little like libraries; his knack of shuffling cards so that, for a moment, they'd move between his hands like an accordion; his slightly effeminate sneezes; the shoe that squelched in the rain.

She loved his tiny room in the eaves, with stacked books and a tea tray for a table and the warm, knitted blanket on his bed. She loved his own love for Oxford—for *his* Oxford, which wasn't the Bodleian or the Radcliffe Camera, but a gargoyle holding its own heart, or a specific willow tree under which she'd lie with her head in his lap. She loved how much they laughed: at wordplay or gestures or child-hood stories, at her naming of pigeons, at sudden downpours they had to run through, at the whipped cream that Teddy acquired on his nose during a shared strawberry sundae and which he chose to wear around Oxford for an hour or two. She loved, too, how he might shout *Go!* without warning—a race, suddenly, over the wasteland or college greens, which Florrie would never win, but it hardly mattered when he'd wait, open-armed, for her.

And Teddy made her feel beautiful. How on earth could he man-age that? When nobody else had ever considered Florrie to be so, least of all Florrie Butterfield herself? But he listened to her, without inter-ruptions. He would lean forward and ask for more from her: her fears and ambitions, what she loved most—and, as she answered, he'd wear an expression of wonderment as if Florrie were made of gold. "How did I find you?" "Potatoes," she replied. He never remarked on her height. He counted her freckles, called them constellations. Nor did he mind the redness of her inner thighs, where they'd rubbed together. And once, on the staircase of the Ashmolean Museum, he'd dropped down a step so that they were nose to nose and he kissed her brow, her cheeks and eyelids—as if paying homage to her.

"Does he want to marry you?" Pinky asked this, on the top deck of the omnibus.

"I think so. Maybe."

"But he's not been to Vicarage Lane?"

"Not yet."

But there was other news, too. On that bus, as they rattled along Broad Street, Pinky said, "Listen, Butters . . ." She was going to secretarial school in London—leaving in two weeks' time. "It'll take six months, they reckon—shorthand, typing, all of it."

"London? Why not Oxford?" But of course, Florrie knew why. This was the girl who, since the age of seven, had preferred sleeping on the Butterfield sofa to her proper bed at home; who'd pulled down her sleeves to hide bruises; who'd learned how to jump out of first-floor windows without hurting her knees, and run. She would never come back to Oxford—or not to live—again.

"I have a Great-Aunt Euphemia, apparently—my mother's aunt. I've only just discovered this, but that'll do. Nearsighted, rich, unmarried and happy to have me. Or she's unbothered by the thought of having me, at least. She lives in a house on Notting Hill."

We're changing, Florrie thought—*she and I; we are about to walk down different paths*. And as they descended from the bus, she grabbed Pinky's wrist as if they were parting at that very moment and she couldn't bear the thought of it.

"Don't be daft, Florrie. We're *us*, aren't we? You and me. London is hardly far these days. And anyway," she winked, "you'll visit, won't you—the three of you? You, Ted and your engagement ring?"

Looking back—as she has done ten thousand times—Florrie supposes it was an incremental change in him; that her understanding came, too, in portions, one by one, like coins. The need to say his name twice before he heard her; the new, increasing lateness; his excuses for not meeting Prudence (too busy, too tired, too late in the day); the sense, too, that it was Florrie, now, who reached for his hand as they walked through the Water Meadow, not Ted reaching for hers. A reluctance to take her back to his attic room on Holywell Street.

"Is everything all right, Ted?"

"Yes. Just . . . thinking."

"What about?"

"Oh, nothing."

She didn't tell Pinky of this. Her friend was gathering clothes, books, pencils; she was making plans to see the Savoy Hotel and London Zoo, to ride on proper red buses. On the platform of Oxford station, preparing to board, Pinky glanced back to Florrie. "Want to come?"

"To London?"

"Stay with Great-Aunt Euphemia and me? Be a secretary? It'll be fun."

But she had Bobs. She had her job at Berriman's—and whilst she didn't name Teddy, they both knew that he was her primary reason for staying behind. *Because I love him.* Because, too, she feared his love would dissipate like a rainbow if she went away.

It's just because he's busy. Or I'm imagining it. And she tried not to notice the tiny, insubstantial signs which started to grow in number until they were, in fact, of substance: how he'd study a teaspoon for too long; how he wouldn't want to sit in the window of a café but chose, instead, a back corner where they couldn't be seen from the street; how he'd look up at Florrie after she'd been speaking for a minute or longer and say, "Sorry, what?" And when Florrie asked for cream on an apple slice, he'd question whether she needed it—gesturing at her waist. "Just a thought," he said.

On the canal bridge, she'd pleaded, "You do still love me, don't you?" (How she'd hate herself for this later, thinking, *Stupid girl.*)

Then, one day, he didn't come at all. She sat on a bench in the park all day—until the interior lights of the buses were reflected in the puddles and a fox trotted past her. *He's had an emergency. He's not well.* But the wiser, tired Florrie knew that he was perfectly healthy; he was just choosing to be somewhere else and watching (perhaps relieved? A little guiltily?) the minute hand of the clock.

Even now, seven decades later, Florrie has never had a proper goodbye. Teddy never gave a reason for his leaving—although she has pulled enough threads together to make a wholly plausible truth.

Homely Florrie. The Butterfield complexion. The large, soft behind of Florrie Butterball. (*Of course,* she thought. *Of course he's changed his mind.*) And it all made further sense on a Sunday lunchtime in late September. Prudence had half burned a ham. Florrie was laying the table—cutlery, napkins, a late rose in a vase—when her mother set down the saucepan and said, "There was talk at church today," addressing the saucepan directly.

"Talk?"

"Clemency Winthrop. Dr. Winthrop's daughter. She's engaged. It's lovely news—isn't it? A wedding! But I don't think we should tell Bobs. I know what hopes he had."

Florrie set down her napkin. "Engaged? To whom?"

"Edward someone. Silver? Gold? No, it was Silver-*something.* These carrots, Flo—have I ruined them?"

Florrie stared at the tablecloth. *But he's combed his hair for me. I've lain in his bed on Holywell Street.*

No, the carrots weren't ruined. Yes, it was lovely news. And she agreed that, no, they shouldn't tell Bobs, for it would burn him more deeply than Clervaux ever did.

34

Dr. Mallory Is Concerned

Florrie—still fully dressed, still wearing a single pale-green shoe—sleeps for nearly six hours. When she finally awakens, she's confused to find there is an afternoon slant to the light in her room, that it strikes the eastern walls, not the west; doesn't she normally wake up in the morning? And why is she not in her night-dress? Florrie peers at her alarm clock, puts it down.

But slowly, clarity comes. It is Saturday—still. It is Saturday afternoon. She had been at the computer till almost five in the morning; later, she'd taken herself down to St. Mary's Church. And, having sat herself upright, Florrie moves through her recent discoveries, lifting them out one by one and holding them up like crystal glasses: the luminous computer screen; Magda by torchlight and *sans maquillage*; the moment when her magnifying glass with its beaded handle had picked out, from an old photograph, an opal ring, nearly as big as a thumb.

Nancy. How could it be her? This timid woodland creature? But it is her. She sent the nightjar card; she pressed those words into it: *I never stopped hoping I'd find you.* Not, then, the words of someone who's loved for years and years, but someone who's grieved for as many. Someone who can't forget.

Florrie glances down. Stanhope's note is still sitting on the carpet. It is folded so that she can't read it from here—which is enough for Florrie to find the strength to push back her bedsheets, adjust her linen dress (a soft mid-green, like peppermint tea) which has gathered around her waist and creased itself terribly, and work herself into her wheelchair.

Dear F,
I've had a sudden thought about someone. Shall we meet
for lunch?
S x

But it is past three now: lunchtime has come and gone.

She sets the note down and worries. There's so much to tell Stanhope. But she can't tell him, not really; she doesn't feel able. (*What colour*, she wonders, *are his braces? What shirt is he wearing today?*)

Then there's a tapping on the door. "Miss Florrie?"

Magda Dabrowski enters the room looking as Magda usually does; that is, no pink velour tracksuit bottoms, no teddy T-shirt or scent of talc. Her eyebrows are, once more, thick, dark and geometric; her fingernails are an extraordinary bright green colour today, not unlike the algae that grows in stagnant water. (Did Florrie dream the other version?) "You okay, yes? I knocked earlier and you did not answer. So I thought, She must be sleeping, and I leave you."

"Hello, Magda, dear. Yes, I'm quite all right."

"So." The carer sits heavily on the mallard chair, swings one leg over the other. "There are no St. Clairs. I tried all the spellings. Once, before I came, there was a Sinclair on the second floor—*sin*, not *saint*; spelled not the same—but they died two years ago." She gives her singular shrug. "Does that help? I think not, probably."

"Oh, it *does* help—thank you. And Magda, may I ask: Did anyone see you doing this? Or did you tell anyone?"

Magda scoffs. "Florrie . . . I can keep secrets. Like you can, yes?"

Part of her would love to pour all of this out, for Renata, like cream from a metal urn: opals and Tapps and nightjars and treble clefs and upturned cars in rivers all caught in Magda's palms, between her algae nails. She'd love to say, *Look*. But she can only shake her head.

"It is fine. You tell me when you're ready—or not at all. Makes no difference."

With that, Magda leans forward in the chair. She lifts Florrie's left wrist across to her lap, where she studies the bruise, looks at its progression. "Better. Does it hurt if I do that?" And she talks in her low, casual, monotonous way—about Georgette and Poland and how her daughter, Ula-bear, is entering a bad-tempered phase so that Magda's *matka* and *babcia* are both in despair—and Florrie responds with murmurs and nods, and gives the impression that she's listening hard, but she is, in fact, thinking of the Babbington stairs. She is thinking of their height and creakiness; also, that they're stairs at all. Because yes, Nancy wrote the nightjar card. But how on earth did she reach the third floor? How did she knock on Renata's door, up in the eaves? She couldn't have done. There's the lift—but it would have made so many pings and clonks that, even in thunder, it would have been detected; also, it only reaches the second floor—and so what might Nancy have done then? Pulled herself up on the banisters? Crawled?

"Magda?"

"Hmm?"

"Tabitha Brimble. How is she?"

"The lady upstairs? I think she is the same. Maybe quieter—but Dr. Mallory helps. He is seeing her a lot. He is here now, I think, because his car is in the car park. That little red one? All I will say is doctors must make a nice amount of money to have cars like that whilst nurses and carers just have beans for tea—but what do I know?"

"Is she shouting now?"

"I don't think so. Not anymore."

"But she did shout?"

"Yes."

"And she's pushing still? I heard she pushed someone, Magda. Do you happen to know who?"

Magda narrows an eye and considers Florrie at an angle. "Is this more research that you do? Like a spy? So—I don't know his name. But I know she just tipped him out and called him all the bad words—like a liar and a cheat. All about the lying. The man wasn't hurt, but it was not a nice thing to happen." At that, she stands, exhales and rotates a shoulder with an audible crack. "Sleeping on that sofa . . . It's not good for me. I reckon they should pay me more for my bones . . ." She mutters in Polish.

"Tipped him out?"

"What?"

"You said tipped him out. Out of . . . what? A chair?"

"A wheelchair—like yours. Except he uses it sometimes, not always. You know how it is."

Suddenly, Florrie does. She knows exactly. "Magda?"

"It is all questions with you today. Should I charge a pound an answer?"

"Did you say that the doctor was still here? At Babbington?"

Dr. Mallory arrives at Florrie's quarters as the afternoon grows old. He enters as he always does—two brisk knocks to announce himself. He is groomed and scented. He seems out of breath, as if he has hurried here.

"Florrie. I've heard you're not well. I'm so very sorry. What is it, exactly?" He moves forward to her and sets his leather bag down on the floor. "Your head? Is your vision all right?"

"Yes, both are fine. It's not that. It's a rather sensitive issue."

"Florrie, I can assure you that there's little I've not seen or heard about the digestive system, or gynecological problems, or—"

"No! No, no. I'm perfectly fine in those areas, thank you. I'm very well in general, as it happens—more well than I've been in a long time, which is surprising, all things considered."

"Then why have you called me?"

"Because I believe I've uncovered something, Doctor."

"Uncovered?"

"About one of the other residents."

The doctor seems nonplussed. He takes his place in the mallard chair and leans forward with his hands cupping his knees. "You've uncovered something? I don't understand."

"Can I ask what you know of Nancy Tapp?"

"Nancy? I can't tell you anything, Florrie—as you know. Patient confidentiality."

"But you do *see* her?"

"Yes, I see her. I see everyone here who needs to be seen—residents, staff. It's what doctors do. After tomorrow, of course, I'll be seeing much less of her—because she's leaving for St. Chad's. Did you know that? First thing in the morning. Florrie, I'm worried. What are you telling me? Are you sure you have no headaches? Any nausea?"

She pauses. She has yet to speak the words that will follow; she hasn't tried them in the mirror, hasn't murmured them to her painted lemons or her prayer flags. She has no idea how they will sound. "I am not sure how ill she truly is."

The doctor settles back. His expression remains unsure but he also shifts his jaw, from side to side, suggesting he's not taking kindly to this. "Not ill? Nancy?"

"Well, I'm sure she *is* ill. I'm sure she does have tumours, because she's terribly pale and thin—and I can hear how awful this sounds, Dr. Mallory, to be doubting her. I hate doubting anyone—and I will feel perfectly dreadful and ashamed if what I think is the truth proves to be wrong. It's not in my nature to be suspicious, you see. But, Doctor, I think Nancy can walk."

He is motionless, without expression. "Walk?"

"I think so, yes. Or maybe we should ask her. Because how do we know that she can't? She says she can't, and she's in the chair, but have you actually examined her? Do we only have her word for it?"

"I assessed her before she came to Babbington. They require it, as you know. A doctor's report is necessary, especially for the accessible rooms. What's making you say this?"

They study each other as opponents do—cattle, or the stags that would roar from the slopes of Achnacross in the autumn before locking horns.

"She must be able to."

The doctor seems annoyed, plucks at his collar. "Why, exactly, must she be able to?"

"Because Tabitha Brimble saw her—walking up the stairs. And she's been trying to tell us all that Nancy is lying, that she doesn't need a wheelchair, but no one's listening to her. That's why she's frustrated. It's why she pushed someone and called him a liar; not because of *him* but because of the wheelchair. People think it's her condition making her say such things but she's actually telling the truth, poor thing; she knows exactly what she saw. And I'd probably shout, too, if no one believed me. I'd push people out of wheelchairs, too."

"Let me understand this, Florrie. You think Nancy Tapp is lying about her cancer, about needing palliative care; that she can, in fact, walk perfectly well. That she walked up the stairs at some point. When did this happen?"

"Midsummer's night. The thunderstorm."

"The night Renata jumped?"

"Fell, Doctor. Fell. And actually, I do believe the cancer; it's just the wheelchair that I think is an outright lie."

The doctor drops back into the chair. There's a loosening to him, a long exhalation, and he scratches his jawline. "How long has it been, Florrie? A week? I'd have expected confusion to show itself before now, but shock can come and go as it chooses; it's not predictable that way. Let's have a quick listen to your heart, shall we? And I'll ask you a few questions, if I may. Can you tell me the year?"

She stares, appalled. *Oh, heavens!* He thinks she is losing her mind. Dr. Mallory is thinking, at this very moment—as he holds her wrist in his cold, pale hands and times her pulse on his pocket watch—that Florrie ought, perhaps, to be moved elsewhere; that he'll have a quiet word with Georgette. And Florrie has two options, now—only two. She can either continue with this—maintaining that, yes, Nancy can walk, and that she's lying to him and everyone else and you'll see that I'm right, you'll see; or she can laugh at herself. She can laugh at this sudden foolishness, blame the hot weather and lack of sleep. She opts for the latter. "Oh, *listen* to me! Oh, Doctor. I'm talking nonsense. I *do* have bad dreams but it's only the heat."

It is the better choice. He sets down his stethoscope, nods. "There's no doubting that these are strange times. They're taking their toll, I know—and on *you* specifically, it seems. But I'm concerned that you did, in fact, bang your head when you fell. Or you might have had some sort of bleed . . ."

"I didn't. I'm fine. I told you—I'm quite well."

"So you say, Florrie. But I'd like to take you in."

"In? To hospital?"

"For an X-ray, Florrie. It's important. In fact, I should have done this before. If there's a bleed on the brain . . . It won't hurt, I promise. It's important we do this, and that we do this quickly—do you understand me? Now, please: wait here. I need to speak to Georgette. But I'll be right back, do you hear me? We can get you in tonight."

"Doctor, please, there's no—"

He rises, goes to the door. "You'll stay, yes?"—as if she's a dog who he knows is only half trained and who will, most likely, jump out of the window as soon as he closes the door.

Of course, Florrie doesn't stay. She's never cared too much for orders—and there is, categorically, no bleed on Florrie's brain. Nor can she go anywhere when Nancy Tapp is leaving for St. Chad's in the morning, when there's so much to do and say. So Florrie waits till the doctor's footsteps have died away and then pushes herself outside, into the fading afternoon light, and across the courtyard; she turns left, grinds over gravel, bounces over turf and arrives at the old wood-shed, the door of which is wide open; in it, there is no Nancy. All her boxes are gone. So Florrie pivots and hurries onward—to the only other place where Nancy Tapp (or Nancy St. Clair, as she was twenty-five years ago, in the newspaper reports) might be now; over cobbles and tarmac and red-brick pathways, past the Grecian urns. Even as she passes the old pig sties, Florrie doesn't slow—although she does think of Stanhope in his armchair, reading. She thinks of his books and ter-racotta tile, his illuminated globe.

35

St. Mary's Church, Saturday Evening

Florrie rolls up the ramp, down the ramp and into the church's half-light. Once in, she finally stops. She catches her breath, or tries to. She lets St. Mary's grow used to her being there.

There's rarely proper silence in the world. One thinks there is—but, if one listens, a pipe will creak or a bee will knock against a windowpane or, in the far distance, someone will clear their throat. There's always one's own body, too; the act of existence creates its own sounds—breath, pulse, the gurgles of digestion. On the lower slopes of the Matterhorn, there might have been true silence if she'd thought to hold her breath.

Yet there appears to be silence now.

The dust and light make no sound. Nor do the stacked Bibles. Nor do the homemade pamphlets, on St. Mary's, printed on royal-blue card. Flowers wilt on the trestle table. The prayer book is closed on its red ribbon marker, already looking different from a few hours ago. All these things are silent. But then Florrie hears a sound.

It's tiny. At any other time, she wouldn't have detected it. But this evening she's more alert than she's ever been—and she knows what the sound is. This is a building of stone: its walls and stained-glass windows cannot make any noise, nor can the font. But the metal grate? That runs on either side of the aisle, with the worn red carpet in between? It's old, as all things here are. It's not evenly laid, in parts. And so, Florrie knows, this grate—with its holes in a fleur-de-lis pattern, and all its dropped pennies and buttons and hair-pins in the cavernous space below it—can rock beneath a person's weight; it can clonk and shudder beneath a wheel or shoe—and when it does, that sound will echo through St. Mary's like a steady knock on a door.

She hears that knocking now.

Florrie herself wheels forward to the top of the aisle, looks down.

At the far end, by the altar, Nancy sits in her chair. Is she praying? She doesn't seem to be. She is facing forward; she appears to be look-ing at the embroidered altar cloth, or the vase of lilies; or is she looking higher? All Florrie knows is that she, Nancy, seems entirely absorbed in her thoughts, for she doesn't turn at Florrie's own clonking and knocking. She seems wholly unaware of Florrie's approach.

Florrie draws alongside her, puts on her brakes. "Nancy?"

At that, Nancy jumps—*Oh!* And on seeing Florrie, she gives a bright smile. "Hello! How *lovely*, Florrie. Will you sit with me a while?"

So they sit side by side, wheel by wheel. And Florrie feels quite unsure of herself. She wants both to stare at Nancy's face and not look at it at all; she wants to speak of what she knows and never say a word. She feels that she's sitting by a friend with whom she ate those biscuits—but also a stranger. "How are you?" she asks.

How are you? Those old three words that have always seemed so foolish when said to Nancy Tapp. But Florrie means them differently, now. *How is your conscience? Your broken heart?*

"Me? I don't quite know. You know I'm leaving tomorrow? By ten, they're saying. So I won't ever be in this church again. I'm saying good-bye to it, Florrie. It's been a good place for me."

My friend. Nancy is, isn't she? No matter what's said, or done? So Florrie tries to settle herself, let her nerves drift down from her, through the fleur-de-lis grating to join the buttons and fluff. "It *is* a nice church. And the churchyard, too."

"Oh, yes—and the churchyard. It's lovely, especially with all those birds, now. Mind you, I do think it's a shame that the Babbingtons are everywhere—Babbington this, Babbington that. Like ants at a picnic!" She laughs quickly, uncertain. "I'm not sure they were terribly nice, actually."

"No?" Florrie has always suspected she'd have been fond of the pig-breeding one, at least. "What makes you say that?"

Nancy blinks her dark eyes. "You don't know? Well, I can't speak for *all* the Babbingtons. But *he*, that one there"—she gestures—"wasn't nice at all."

Florrie's attention is not drawn to the wooden cross or mahogany pulpit but to the nearest, largest Babbington plaque, set high on the north-facing wall. *Richard Babbington Esq. late of this parish*—his attributes carved out in stone for fifteen lines. *He was just, honourable, a leader of men, who enacted the finest qualities that the Lord may bestow on a man.* She can't find any hint of unkindness. "But he *sounds* nice, Nancy."

"Doesn't he? I know! But honestly, you won't believe what I found. I looked into it, you see—the Babbington family, and the history of this place. Whilst I waited, you know. And it seems that Richard Babbington is not what this plaque claims him to be. Do you know how his fortunes were made?"

"Mine ventilation?"

She squeaks at that, like a vole. "I thought that, too! And he *did* create some sort of bellows or pump, that's true. But before that, I mean! You'll never guess."

In appearance, Nancy seems no different from the last time they met. She still has the quick, searching eyes; still the pearl earrings, the neatly combed hair. Still the restless hands that move over each other, like a mouse's paws. And that girlishness, too, is no less so that Florrie wonders now if she's made a mistake, a terrible faux pas. How could *she* have hurt Renata? *Florence, you've got this wrong.*

"Slaves! Can you believe it? I just couldn't, at first. But it's perfectly true. I used the computer and there it was. They don't tell you *that* in the Babbington brochures!" She fans the air once, dismissively, as if an imaginary brochure had floated by. "No, it's the ventilation they tell us about. And I've wondered, in my little room—with all my cardboard boxes—if, having built his fancy house with its stables and icehouse, and having married his pretty wife, he'd paused over dinner one night—a fine roast pheasant, perhaps, with a nice glass of red— and suddenly felt that maybe the selling of people might not be the Christian thing. So he decided to do something else. I wonder if he saw those poor miners and thought he'd help *them*, at least. Anyway, those are my thoughts."

As for Florrie's thoughts, they are this: *No, I haven't got this wrong.* For Nancy may still be smiling as she speaks; she may still be turning her paws over and blinking those bright eyes, but there is, now, a shadow in her voice. Speaking of Richard Babbington Esq. has beckoned forth a brand-new sharpness. (Certain words—*pretty, Christian, a fine roast pheasant*—had almost been spat out.) And it suddenly seems possible that there is, beneath this girlishness, a different, harder Nancy Tapp; that just as the wheelchair isn't the truth, neither is her sweetness. And it's at this moment that Florrie hears someone (who?) say, "I know."

"Know what, dear Florrie?"

"I know what happened at the Nightjar."

Nancy is suddenly still. Indeed, she stops moving so quickly that one hand is left to hover, in midair. She stares, without blinking, at the altar cloth. And, oh, how right Florrie is. The little brown bird and Arthur, anniversaries and the *F* like a treble clef: Florrie has added these things up like marbles to reach the right number, which is, put into words: *Nancy, it was you.* Yet Florrie doesn't say this.

She chooses this, instead: "And Maeve Bannerman. I know who that is, too."

Nancy lowers her hand. "Do you? Ah."

And with that, there's a change in the air. Florrie is aware, suddenly, of an enormity of power in the woman by her side. She is skeletal, yes. She is ill. But something is starting to radiate from Nancy now—hatred or rage or something even darker. It feels physical, with its own temperature. It seems to literally darken the church. And how Florrie feels now—uneasy, tense—is how she might feel when standing at the foot of a concrete dam that holds back a winter reservoir, thinking, *If this breaks, I will be swept away.*

She finds her own, small voice. "I'm so very sorry for your loss."

"Are you? That's kind. But you are kind, aren't you? Those custard creams. I meant that, you know; I was touched by that gesture. Most people stay away from the dying or the grieving because we make them uncomfortable. But not you. You've always been so . . . thoughtful. You're such a cheery soul—and it doesn't do, I know, to envy; but, oh, I've envied you, Florrie. Not a care in the world! As light as a cloud—or a powder puff! But you're no fool, I know that much. May I ask you something? Under the yew, on Sunday morning, you said Renata *fell*. Fell, not jumped. Why did you say that?"

"Because she didn't jump. I've never believed that."

"Why not? Because you took her a jam jar of flowers and she was grateful? I saw you do that, Florrie—collecting petunias and daisies that morning. Another kind gesture of yours, dear. But if I may say so, a lively conversation over some buttercups is not enough to stop someone from walking in front of a train or taking pills and running a bath. My husband—my second husband—had made dinner reservations for the night he died in Belsize Park; do you think that stopped him?" She looks down at her opal ring. "You say you know what happened at the Nightjar? How? From newspapers?"

"Yes—on the computer. It was a nightclub. Three girls went there."

"A nightclub? A brothel, of sorts; a disgrace of a place. Three girls did go there, yes. How old were they? Do you know that?"

"Sixteen at the time."

"No." Nancy raises a single finger, in correction. "*Two* were sixteen. The two girls who died were sixteen years old. But the one who didn't die? Who was driving the car? She was eighteen months older. Another three weeks and she'd have been eighteen years old—an adult, in the law's eyes. *Two* were sixteen. What else do you know?"

Florrie tries to remember. But it's hard to remember things clearly when one's heart is banging like a metronome and one's companion is speaking with such bitterness, opening and closing their hard, pale hands. Only fragments come to her: a courtroom and midsummer, a property tycoon and a Volkswagen Corrado that the girls borrowed from Meredith's brother.

"Borrowed? Oh, she *said* that. Stole. Maeve took that car without permission—so what does that make it?"

"But the judge said—"

"Never mind the judge. The judge knew nothing. He was taken in by her big blue eyes, her pleading. Oh, I didn't mean it, Your Honour. No—Maeve stole it. And she'd stolen more than that in her time— but I doubt the papers have told you that? That she'd been placed into care and passed from family to family? As wanted as a disease? She was trouble from the start, that one—bitter, sharp-tongued, answering back. She met Polly in Liberty's in London—in Liberty's! *Her!* She was only there to steal, I can promise you that. But somehow—God knows how—she and Polly liked each other. They became friends . . ."

No, she hadn't known—about the thieving or the care home. Neither of these things had been in the newspapers. One gets facts in such places, perhaps—times, statistics, court rulings, who exactly said what—but one doesn't hear about all the different bedrooms that a girl called Maeve must have known in her childhood; one doesn't hear of the small bag that must have held all her belongings—clothes, a book, a toothbrush, her one-eyed furless bear that she keeps, even now, on the third floor. One doesn't learn what she must have liked in

Polly or what Polly liked in Maeve. Adventure? Robustness? A shared
sense of humour? A soft, strange, easy recognition that these two girls
were of similar soul and substance and would, perhaps, be friends all
their lives?

"What of Meredith Trott?"

"Meredith? Sweet girl. She and Polly had known each other since
birth. I'd been expecting Polly when Charlotte Trott had been expecting her twins—and we'd take tea together, compare notes on our
pregnancies, as mothers do. They went to the same boarding school,
our girls, had the same toys. And they could have been sisters, because
they had the same colouring—fair, with blue eyes. Smart girls, too—
never any trouble. So you can imagine how we felt when that wretched
Maeve arrived . . ."

The dam, she thinks, is straining. It creaks at its joins, its weakest
points. But Florrie can't leave or turn away. She has so much more to
ask; and Nancy, she's sure, has so much more to say—and so Florrie
looks squarely, without blinking, until Nancy's gaze meets her own.

"You sent the card, didn't you? With the nightjar on it?"

For a moment, she thinks this woman will object—a horrified
gasp, a scornful *Ha!*, or the squeaked protestation of a cornered mouse.
But instead, she starts to smile. "Aha! I knew you'd ask about that. I've
known you've had it, you see. I saw it—when I met you and Stanhope
outside the church. I saw the envelope wedged between your thighs,
Florrie. Hardly very ladylike—but then, nor am I these days. Since
then, I've been wondering about that card—what you might know, or
not know. As I say, you're no fool, despite appearances."

"Why did you send it?"

"Why? Because it's what one *does*, isn't it? Send cards on anniversaries? I'd have sent one every year if I'd known where to find her—to
remind her of the date when she killed my child."

"And why those seven words?"

"What other words were needed? I wasn't going to ask about her life or comment on the weather. I wasn't going to send her love or best wishes. And perhaps I wanted to frighten her, too—which I'm not proud of, Florrie, you must know that. But I wanted her to look over her shoulder. I wanted her to feel afraid."

"Nancy, did you push Renata?"

"Renata? No. But did I push Maeve Bannerman?" Nancy considers this; she moves her head from side to side, as if trying to decide which coat to wear. "Did I? Yes, I suppose I did. But did I *intend* to? Now, that part I can't truly answer. I had every intention of seeing her, at least. I waited till ten past one in the morning—the exact time, you see, that she killed my Polly—and I let myself in by the back door. How lucky I was to have had thunder! I didn't even need to creep about— not really. And so I climbed the stairs to the third floor, knocked on Maeve's door. She was shocked, of course, to see me walking—and she didn't recognize me at first. Why might she? Twenty-five years is a long time. We all look different; we all grow shorter or fatter, turn grey. But she recognized me eventually, and started backing away . . . She was right by the window—which was already open, by the way. And all the while she was saying how sorry she was, of course—'It was an accident; I didn't mean to'—just as she'd said in court that day. 'I've lived with it every day,' she said—as if *I* hadn't! And I didn't take kindly to that, I'm afraid. And *then* she started saying that I was in the wrong—*I* was! In being there! In not making peace with what happened. Those were her words: *making peace*! She told me she had a right—a right!—to a happy life. Marcella's boy—Jay? She told me they were in love with each other—in love!—and that I wasn't being fair, and I felt so angry at that, so very cross, Florrie, that I grabbed her by the shoulders, like this"—Nancy mimes it, grasping the air—"and maybe I only wanted to shake her or maybe . . ." She lowers her hands. Her eyes grow glassy, as if watching the fall for a second time. "Maybe I *did* mean to push her. I don't know. But I *do* know that I can't say I'm sorry—is that dreadful? Perhaps. But I just feel nothing about it—even now."

Nancy sighs, looks down. She considers her fingers and knuckles, as if looking for some physical mark of what they did.

"We talked of Richard Babbington. That's apt, I suppose. For I don't know if he ever asked for forgiveness for what he did, how he made his money—but only those poor, abused souls that he helped to enslave could ever offer it. Only they could pardon him—them, and no one else. I understand—I do—why we have judges and juries. Before Polly died, I saw no possible argument against it; to ensure a fair trial, isn't that what they say? But let me tell you this: there is nothing fair about a girl who'd been a nuisance in our lives already at that point—a wretched mess of a girl, answering back—getting into a car with my daughter and her best friend and driving them off the bridge at Molesey; there is nothing fair about that girl being *forgiven* for it. Forgiven by strangers. Forgiven by a jury who saw her sobbing in the dock, who heard her regret and her *Oh, I'm so sorry*; who heard about her difficult childhood—but who has an easy one? They forgave her. It wasn't *their* business to do that: it was *mine*. I was her mother. I was the one who lost her daughter. Later I lost my Max, too. Do you know what the judge said, Florrie? That no good would come from jailing Maeve; that he'd heard her sincerest regret and felt that one life, at least, should be saved from the wreck. No good would come? Punishment would come. She was a thief and a liar and a failure in life: it was *all* her fault. Maeve . . . I saw her outside the courtroom after the acquittal, pale and fainting for the press. Saying how sorry she was. Woe is me. And I managed to say to her that I'd never forget, that I'd not let *her* forget, either. But then she disappeared—vanished. She was eighteen by then and I lost her. I looked for her, of course; I went to the last of her foster homes. I checked phone directories and hospitals and church records, in case she got married. And before you ask, Florrie, it wasn't because I intended to harm that girl. I'm not a monster. Oh, I hated her, certainly—and I've lost count of the times I've wished that she'd died, instead of Polly—or Meredith, who was a sweet-natured girl. But I never intended to physically hurt her."

"Then why look for her at all?"

"Because I didn't want her moving on. I didn't want her to leave the Nightjar behind her, like it didn't happen—like she didn't leave her two friends to drown in that damned car. Why should she? When Polly and Meredith couldn't leave it behind? When I can't? When the Trotts can't? When my Max could not? Why should she—the one who caused it—live any kind of happy life?"

"And do you think she's done that? Do you, Nancy?"

"Been happy? Perhaps not. But that Maeve has any sort of life at all seems so very unfair, in my eyes. Why is *she* here, still breathing, when my darling Polly is not?"

The waste, thinks Florrie. All the terrible waste. It almost takes the breath from her lungs. "But then you found her."

"Me? Not me. A friend. I received a telephone call that she'd turned up, just like that—at a residential home in Oxfordshire, of all places. That was it: I wanted to see her. You can't imagine how much I wanted to see her and to not lose sight of her again. The manager of Babbington Hall . . . How well she's done for herself, I thought. So I enquired about a room. But they were fully booked—save for an accessible room."

"Ah. So the wheelchair . . . ?"

"A ruse. But I think you know that. I knew that if anyone would spot it, it would be you. These things take practice, don't they? Reversing! So hard! You're so adept at it, Florrie. But I suppose you have the arms . . ." Nancy examines her sleeve. Something has caught her eye—a speck of dust or a stain, which she brushes at. "I know you disapprove. I can understand why—pretending that my legs don't work when in fact they are perfectly fine. And I do feel bad about *that*, at least. But do you know something? I can't be truly sorry. Because there hasn't been a day that's gone by when I haven't imagined how my daughter might be if she'd lived. I've imagined her wedding day. I've imagined her having her own children. I see dresses, even now—even now, a quarter of a century later—and I think, Oh, Polly would look so pretty in that! Every birthday. Every Christmas. Every Mothering Sunday."

She is quieter now. Speaking about the wheelchair has softened her, slightly; no words have been spat like cherry stones. And Florrie (despite thinking *Do be careful*, as if entering a field with livestock in it) leans forward, at this moment, and touches Nancy's arm. "You must tell the police."

"Must I? Why, Florrie? What difference would it make?"

"Because it's the right thing to do—to tell the truth. Renata didn't choose to fall."

"So what? The likelihood is that she'll die. The outcome can't be changed by me speaking to any policeman. And even if I *did* go to the police, even if I stood up and caught the bus into Oxford and confessed to both of them, what is the point when I've got three months of life left in me, at best? Three months! I might be able to walk, Florrie, but the tumours are all real enough. I'll die before any trial. I'll die before they can even complete the paperwork—so really, there's no point at all."

They look at each other. Florrie thinks, *A powder puff.* It has been one of the common misconceptions about her, in her lifetime; that her perky nature and enjoyment of small pleasures means that she's simple, insubstantial, that if one were to dissect her one would find only air. She has a tendency to name potted plants; she must, therefore, have no knowledge of art. She liked to paddle on shorelines, no matter the season; she can't, therefore, care for political debate. All the *fripperies*—so they've been called in previous years—such as her penchant for lace or the pleasure she takes in a single crocus or the fact she could do forward rolls into her forties—have made others think her childish or beneath them.

She still has her childish side, it's true. She is oafish and plump and marshmallowy. But she's her parents' daughter, too. And whilst her mother was, yes, the twirling, gentle, daydreaming sort who left out milk for the Upper Dorbury hedgehogs, there was no doubting that Sergeant Butterfield was as sharp as they come, with his books and newspapers and interest in the planets that looked down on Vicarage Lane at night. Florrie comes from both of these people. And so, yes, she may like pink clothing and broderie anglaise, but she's also had no real difficulty in discussing gun control with the American ambassador to Portugal or interrupting Lieke in her own language. She came to understand Newton's laws well enough.

Therefore, she hears the words. Just as, once, she stiffened on hearing *as she intended*, so she stiffens now. Nancy said *confessed to both of them*.

"Nancy? You did something else?"

She looks up. "What?"

"Both. You said both of them. There were two accidents, then? Two falls?" And as soon as Florrie says this, her skin tightens as if a cold breeze has entered St. Mary's. "Oh, Nancy. Please tell me you didn't push Arthur, too?"

The woman is no longer looking at the Babbington plaque, nor the cross, nor the windows, nor the lace altar cloth. She is posing, as if for a portrait; the shafts of sunlight catch her left-hand side. How beautiful she might have been once. She might be beautiful, still, if she wasn't narrowing her eyes at herself, shaking her head in self-chastisement. *Nancy, you absolute fool.*

"He knew you could walk, didn't he? He saw you."

"Nosey old devil. Always smoking his pipe outside my window. He'd snoop—your friend. You think the Ellwoods are bad? At least one can hear them coming. Arthur would just . . . appear at a window. So, yes, he saw me walking. He came to see me a few hours later. Called me a fraud. Said that he knew of others—in wheelchairs, like you, Florrie—who were longing to come to Babbington Hall, desperate to find an accessible home that didn't feel like some sort of institution, and that I was wrong to be using up that room. He called me a liar."

"It *is* a lie."

"Others lie all the time, Florrie—or haven't you noticed that? Do you think that's entirely Marcella Mistry's face? That the Rosenthals can even stand each other? Renata Green doesn't exist; that whole woman is a fabrication. There are far worse crimes than a false-hood, Florrie."

"Thou shalt not lie. Or kill."

"Oh, please. Do you think that means anything to me? I told you that under the yew tree, remember? I come to church, yes, but I don't find solace here—not really. To be honest, if anything, it tends to make me angry. Because where has He been? Where was He when Polly was drowning? When Max stepped off that platform? Where was He when I was diagnosed last winter? Yes, I pushed Arthur. I intended to, too. I suggested we meet by the stone cherub because no one would see us there. And for what it's worth, I did more than push Arthur. I pushed him, yes, but he was still groaning. So I hit him with a stone to get the job done, because I wasn't going to let him ruin my plan. Then I untied his shoelace and walked back to my wheelchair and called for help until someone came. But what does any of it matter now?"

The dam, she thinks. It is cracking. Leaks are starting to appear—spouting in one, two and three places; four and five and six—and there's no saving it now. The dam will give way; Nancy is rising slowly in her chair and all Florrie can think is *get away from here*, as she thought with the buffalo in Africa, or when floodwaters came, or when a riot broke out in the sun-baked marketplace and she saw the glint of machetes, held up. So she fumbles backward, finds her wheels' rims; she turns on the spot and pushes herself forward with all her might—and all she wants now is the evening air and solitude and the thick emerald moss that grows on the gravestones on the south-facing side, or for a room with a map of Hadrian's Wall, or the damp, safe smell of the compost heap. *Push*, she says. *Go go go!* Florrie would run, if she could.

This all means that she moves too fast. As on the night of the dropped mulled wine, Florrie moves before she's ready to, forgetting that the aisle is uneven and that the wrought-iron grate is an inch or so lower than the carpet, and she forgets, too, that by turning so quickly her weight is unbalanced—one bosom is almost over the arm-rest, the other is forward, close to her knees—and so she starts to topple in this act of turning. She says, "Oh, oh!"—as if these words might help. And at the point when she feels that gravity is taking over, she thinks of Jack Luckett with his rifle in Northern Rhodesia saying, "No sudden movements . . ."

Too late. Florrie is upright and then she is not. She finds herself lying on her front without her spectacles, without a hearing aid and with a terrible, fiery pain radiating from her chest. She can hardly breathe for it. She wails once—frail, instinctive. She wheezes, "Help."

A voice is brought close to her ear. "Oh, Florrie. I'm sorry—I am. But I'm just not strong enough to lift you." And she wonders, then, if she is being assessed by Nancy. One final glance before a sudden coup de grâce? But there is nothing more. No words, no touch. All that's left to hear is the slow, methodical squeak of Nancy's wheelchair as it rolls past her, over her spectacles so that they crack and fracture, and makes its way up the aisle and into the soft, lovely twilight of Temple Beeches, leaving Florrie alone in the darkened church.

36

Other Holy Places

She is cold. That's as much, at first, as she's aware of: a coldness soaking into her bones. Also, there's something hard against her cheek (a flagstone? metalwork?) and she can detect a damp, ancient smell that reminds her of something she can't quite place— like cellars or buckets, old troughs.

Florrie knows, too, that she's inside. But where? Which stone floor is she lying on? Which holy place is she in? For there's a hushed, calm sense of holiness to it. A cave? Perhaps it's a cave. For Florrie's entered caves before; she's left the bleached, midday heat of a desert to find dust and a form of silence. Is she near Siwa Oasis? With Hassan sitting by her? Possibly. But it is too cold for that.

A temple, then? Or woodland? Or All Saints' Church in Upper Dorbury, in which the coffins of her mother and father and brother were all, in time, placed on a stand? Or perhaps she lies on the tiled floor of the British Museum. Or on the splintery boards of Miss Catchpole's classroom. Or she's in the little church at Achnacross where, on the grounds, a stone cross bore the names of men who'd died in wars or shipwrecks, and she'd thought, *It should have been me, not them.*

But then it comes to her: She is in St. Mary's in Temple Beeches. She is eighty-seven. She is lying on the floor and she cannot get up. Florrie tries to move—she attempts to lift her cheek away from the grate, to push down through her palms and arch her back. But she hasn't the strength to do these things. Her left leg, or what remains of it, thumps like the tail of a dying dog.

She tries, instead, to call. It is hard to be loud when one's lying on one's front, when all one can see (or half see, without glasses) is the dark, cavernous space beneath a pew. But she tries. "Help! Can anyone hear me? Reverend, are you there?"

I am on my own. There's nothing I can do. She can only wait—yes, wait, that's it, for it is evening, and so the time will soon come to lock up the church; the vicar will come with his single, huge key and, before locking, he'll call out, *Hello? Anyone there?* She'll answer him. Reverend Joe will find her. He will kneel by her side and say, *Florrie, hold on.*

So she waits. She stays where she is. And she imagines how she might look, from above: her floral skirts fanned out, her arms laid out in opposite directions so that one is raised above her head, palm down, and the other is by her side, palm up—the pose of a swimmer, perhaps. All the polished pews around her. All the dark corners and old, carved stone. The stained-glass windows have folded away their colours for the night, as flowers do.

Is this her dying place? Where her life will fold away also? The thought comes down beside her. If it is, there are worse places. There are far worse ways, too, to die. And it surprises Florrie that she isn't afraid of this thought, that it doesn't make her try, once more, to use her elbows and knees to roll over. She simply thinks, *Maybe.* And what she sees, as she waits—for Joe or for death, one or the other—is her gratitude. This, too, is a surprise to her. Florrie has always, of course, been grateful; but how easy it's been in her life, to think of what she didn't say, what she didn't do, of the falsehoods and failings, the wrong words or wrong turns; the *what if*s of her life; the *if only*s. All the things that she wished hadn't happened. All the things she'd say she was sorry for.

What she sees, instead, is the luck. Under the pew, Florrie sees all the small miracles and coincidences that, if they'd happened a moment sooner or later or not at all, would have meant a different Florrie and a different sort of life. Thank goodness, for example, for a bicycle thief; that someone, a hundred years ago, had lifted a cherry-red Pashley and Barber from the railings outside the Sitwell house so that an inconsolable Prudence had called for the police. Thank goodness for the multitude of unfertilized eggs between Bobs's birth and Florrie's conception, which meant that Florrie was, in fact, made at all. And she is minded, even, to say thank goodness for her broken, ruined heart, which, in her adult life, had taken her to Victor—to deltas and markets and a balcony in Havana, and the chance to dance to the Beatles' music on a wireless in Kampala, barefoot and half drunk on dark rum and, above her, fruit bats on the wing. Thank goodness that the girl from Pepper Street forgot to bring a pencil; thank goodness that Philippa Sitwell married so badly that she could leave her husband without regret and come to Vicarage Lane. And Florrie will always, always wish there hadn't been Clervaux; she will wish, always, that a man called Sergeant Butterfield had chosen not to chase a drunk into the snow and call out, "Drop the knife, lad. That's it." But thank goodness these men have existed. Thank goodness they ever trod on this earth, looked up into the quince tree or showed her the joy of snowball fights or crystallized ginger. Thank goodness she loved Teddy. Thank goodness that, in an attic room in Holywell Street, she'd nodded. *Yes, I'm sure.*

For this, too, is what she knows: Florrie would not change a single thing. If she was born again? If time could be wound back into itself, like a hosepipe in a garden, so that she could be taken back to the house on Vicarage Lane with Gulliver and tea trays and the snowdrops by the back door, how would she live the life that was, once more, waiting for her? What would she avoid? What would she do the same? And what Florrie sees is what she always knew: that her life cannot be seen as a normal kind of life; that some might tilt their heads and think, What a shame . . . But the love! Oh, the *love* in it: for her family and Pinky and those six wonderful men. And the love, too, for cracks in a pavement that a daisy will grow through; love for jackdaws or whisky or *les croissants aux amandes*, for rainfall or that lovely *pat-pat-pat* of the Nepalese prayer flags catching the wind, or the way her own body has endured despite having had half a leg chopped off, burned and thrown on a flowerbed. *How wonderful*, she thinks, *that I've been here at all.*

And above everything else, Florrie sees *her*. She sees a small, bunched face that she'd held in her arms for sixteen minutes—no longer. But oh, the *love* in that too-short time. And if she could live this life a second time, she'd do it all the same because of that face, because there must never be a world that does not have Joy in it.

Joy. Florrie smiles in the dark. She thinks of the woman called Gladness whose bosom applauded itself when she laughed. "I am named," Gladness told her, "for what I brought to my mother"—before cutting back into a papaya. *Here, Florrie—eat.* And as she ate, Florrie was suddenly so close to sharing all of it, to saying, Yes, I understand that—the wish to bestow, on one's child, a name that shows what they have brought you. But to bestow a name, too, for what you hope that child will find in their life. *Joy*—named, in those sixteen minutes; named for what Florrie wanted her to have. Joy, in abundance, and laughter and contentment. Sunrises and sunsets. Every kind of love.

Florrie sighs.

To sleep. To rest—after so long. It seems, now, such a small and easy thing. Arthur, she knows, had died like this. He hadn't fought or protested. He'd lain on the grass, beside the stone plinth, and as people urged him to stay, not to leave them, he imagined his son kneeling beside him and saying, *It's okay, Dad. I know.*

Does he wait for her now? Or beckon? Does Victor pat a chair beside him and say, *Ah, Mrs. P—come and plonk yourself down?* She likes to think that he does. She likes, too, to imagine who else might be waiting for her—all those known, missed faces that she's loved with all her heart. (*What took you so long?* asks Jack Luckett. Prudence smiles: *There she is . . .*) But Florrie thinks, too, of unknown faces; of two nameless, faceless people she's never met and yet she knows exactly who they are. She has never blamed them. (How could she have done? When they have loved Florrie's most beloved person? When they've made birthday cakes for her, tended to grazes? Kissed that little bunched face every night and watched it change into womanhood—change, yet stay the same?) Florrie has sent them love, too—from the church in Sanct Spiritus and Achnacross, from the banks of the Nile, from Kew. She sends it now, on the floor of St. Mary's. *Thank you.* (They answer, smiling, *No, thank you.*)

Perhaps, then, it is time.

Florrie closes her eyes.

She gives a single, slow breath that is not like her usual way of breathing—deeper, with more meaning, as if something else has taken over the workings of her lungs. She no longer feels so cold. She feels less aware of her physical self—and she thinks, *Bobs? Pinks, is that you?*

For someone is saying her name.

Someone is saying, "Florrie? Oh, Florrie, no." There's movement beside her—the sound of fabric upon fabric, the knock of kneecap against something harder, and she can hear someone's breathing—in and out, laboured—and the voice is suddenly nearer to her now: "Oh gosh. Florrie?"

She knows, then, who this is. And she'd thought to stop swimming; she'd thought she was ready to drift down through the water, away from the sunlight, to let her bones settle, soundlessly, onto the sandy bottom and let herself be dismantled by time, in the dark. But here he is, fumbling beside her. Here he is, saying, "Florrie? Can you hear me?" And she finds that, in fact, she isn't ready. She will not sink down or stop swimming; she still wants her life and all that's to come. And Florrie rises now, like a diver. She breaks the surface noisily—wide-eyed, with appetite—and grasps Stanhope's hand as she fills her lungs with air.

37

The Meaning of Joy

Florrie discovered that she was carrying Teddy's child in the autumn of 1949. She'd thought it was grief, at first. She'd learned of his engagement to Clemency Winthrop, sat down to the roast ham and felt nauseous; she considered the small physical changes that followed to be her despair in manifest form. But by October, Florrie started to wonder. By early November, she looked at herself in the bath and tested her abdomen with her finger: it felt harder, bouncier, than it usually did.

He had, of course, to be told. She had to do that, before anything else. So Florrie—claiming she was taking more shifts at Berriman's—began to search for Teddy everywhere: in museums and parks and theatre lobbies, in the ice cream parlour on Bear Lane. She loitered outside Brasenose. She peered through the windows of Cadena Café. In the end, on a hopeless, rainy day, she planted herself outside his flat on Holywell Street. He never came. Nor the next day. Then, at last, he did come—holding an umbrella as high as he was able as they ran, side by side, squealing through the rain. And Florrie saw how happy he looked. Also, she saw how happy *she* seemed to be—Clemency, in her fawn coat with its deep-orange lining and her neat buckled shoes. And Florrie knew it wasn't possible; that she couldn't step forward and say the words, unbutton her coat to reveal the early proof. She couldn't do that. She wouldn't. Because, firstly, what had Clemency Winthrop done to deserve being hurt? And also, what good would it do? Edward Silversmith would marry Florence Butterfield out of obligation and shame—not out of love. And Florrie didn't want that. She saw no happiness in being married to a man who'd dream, at night, of someone else; who'd watch Florrie and their child with a heavy heart and think of the other, better life he could have had.

What to do? She could not tell Dr. Winthrop, of course. She couldn't tell Prudence, whose headaches came and went, or Bobs, who'd been melted down like wax and lay, wheezing, in his childhood room. Briefly, she did think of telling Aunt Pip—because Pip had, Florrie felt, unknown depths to her; to look at Pip, drinking her beer, was to look across the surface of a flooded quarry, in that one could sense stories, the sunken evidence of men. But even so, Florrie couldn't approach her aunt at her sewing machine and whisper, Can I talk to you? All in all, it was a blasted house. War and the work of a bone-handled knife had left survivors who were only getting by.

But there was Pinky Underwood. There would always be her. And when Florrie stepped off the train at Paddington and sank onto the concourse, too distraught and exhausted to stand or speak, Pinky had just sat down with her. She'd put her arm around Florrie and said, "I'm here, Butters. We'll be all right." How Florrie had loved the word we.

This, then, was the plan. Florrie could not stay on Vicarage Lane. She couldn't blame it on food for much longer or hide it from the staff at Berriman's store. She'd announce a desire for secretarial skills and join Pinky in London, in a house on Notting Hill. Pinky's great-aunt Euphemia—inscrutable, enormous, the rumoured mistress of kings and army generals—had put a mattress in the linen cupboard, amongst the bedsheets and towels. When the bump grew too large to hide, it was agreed that Florrie would move elsewhere.

"Somewhere else?"

But they knew. They'd heard rumours. And in Great-Aunt Euphemia's attic—which was Pinky's home for more than a year in the end, her place for practising shorthand and typing—they discussed those rumours beneath a shared blanket: tales of grey dormitories in which girls screamed and laboured, in which cold water was sluiced over open wounds, and where the Bible was quoted in a terse response to each request for water or a pillow or warmth. They'd heard, too, about the richer, older, better parents who would come, arms open. It sounded like the worst of all places. But what else could Florrie do? Without Teddy or her own money? Without enough beauty or intellect to marry a man who'd raise her child as his own?

The Hackney Home for Mother and Child.

Florrie was sick into a bowl. Pinky put her arm around her and said, "I know you've not got Teddy. But you're not on your own."

She had, therefore, to tell some lies. Had this been the hardest part of all? Not quite, of course: that was still to come. But how hard it was for Florrie to return to Vicarage Lane, sit at its kitchen table with Prudence, Bobs and Aunt Pip—all such kind people, all generous and trusting, all so very tired—and lie to their faces; how hard it was to look into her own mother's eyes (those round, brown eyes like a dairy cow's) and talk of a secretarial course that she had, in fact, no intention to take. "Pinky's already down there."

"A secretarial course?" Pip nodded. "Not a bad idea. How long for?"

Florrie could have answered exactly. She could have offered five months, three weeks and nineteen days—or thereabouts. But instead, she lifted her teacup. "Five months, I think. Maybe more. I'll probably spend Christmas down there—with Pinks. Would you mind?"

"Mind?" Prudence considered this. "How kind of dear Pinky's great-aunt. Have we met her? I can't remember." She insisted on offering money. ("Your father would want you to take it, Flo.") But Florrie was insistent; she'd use her own savings—pocket money and earnings from her job at Berriman's, shillings that she picked up from gutters, park benches.

In London, Florrie ballooned. At five months, her waistbands had grown tight; by six, her belly acquired a central seam, like a plum, and its own dusky blush. By day, Pinky was at secretarial school. Florrie, with no company except her fear and shame, would spend her days in the park or museums, her hands pressed deeply into her pockets to hide the lack of wedding ring; in the evenings, Pinky would sit Florrie down in front of her Empire Aristocrat and teach her everything she'd learned that day. ("This key with this finger—see?") Florrie tried to avoid her host. But one wet afternoon, Great-Aunt Euphemia emerged from her drawing room—six foot in height, very upright, a voice like a bassoon—and asked Florrie to read to her: "I can't see the print too well these days—and you have time on your hands . . . for a few more weeks, at least."

After four and a half months of London, and nearing eight months of pregnancy, the time had come. What is there to say about the Hackney Home for Mother and Child? What might she wish to say, or remember? Pinky carried Florrie's bag, clutched her arm all the way so that they almost felt like one person. On reaching the building, they looked up—and Florrie might have thought it a prison if she hadn't known better, for there were bars on the windows and huge, heavy doors, an air of desperation to the place. A man on a bicycle spat as he passed them.

"Well, here we are."

Later, she'd bury it all. Florrie would choose—that is, she'd actively decide—to pack away what she saw and smelled at Hackney, what she heard at night when she could not sleep. She'd choose to forget the names of girls, the abrasive soap, the stiff, brown cloth of uniforms that caused a rash in the crook of her elbows. She'd drown the letters she wrote to Vicarage Lane in which she'd lie—*The course is wonderful*

and London is such fun—when in fact she wanted to write of the creature that pressed its knees against her spine in the evenings, or hic-
cupped on occasion. She wanted to ask Prudence if she, Florrie, had
moved this way inside her, or if Bobs, not Florrie, had been the more
active one. She wanted to write to Teddy—not with reprimands or
pleading, not with talk of love (for where was that now?), but to tell
him that this was happening to her; it mattered, to Florrie, that at
least he knew. Above all, Florrie would lower the screams and pleading of others and her own fear (for she was so afraid in there) into the
deepest part of herself, like a bucket into a well.

Pinky kept her word. Pinky was the hand clutching hers through-
out this time—visiting on Saturday mornings with licorice sticks or
fresh apples or hefty books on typing skills or letters from Vicarage
Lane that had been sent to Great-Aunt Euphemia's house and which
began *Our dearest Florrie.*

"How is it?" Pinky would say, whilst eyeing the nuns and barred
windows, the teary eyes of her best friend, and guessing perfectly well
how it was. But Florrie didn't have the words, nor did she want to have
them. So she'd ask for Pinky's stories instead—for tales of the London
she wasn't seeing: the theatres, Westminster, Horse Guards Parade,
sugared almonds that Pinky would sample in Harrods with no intention of buying. Florrie heard about Pinky's beau—an ophthalmologist
called Jeremy Topham who'd helped Pinky on Tottenham Court Road
when her umbrella had blown inside out, nearly carrying Pinky away
with it. "He offered me his. Or rather, he held his umbrella over both
of us. Walked with me, down to Charing Cross."

"What's he like?"

"Funny. Unobservant. Smells a little medicinal. The kindest man
I've ever met. Florrie, do you mind?"

"Mind?" How could she possibly?

"When this is over, Butters, we'll buy gloves on Regent Street.
We'll go to the cinema in Leicester Square—a matinee!"

When this is over. As if it ever could be—although Florrie was still trying to believe it might. And on other days—those that weren't Saturday mornings, when Florrie wasn't allowed to be visited—Pinky would sometimes cycle down to Hackney simply to sit on the bench outside with her collar turned up against the weather, arms folded around herself for warmth. She'd wait for hours sometimes—just to glimpse her hefty, lonesome friend at the window of the fourth floor so that they could hold up their hands to each other as one might in a mirror, to one's own reflection. Hello, they'd mouth at each other. *Friend* is too small a word.

Her labour lasted for four days. Florrie sweated in her bed, snatched minutes of sleep between her contractions. Nuns lifted the sheet at intervals, shook their heads—and carried on. Once, they gave her water; once, someone felt her pulse. On the third night, Florrie opened an eye to find a doctor was there, and she said, "It's hurting me. Please. Is there anything . . . ?" But he answered the nun, not Florrie. "She's wide-hipped, this one, and young. A first offender, yes?" He snapped off his gloves, turned on his heel. "She'll be fine. Next one?"

This has happened before. It was her only solace, as Florrie tore at her stiff, featureless smock or grasped the metal bedframe. So many other women had gone through this: Prudence and her grandmothers, Mrs. Fortescue, Mrs. Patchett; even Mary Underwood. *I am not the first.* She thought of the places, too, in which babies had been born—in African shade or igloos, palaces or country lanes, farmsteads or prairies or in quiet, suburban bedrooms with bay windows that looked onto the mown, green lawn of a cul-de-sac. She imagined all the ceilings that had been studied, all the gods that had been implored. And in the last minutes, she understood entirely why she'd heard others in the building plead for their lives.

Florrie's daughter was born in the early hours of the first day of April. Physically, Florrie felt destroyed, on fire; yet those first, frail cries were enough to rouse her into a hard, animal clarity so that she crawled across the bed, held out her arms as a beggar would. *Let me see. Give her to me.* Was this request met peaceably? Had they been too afraid of this wanting, bloodied creature with capable forearms and, for a time, acquiesced? The answer doesn't matter now. But for sixteen minutes, they were together. For sixteen minutes, with the rain against the nighttime window, Florrie was able to look and breathe and feel this stranger who'd emerged quite suddenly; she'd expected recognition, to think, *There you are.* But Joy was her own tiny person—entirely unexpected, or so it seemed, in the end.

Outside, in the darkness, London began to stir. People woke and lights came on. But inside the Hackney Home for Mother and Child, these two wide-eyed Butterfields had all they needed in this world: milk, warmth, the exchange of breath, the mother saying *That's it, there you go . . .* and dabbing her child's damp chin with a square cotton cloth. The child stretched out her leg, as if seeking the membrane she had known all her life and Florrie, seeing it, recognized this movement. It had happened inside her; she'd felt it, in her sleep.

In the years to come, she would be asked, "What happened to you, Florrie? Tell me." It would be assumed—by all of them, by Dougal and Hassan and the Ellwoods, by Victor Plumley—that a man had broken Florrie's heart, somewhere down the line. But it wasn't that. Teddy blasted her open, yes; he showed her that people can lie, and change, and treat you badly—and she felt like such a fool, so undone by him. But it was this creature's work, not his; this little human—with her mewling mouth, her gathered frown and matted hair, her flexing hands and hard, furious suckling—who broke and mended everything, who changed every coming hour of Florrie's life as a field's whole lifetime and purpose is changed by a scattering of grain.

The nuns came far too soon. "Come on, now. Give her to me, Florence—to *me*. Her parents are downstairs. Florence!"

Immediately, she fought. She snarled at them. But they pried her arms apart, like machinery, and Joy protested in her own frail, wavering pitch as she was lifted away from the warm, still place she'd been resting in. Florrie stumbled out of bed. She staggered into the corridor, still bleeding, and brayed like a mule for her daughter, who she could hear crying somewhere in the distance (*Why are you letting this happen to me?*). And when she reached a locked door, Florrie bucked and kicked and punched through it, smashing its glass, slapping and biting those who tried to stop her until she'd made her way through to the stairwell where she grasped the banister and bellowed into the cold, echoing void of it, her cries amplified so that every single woman in that building must have heard Florrie, covered her ears and murmured to herself, Don't listen, it'll be different for you. One nun— barely older than Florrie—had met her in the stairwell. She'd taken Florrie's wrist gently, as if to take her pulse. "Enough of this. It's the best thing for her, isn't it? They're nice people and they'll take good care of her." But this only summoned the last, great monster inside Florrie—the behemoth, bloodied and furious—to lunge at this nun and tear her, bite. She tried for her eyes with her crimson thumbs.

Mine. She is mine. Give her back to me.

There was a female scream. Then male voices.

A needle was pushed into Florrie's arm and the world went black.

So it was for nine days. Florrie would flail, as if in a fever; they kept her tethered, slapped her face and told her, "Shame on you. For shame!" There were, she sensed, no windows. She was in a basement or a cave.

Over her bed she heard conversations—muttered, brittle—of moving her elsewhere, of this girl needing a different kind of care. "She's gone mad with it. Send her across. We aren't keeping her *here*." And Florrie, blinking through swollen eyes, did not care where they took her. She had no wish to protest. She had no wish for anything now, except to lie in a place, any place—a ditch, a grave, a wrought-iron bed—and not move for years, except for the act of breathing. She was leaking milk and bleeding; she could not lift her head.

Others, though, could still protest on her behalf. And Florrie, even now, cannot be sure if what she remembers is the truth or imagined, or a conjoining of the two, but it was Great-Aunt Euphemia who ended it. She entered the room like a warship with all the smaller boats falling back, afraid. ("You know," said Pinky later, "that they'd chained you to that bed? Arms and legs.") And were there objections to the arrival of Pinky's great-aunt? Raised voices? Did Euphemia threaten the doctors and nuns, in her slow, menacing voice like a gathering storm? *You will not try to stop me. Understand?* All Florrie knows, with certainty, is that it was her—Euphemia, a magnificence of a woman—who physically lifted Florrie and carried her home in her arms.

Is Florrie being carried now? She can't be sure. There is touch, certainly—on her arms, on her forehead. She feels, again, a needle. *Right. Ready? On the count of three.* And is her baby still with her? Florrie can feel her warmth against her, hear the tiny animal sounds of contentment that she made as she suckled hungrily, a single hand opening and closing. My baby girl. My joy of the world.

But then she knows that Joy is gone. Joy, in fact, is elderly. And Florrie opens her eyes enough to see blue lights, the sleeves of strangers moving across her, and she can only blink, watching this as if through a lens or from a different room.

Bring me my box. She'd like her cheese crate with her now—the one with *Botley and Peeves* on it. *Est. 1816.* And, if she could, Florrie would like to move through this box with both hands, sifting through all her lifetime's treasures—the emerald without inclusions, the napkin from the Sunshine Hotel, the worn copy of Baudelaire that she'd read, in French, on the Pont des Arts, the postcard from Zermatt, the sepia photograph of the Butterfields with the quince tree behind them and Gulliver, at the front, intensely *en lavage*; she'd put aside her dried Scottish thistle, her name in Arabic, the announcement of her engagement to Victor Plumley, the garnet necklace that Pinky had worn for over fifty years, the handwritten Sitwell fruitcake recipe, her father's police badge and Bobs's last copy of *Wisden's Cricketer's Almanack*, in which he's written his name with an exclamation mark—*R. S. Butterfield!*; the rose-coloured shell that, if pressed to one's ear, sings of a southern sea.

She'd keep going down, through it all. These treasures would build at the side of her—as earth does beside a mineshaft. For what Florrie loves most of all lies at the bottom of her keepsake box: a small square of greying cloth—a rag, an off-cut—which had, for a few months afterward, retained a sour, milky scent and bears, even now, the ghost of birthing blood. It isn't much to see. But it touched Florrie's daughter; on its thinning weft there may, even now, be an atom or a fragment of her daughter's breath. And, knowing this, Florrie has never let go of this square of cloth: for seventy years, she has taken it to every house or foreign country, every form of home. And she's kept it, always, near her bed so that, at night, she has been able to lie on her side and feel it, in the darkness: small, strong, wonderful and beating like a heart.

38

In Which Everything Is Revealed

Florrie stays in the hospital for six days. "You're lucky," the doctor tells her. She has two cracked ribs from the fall; there's bruising on most of her—her abdomen, her left arm and leg, the left-hand side of her face—which shows itself quickly like ink on blotting paper, changing her complexion to yellows, blues and greys. The pain comes and goes, as her medication does. And, at first, in this narrow bed beneath these off-white, perforated ceiling tiles and strip-lighting, Florrie is only aware of a bone-deep tiredness. All she wants is to sleep.

But as the days pass, Florrie stirs. She watches the light in the hospital room, how it changes during the course of the day or when the nurses enter. Sometimes the blinds are half open; sometimes, half closed. And one day (which?) Florrie opens her eyes to sense a new difference, an addition to the room that hasn't come before or which, at least, she hasn't been aware of—and she finds Stanhope sitting in the padded plastic chair. "Hello," he says, as if nothing strange has happened. Both his shirt and braces are the palest shade of blue.

He comes to see her every day. When he is there, he reads to her; from Shakespeare but also poetry, magazines, the lives of Roman emperors, an article from the *Oxford News* about something so light and lovely (a summer fete, an open-air production) that he looks up, having read it, hoping that she'll smile. He informs her of Wimbledon—whose serve is top-notch, who seems to have the best double-handed backhand. He adjusts Florrie's pillows carefully and says, "How's that?"

He says nothing of nightjars, nothing of treble clefs.

She herself says nothing at all for three days. But on the fourth, Florrie cracks open her mouth like a seal and says, "You found me."

"Yes."

"How?"

He tells her he was concerned. "Magda said you were sleeping. But later, I couldn't find you anywhere—the dining room, the terrace, the library, the compost heap. I peered through your window and you weren't in your room. After that, there was only one place I could think of. Reverend Joe had locked the church, did you know that? He was walking away, whistling—but I stopped him, told him that you'd vanished. So he unlocked the church again, let me look inside."

Later, she will thank Stanhope with words. But, for now, Florrie is wordless. She only opens her hand and Stanhope, understanding this gesture, moves a little closer. Gently, he fits his hand around hers.

"Your note . . . under my door."

Stanhope nods, understanding. "Florrie? Are you ready? Because there is more to say, I'm afraid. It wasn't just Nancy, you see—not quite."

Stanhope tells her that he'd been unable to sleep. That night—in which she, Florrie, had turned up in her dressing gown, speaking of anniversaries—he'd gone back to bed but felt wide awake. "So I decided to take a sleeping pill. Except I didn't take it because a thought came to me, as I reached for the bottle. I remembered when Dr. Mallory had prescribed those pills to me—oh, a while ago now. December, I think. Anyway, I'd remarked on his bag—that lovely leather bag with its embossed letters?" The initials, Stanhope tells her. "They were M. T. The M at the beginning, not the end. Mallory is the doctor's Christian name."

Just as the Reverend Joseph Poppleton had taken a disliking to formality ("Call me Reverend Joe, or Rev, if you like"), so it had been

that, long ago—long before either Stanhope or Florrie had arrived at
Babbington—Dr. Mallory Trott had decided first-name terms was
the better way of it; that the informality allowed for a better professional relationship. One would trust a doctor more, perhaps, if one
called him Mallory. And who'd ever thought to question it? No one
at Babbington knew. They only missed Dr Laghari, accepted that her
replacement—with his slightly oiled hair and red sports car—was here
temporarily, and so didn't need to ask too much about him. Dr. Mallory, then—to staff and colleagues and patients.

"He told you," she whispers, "his surname was Trott?"

"No—but I went back to the computer. Typed in the name of
Temple Beeches surgery and there he was, looking back at me. Dr. Mallory Trott."

"But the parents weren't called Mallory. They were Charlotte
and John."

"Twins. They had twins, remember."

"Meredith and Mallory . . ." She tries out their names under
her breath.

And the rest? How all these fragments of loss and sadness fit
together to make a clear, sensible whole? "Ah," says Stanhope, smiling
a little. "We have the Ellwoods to thank for that." Because the day after
Florrie's fall in St. Mary's, the woman called Nancy Tapp—dressed
for her departure, in a grey silk dress with diamante earrings—had
announced in Babbington's reception that she had something to say.
At that, she'd risen from her wheelchair and walked—walked!—down
to Georgette's office so that all the witnesses (Reuben, Velma Rudge,
Aubrey Horner and the Ellwoods, naturally) had gasped at once, and
in various pitches—as if part of a church choir. Georgette closed her
office door. But when might that have stopped Emily and Edith?
Never, is the right answer—and they wouldn't be beaten now. So they
listened (Who knows how? By pressing wine glasses against the wood
paneling? By bringing an eye to a rusty keyhole? Or by adopting the

stance of a circus troupe—Edith sitting on Emily's shoulders, say, or Emily cupping Edie's foot—so that one of them could, in a precarious fashion, peer through the crack above the manager's door?), and, like this, they heard all of it. They heard her say, "Georgette, I'd like you to record this, please." For in the aftermath of St. Mary's, Nancy Tapp had decided that, yes, she would confess. She wished to be fully known by others before her death.

Through the Ellwoods, Stanhope also learned this: that the grieving twin brother of Meredith Trott and the seething mother of Polly St. Clair had never, in fact, lost touch. They'd sent Christmas cards. They'd telephoned each other on birthdays and anniversaries. And life had rolled on, year after year, but they would still speak of the Nightjar as if it had happened recently—amazed to find that their daughter and sister would, if they'd lived, be twenty-five now, or thirty, or forty. And they'd wonder, every time, where Maeve Bannerman might be—if she was married, if she'd borne children; if she was living a happy life. And Nancy Tapp, as she became (having married a friend of her late second husband), always hated the thought of that. Why should Maeve be happy? Why should *she* have survived?

Then one day, a Dr. Laghari in rural Oxfordshire—rounded and attentive, already overdue—headed off on her maternity leave so that a replacement was required, and, by chance, it was a certain Dr. Mallory, a locum from the south, who'd walked into the reception area at Babbington Hall Residential Home and Assisted Living to tend, specifically, to a sour Marcella Mistry, who'd been complaining about indigestion from the Babbington food—and in this way he'd found (can you imagine?) Maeve Bannerman herself, standing in the courtyard with a bright smile and her arm outstretched, waiting to greet him ("Dr. Mallory?")—and wearing a badge that said R. GREEN—MANAGER. A blonde Maeve now, and older. But she had been Maeve all the same. So that night he rang Nancy—who had, at other times in her life, been Nancy Hart, Nancy Cartwright and Nancy St. Clair—and said, "You'll never guess. You won't believe it."

"The coincidence of it! Anyway, moving on . . ."

The Ellwoods (swaying like a stack of plates, or so Florrie likes to imagine) had kept listening, in the corridor. And they heard that Nancy had wanted to see Maeve again, after all this time. To be a resident at Babbington Hall: that's what she wanted—so that she might be able to see her daughter's killer on a daily basis, watch her laugh and stretch and descend the stairs and pause to feel the sunshine, all the things that Polly had been denied by that girl. But Babbington, she'd discovered, was full. That is, it *had* been full—until Dr. Mallory learned that a man called Dermot Dunn was leaving and an accessible room would become available in the springtime. And what did it matter that she, Nancy, could walk perfectly well, despite the tumour that was growing inside her? She could always lie. She could ask Mallory to help her to do so—with paperwork, phone calls, his own lies. And so Nancy arrived with the crocuses, pushing herself up the gravel drive without having any real understanding of brakes or pivoting, or how to approach a ramp.

Florrie looks away, to the hospital floor.

"Florrie?"

She's thinking of those custard creams. But she thinks, too, of sitting beneath the yew tree with their hands like pancakes, in the dappled light. "She urged me to speak to Dr. Mallory. If I'd seen something that troubled me."

"Did she? Well. That's why. They were keeping an eye on you, Florrie. They weren't sure how much you'd seen that night."

How sad this makes her. "What's happened to him?"

"The doctor? Charged with assisting an offender, apparently—although Nancy is claiming he did nothing wrong, that it was all her own work and she duped him entirely. Either way, I don't suppose he'll stay a doctor."

And, as if the truth is a cave that they must hold their breath to enter and move through, so neither Florrie nor Stanhope can stay in there for long. In the days that follow, they speak of Nancy for a moment or two and then surface, inhale, grateful for the air. And they move their conversation onto other matters—the Babbington jackdaws or Clive's latest sweet creation, or how a minibus trip is planned to a distant arboretum in the autumn, which is a lovely idea. How, she asks, is the compost heap? Then, when they're ready, they take a deep breath and dive back down.

"Did she mean to do it, do you think?"

"Mean to push Renata from the window? Georgette asked her this. And Nancy didn't really answer—or not so that Edith could hear. But she confessed to killing Arthur—to choosing to kill him, deciding to do it because she didn't want him to *spoil things*. So I rather think that, yes, she chose to push Renata, too."

Cards are received—from Georgette and Aubrey and Marcella, of all people. The Ellwoods themselves are clearly so enthralled by everything, so delighted that there's so much to speak of now (an attempted murder and an actual one being far more interesting than Velma's latest shade of rouge or the flaking paintwork in their kitchenette), that they appear to have sent Florrie a congratulatory card. Inside, it's bestowed with exclamation marks. *Get well soon! We can't wait to hear all about it!* And she smiles to read it, feels a certain fondness. "You know, I think they miss you," says Stanhope. "Everybody does."

And in those last few days in hospital, two other visitors come. One afternoon, she looks up to find her doorway is filled by a beard, a dog collar and a Motörhead T-shirt; in his hand, Joe carries a packet of crystallized ginger. "Knock-knock? May I come in?" And it's a lovely hour or so that follows: she delights in Joe's stories of before he found God (that is, before he heard God's voice whilst working the door of a gentlemen's club called Legs Akimbo—and why not? When the Big Guy is everywhere?). He tells her of nightclubs and drug busts, of nosey urban foxes, of a sunrise that was so beautiful that a reveler stopped on the pavement and stared.

But also Joe takes her hand. "I owe you an apology, Florrie." For he'd known Renata had once been called Maeve Bannerman. Only the day before her fall, she'd confessed it all to him—the Volkswagen, the two friends, the bend in the road; she'd cried at his kitchen table over her mug of tea. Joe knew what the nightjar really meant. Indeed, he'd been working in Soho when the Nightjar case had happened; he'd been working nearby, too, when it had burned to the ground. "And so we talked and talked, that day; Renata cried, and I did, too. By the end, she was smiling. It was the first time I'd seen her smile, I think—properly, I mean. And I thought that I'd helped her, Florrie. So when it looked like she'd jumped, a day later . . ." It shook him, he told her, to the bloody core. "I'd packed up, thinking to leave Temple Beeches. Thinking to leave the Church entirely—because what sort of vicar misses that sort of pain in someone? Makes it worse, even?"

"But she didn't jump. You did help."

He smiles sadly. "I hope I did. But, still, my apology, Florrie: When you came for tea? You and Stanhope? It was so hard, not to tell you what I knew. I wanted to—I really did. But Renata had my confidence, of course—and she was so frightened about anyone else knowing about Maeve, or about the Nightjar business, that I half thought to steal that bloody card from you! Keep it out of sight. But I'd have Him Upstairs to answer to . . ."

What a story it is, she thinks. No apology is needed.

"You're not leaving, then?"

"The Church? No. Nor Temple Beeches. Too fond of the congregation, as it happens. And woodpeckers come to the feeders now so I can hardly leave them, can I?"

Florrie pats his hand, as a grandmother might.

And Magda comes, too. She ventures into the hospital room—in neither her uniform nor velour tracksuit bottoms but in holey jeans, a black jumper that hangs loose, revealing a shoulder, and with only a modest amount of makeup so that, once more, she looks like a version of herself. She brings flowers, too—wayside roses that she's wrapped in wet paper towel. "I was scared," she tells Florrie. "When I heard, I thought, *Not Florrie.* The others? No problem. But you? Please, not you."

All this happens in these six days. All these questions—and truths, at last. But there's one question that Florrie does not ask. She doesn't dare. For she is afraid that she will hear what she doesn't want to hear, what she knows she'll be undone by. And it's only on her last day at John Radcliffe Hospital—as Stanhope reads out a crossword clue to her, taps his jawline with the pencil—that Florrie decides, at last, to ask it. "Renata? Stanhope, how is she?"

He lowers his pencil, shakes his head. "Still nothing. Still no change."

Everything's changed except that.

It hadn't been, then, her dying place. The iron grate of the aisle of St. Mary's, Temple Beeches, hadn't been the place where Florrie Butterfield's story ended. But it might have been. She remembers—here, in her hospital bed—how it felt, in the end, like a quiet choice: she'd been minded to stop trying; she'd wanted to truly rest.

But Stanhope had found her. As Joe ran for assistance, Stanhope had folded himself down onto the thinning red carpet, taken Florrie's hand and kindled her back into living, convinced her to stay in this world. So she did. She is still here—and Stanhope is still here, too, in a combination of turquoise, peach and pale yellow that gives him a slightly tropical air. And she thinks how much her parents would have liked him. Pinky, too, would have heartily approved. ("Nice and tall, Butters. Balances you out.") And perhaps it is the candour of Renata's story; or it is being in hospital—where one sees the reflection of one's life in all its metalwork, where one stares at what really matters;

or perhaps it's just because Florrie has grown so very fond of Stanhope that she finds herself saying his name. He looks up from the *Oxford Mail*.

"Do you need the nurse?"

"No."

He manoeuvres his chair nearer and says, "Florrie? What's wrong?"

Like this, she tells Stanhope all of it. She speaks of bandstands and linen cupboards, of Hackney and Joy, and how, one night, for sixteen minutes, she was the mother of the most beautiful thing in the world. And what Florrie finds, in doing so, is that this telling doesn't hurt her; that what she lifts into the light, onto her hospital bed, isn't a sharp-toothed pike at all. Rather, her tale seems oddly small; not in what it means, or what it's always meant to her, but in how these words are, somehow, easy to say. *I have been afraid for seventy years.* Yet here she is, aged eighty-seven, finding no pain, or very little, in speaking of *what happened*, of *that London thing*. She is wanting, in fact, to speak of Great-Aunt Euphemia; she is wanting Stanhope to know the truth about her scars. And she is rushed with such tenderness then (For what? For *It*, for Pinky—and for her own self, perhaps, for the younger, heartbroken Florrie and *this* Florrie, too), that she thinks to cup her story, gently, in both hands, as she'd carried Gulliver's shrew once, released it into the bramble patch. She thinks to cradle it, like a small, brown-feathered bird.

Stanhope listens to the end. Then, having listened, he only takes her nearest hand in both of his own, as if holding a candle. "Oh, Florrie," he tells her. "Oh, my dearest love."

39

By the Compost Heap—Part Three

T he months pass and late September comes. In the orchard, there are apples. The beechwoods have turned to a deep, coppery hue; in the churchyard, the blackberries have mostly come and gone. Underneath her wheels there are fallen leaves that, softened from rainfall, will sometimes stick to the tires and rise into her hands like an unexpected gift, and she never minds this. She will peel the leaf away and look at it for a moment—its edges and veins, its mottled hue.

All seasons have their beauty. But Florrie has always loved this time of year. Easy to think that it's meant for endings, with the rotting away of the summer fruits and the lessening of light; but she has never thought so. This month, for her, has never lost the thrill of a new school year; in it, she's found conkers and mushrooms, the leafy preparations of a hibernating mouse. In India, it marked the end of monsoon season so that pavements and awnings and the backs of cattle steamed in the sunshine, the last of this year's rainfall evaporating like a dream. It is her birthday month—eighty-eight, which sounds both impossible and rather lovely. Out she came, arms open, all those years ago.

How well, too, September suits a compost heap. It is, she thinks, looking splendid: all the warmest colours are here—russet and fox-fur, chestnut and gold. After a wet August, in which heavy rains flattened the grass cuttings and caused the compost heap to sink to half its size, there's been a reprieve with this lovely autumnal sunlight and these colours have bloomed with it, like ink on a page. How wonderful, too, it smells. It is earth and vegetation, sweetness and rot. It is Vicarage Lane and the deep Scottish woodland. It's the smell of Babbington Hall.

They sit here, facing each other.

She sits, of course, in her wheelchair. For Stanhope, however, the cracked plastic chair with its bird droppings is gone. In its place, Franklin has provided a sturdy wooden chair with a removable cushion—so fine that, at first, Stanhope felt marginally guilty about it having been brought down here specifically for him, and he wondered about moving it up to the terrace so that others might sit on it, too. But nobody seemed to mind. Indeed, nobody else sits outside these days, disliking the new chill in the air. It's just Stanhope and her.

There is a small trestle table between them. On it, there sits a chessboard; a scattering of pieces are left in play with the rest lined up at the table's edge—knights, bishops and a single queen, watching from the side. Stanhope considers his move. He frowns a little; he puckers his lips in concentration. "Hmm. Tricky," he says. And it's a bishop that he lifts, gingerly, to take Florrie's remaining knight.

What a thing. Oh, it has been. If someone had sat down with Florrie—in her childhood or teens, in her fifties or sixties, or in the days after her left leg had been removed—and said that all this would happen in her late eighties, she wouldn't have believed a word of it. But it did happen. And on her return from hospital, Florrie (feeling oddly embarrassed, shy) had ventured into the dining room with Stanhope by her side to find, at first, a hush at her arrival—as if she'd been the Queen, or a stranger to them all. But then the Ellwoods stood up and started to applaud enthusiastically; others came toward her with fluttering hands. "We were so worried! How on earth did you *know?*" Even Marcella Mistry had squeezed Florrie's shoulder as she'd passed her, which was her own version of rapturous Ellwoodian applause. It had been too much to take in the beginning. Florrie took herself off to the accessible lavatory and cried a little—cried for her parents and her

missing leg, for Stanhope and for friendship. "Thank you," she said to
the turquoise paper towels.

Now Stanhope looks up, finds her watching him. He smiles with
his penny-bright eyes. "All right? Not too cold?"

"No. Just right. You?"

"Just right, too."

They consider each other, as if still surprised by this—which they
are, she supposes. They will always be surprised. She moves a pawn
forward, flexes her toes. "There."

So much, Florrie thinks, has changed. Love will do that, of
course—love, and the naming of it. He first told her he loved her in
Latin ("*Te amo*, Florrie")—as if testing himself, or still too bashful to say
it properly. The English version came a week later, as they were sitting
on the white-painted bench, watching the wren as it fossicked in the
undergrowth—and how simply he'd said it, as if his love for her was as
much a part of the world as rivers or sunshine, or the wren itself. They'd
smiled at each other, did not look away. Oh, how she loves him, too.

But there have been other events—quite beyond the pair of them—
that have altered the mood of Babbington in these past few months
so that even the wood paneling seems lighter in colour, despite the
shortening of days. The Rosenthals appear to bicker less. The mah-
jongg group has disbanded after a spat about Sybilla's dragon tile and
it's been suggested they start a poetry club instead. As for Franklin, his
trousers are as low as they ever were, but he's worked hard in the farthest corner, stripping back all the bindweed and ivy from the stone
cherub so that it, the cherub, can be fully seen now—it's lovely, in its
way, with plump, filled cheeks—and he's thinking, in time, of sow-
ing wildflowers there. ("Pollinators," Franklin told them solemnly, as
if making a promise with that one word.) And in early August there
was a new arrival: she—Patsy Lavoisier, a former actress with the gestures to match—has taken over Arthur's old quarters. At first Florrie
thought, *What of Arthur? Where will Arthur live?* But Arthur, physically,

is not coming back. And anyway, she knows that he would find Patsy a delight, as Florrie does: for Patsy, too, clasps her hands together at the sight of a teacake; she will halt others, theatrically, to avoid a snail on the path. Moreover, she appears to have taken a shine to Aubrey; he, in return, appears to have turned into a schoolboy again, picking up anything she drops with a flushed, breathless excitement, daubing himself with eau de cologne.

"It must be catching," said Georgette with a knowing wink. She, too, has a certain glow.

And this: In the aftermath, Florrie had made a request. It was met with a frown. "It's not," said Georgette, "what we tend to *do* . . ." No one had made the request before. But sending love, in this instance, seemed peculiar to Florrie; why not show that love in person? Why only imagine it crossing the courtyard and using the lift when she herself could do those things? The Brimble family were asked. No, they said—they had no objection; nor did the nurses on the upper floors. And Tabitha Brimble herself had nodded at the suggestion so that when the lift pinged to a stop, on the first floor, and its doors opened, Florrie found that Tabitha was waiting for her—arms outstretched, like a long-lost friend, and they'd sat in the bay window with the whole of Oxfordshire before them, making conversation about the beauty of the trees and the owl that lives within them, or listening to piano on the radio. "You'll come back?" Tabitha asked her. "Yes, please," said Florrie. Every Sunday morning, they sit, side by side.

Was Nancy's death a change, too? To Nancy it was, of course. But Florrie heard the news from Dr. Laghari and, afterward, felt strangely altered—as if she, too, had lost something she couldn't name, or express. She didn't talk to Stanhope of that loss. But she thought of it, staring at the painted lemons. And she decided to remember Nancy as she had been, that day—smiling across that plate of custard creams.

"Your move again, Florrie. I think you're about to take my queen, but never mind. It can't be helped."

Florrie considers the board. But then, in the distance, she hears a voice. It comes from her right so that she turns toward it, looks beyond the crisping beech hedges and the last of the roses to the brickwork path that leads toward the church. A man is standing very still. His arms are held out in front of him, very straight. Is he young? Perhaps not—but nor is he old. He's bearded, thick-haired, wearing a cable-knit jumper that makes her think of fishermen, although she doesn't suppose that he's ever been a fisherman, having lived in Bourton-on-the-Hill for so long, which is nowhere near the sea. Nor is Nepal—although it has fast, crashing rivers in the Himalayas that she remembers drinking from. Snowmelt—so cold that Florrie felt that water inside her. There must be fish in those waters; perhaps he fished in them. And this man—Jay, who did receive a letter from his mother, in the end, stating that Renata had survived an attack from a resident—continues to stand without movement; he is a statue, in his stillness, with the breeze finding his hair. His arms remain outstretched toward someone else—someone who, for now, Florrie cannot see. He says, "Slowly, now. That's it." And Florrie waits, holding her breath, as one might wait for a mouse to appear, or for clouds to move away from the moon. She waits. She waits. She keeps waiting. And it's the stick that appears first; it feels its way ahead of Renata, grounding itself into the brickwork before the rest of her moves, slowly, into view—the woolen coat too large for her, the unpinned, darker hair. "That's it. Slowly . . . There you are."

"What she has been through?" so they murmur, in the corridors or on the Babbington minibus, going back and forth to Oxford. "Oh, that *poor* thing!" And they mean, mostly, the fall. But Florrie looks now at Renata (as she seizes the sleeve of Jay Mistry's jumper to balance herself, draws herself into his chest with half-closed eyes and a private smile) and thinks of all the other moments she's endured—from care homes to guilt, from midsummer evenings to the sorrowing dreams of Paris and the life she could have had. All the self-blame. All the lonely hours. All the fixed, hard belief that one doesn't deserve more than a solitary life. And it was with this understanding that Florrie, in late August, had moved a jug of pink lemonade, leaned across a table and cupped Renata's face in her hands and said, "Tell him. You must. Tell him all of it."

Stanhope, too, is watching this. He's smiling as he does so; he has the gaze of someone who understands that this is, for them, a beginning, too. Renata will not work at Babbington again. She will visit, sometimes, as she visits today—for she has friends here, and memories, and Jay's mother to know in a new capacity. But she's not its manager anymore. Renata will, instead, see Paris. In time, she will feel different winds in different places with Jay beside her, or not far behind. And at this moment, as if he senses their gaze, Jay turns toward the compost heap. On seeing them, he smiles—and, keeping one arm around Renata, he raises the other in greeting. Stanhope, still smiling, raises a hand in return.

"Your turn, Florrie. Checkmate, I think?"

But then the breeze strengthens. A sudden, noisy gust comes in sideways, catches them off-guard. A pawn is blown over; fronds of Stanhope's hair are blown vertically and the paper napkins peel away from their table and skitter off toward the compost heap, like a concertina, most of which Stanhope manages to pin down with his walking stick. They exclaim their surprise to each other; they glance around, as if there might be a reason for this unexpected gust. "I wonder if we should move inside. It's all getting a bit . . ."

He starts to pack away the chessmen. But Florrie, for a moment, cannot move. For a feeling has settled around her that is not new, as such; she's had it before—in Cairo and at the Sunshine Hotel; eating *stroopwafels* with Lieke; here, in her kitchenette in the old apple store. But she's never been sure of what this feeling is. It's always been warm, and unexpected; it feels companionable, too—so much so that even on her own, she's turned around, as if half expecting to find somebody is with her. What *is* it? This . . . contentment? That's arrived as a pigeon might? And it occurs to her, then, that this feeling might be love. Not *her* love—for she knows exactly how that feels. Rather, she wonders if it might be someone else's; if this love might have been folded by someone, packaged and wrapped up in string and sent here, to find her (*her*, of all people)—across the continents and oceans, the fields and motorways. Could that be what this is? Is there someone out there who, moments earlier, set down their teacup or turned in their sleep, or watched their grandchild running across a lawn and felt so full of love and gratitude that they took that love, as if it were a proper object, and sent it to a woman they've imagined and loved for their whole lifetime? Without ever knowing who that woman is? Had they released that love from an upstairs window? A church? *Go. Find her. Wherever she might be.*

Yes, thinks Florrie. That's exactly what this is. For sometimes, one just *knows* things, despite all sense and reason; one knows, in one's heart, that such things are true.

"Florrie? Shall we?" His hair, in parts, is still vertical. He smiles at her, with his face like a saint, like a book that's open on its pages. And Florrie smiles back, takes off her brakes, and she and Stanhope make their way, side by side, back toward Babbington Hall—past the urns and the last of the roses, and the stone cherub, beneath a blowing sky; and they speak, as they go, of small, passing things which fill her heart entirely—rosehips, pumpkins, a loose brick to be careful of, the spring bulbs that are waiting, waiting, in the ground, and won't it be wonderful to see them, in time? The snowdrops and crocuses? Bluebells, even? How lovely the faint crescent moon looks above the church tower so that they pause for a moment, admiring it.

On reaching the French doors, Stanhope opens them for her. "After you, my darling."

"Thank you, my love."

Florrie and Stanhope go inside for tea.

ACKNOWLEDGMENTS

I could not have written *The Night in Question* without the financial support of the Royal Literary Fund. Their generosity, and their unwavering belief in the potential of each writer, is transformative—and I know this book only exists because of them. Particular thanks must go to Steve Cook and David Swinburne from the RLF's Fellowship scheme; to Eileen Gunn, through whom I made my bursary application in 2019; to the RLF's bursary committee for their decision; and to Professor Jean Webb at the University of Worcester, for her professionalism and friendship.

So many people are deserving of heartfelt thanks. My agent, Cathryn Summerhayes, is a writer's dream. (Dear Cathryn, *diolch â'm holl galon* for seven years of patience, encouragement, fighting in my corner—and for guiding Florrie home.) I'm grateful, too, to everyone at Curtis Brown for their expertise and support. Extra thanks must go to Katie McGowan, Georgie Mellor, and Grace Robinson in foreign rights; to Annabel White and Jess Molloy; to Lisa Babalis (whose first reading of this book made all the difference); and to Vivienne Schuster—as always.

The brilliance of my editor, Francesca Best at Transworld, has been matched by her vivacity and kindness: Francesca, thank you. Deepest thanks, too, to the wonderful Alison Barrow, Frankie Gray, Vicky Palmer, Lara Stevenson, Hannah Winter, Larry Finlay, and Bill Scott-Kerr.

I'm so fortunate and proud to be published in the United States by Union Square & Co. Huge thanks to my editor Claire Wachtel for her passion, talent, and belief in this book. Thanks, too, to Barbara Berger, Alison Skrabek, Gavin Motnyk, Sandy Noman, Jo Obarowski, Lisa Forde, and Kimberly Glyder for all their hard work and kindness. And I am so grateful to Sarah Scarlett, who matched Florrie with Union Square & Co. in the first place: Sarah, thank you. I know Florrie is setting off on her American adventure with a wonderful team by her side.

Thanks are due, too, in other places: to fellow writers Annie Ashworth, Sarah Bower, Emylia Hall, and Meg Sanders for their encouragement and wise words; to Alex Roddie, for the same—and also his advice on Zermatt and the Matterhorn; to David and Gail Wright, for their generous insight into the diplomatic service; to Karen and David Mander, for providing the loveliest of writing spaces in Treetops; to Pete Savin and Scott Vanderbilt, for cheering me on in the wild Northumbrian weather and also for Latin advice; to Kimberley Atkins and Charlotte Brabbin, whose early passion for this book has made them a part of it; and to Miriam Bannon, for more than I can say. Heartfelt thanks, too, to all my dearest female friends: their love, humour, energy, and propensity for silliness can all be found in Pinky Underwood.

My much-missed grandparents are named at the start of this book. I have much to thank them for—for their enjoyment of books and writing, as much as for their grandparental love. But, as I write these acknowledgments (at night, in a quiet house, with only a single lamp's light), I send out a particular parcel of love to my maternal grandmother, Claudia Dick. She helped me to write this book.

Lastly, to my parents, my brother Michael, my stepmother Susie, and wider stepfamily, my uncles, aunts, cousins, in-laws—and my husband, Oliver: thank you. Florrie's pride in her family, and her love for them, is entirely my own.